Michael Scott Rohan was born in Edinburgh in 1951, of a French father and Scottish mother, and educated at the Edinburgh Academy and St. Edmund Hall, Oxford. He is the author of twelve fantasy and science fiction novels, including the award-winning Winter of the World trilogy, and co-author of three more, as well as several non-fiction books. His books are published in the USA, Japan, Israel, Russia and throughout Europe. Besides writing novels he has been a *Times* columnist, edits reference books, reviews CDs, videos and opera for *Gramophone* and other magazines, plays with longbows and computers, drinks beer, eats Oriental food, keeps up with hobbies including archaeology and palaeontology, sings, argues and travels a lot. After many years in Oxford and Yorkshire, he and his American wife Deborah now live in a small village near Cambridge, next to the pub.

Find out more about Michael Scott Rohan and other Orbit authors by registering for the free monthly newsletter at www.orbitbooks.co.uk

Also by Michael Scott Rohan

The Winter of the World
THE ANVIL OF ICE
THE FORGE IN THE FOREST
THE HAMMER OF THE SUN
THE SINGER AND THE SEA
SHADOW OF THE SEER

CHASE THE MORNING
RUN TO THE STARS
MAXIE'S DEMON

With Allan Scott
A SPELL OF EMPIRE
THE ICE KING

The Castle of the Winds

A Winter of the World Novel

Michael Scott Rohan

www.orbitbooks.co.uk

An *Orbit* Book

First published in Great Britain by Orbit 1998
Reprinted 2002

Copyright © Michael Scott Rohan 1998

The moral right of the author has been asserted.

*All characters in this publication are fictitious
and any resemblance to real persons, living or dead,
is purely coincidental.*

All rights reserved.
No part of this publication may be reproduced,
stored in a retrieval system, or transmitted, in any
form or by any means, without the prior
permission in writing of the publisher, nor be
otherwise circulated in any form of binding or
cover other than that in which it is published and
without a similar condition including this
condition being imposed on the subsequent purchaser.

A CIP catalogue record for this book
is available from the British Library.

ISBN 1 85723 570 3

Typeset by Solidus (Bristol) Limited
Printed and bound in Great Britain by
Clays Ltd, St Ives plc

Orbit
An imprint of
Time Warner Books UK
Brettenham House
Lancaster Place
London WC2E 7EN

DEDICATION
Richard Evans, 1950—1996

In 1979, when I was a young writer nervously setting out to sell my first science fiction novel, *Run to the Stars*, I was lucky enough to be recommended, by Robert Holdstock among others, to an editor called Richard Evans. This was the dynamic character, I was told, who was discovering and developing new talent among British authors.

I was rather surprised to find this super-editor a quiet Welshman hardly older than myself, a chain-smoker with a nervous, good-natured manner and a rather diffident chuckle. All too soon, I discovered these concealed a cheerfully wicked sense of humour and a razor mind, as he simultaneously praised the book and tore it apart, leaving me both shrivelled and encouraged – no mean feat. In the end he bought it, and we began to meet regularly for long and hilarious lunches, in which just about everything imaginable was discussed; and somehow, although we didn't like the same music, politics, or even beer, we managed to become good friends.

One subject Richard often returned to was his scorn for a lot of the contemporary fantasy he was offered, Howard rip-offs and clones of Tolkien, which he loved; he was insistent that I should do something in the heroic vein, but different. Well, I said, still tentatively, there were these ideas I had been gassing about – all sorts of historical dark alleys, from the migration theories of Thor Heyerdahl (flawed but fun), Atlantic crossings by the Welsh, the Vikings and others, the peculiar resonances between Norse and Native American mythology, the first arrival of men in the New World, how primitive cultures thought of metalworking as magic, and what if the Ice

Ages were a living menace, a bid by elder forces to regain control of the world . . .

'Wait,' said Richard, simply; and very soon after he moved to the firm of Macdonald (now Little, Brown), there came an electrifying phone call. 'That fantasy novel you were telling me about . . .' And so the Winter of the World series was born.

And, when it had been hammered out to Richard's exacting standards, thanks to him and his equally convivial and sharp-minded associate Toby Roxburgh, I had what many authors only dream about, a generous contract for all three novels. Bringing them to life took fully four years, during which time Richard was immensely supportive, guiding me through the dark ways of production teams, printers, sales and marketing, while keeping a keen eye on the work. Every manuscript came back with sheets of devastatingly sensible and perceptive comments, which often had me tearing my hair and resulted in spectacular arguments, but for which I was deeply grateful.

He was not an obtrusive 'creative editor' type, though. I cannot remember Richard suggesting a single idea; his gift, or more correctly his great skill, was making me come up with better ones. He was especially helpful and sympathetic when, during the writing of *The Forge in the Forest*, my father died very suddenly. He bore the brunt of my occasional explosions when something went wrong. And nobody was more delighted than Richard when throughout the following decade the trilogy sold across the world, in nine countries and eight languages, and hit the bestseller lists in many of them, Britain included.

All this while, of course, he was doing just as much for many other rising writers. Our friendship remained a professional one; he only once visited my house, and I never saw his, or the young family he was so proud of. His work was so harassing he deserved to escape from authors at home. Nevertheless, he was one of the faces my wife and I always eagerly looked for in the crowds at conventions;

and when *The Winter of the World* won the IAFA Crawford Award, the bulk of the prize went on a very large dinner with close friends, and Richard chief among them.

Richard bought most of my later novels, and I moved with him to other publishers. Even when he was not directly involved in a book he would take an interest, and offer advice when asked. When he could not buy one particular book he liked, he was even influential in getting it accepted by another publisher. In the 1990s, he became seriously ill; when he recovered, it is no exaggeration to say that a wave of relief went through the British SF and fantasy field. In summer 1996 I saw him, looking fit and lively, bustling about for his first trip to America since his recovery; and on his return, barely off the plane, he collapsed and died shortly after, aged only 46. He is sadly missed by everyone who knew him, and had cause to be grateful to him; I am only one among many.

He was excited to hear I was returning to the Winter of the World, and looking forward eagerly to reading this book. All I can do now is dedicate it, with deep and lasting gratitude – not to his memory, that feels inadequate. To Richard himself.

Acknowledgements

To the stalwart editorial team, Tim, Colin and Lisa, many thanks for all manner of things; and to Nick Ross and the others in production. To Olavinlinna Castle, Savonlinna, Finland, and its staff (and its mosquitoes) for research assistance. And, as always, to my wife Deb.

Contents

Chapter One	Fair of Swords	1
Chapter Two	The Hand of the Ice	30
Chapter Three	Trail of Ashes	59
Chapter Four	The Light in the Marshes	99
Chapter Five	Faces in the Reeds	144
Chapter Six	The Hill of the Winds	173
Chapter Seven	Light Airs, Dark Waters	216
Chapter Eight	A Lord and a Lady	261
Chapter Nine	The Voice of the Winds	300
Chapter Ten	Ice and Steel	337
Chapter Eleven	Armour of Proof	378
Appendix		431

Prologue

Of the mastersmiths in the Northlands that were, and of their marvellous skills, the Winter Chronicles tell many tales. Greatest is that of Elof, called Valantor, but there were others who, mere men though they were, also forged for themselves an enduring name in its pages.

One there was who might have become a master among masters, yet in the end was counted the worst of failures, betrayer of his craft and squanderer of his inborn power and talent. So judged his fellow mastersmiths, who set down his story. Yet written in the margins beside it, in a hand unknown but always faithfully copied from manuscript to manuscript, generation to generation, is the simple phrase, 'There is more to be said.'

Much more . . .

CHAPTER ONE
Fair of Swords

THE ICE LAY EMPTY beneath the cold moon, as if seeking a mirror for its own no less jagged and barren beauty. From sky's end to sky's end of that immense glacial wilderness nothing stirred save the pale sky-shadows, and the pattering wafts of powder snow. And yet faint shimmers of light glanced among the cold crags, and voices awoke. They sang in the glassy air like the chime and fall of icicles.

'He is coming.'

'We must see him, speak with him. We have taken too much on trust already.'

'He will be here soon. He is making preparations. There is so little time, with these vermin. To dwell among them . . . I am weary.'

'Soon others will carry on.'

'He will be overawed.'

'Yes.'

'In the right way! Nothing must go wrong now.'

'Then you had best turn south again. At once!'

It was a dream that woke him, as he nodded over his work. Suddenly, sharply, so that his heart raced and his breath came shallow. He seldom if ever remembered dreaming, and it shocked him. He looked around wildly, and saw that his work was cooling evenly, and the workshop was quiet. Through the open upper half of his door the sky was black, the stars pale; but suddenly a brighter light streaked between them, a brilliant, instant slash across the sky, rising to the zenith and falling away. 'A starstone,' he thought sleepily, stumbling to the door. 'They don't usually last that long.'

But when he reached the door it had gone. The cold air on his cheeks woke him a little, and he stretched, yawned, groaned. Nothing met his eyes but the fading stars, and the moon impaled upon the distant summits, spilling its thin glare down their flanks. Around the horizon, like veils it drew before the dawn, fluttered the faint colours of the aurora; but a colder light shone beneath. He knew what lay there, not so many leagues distant, but rarely in his life had he given it much thought. Yet could it have been *that* he dreamt of – and the voices? He searched his memories anxiously, but they were already fading. He could remember only an urgent command, to go south. And that was nonsense, if ever he'd heard it. He'd never been to the South, where it was so hot men had red hair; and he never wanted to.

So it began, as he told it, and as the Chronicles record. Perhaps it was only in looking back that he added meaning to that vision, and those words to the voices. Perhaps, though, some faint echo did reach into his sleep, of the powers that were stirring, the wave that was rising and was soon to sweep him away for ever. But a sudden sizzling creak from the furnace caught his ear, the first faint contraction he awaited. It drove away all other thoughts. Seizing the great tongs that stood ready, he knocked free the catch of the small door and swung it squeaking back. Shading his eyes against its withering breath, he plunged in the tongs and pulled out a chunk of metal, strange and uneven in shape, glowing dully in the near dark. He turned it this way and that, inspecting it by its own light, absently humming a slow tune. Then, without haste, he carried it to the great anvil, braced it against the heavy round-topped swage he had set up, and reached for the largest of the hammers he had ranged out ready. A tap or two and his hand went to a smaller one, and some time after that to a file. From time to time he thrust the metal back into the furnace, to renew its glow; he needed no other light. And as he tapped and scraped and shaped he sang, softly, in a tuneless baritone; words of holding, resisting deflecting, defending. He never faltered, and he never looked. Every tool lay under his hand as he reached for it, every word flowed, so that his mind and his eyes never for an instant left his work. For he was a mastersmith, and the virtues within him poured into the metal he was forming, and made them, for that moment, one.

At last, as the darkness itself receded and the morning mists rolled over the town, he straightened up, sighed, plunged the darkened metal into the open fire once more, and then, with careful calculation, into the trough by his side. Steam squealed, the tongs shivered an instant in his grasp like something alive, and then there were only bubbles. He pulled the metal out and dipped it into a narrower jar, raising throat-stabbing fumes from which he retreated, and then into a sandbox. Enough for now, he told himself, as he washed away the sand and the corrosive pickling stuff. Polishing and decorating could wait. He would try it out now.

Exulting, he stormed through to the back of his workshop and the little rooms where he and his apprentices slept. Even in the dark he knew Olvar was there, snoring gently to himself, a long contour of darkness like a miniature hill. 'Hoi!' barked the smith. 'It's done! Up, up and into the saddle, you lazy slugabeds! It's a bright day beginning!'

The hill gave an uneasy quiver, snorted, broke wind, sighed happily and shrugged deeper into the worn fur covers of the cot. The smith growled and aimed a boot somewhere just below the summit. It was like kicking a rock, but a head shot out from under the cover. 'That wasn't necessary!' complained a richly petulant voice. 'I was just—'

'Getting ready to sleep out the morning? No, I do you wrong. You'd never have missed breakfast – or breakfasts, in your case,' added the smith cheerfully. 'Well, today you can earn your bacon for a change. Up and out!'

Olvar heaved his dark bulk upright. His cot complained bitterly. 'I warn you, Master Kunrad,' he yawned. 'I'll be working up an appetite.'

'Then you can start on your own toes, and keep going.

And you, Gille – *Gille?*' The other cot stood empty. The mastersmith swore, pulled his heavy sheepskin jerkin off the hook and stamped out of his back door, across the rutted alleyway to the stables opposite. The air within was warmed by the beasts who nodded peaceably in their stalls as he strode by to the raised hayloft at the end and kicked the wicker panelling hard. There was a yelp, a flurry of hay and a slight, swarthy youth sprang upright, stark naked and staring wildly around. Then he blinked at the smith in the odorous dimness and sighed. 'Oh, it's *you* . . .'

'Yes. Not her father, not this time and bloody well lucky for you too!'

The young man shrugged elegantly. 'I'm just a poor prentice. I can't afford to marry and settle down. What am I to do?'

'Take up knitting! If you're trying to pretend you can't afford clothes. Put some on or I won't be able to face my sausages. Who is it this time, anyhow?'

'*This time?*' A round-faced young woman sprang upright beside him, clutching a crumpled gown as rather inadequate cover. The smith blinked.

'Oh – er, hallo, Stejne, isn't it? Well, yes, this is rather a popular place—'

She shot a smoking glance at Gille, who had been frantically gesturing at the smith. '*Popular!*' He gave her a studiedly boyish half-smile and a little shrug.

'You wait!' she snorted and turned away, making the gown even less adequate. But she took rather longer about stalking off through the hay than modesty demanded, giving Kunrad ample chance to admire the curves of her back; and as she passed him she launched a glance of a different kind under her long lowered lashes. It made him pray to the Powers that Gille hadn't noticed.

'Whew!' said the young man, hopping on one leg to get straw out of his shoe. 'See that, did you? Isn't she a peach? I reckon you could—'

'I could use a better couple of prentices!' snarled the mastersmith, making as if to cuff him on the ear. 'One does nothing but sleep and eat me out of house and home, the other can barely lift his hammer of a morn because he's been banging away all night!'

Gille ducked away easily. 'You should talk! But I can still make you songs and verses for your great works, better than your own—'

'And one of these days you're going to make more than that, and who'll have to cope with the father? Aye, fine, you're a ready wordsmith, but I wish there was some way to keep your head and throw the rest of you away!'

'Wouldn't have a lot to sing about, then, would I?' grinned Gille, flinging his shirt over his shoulder as they came out into the alley. 'Anyhow, this is all your own fault for rising at such an hour! Look, the sun's not even through the mist yet, and an hour or more till breakfast.'

'I haven't been to bed. I've been working. And we're going to make good use of that hour. Get Olvar and—' Kunrad grinned. 'Come help me into my armour! Oh, and get some clothes on. Working clothes!'

'These *are* my working clothes!'

Nevertheless Gille was soberly enough dressed a few minutes later, as he and Olvar led the mastersmith out of his front door on to the open green beyond, beneath the high gate in the palisade wall of the town. At every step he clanked, but he was already moving more freely, testing and flexing the joints. As they passed the door he did a clumsy little dance step, and the mailrings and the plates and gadlings chimed faintly in harmony. The prentices stood back admiringly. 'Something to see it all together at last!' rumbled Olvar. 'Ready for the big fairday! You've fixed the gardbrace, boss?'

'It was in the cooling,' nodded the smith, noting that the recut lining held the helm exactly level and unmoving on his head, and the visor's browpiece no longer showed that slight tendency to tilt over his eyes. Mist droplets were collecting on the mirrored surfaces, beading the delicate inlays, trickling away down the fine fluting that both strengthened the plate and ornamented its flowing profiles. 'I was too hurried with the first ones. This time I've been more careful. Well, shall we see?'

The prentices exchanged glances. Gille hefted the big, roughly made sword he carried. So did the smith – and took a swing at him. Gille ducked it as easily as ever, and as the glittering arm passed he struck at the opened shoulder joint. The long blade struck the ornamented shoulder armour, and skipped off across the new gardbrace, the one unpolished point, to slither feebly down the smith's back. 'Perfect!' whooped the smith behind the stern features he had moulded on to the visor's facemask. 'Another!'

Gille, recovering, drove at the chest armour. His point struck, driving the breastplate back on the fine mail beneath. It linked, stiffened and spread the force, and the smith parried skilfully. 'Hardly felt it! Another! You now, Olvar!'

The burly prentice swung up his sword with stolid unconcern and brought it down on the high crown of the helm. The smith disengaged easily, and it clanged and clattered across the other shoulder. 'Featherlight!' jeered the smith cheerfully. 'Come on, laddie, you're holding back! These are blunt edges, remember? Put a bit of weight behind it or you'll get no breakfast!'

Like most of the smith's threats, this meant nothing and Olvar knew it. His cut to the left thigh clanked away of its own accord, off cuisse and greave, to stick in the turf. 'Ha!' growled the smith suddenly. 'I'm going to chop off your head, you great useless lump of buffalo lard—'

He whipped his sword back with enough forceful intent to startle a more imaginative man than Olvar. As the mastersmith twisted back, swinging the blade high to deliver what would be a devastating blow, the prentice lashed out in a wild clumsy parry. But the sword quivered at the crest, did not fall. The mastersmith gave a strange choking cry; and then the edge of Olvar's sword, with all his huge strength behind it, smashed into the loricated plates that shielded his side, with a noise like new forging. Appalled, the big prentice let fall his blunted blade. But even as it struck the ground the smith toppled with it, like a steel statue, flat on his back, jingling as the helm bounced off the hard earth.

Gille sprang over him, fumbling with the helmet straps and gibbering. 'Olvar, you idiot! Master! Master Kunrad, are you killed? Olvar, oaf, wantwit, don't just stare, go fetch a healer, you sow's head! Fetch Mistress Metrye, and the Guildmaster – run!'

A gaggle of inquisitive neighbours carried the mastersmith to the healer's house on a door, still in his magnificent armour. Everyone had browbeaten the prentices so thoroughly that they were shaking too much to remove it. *En route* Gille managed to unlace the tabs of the plate collar, spilling out the smith's dark tousled curls but, mercifully, nothing worse. Kunrad's face, normally best called amiable, was unmarked, but very pale. He groaned suddenly, and his carriers almost dropped him. But he raised himself on one elbow, and said thickly 'Twist the catch about, idiot!' and dropped back with another groan.

'Master!' moaned Gille. 'What happened? Why didn't you move when that ox Olvar—'

'Not . . . fault,' said the smith clearly enough. 'Mine . . . 'nother flaw . . . tell you 'bout it when . . .' His voice uncoiled like a broken spring.

'He's cracked a rib or two and rattled his brains,' said the silver-haired woman severely. 'Which if he is very unlucky will leave him little better than you two morons. But it's much more likely he'll be his old self in a day or two, with rest.'

Gille breathed out. Olvar sat down hard, and almost destroyed the bench. 'Thank you, mistress,' said Gille. 'Well, at least his armour is well proven. I thought he'd been cut in two with *that* blow!'

The old woman picked up the breastplate, angled it to the window and sniffed. It mirrored the painted planks of her house, wild images of seabeasts she had never seen, and shipbattles her father had fought in; but to the prentices' sight it showed something beneath, a burning shimmer like sunlight on clear water, transient yet somehow embedded in the metal. To her eyes as well, they realised; for often healers had a touch of smithcraft in the blood. 'Strong stuff indeed, by the look of it.'

'Masterly!' breathed the Guildmaster. Like Olvar, he was one of the copper-skinned men whose forefathers had first come from over sea, and his narrowed eyes were like coals above his cheekbones. 'Getting it ready for the spring market, was he?'

'His great project,' said Olvar hollowly. 'His dream. Beyond any fair I could think of. The greatest armour that ever smith since Ilmarinen made, it was to be. He's crafted suit after suit till he came to this pattern, all the time he could spare from supporting himself and us – and then he's made three of the type, shattered half the pieces testing and stuck the best ones together.'

'Testing,' huffed the Guildmaster, who headed all the local guilds and hence the town. 'Like this?'

'And on us, sometimes,' said Gille, wincing at the memory.

'So?' mused Metrye. 'Then I suppose he's earned what you gave him this morning.'

'He said it wasn't our fault!' protested Olvar.

'Did he?' grunted the Guildmaster. 'Well, he ought to know, I suppose. I still don't know what prentices are coming to. Rack and ruin, no discipline – it's a proper household that young fellow wants. Thirty-six and still unwed – you should encourage him!'

Gille recalled that the Guildmaster's eldest girl was among the many who had tried to snare Kunrad, and the few who had succeeded, briefly. 'It's not as if we don't try, sir,' he said lamely. 'I mean, we'd be glad of a woman's touch around the house, us.'

'Decent cooking,' groaned Olvar.

'And filthy clothes washed and backsides run after,' said Metrye sardonically. 'A fine prospect for some poor innocent, I'm sure. No wonder they never stay with him long.'

'Something to take his mind off work, anyhow,' said Gille sourly. 'That's why. He gets lost in it. For a week he's head over heels in love, and then he gets some new idea – about the armour, usually – and, well, just forgets about them. Along with eating, washing, sleeping, you name it, for days at a time. He doesn't mean to, he doesn't mean any harm! But then they see what he's going to be like.'

'And they give him the breeze!' grunted Olvar. 'And he doesn't notice that, either.'

Metrye, with two husbands behind her, wrung out the damp cloth on the smith's brow. 'Then he can't really have cared. Nor they. A shame there aren't more woman smiths!'

'Woman – ridiculous idea!' growled the Guildmaster.

'Well, I can't think who else is going to land him,' said Gille. 'Not while he has this idea set in his mind, anyhow.'

'Lucky to have anything still set – ah, he's coming round.'

Kunrad rolled on his side and was promptly and noisily sick. But after he relaxed, and drank some of the wise woman's herbal infusion, he seemed to recover his wits quite quickly. Until, that was, Olvar, still in anguish, asked him what had gone wrong with the armour.

Kunrad stared blankly. 'Wrong? Well – oh yes, something did . . . I suppose. But . . .'

'What, Master?'

'Why . . .' His face mirrored Olvar's anguish. 'There was something. I know that. But I can't remember what it was. Not a thing. Not a damn thing!'

'Common enough,' said Metrye, brushing the prentices back from the couch like so much fluff. 'A wound or a dunt on the head'll often blot out the memory of it. You take your rest and don't fret your stupid self, and the chances are it'll come back to you in a week or two, when all else is healed. Lie back quiet, now, and bless your luck your brain didn't run out your ears!'

Kunrad did his best to take her advice. The grating pain

in his ribs every time he breathed made that a lot easier. Leaving a problem alone, though, was not in a true master-smith's nature. Even when, strapped up and bandaged, he was allowed back to his own bed, it kept him awake all night, as much as the aches and pains did, or the aftereffects of Gille's cooking. When he did sleep, too, he dreamed again, feverish dreams in which he chased an empty suit of armour that danced eerily through a spectral landscape, lush and pleasant one moment, but the next falling away to reveal the stark bones of the Ice. The awful thing dangled the answer in his face, mockingly; but when he awoke, the bandage sweat-soaked and tight over his swollen ribs, he could remember nothing.

Nor could he still, by the first day of the great spring fair, some five weeks later. The bandages were off, the bruising yellowed and healing, the ribs no worse than tender, but the inner itch was still there. Kunrad was back at work, polishing up the blades and hafts and hauberks that made up his stock-in-trade, for this was the occasion of the year, not only in the town of Athalby but in the whole of the lands around. It would draw buyers from all across the Northlands, from the seacoast to the mountains, from wandering bagmen peddlers to the great merchants who traded between cities, and still sometimes with the hostile South. There, he had heard, the sothrans despised and mocked the idea of true smithcraft. They called it a superstition of half-savages that crafted metal could be infused with virtues, strengths that went beyond the merely physical, influences that could strengthen or direct the purpose of the metal artefact, sometimes in very powerful ways. They scorned it as they did all things northern, yet they were still ready enough to pay high prices for the work itself. Merchants had made a good profit from his work there, he knew; well, let them! They earned it by the trouble of such a long journey among such nasty folk. If they bought from him again, as they always did, that was enough. Of course, the price might go up a little . . .

It was at a past fair that Kunrad had found his path in

life, very early. He was born in Athalby, a quite large town in the rising years of the Northlands, some two centuries after their first painful settlement. In those days there was no Great Causeway across the Marshlands to the South, the land of Bryhaine, and both lands still stood in fear and distrust of their neighbours. This was made more so as the Northland settlers intermingled with the rustic, peaceable folk who came across the sea to settle there, and took on the copper hue of their skins, which many in the South despised. But to the people of Athalby both the sothrans and the Great Ice seemed like very remote menaces, problems for others to get concerned about. They were, by and large, a quiet, stolid folk, hard to impress, harder to daunt, well-nigh impossible to panic and proud of it, shaped in the tough image of their land.

This lay well to the north and inland, a wide lowland on the southern margins of the Starkenfells, beneath the crook of the arm that the mountains of the Meneth Scahas thrust out northwestward, barring the advance of the Great Ice. They sheltered Athalby and its surrounding villages and farms from the worst of the chill winds, and broke rainclouds upon their slopes to send down a maze of small rivers and lakelets. Other, less welcome streams flowed in summer, swollen with meltwater from the vanguard of the glaciers. The mountains were young and sharp, their rock new. On the higher ground its jagged bones showed through the thin earth, and few trees grew, or much except scrub and heathers and mountain herbs. The rich silt the streams brought down kept the lower ground fertile, but it was never lush, with only small patches of woodland, stunted and wind-bent. It was not especially attractive country. Indeed, the townspeople themselves said that its chief virtue was that it was impossible to get lost, because the country was exactly the same no matter which direction you went. They also joked that Athalby stood at the centre of the world, because no matter how you rode around it, you always seemed to stay in the same spot.

With such reflections, repeated endlessly to one another and even more often to strangers, Athalby folk contented themselves through long and generally peaceful lives. They were not a people to be much concerned with the need for adventure, or change; the seasons were variety enough for them, and the increase or otherwise of their flocks, harvests and families. The frequent markets and fairs, of which spring was the greatest, furnished all the trade and society they required, and a wide range of diversions. It was to one of these that Erlik, Town Smith of Athalby and one of its most solid citizens, took his young son Kunrad, who till then had seemed another of the unexceptional breed.

The first the Chronicles show us of him is a small boy watching a friendly contest of arms, mailed riders sweeping by with lances couched to meet in jangling disorder, or rising in their stirrups to loose long arrows at tiny targets on wands beside the track. Others on foot contest with swords and bucklers, setting the air alive with the toneless music of metal. It is a sound his home is already full of, but there it takes on a newly exciting life. The fighters are the armed guardsmen of various towns, the nearest the Northlands ever came to armies; and the boy watches them, mouth agape. Yet he is held, not by the battling, as many boys would be; but by the beauty of the weapons themselves. And most of all by the bright armour, the rippling shirts of mail, the shining plates at leg and breast, the gaudy shields and the polished helms. They fasten themselves in his mind, these shining skins of metal and their companions and tormentors the bolt and blade. These are friendly contests, and he sees nothing of their killing quality, only their bright power and the skill with which they can be wielded. Wonderful things they seem to him, attributes one should be born with, instead of flesh and bone. And yet, they are so very crude. So many small details he notices that could be better shaped, so obvious that he wonders why others have not corrected them. All the way home he prattles about them, and Erlik listens patiently; for even an Athalby mastersmith has to have some imagination, and he sees the beginnings of a powerful talent in his little son. A very profitable one, too.

In due course, it is recorded, Kunrad became one of his father's prentices, and gave good proof of his promise. Erlik was a sound teacher, and by his teens the boy was already an able metalworker, adept at all the ordinary tools and utensils, charms and trinkets the townspeople demanded of a smith. It was not only his way with the metal, though, but the strength of the virtues with which he imbued his work. His steel hoes dug better, and the plants around them flourished; his silver flagons kept the wine fresher. He made everything well; he became a very good smith for all purposes. Erlik, feeling the onset of age, would have been happier if the boy had actually shown more enthusiasm for all these everyday wares, on which his own fortunes had been founded. But what really held Kunrad's attention was the shaping of fine swords, and knives, and axes, and pikes, and arrowheads, and above all armour; and it was always on these that he chose to use the skills he learned.

Erlik, an unwarlike man, found it slightly unnerving as his smithy began to fill with beautiful, lethal objects, not least because they kept their edge all too well and found their mark with bitter accuracy. In part this was due to the cool perfection in Kunrad's forging, but there was more to it. A quality in himself flowed out into them; and Erlik and his wife, who no longer dared sit down in the smithy without looking carefully, began to worry about where the boy had got it from, and how he was going to turn out.

They did not have to. As the years passed, and he grew from capable journeyman into burgeoning master, he began to study the arts of battle, and even fought in occasional friendly tourneys and trials. It showed in his craft; but on Kunrad himself it had little effect. His prentice piece had been a plain but beautiful knife, of undeniable skill, but too like a dagger for Erlik's taste;

and when at twenty-four he became the youngest candidate for mastery anyone could remember, it was with a hunting sword of conventional falchion shape, broad and heavy, but inlaid and entwined with traceries in many metals, a forest of swirling vines and creepers entangling the figures of foresters, hounds and game, great beasts whose images he had found only in books, all frozen in an instant of pursuit and flight. And beneath them, for the eyes of the masters who marvelled, there was another tracery deep within the metal, fleeting webs of light that spoke meaning to their minds and hearts directly, and to the craft they themselves held. These were the subtle virtues a smith could pass into the works of his hand, to make it more than the mere metal form, a living instrument of its purpose. The masters read them in the light of their own craft, and were borne up themselves into the unending quest the fine gold and silver inlays depicted, eager as the fine edge to cut at the quarry. They were silent awhile as they passed the blade from hand to hand; and then without a ballot, in standing acclaim, they welcomed the gangling young man into their company.

But though his home bristled with spike and blade he never showed any urge to use in earnest the creations that were beginning to make him a name, first in the region and then further afield. He remained the generally quiet, amiable character he had always been, hard-working and serious-minded, and if there were hidden fires they were unleashed chiefly on his work. When his parents died in one harsh winter he declined to follow Erlik as Town Smith, forfeiting riches and a fine house, but freeing himself to his own pleasures. He made the things he liked best, worked hard, lived simply, drifted in and out of several hopeful matches, and eventually, when he had a little money saved, brought in two prentices. The most hopeful candidates went to richer smiths, so he chose those less accomplished but most serviceable to him, Olvar for relentless strength and patience, and Gille for the finer decorations and the wordcraft that could weave and intensify the virtues of a work, the spells that were sung over it.

So it is the Chronicles return to him, a man in his prime who seems to mark time in all the common concerns of life, that he may still pursue the vision of his childhood. Small wonder he rarely dreamed, for his dreams were what he lived and thought about, and what he wove under his hands. Such folk are most often the happiest; but as he made ready for the fair, that dancing vision of imperfection tormented him still, a torment he had never learned how to bear.

As usual he took no booth at the fair, for its centre was just beyond the gates, and his door could be seen from there. He had chosen the house with that in mind. The prentices were busy hanging a banner from his eaves, and staking out a double line of swords and other weapons like a bizarre fence to lead in his buyers.

'Get yer wares!' chanted Gille, bedecking them with signs. 'Get yer luverly pig-stickers! Gizzard-slicers and gut-grallochers! Gall-churners and codpiece-collopers! All hot, all hot! Get 'em while they're fresh, afore they get you! Don't drop 'em on yer toes whatever yer do! All hot, all hot!'

'Shut up!' grunted Olvar. 'You sound too much like the pie-seller. Or that girl with the hot rolls.' He scanned the gathering crowd hopefully. So did Gille.

'Look, if she turns up, I'll take her and you take the rolls, right?'

Olvar gave him a withering look. 'In a pig's ear, brother prentice. Food's not all I think about, you know.'

'Maybe not, but what about that time you almost choked? I told you, you can't do it *and* eat—'

'A man can try. Listen, you, the master said we could go look around the fair for likely customers, when we were ready. So I'll go now.'

'Hey, why not me first?'

'Because food's all he's after,' grinned Kunrad, coming out of the smithy, wiping a newly filed spearhead on his leather apron. 'It's too early in the day for your pleasures, yet.'

'It's never too early!' protested Gille, but he subsided.

'Besides, yours are more expensive,' said Kunrad cheerfully. 'Look alive now, or you'll put off the customers! Sell a round dozen of swords today, or a couple of the heavy mailshirts and you can have a silver penny for tonight, and ache for days after. Set those arrows out handsomely, there. Even with the weeks I lay ill, we've got a fine stock. Shift it all and we can spend six months or so *really* getting to grips with that armour!'

'Yes, master,' sighed Gille. 'I can hardly wait.'

Olvar, though, was back unexpectedly within the hour. He was greasy about the mouth, and licking it off his fingers, but it was news he was alive with. 'They're all talking about it!' he announced. 'There may be war with the South!'

'There's always going to be war with Ker Bryhaine!' sighed Gille. 'It must be so boring down there in the boggy borderlands they spend their time cooking up squabbles!'

'Never seems to come to anything!' agreed a merchant, to whom Kunrad was showing some heavy horseswords. 'I've heard the rumours, too, but they don't amount to more than a skirmish here and there—'

'It's coming to something this time!' interrupted Olvar, looking almost excited. 'There's a lot of trouble with corsairs at sea, ships taken from north and south, and each one's blaming the other, either for the corsairs or not doing enough about them. There's toing and froing on land as well, raids and suchlike!'

'What, across the Marshlands?' grinned Kunrad, clinching his sale. 'They'll soon get tired of that!'

'If they live long enough!' shivered the merchant, slowly counting silver from his purse. 'Twice I've been across that godawful place, in a caravan the size of a small town, mark you, and we still lost men every night! Weeks it took, and I don't think I got an hour's sleep at a stretch without some horrible sight or other alarums. It'll be a while before I ride those paths again, for any profit!'

'Well, you'll have good protection at your saddlebow

when you do!' said Kunrad. 'Now upon this blade there are virtues of breaking barriers and cleaving a sure path, as I said, as well as mere breaking of heads. And the silver tracing on the guard's a fine specific against bogles and bump-in-the-nights!'

The merchant winced as he put down the last coin. 'Let's hope so! All very well for you to joke, but you haven't seen them. I'd sooner wield the sword against them than sothrans, that's for sure. The redpates aren't such bad fellows in their way. But I'm sure it's all talk. Why should sensible men fight? There's little enough profit in war for either side. Why, there's a sothran lordie here to the fair, friendly and freespending as you like, and he's pouring scorn upon it!'

'Is there now?' exclaimed Kunrad, rubbing his hands. 'Olvar, you lout, now that's the kind of news you should be looking to bring back, and not a pack of rumour! Up, off, away the pair of you, waylay his wealthy worship and invite him hither in ways he can't resist! From all I've heard, these sothran lordlings are always after new wargear. Merchant, that's worth a stoup of ale – will you seal the deal on one?'

Soon after the merchant left, with his weighty purchase bouncing at his back, there was a stir in the crowd, and the prentices reappeared at the head of a small entourage. Kunrad smiled as he saw the tall figure they led, striding eagerly across the trodden grass as if it was his own homefield, with a gaggle of what were evidently servants and soldiers at his back. A rare sight, a sothran so far north, let alone one of their ruling lords, and one that reassured his heart. Not only because this might be his best customer ever, either.

Kunrad was not the kind of man to take joy in any profit a war might bring him. He saw weapons as matters of defence, of shielding the just and enforcing the right. For those, sometimes, men had to fight. Against savagery and barbarism and the greater enemy, the Ice and the evils with which it sought to flood the world – there, too, men had to fight, and he was happy to give them the means. A war, though, between two civilised peoples, lately neighbours under one king – it was not to be thought of.

Very likely that was why this lord had come here, so far north. On some kind of embassy, perhaps, sent by the sothran Syndics or whatever they called themselves to reassure people, to calm their fears and remind them Bryhainers were not all tomato-haired devils.

If so, the smith decided, he was a good choice. The lord's hair was nothing more outlandish than auburn or light brown, streaming back over his shoulders as he walked. He was as tall as Kunrad, towering over Gille and most Northerners, and a lot more lithe. He would be considered handsome, too, the smith realised as he drew closer – uncommonly so, in a lean, hawk-nosed sort of way. He walked easily among the crowd, without any hint of the legendary sothran arrogance. When he saw the smith waiting at his door, he stepped ahead of his followers and saluted him politely. 'Merthian Laithe, of Anlaithann in the Southlands. Do I have the honour of addressing—'

Kunrad smiled to himself. Very neat! Merthian had phrased his name so as to avoid mentioning any title which might offend Northerners, but leaving no doubt that he had one – Lord of Anlaithann, probably, wherever that might be. It would do no harm to return his politeness.

'Kunrad Erliksson, Mastersmith of Athalby, to serve your – lordship.'

Merthian smiled back and nodded to the burly soldier with a head of russet hog's bristles who had unobtrusively moved up to his side. 'We've been hearing about you along our road – eh, captain? It's a pleasure to meet you.' And he bowed.

That was not a gesture Northerners went in for, but Kunrad was not going to look like a yokel in front of the crowd. He bent awkwardly in return, ignoring Gille's stifled snigger. 'If it'd please your lordship to look over the works of my hands—'

'If they're anything like the others I've seen, it certainly will!' said the newcomer cheerfully, plucking curiously at one of the hedge of swords.

'Just workaday blades, those,' said Kunrad. 'Decent and sound for a fair price, but naught special. I've better within.'

Merthian straightened up and sighed. 'Workaday!' He looked at the smith a moment, then drew his own sword and offered it, hilt forward over his arm. 'This is of Northern make, and what it cost me, I dare not tell you! Eh, captain? What would you make of that?'

Kunrad took it, weighed it in his hand, tapped it against another, checked the balance, peered at the hilt a moment, and swept it back and forth in great whistling slashes that made the captain stiffen visibly. Merthian just smiled. Then Kunrad held the blade away from the light, twisting it slightly, and gave a considering nod.

'It's a decent enough piece,' he admitted. 'From Dunmarhas down south, by the master's mark, about seven years old. Good springy steel, well forged, with a harder edge added. It's seen some use, it's well sharpened bar a few nicks. But the pretty hilt, now—'

'Ah!' murmured Merthian, exchanging looks with the captain.

'The hilt's sothran work. Well enough in its way, but weaker. It'll give, and soon.'

'But that is newer!' protested the captain.

'Look for yourself! There's already fine cracks about the base of the guard. It could be far better shaped to the hand, too, offset a touch to lessen the strain on your wrist, and end the wear where your thumb falls. I've guards and quillons that'll shield your fingers better, but I'd go for a finer blade altogether. This one's a shade short for a man of your stature. And a touch too rigid near the point – too ready to snap at the right blow. Too wide at the hilt, also, with the fuller – that's the blood channel – too flat. And the tang overly narrow, by the look of it. And the same type of simple edge all the way along – nothing to catch or snap the other blade, nothing

– oh, there's far more you can do. And virtues – well, one against rust, that's usual, and one of easy drawing and sheathing, and one of straight cleaving, but no more, and none as strong as they might be—'

He stopped. The captain was chuckling, quite openly. Merthian held up a hand. 'Enough! Please excuse him, Mastersmith. We don't talk much of such things in the South, but I – well, I'm not a man to mock what others believe in, simply because I don't understand them. So tell me about . . . virtues, by all means.'

'Little more to tell,' said Kunrad, mollified. 'Fair enough, but you can do better. But for the hilt, they might issue a common soldier such a sword here. Decent, but, well, as workaday as those.'

'I was afraid you were going to say that,' sighed Merthian. 'I saw some other work on the way North, a couple of your pieces included. Well, show me something better, by all means; but I'm seeking all manner of arms for my housetroops as well. So we'll set a price on these workaday ones too. A quantity price, of course.'

Gille and Olvar exchanged eager looks. Kunrad ushered in his guest, sizing him up as he did all customers. He found him a younger man than he first appeared – bright-eyed, pale-skinned, clean-shaven, no more than thirty. Well dressed in a quiet way, in rich green riding coat and hose; only the touches of gold at throat and cuffs, the single heavy ring and the fine tooled leather of belt and boots suggested special wealth. A casual wealth that needed no display, just as the very ease of his manner suggested he was used to command. The Lord Merthian evidently had nothing to doubt or prove, but he did not seem complacent about it. He was looking around the cluttered smithy with keen interest all over his fine features. Gille might have some competition with the girls tonight, thought the smith cheerfully, and warmed to his guest even more when he ignored the one good chair and slumped comfortably down on a bench.

'Can I offer your lordship some wine?'

'You can, Mastersmith – though with no offence to Northern wine, I'm happier yet with Northern ale. The captain here certain is! And by the way, plain Master Merthian will do very well. If truth be told,' he grinned, as Gille filled the best pewter tankards from the house barrel, 'it's something of a relief to be free of all the honorifics. I find the North refreshing – in several senses, eh? Your health!' He wiped foam from his lips. The captain belched happily. 'Now, what can you show me?'

For the next hour a succession of Kunrad's best swords were brought out, laid on the table, tested, compared, priced and mused over. Merthian plied him with questions about them, the considered kind of questions that spring from knowledge already wide. Evidently he had a deep grounding in the art of swordsmanship, and one based in experience, although there was nothing bloody or violent in his talk. The smith responded readily, for he rarely met anyone with whom he could share his enthusiasms so fully. Before long, fascinated by Merthian's experience and his sothran viewpoint, he was questioning eagerly in his turn. Time passed, ale flowed, and almost in passing two of Kunrad's finest swords were sold for little less than his asking price. They had hilts gilded and jewelled, the grips bound with finest doeskin on a base of hide boiled and hardened to form, and blades made like great tapering leaves but edged like razors, with cunning shapings and serrations at the top and strong, lethal points. The price was not low, and the captain spluttered into his ale; but Merthian paid without demur.

Not content with that, he picked out a great pack of lesser weaponry, the greater part of what Kunrad had made ready for the fair – so much that the captain and two of the followers had to be sent back to Merthian's lodging for a deep bag of gold coin, stamped with the image of the Raven and Sun on one side, and with the image of a towered city on the other, impossibly great to Kunrad's mind. Still they talked, with Kunrad eager to draw on Merthian's experience; and it was to armour the talk turned. The prentices dragged out jingling mailshirts and lighter cuirasses of overlapping plates; and although the sothran shook his head a little at the prices, still more gold changed hands. At last Merthian took Kunrad up on a point about the padding of overlapping sections, and the mastersmith could not resist a reference to his great work.

Merthian's eyes gleamed. 'May I see it?'

Kunrad havered. 'Well ... it's not ready. Nothing like. There's a lot still needs doing ...'

Merthian spread his hands. 'Does that matter? Oh, I know you craftsmen, you'd sooner astound me with the finished piece. But I shan't be back this way for a long time. If ever. I too have a great project in my life, a work of order and peace, and it will hold me in the South for years to come. That is, if it succeeds; if not, well, who knows where I may be? My friend, this armour's evidently the peak of your achievement, the end result of all we've talked about. You wouldn't deny me this one chance to see it?'

The smith, as his prentices knew, was a kindly man by nature, and he had his common share of vanity. He had also had a little more than his share of ale. With a sigh he rose, angled the shutters so the sun, now sliding down into the afternoon, fell on the back of the smithy, and with a slight hiccup drew aside the heavy curtain that hung there.

Merthian sprang up with a yelp of surprise. The stolid captain, who had been consoling himself with the beer, gave a long low whistle and swore. Even Olvar and Gille stared, for seeing the armour complete in cold mist, with pieces left unpolished, had not prepared them for the sight of it in the full sun. In the time that had passed Kunrad, pursuing his quest for the flaw, had replaced the damaged parts with his spares, and completed the polishing and the decoration. It stood there now, ranged on a frame as it would be worn in life; and the sunlight struck it now with such blazing force that it seemed to sound in the ear as well as the eye, a great clash of silver cymbals.

This was the form of it. A full suit, covering the body from head to foot, so that as it stood there, arms outstretched and masked helmet bowed, it looked like the statue of some ancient hero. It shone black and silver there, bright plates of ornamented steel founded on a base of mail that at first looked plain and dark, but shimmered with an elusive light in the steady sunbeams. It was as Kunrad had intended, both a stern image of martial strength and a thing of beauty in itself. Yet there was more, as he began to see for the first time, watching the others' reactions. He had worked, perhaps better than he knew. He had envisioned something that would suit a leader of men; but in uniting the strength and beauty he had imagined with other qualities less obvious, maybe, he had created something that embodied leadership in itself, a vision of sheer power almost independent of the wearer.

There were two kinds of armour worn at that time, mail of interlinked rings or overlapping scales, and plate, that enveloped the body in stiff forms of solid metal. Mail was lighter and more flexible, but even with aketons – coats of padding – or light plates of stiffened leather beneath it, it could not withstand the heaviest blows with the edge, or the piercing of spear or crossbow bolt. Rings might be driven into a wound, and worsen it. Plate armour would turn almost any blow, but at the cost of weight and stiffness. Also, for all the time and patience it took to make mail, plate was more expensive, and much subtler, because elaborate joints of many elements, given archaic names such as poleyns and couters, had to be fashioned and worked for every flexion of the body, often down to the very fingers. Kunrad had chosen both. His work was founded on a mailshirt of the pattern commonly worn, the long hauberk reaching almost to the knees, with mailed gauntlets and leggings; but uncommonly light and fine in its fabric, and shaped by his own subtle and complex craft.

'The rings are small,' he said, 'but shaped and riveted

each against its neighbour, and in places double-layered, so that they interlock if driven back against one another. There is a virtue upon them to enhance that.'

'What makes them sparkle like that?' asked Merthian wonderingly. 'What manner of decoration?'

Kunrad smiled. 'Not for appearance alone; nothing here is. Each ring is coated with black forge-enamel, baked hard and glossy – that is against corrosion. And they are lined with a dust of tiny gemstones, won from fine river-sand and little greater, so that they move freely against one another. That is what takes the light. So that while the shirt hangs thus, yes, it sparkles; but when its wearer moves—' He took one arm gently, and the onlookers gasped. The cold glitter rippled like liquid fire.

Over the mail he had set garnitures, plate pieces to protect the most vulnerable areas, yet leave movement as free as possible. This again was not uncommon, but Kunrad had created these in his own fashion. Instead of a solid collar and breastplate there were jointed assemblies, like poleyns that followed the contour of the body, flexing and sliding over one another to follow its movements, and overlaid layers of lames, bands to protect the outer surfaces of side and thigh. These plates were not plain things, but shaped with careful skill, relying almost always on shape and angle for their strength, rather than sheer weight of metal. And they were made beautiful in themselves, richly but finely ornamented with fluting, moulding and inlays; yet every moulding had its own purpose, to block a blow or turn it, or to strengthen some other piece that might be driven back against it. The shoulder and arm assemblies, gardbrace and vambrace, seemed solid at first sight, yet beneath the beautifully shaped outer shells plate and mail flowed together as freely as a second skin. Gauntlets of mail with leather palm and finger panels covered the hands, but topped with more interleaving plates on springs of steel and whalebone – flexible till struck, then bedding, locking, impenetrable. Here as elsewhere the rivets that provided both fixing and hinge between plates were shaped, not for mere decoration as in ordinary fine armour, but as defences in themselves, shaped to deflect a blow in directions carefully considered. The inlays were of gold and silver, alongside glossy black enamel and the duller niello shading that added richness to the mouldings. They enhanced the shape of the armour, and its flowing movement, the free flexion of its joints, the commanding features of the visor-mask beneath the high-crowned helm.

'Yet none of this also is mere decoration,' said Kunrad quietly, contemplating it. 'There are virtues in the inlays also, more than the bare steel could contain. It may have many virtues forged into it, the turning of blades and the blunting of edges, the breaking of points and the baffling of blows, dispersing their force among its own springy sinews. For those, steel more than suffices. But to make the suit act as a whole, to have it follow the body of its wearer like his own skin, to lend it lightness and life and a flow like those of the flesh and blood within – there the finer metals of the patterning must serve, as the nerves do in the body of bone and flesh.'

'I would not find that too hard to believe,' said Merthian, no less quietly. 'Even as it hangs there it seems alive, ready to move almost with a will of its own. And a strength, as if it could lend that strength to the wearer, to put fire in his friends' hearts and fear into his foes'. That is armour for a leader.'

'To that end I designed it,' answered Kunrad.

They contemplated it in silence, swaying slightly on the cool breeze, the tall helm brooding in silence over the strength it crowned.

'Did you have any wearer in mind, then?' asked the sothran. 'Is there a famous face in those features, some great man of the Northlands, some hero?'

Kunrad smiled. 'We have few enough of those in these times. No, no one man; though if one such comes along, in my lifetime, I would gladly be the smith to craft him something fitting.'

Merthian looked puzzled. 'But this—'

Kunrad winced slightly. 'It's . . . unfinished. There are problems within it. Perfecting it will teach me the shaping of something better, in time.'

Merthian shook his head wonderingly. 'Smith, to me it appears perfect. Perfect! Smith – this also I would like to buy.'

Kunrad stared. 'My – Master Merthian, I'm sorry. It's unfinished, flawed. Besides, it's not made to your stature, as it should be. I made it to mine, so I could prove it.'

Merthian rose to his feet. 'We're of a height, you and I – very close. My shoulders and breast are not so large-made, but a trace of padding will amend that. I can tell you now by the sight alone, that suit will fit me more closely than half the sothran armour I own. As to the flaw – Powers, man, I have talked enough with you to know that what you call flaws are beneath the notice of any ordinary man. They need not affect the price. Smith, I want that suit, I will not haggle. Your price is mine! Name it!'

The prentices' eyes glittered, but Kunrad writhed. 'Master Merthian! Do not make me refuse you again! In all conscience, I cannot. I'll gladly make you one like it, when I've done, for a fair price – or a lesser one for you, as outwardly fair as this, even now—'

'And how long would that take?' demanded Merthian passionately. 'Smith, you heard me. My project calls me, as yours you; but mine must be launched within months. And then I cannot come back till it is done, and that may be years. And smith, I need that armour for it. Need! Do not think I am a child with a shiny toy under its eye. I have men to lead, I must be in their eye at all times. Even in the heat of battle I must be clear to them both in their eyes and in their hearts, a living standard and a banner they will flock to. Can you make me another suit to let me be this, in three days?'

The smith shook his head. 'Not in three weeks, Merthian. I am truly sorry.'

'Then if I do not have that one, I am nothing. Come, man, at least give me a fair chance! You showed it to me, you never said then that it was not for sale. At least name some price, however enormous!'

Kunrad held up a hand. He was breathing hard, and he ran fingers through his already disordered hair. 'A price? What could I have of you that would persuade me? There are things you don't begin to understand, that nobody but a smith truly could. A hundred thousand of those gold coins, a thousand thousand; your castle, your lands even, wherever they are—'

The captain was on his feet and drawing his sword, barking something in the sothran tongue. Gille gave a nervous yelp, but he reached for one of the swords on display; Olvar's hands closed on the tabletop, ready to heave it over. The sothran servants crowded into the door. 'Down on your knees, you Northland hound!' the captain was shouting. 'You baseborn bastard, you dare insult my lord Merthian, the—'

Merthian's long fingers closed about his sword-arm and stopped it without any visible effort. 'No, captain! We are guests here! I would sooner think the Mastersmith meant no insult.' He waved the servants back.

The smith shook his aching head. 'No insult to you! Though some might feel insulted already by such insistence as yours. I was going to say such things wouldn't be enough, that was all. But yet, we'll call it that, if you must insist on a price for a thing that has none. If that'll end it.' He gave a weary laugh. 'Nothing less. That sum, or your castle and your lands. And I wish you a safe journey back to them, Merthian. I am truly sorry.'

Merthian shut his eyes. 'Perhaps I do not deal in this as fairly as I would wish. If you knew what is in my heart, and what I must do – if I were only free to tell you, you would at least forgive me my refusal to take your answer. Smith, if you were to help in this project of mine, in this way and others – then, yes, when all is brought to fruition, then I *will* give you what you ask. The gold. Or, yes, the lands, that I love dearly, and that are worth as much or more. And I swear that! By the name of my father who left me them I swear it. I will write it in blood if you desire!'

There was a moment's silence in the smithy, and the noises of the fair outside seemed like an intrusion from another world.

'Master Merthian,' sighed the smith, 'it is I who cannot explain matters as they demand. Keep your lands, as you should, and as I must keep this armour. For it is as much the same to me, and more. The work of my heart, a part of myself, with all that I have poured into it; and it must be completed or I will never know rest again. Could I sell the reflection out of my mirror? As I said, I can make other armours, I will make one for yourself before all other men, if you still wish it. This one, though, this must never leave me; and though it gives me pain, the whole Southlands and Northlands together would not buy it of me.'

Merthian shook his head, his hair flying in his eyes, and his voice was cold and controlled. 'There are concerns here I do not understand, clearly. I try to respect another's beliefs, as I said; but this seems to me beyond all reason, to feel that what you make is part of yourself. Believe in the Powers if you will, I do myself in some wise; but this ... this religion of metal, this divinity of steel! A savage superstition, as if you worshipped stock and stone like the brown-skinned men you have taken among you. That you should clutch it to you is reasonable enough. Men need faith, however unworthy or demeaning. But that it should prevent you acting sensibly – ah, well. I waste my words, as before. My servants will take up what I have bought, and I thank you for that, Mastersmith, and the good ale. Perhaps we will meet again. Come, captain!'

He bowed, as politely as before. Kunrad, red in the face, bobbed curtly in reply, but Merthian was already turning away, with the captain stalking at his heels, hand still ostentatiously on his sword-hilt. They stepped out through the door into the warm light outside, and the servants, laden with clanking bundles, closed in behind them. None of the sothrans looked back. Olvar let out a great breath, and Gille sat down as if his legs had begun to shake. Kunrad twitched the curtain violently back into place, and slumped down at the table. Nobody said anything. The atmosphere of Merthian's departure still hung heavy over the smithy.

At last Kunrad reached for his alemug. He took a sip, then he stared at it distastefully and put it down. 'A lesson for a smith. Beware of vanity, and overmuch ale among your customers. And never, never show anything you are not prepared to sell. There I've offended a good customer and a fine fellow, as he seemed, and ruined my pleasure in the day.'

'He had no call to be so greedy,' said Olvar soberly.

'That's so!' agreed Gille angrily. 'With the manners of these sothran lords I've heard about, he should have taken no for his answer, and never let matters reach this pitch. He just wanted the thing so much.'

'I suppose so,' said Kunrad unhappily. He smiled ruefully, and hefted the bag of gold. 'Ah well. At least we've a fine profit out of the day.' Shutting the outer door, he and Olvar began to heave a spare anvil off the trap door that hid his strongbox. He stopped, and, delving in the bag, tossed a gold coin to Gille. 'I'll keep my word to you both. That's the worth of a silver penny each, and more.'

Gille caught it almost absently, and sat turning it over and contemplating the design. 'I wonder what his great project was?'

CHAPTER TWO
The Hand of the Ice

'**AND** THAT CONCERNS YOU?' demanded Haldin, putting down his alemug. 'I shouldn't let it. If he's as decent as you think, he probably regrets the brawl himself, no less. Anyhow, you haven't driven him away.'

'He's still here?' Kunrad looked up from his plate.

'Oh aye. Still in his rooms at the *Golden Seal*, says old Kulle, till the fair's done; so he'll be quitting in the morning, most like. I've seen the man around once or twice – sold him a dozen swords yesterday, in fact. And a parcel of helms.'

'You too?'

'And Galdred here, a pile of those cheap mailshirts of his – eh, Galdred? And Makke of the Barns, and Bure from Hroby, Tovte the Axewright – every weaponsmith hereabouts, just about. Said he was buying for his housetroop.'

'Yes, to me too. Must be a fair number.'

Haldin nodded. 'Could be two, three hundred or more, if he's a powerful wight. These sothran lords are rich, boy. You should see the place, sometime.'

Kunrad smiled weakly. 'I don't think I'd get on with them, if present experience is anything to go by.'

Haldin laughed. 'You're letting it get to you, my lad. You'd be fine, long as you didn't push your food about the plate like that. They're long on manners and deportment. Now me, when I was eating with the quality, every time I slurped the soup through my whiskers, know what?' He prodded Kunrad painfully in the ribs. '*I wiped 'em neatly on the tablecloth!*'

Kunrad couldn't help joining in the happy guffaws

around the table. Haldin was the man who had stepped into his father's shoes as Town Smith, a mastersmith of ordinary ability but wide experience and far travelling, and a friendly counsellor to all the younger smiths.

'Pay no need to the ignorant old buzzard!' chimed in Tarkil the Goldsmith. 'What's he think the serving-girls' shifts are for?'

'What's a tablecloth?' demanded Galdred.

'What's a shift?' demanded Haldin. Guffaws again all round.

'Not in front of the lad!' said Kolfe the Farrier in mock reproof. Kunrad shook his head and chuckled. Few of his fellow masters were really old, Haldin a vigorous fifty, but they made a point of treating him like a babe in arms. All the same, their plain banter and the sense of support behind it was making him feel far better than he had done for the last couple of days.

Not that the fair hadn't gone well. What Merthian had left, a host of other buyers cleaned out – eager, it seemed, to buy at the same place as the sothran lord. He and the prentices had sold all they had and what little more they had time to craft in the two days remaining, and the strongbox was now crammed. For most of the time he had been too busy to give Merthian a thought, but he had been obscurely unhappy. When his guildfellows began plying him with questions around their fairtime feast, it had all come back. The universal opinion, though, was that Merthian would have been lucky to escape any of them without a boot in his sothran breeches; and that Kunrad should forget it, enjoy his gold and get on with perfecting that armour.

Nonetheless he left the feast as early as he decently could, and as sober. As the tall doors of the Guildhall, with their painted emblem of Ilmarinen forging the lightning, closed behind him, he pulled his old fleece jerkin close and strolled off down the main street, sniffing at the air. There was a heavy, oppressive feel to it, a brooding hint of coming thunder, and he was eager to get home before rain turned the trodden clay and stones to mud. The night was quiet now that the fairtime revellers had gone to their beds, or in some cases gutters, but he was faintly aware of distant stirrings, and the sound of hooves in nearby streets.

Unknown to him, all across the town men were slipping out of lodgings and stables where the casual faircomers slept, donning armour, buckling on weapons, climbing on to horseback, gathering at street corners and byways. They were quiet about it, quiet and calm, and ready to quieten others, so that he heard only the occasional voice raised. Common enough in fairtime, that meant nothing to him until he reached the margins of the green common before the gate, and saw the men who milled around there.

Men, and the gleam of swords in the near-darkness. Nobody fighting, not exactly, but people shouting, waving, protesting – folk held at swordpoint, he realised, voices he knew, his neighbours. Amazed, struck with that sense of the unreal which surrounds sudden crisis, he took a step closer. Only then he saw there were other men prowling about the common. One loomed up in front of him, sword in hand, mouth open to challenge. Kunrad, outraged, slapped the blade aside and swung a fist into it. The man was stretched flat on the grass, unmoving. Rubbing his knuckles, he trotted on, then stopped uncertainly at a rending crash of masonry, another, hollower, and a roar of rage – Olvar's. He stood a moment, then swore and ducked back, searching around on the grass for the stunned man's sword. Fire flashed up behind him, and he found the blade by its glitter. He plucked it up, took a deep breath and ran headlong for the crowd. The fire was flickering around his own doorway.

All the faces were turned towards it, swordsmen and captives alike and pale. Only as they heard him run up they turned, but in the black of the smith's guild he was hard to see, and so the blows aimed at him were too late and too weak. The sword felt good to his hand, and he swung it around him in two great slashes, back and forth.

The swords that struck at him were hurled back on their wielders, sending them flying, or dashed from their hands, or shattered, and he had a passage clear to the doorway. The door hung loose, lock and hinges dangling broken. He clutched at the frame in shock.

The flames rolled out from under the lintel, across the ceiling, tasting the wooden rooftiles. The inside of the forge was lit bright. Neither Olvar nor Gille was anywhere to be seen, but the wall of his hearth was shattered, and blood trailed among the debris. The spilling coals had started the fire. In the shattered wall lay the spare anvil, as if hurled aside by straining men, and the trap door was smashed asunder. Beyond it, at the back of the forge, fire licked at the sagging curtain that had concealed the armour, torn aside now and half fallen. A man stood there, with his back to the smith.

That much Kunrad saw, in the one instant. Then there was an almost musical chime in his head, a point of bitter pain, and the light exploded out at him. He was dimly aware of something rushing up, and the impact, the gritty pain against his lips as he grovelled. There was a duller pain under his chest; he fought to breathe. The strength was out of his limbs, and he made swimming motions like a baby as he fought to raise himself. Something cracked, loudly, and flaming splinters dropped around his face. Men were stepping past him, over him, and he could do nothing to prevent them. With a tremendous effort he managed to lift himself on one elbow, ignoring the ache in his skull and the sickly warmth that dribbled down his chin. He looked up, out of the forge, the way the men had gone.

He saw Merthian, no great ways away, dressed in dark riding gear, with a sword in his hand. He was looking half over his shoulder, back at Kunrad, and the look on his face was remote and deeply unhappy. He turned, and angled the point at Kunrad as he lay. He seemed to hesitate a moment, then turned sharply away and vanished into the dark. It came rushing in on Kunrad, and he felt his arm give.

He was vaguely aware of something dragging at his ankles, worsening the pain in his chest, and he tried to kick against it; but then he felt cold, and his ears rang, and the night dropped away under him.

Light burst in on him, and he sat up abruptly, or tried to. A firm hand pushed him back on the rough bolster. 'You lie still!' said Metrye's voice, severely. 'Two such knocks in two months, you'll be lucky not to become touched as it is. No more than you were already, anyhow! At least this one wasn't too hard. Didn't put you out for long.'

He coughed, and winced. 'Chest – hurts.'

The old woman snorted. 'Oh, that! Just bruises when you fell, and luckier still that it wasn't on any of the sharp bits.' She gestured at the wall. 'Your sword.'

'*My* sword—' He stared at it. 'No wonder it felt right . . .' Then the whole vision came rushing back.

'The forge!' he choked. 'The boys – Olvar—'

'Here and well,' said Metrye. 'Trust them!'

'We're well, boss,' echoed Olvar's voice. 'They damn near caught me with the anvil, but Gille pulled me loose. You too, after they conked you.'

'Looking after his own skin all the while, I'll be bound!' said Metrye acidly.

'No . . . did the right,' said Kunrad thickly. 'Nothing else 'gainst so many . . . but the forge?'

'Bit singed, boss, but still sound. Like you always said, when you've a roomful of fires you don't build a place to burn easy. Heyle the Glover's roof caught, though; and the butcher's house behind, and the builder's yard, and a clothworker's house. They raided them all, powers know why. More mess than looting, like they were drunk or something. Though they went right by Ennar Goldsmith's without so much as a glance, they say. Our house came off lightest, except . . .'

'Except there's stuff gone,' said Gille miserably. 'All the weapons we had left, just about. And . . . and the gold.'

'The . . . gold,' Kunrad twisted his neck to try and

avoid the pain. Evidently he had been hit at the base of his skull. 'Weapons? We hadn't much ... *The armour?*'

Silence was his answer.

Metrye squawked in protest and astonishment as Kunrad twisted violently around, sat up and dropped unsteadily to his bare feet on the boards. 'The armour,' he mouthed, feeling the puffiness of his lip. 'Get the mastersmiths! Have Haldin ... and the Guildmaster, get him ...' His voice faded, and he swayed. But even as he wavered his eyes focused on the prentices. 'Get them! Now! Run!' He slumped back over the board bed.

By the time they arrived, though, he was sitting up, pale but composed.

'Glad t' see you're well enough,' rumbled the Guildmaster, patting his shoulder. 'Louse-ridden business! Though it could've been worse. No lives lost, at least.'

'Dunno what things're coming to!' said Haldin grimly, twitching his whiskers. 'Within our own bloody walls! I mean, here's these fellows, just like ordinary comers to the fair, in their ones and twos mostly. Then all of a sudden they're up and in a bunch, ten or twelve, maybe more. And any man gets in their way they knock cold or scare shitless. Much use the guards turned out!' he added, looking accusingly at the Guildmaster and Kennas, the guard captain.

'We couldn't help it! We're more concerned with thieves getting in, and rightly so, this time of year. My lads were all around the walls, no more'n three or four on the gate. They winged a couple with arrows, they think. Hadn't time for more.'

'Well, maybe that'll help put the finger on the bastards,' grunted Tarkil. 'Small chance otherwise. They had the sense to be smart about it. Raid a few of the houses nearest the gate, break out and gallop off, bang. Nobody knows who they were. Seems they're right, all these southern tales about bandits getting bolder.'

'No,' said Kunrad flatly. 'Not bandits. That's what they wanted you to think; that's why they raided the other houses too, or pretended to. I saw their leader. And I knew him.'

There were cries of disbelief as he told his tale. 'A man as rich as that? Why'd he stoop to petty plunder?'

But as Kunrad told his tale his fellow masters grew grimmer still. They knew the young mastersmith from childhood, and they had heard his tale that night. 'It makes sense enough,' admitted Haldin unhappily.

'And there's proof,' said Kunrad. 'I took that sword off one of the raiders, and thought it felt well in my hand. Small wonder. It's one of mine. A cheap one, that was bought for his men.'

'One thing, though,' said the Guildmaster, his heavy brows knitting. 'You saw him. He knew, and he had a sword. Why'd he let you wake up?'

Kunrad had been chewing that one over himself. 'I think he considered it, Guildmaster. Maybe he thought his man had dunted me worse than he had. I was bleeding hard at the mouth, I think. And he expected the smithy to burn down over me. And, well, he didn't look too eager to do aught worse. Sounds as if his men had orders not to kill, too, doesn't it? Not if they could help it, anyhow. Maybe because he's a lord and a sothran he didn't feel it mattered so much if one man recognised him. That nobody'd dare come after him.'

The Guildmaster nodded, then rounded on the guard. 'Kennas! Get a patrol down to the *Golden Seal* and—'

'He quit last even,' said the captain flatly. 'Saying he was anxious to be on the road.'

'Well, he can't have got far yet!' thundered the Guildmaster. 'Muster a riding, all the men you can raise, citizens too!'

'Get me a horse,' said Kunrad.

'He hit harder than he thought, that man!' barked Metrye. 'You're riding nowhere!'

'I know them, remember? There'll be lots of folk on the roads, southward especially. But I saw some faces – marked a couple, too.'

'I'll ride along, then,' said Haldin, 'with your lads, and look after you. Not named Bold-Counsel for nothing, are you? We've come near enough losing you already.'

It was less than an hour later that the riding swept out of the gates, and the sun still barely over the mountains. Scouts and trackers had already gone before. The riders, twenty guards and sixteen townsmen, made a great thunder as they went, with women waving and children shouting, but a half-mile or so beyond the gate they petered to a rather shamefaced trot. There was no obvious trail, and the captain cast about for his trackers. They rode in a few minutes later, but not from the direction everyone was looking.

'Northward?' protested Kennas, taking off his helmet to scratch his white hair. 'Why in Hella's name should they go that way?'

'To throw us off in the dawn light,' suggested the scout. 'So they could turn south later. And they've been trying to mess up their tracks somehow. Didn't work, though. They must think we're thick, these carrot-heads!'

'They'll still be that far ahead!' snapped Haldin. 'After them!'

As they rode, he saw that Kunrad was dangling something from his fingers, a pierced circlet that twisted on a fine chain. 'A direction bracelet, lad? When you know the land around well enough?'

'One of mine. I was hoping it would follow my will, and the armour,' said Kunrad. 'And there is something – but on horseback it's hard to be sure.'

'We'll have their spoor soon enough, Mastersmith,' chuckled the guard. 'And by Raven's burnt beak, they'll need armour when we catch them up!'

'They'll all be trying to cram into the one suit!' crackled Haldin. 'We'll just trim off what sticks out!'

'You'd better be careful,' said Gille.

There was the usual chorus of sneers at anything he said. 'No, he's right,' said Kunrad. 'That swift uprising, the care they took not to kill. That's discipline, not banditry. I think we may be dealing with proper soldiers here.'

'Like enough,' said Kennas crisply. 'But so are you, and there's twenty of us. So if you good citizens will just be content to follow orders and leave it to us, why—'

'Halt!' One of the scouts was shouting, while another, dismounted, was sniffing around on his knees like a dog. 'Over here!'

The column reined in, grumbling and swearing, shivering in the icy air, while Kennas rode up to argue with the scouts. Kunrad took a second to steady the bracelet, on which he had set not only the usual virtues of wayfinding, but of seeking a destination. The armour was his destination, he told himself, wherever it might go in the world. And as he gave word to the thought, he knew it was true.

The bracelet twirled a little, and then it steadied. He looked along the line of it, and raised his eyes. He was dazzled. The climbing sun glittered cold on the sharp mountain peaks.

'But they can't have gone that way!' protested Kennas. Haldin tapped his arm, and pointed to Kunrad's outstretched hand.

The captain knew better than to contradict a mastersmith. 'Ride on, then!' he barked. 'Thought they'd put us off, doubtless! Ride!'

'Doing a grand job, aren't they?' Gille muttered. Olvar nodded; but Kunrad, tucking away the bracelet, was already riding ahead, and they had to spur their mounts to follow.

All that day they rode, and the land around them became less familiar, more windswept, more barren, as it rose. Grass gave way to heathers, and the heathers grew harder and scrubbier. The soil was growing thinner, the plants browner despite the clear spring air. They clung to the bones of the barren land as if the wind would carry them away, and it occurred to Kunrad that anything dying here would soon be covered in low grasses, lichens and mosses, and add one more featureless hummock to the bleak vista. In such a place, and in the clear light, the horsemen's trail stood out clear enough for all to see, and it did not turn. The mountains were looming high above them now, closer than most men had ever seen them, and when they stopped to water the horses at one of the many deep-carven streamlets, Kunrad tried his bracelet once again.

'Always north!' said Haldin, a little too cheerfully. 'Sure you didn't use a lodestone by mistake?'

Kunrad glared at him. 'All too sure! There – see?'

Olvar squinted. 'That's a pass of sorts, there. Swear to it.'

Kennas looked around sharply. 'You mean, *through*? Be damned to that!' All men knew what lay beyond those mountains, and a distinct chill lingered in the sunny noon air to remind them of it. But he was a brave man, or was obliged to be. 'Well, we'll take up their little bluff!' he said. 'Though they must be damnably far ahead, if they're out of view in this bare country. A killing pace they're keeping up! Still finding that trail, lads?'

'Yes,' said the lead scout. 'Though it's odd. Very blurred and mucky, in this damp land. But still clear.'

'Well, we haven't time to look closer!' He didn't need to articulate the thought; night, finding them under the shadow of those peaks. 'One good ride and we should be on their heels. Maybe even have sight of them soon!'

'Let's hope so!' said Haldin softly. 'It would make a difference.'

But as the afternoon wore on the land ahead remained empty. Only birds flew, wheeling and croaking in the distance, and small beasts scattered from the riding's path; though not very many of those. And it was as if the soil began to slip from under their hooves, and they found themselves riding across barely covered scree-falls that would give way treacherously now and again. And then, up ahead, they saw the scouts rein in so abruptly their mounts reared and plunged, and the riders sprang to earth. Then they frantically flagged the column down.

'Now what's amiss?' roared Kennas.

'A camp!' called the scouts, wheeling their horses and stooping to peer at the ground.

'*What?* They haven't had time to camp – unless . . . You bloody fools! Have we been following an old trail?'

'It was still half dark when we picked it up!' wailed the younger scout, as the column closed in around him. 'All muddied! But there were clear tracks, and fresh!'

'That's right!' protested another. 'At least . . . that's what we thought!'

Kennas, beyond speech, tore off his helmet and dashed it to the ground.

'That's no way to treat my good work!' protested Haldin. 'What's going on, anyhow?'

'They came this way *before* the raid!' snarled the captain. 'Before the fair, I'll be bound! Sothrans come to see the sights, that's all! When, you trollscuts – when?'

'Well – three nights since, by the ashes! But there're these tracks—'

Kunrad closed his eyes a moment. 'The night of the first day? Just after we quarrelled?'

'Fresh trail!' shouted a scout, who had cantered away down the hill. 'Fresh beyond doubt! They're headed eastward and south, along the mountain edge. A lot of them, the whole damned column!'

'So they did retrace their tracks to put us off, eh?' muttered the captain. 'Damn-fool trick. Well, they're making a hell of a pace – those big sothran horses, probably. Not much chance of catching them up, but if we ride—'

'Fresh tracks!' shouted the young scout, from the other direction. 'Over here! Only a few, but fresh!' He was pointing uphill.

'What?' roared Kennas. 'You're blind, boy!' But he rode over, came back, and dismounted to pick up his helm.

'Beyond me,' he said, trying to polish the muddy gravel off it with his glove. 'They split up, it seems. Most turned eastward, but a few more paddled around here somewhere. What a place to!' He looked around and shuddered. They

The Hand of the Ice

were at the mouth of a wide valley, its sides rounded and scoured as an old mixing bowl. The soil was thin, more a mix of stones, with occasional long strange heaps like giant wormcasts, and scattered boulders. 'Hoped to decoy us up into that forsaken hole, evidently.'

'It'd make sense of a sort,' said Haldin. 'Just enough of them slink off with the plunder, somewhere easy to give us the slip. That leaves us to chase after a bunch of lilywhites out for a constitutional, and what's to prove otherwise?'

'Right, Mastersmith! The others have probably slipped back around a corner somewhere and followed after the rest, some other way. Well, the day's wasting . . .'

Kennas stopped, his mouth twitching. The bracelet was pointing resolutely uphill.

'Bugger that thing! With all respect, Mastersmith – Mastersmiths! But there must be something agley here. We can't go on up there! If the land goes on like this we wouldn't be able to use our horses. And besides . . .'

'Besides, night's coming on,' said Olvar.

'*Yes!*' snarled the captain, tugging at his short beard. 'Yes it bloody well is! And I couldn't be sure of holding the men here, not the citizens nor my lads either, and do I blame them? In Tiure's armoured arse I do! Listen, you're the guildsmen present. Either I can go after the main band, back eastward, though it's little hope I hold of that – or I turn about and go back. They might be doubling back to attack the town again, after all.'

'Ach, that's nonsense!' protested Haldin, but with scant enthusiasm. 'Small chance of that, and you've more than enough men back there to cope.'

'Yes. But not these lads; and the town's more to them than this hunt, small chance or not. You can doddle around here as you like, Master Kunrad, but the men won't.'

Kunrad heaved a sigh. 'I think you should turn back, captain. What the bracelet shows me is mine alone.'

'You're not going to stay?' spluttered Gille. 'That was one dint too many!'

'The lad's right, Mastersmith!' exclaimed Kennas, horrified. 'I was prating only, I didn't mean—'

Kunrad nodded. 'There were only three or four tracks, you said? Then a few more of us should be enough.'

'If they're all we meet, maybe,' muttered the captain. '*Hoi!* We're turning back, lads. Volunteers to stay on with the mastersmiths?'

'Well, I see I'm one,' grunted Haldin. 'Me and my promises!'

Nobody else spoke. '*All* right!' said the captain. 'Sergeant, take command! Piss off out of it, and watch out for that main band! Masters, we'd best be riding now or not at all – and yes, I do bloody well have to come, if you do!'

'Thank you, captain,' said Kunrad awkwardly, as they watched their force wheel about and go scattering and stumbling down the hill, rather too fast. Men were looking back; but none of them were stopping. 'I won't forget this.'

'Believe me, neither will I!'

'Nobody thanks us, you notice,' muttered Gille to Olvar. 'I don't remember volunteering either, do you?'

'Comes with the guild colours,' said Olvar, though there was a faint fleck of concern in his voice. 'All part of the job. Boy! Sharpen that chisel! Boy, walk into a daggertooth's den! Life's rich tapestry.'

'I think I'm coming unravelled,' was all Gille said. But the others had already turned their mounts uphill, and he was acutely aware of being alone. All he could do was follow.

It was another world the valley led them into, a world where life clung grimly on to the edge of uncompromising stone, in case the whining wind should sweep it away. There was no warm life in earth or sky. There were only a few patches of trees, scrubby firs huddled against either flank, their gnarled roots climbing over jagged boulders like fingers clutching their last handful of sustaining soil. Higher up they shrank to low creeping shrubs, gnarled and tangled and as coated with brownish lichens and mosses as the stones around; so that when they finally gave way, lost ground and vanished, it was hard to notice. But as the searchers approached the crest of the valley slope, only the rocks remained, tolerating the lichen and the few leafy things that shivered in their shelter. The rocks themselves seemed to change at the crest, quite suddenly, in the compass of a step, from a shovelled jumble of scree to a more shapely weathered roundness, but one which gave no shelter or respite to life of any sort. The trail was still clear, but only in pebbles scarred or tossed aside; there was no bare earth to take imprints. They felt, all of them, as if they were crossing some kind of subtle border into a region where they had no place, a country of stones.

It had a bizarre beauty in its fashion, crowned by the majestic mountain flanks, blackened and glossy, with their jagged snowcrowns glistening against the grey clouds. A passing raincloud trailed its veils across the summits, and the raindrops glittered in the low light, as if turning to ice even as they fell. The mountain walls dropped away with breathtaking steepness to this smooth-sided cleft and its barren floor, a wide expanse of wind-raked gravel as flat as any made by man. Sprawled across it lay stones of weird shapes, boulders rolled round as polished gemstones mingled with great jagged things, raw and stressed, that suggested the debris of a battle between immense forces. 'So it is, I've heard,' Haldin whispered. They all whispered instinctively, for the valley's voice was the wind. Not even a bird cried out. 'The . . . the Ice pushes the great boulders as it moves, grinding them to gravel and silt eventually as a river does. But at bleakest winter, its meltwater freezes to the very surface of the rock, and tears great chunks loose, like a beast with its fangs. So it rips at the very fabric of the earth itself. It did here once, before it withdrew.'

Rivers ran between the stones, slow, narrow channels that crossed and recrossed like veins in an ancient hand, gnarled and strong. They were green, a thick pallid green like oily paint, but not even with the small scummy life of pond and ditch. When Kunrad let it drip through his fingers a coarse sediment clung, heavier than wine-lees; and when they sipped a little, the strong mineral taste made them spit. That was all the colour, ground from the green granite beneath. The horses would not touch it. Ahead of them, at a bend in the valley, stretched a wide pool of the same dismal shade, so heavy that even the wind seemed unable to ruffle its pale surface. From here, like an artery, all the streams ran; but as they advanced they saw others, smaller, cascading down into it, a web of tiny rills and waterfalls scouring down a steeper slope of tumbled stone.

And then, as they raised their eyes, they saw above it the source of all this, towering high against the mountain-slopes, filling the upper valley with a mighty wall. Not a straight barrier; its ramparts were jagged, its face irregular, inward sloping, deeply undercut. The sun had eaten at it, the wind weathered, the earth besmirched. Holes and channels riddled it like suppurating sores, running green streams of infected meltwater. Blocks and cascades fallen from it strewed the bleak ground, and shrank slowly to feed the artery streams. Cracks and chasms opened where the earth beneath thrust up in resistance, or sank away beneath its tyrannical burden. Yet all of these attacks it scorned in its sheer enormity, grinding down weakness and strength alike, renewing what was torn from it with an infinity of resource, like a fortress which was all wall, with no hollow heart.

It lay there in timeless stillness; and yet the terrible tension in it, the crouching, contained menace, struck straight into their minds. In the face of the giant glacier they saw a torrent barely held in check, the vanguard of a vast army ready to sweep down over all in its path. The sheer scale and power of it would have been awesome enough to them, even without the knowledge of the dark implacable wills that lay behind it, that turned its jagged rim to an outstretched hand with reaching, clawing fingers. Like a monstrous pale arm indeed it crooked around the mountain face, scaled and scarred with crevasses and encrusted moraines. But they knew also, in this their first sight of it, that it was only one limb of an uncountable number, and not the largest. That it was less than a fingertip of the vast cold hands that closed around the world, and sought to clasp, to crush it tight and eternal within the chilly grasp of the Great Ice.

It was Gille who managed to break the silence. Without wholly realising it, they had reined in and drawn together, like infants clutching hands in the face of the menacing unknown. 'Why – why on earth would they *ever* have come here?'

The captain audibly struggled for control of his voice. ''Cause we wouldn't, laddie. And there's been no trail leading out, has there? So either there's another way – and I don't mind admitting I'd be glad to find it. Or they're still holed up here somewhere.'

'I shouldn't have dragged you here!' said Kunrad shakily. 'No hunt was worth this.'

'But you don't say you wouldn't have come yourself, you obstinate bugger!' grumbled Haldin. 'Don't worry. I feel the same way. I want their hides, and not least for dragging me here. It's my business too.'

'My town,' added Kennas. 'Same goes. But it feels like – Powers, I don't know the words!'

'That now you've seen this,' suggested Gille softly, 'the world's never going to look quite the same, ever again?'

The captain turned in surprise. 'You too, lad? Well, all of us, maybe. But there's more folk than us to consider. There's still a trail to follow. Let's be about it!'

'Have we long enough before dark?' Kunrad wondered.

'There's a good three hours left in the sun!' said Haldin. He unlashed the great beard-axe he carried at his saddlebow, and laid it across his knee. He seemed to draw strength from that. 'Long enough to get up to . . . that, if we need to. And back! Let's go!'

But by the time they reached the margins of the lake, Haldin's guess had proved a bad one. The shadows under the high peaks grew deep much sooner than usual as the sun fell, and the wind that scoured down the valley brought racing tatters of grey, spitting cold drizzle. They were becoming thicker, and the drizzle hung like curtains beneath them, pitting the still green surface of the great pool. The trail led right to its margins.

'They didn't ride through that, surely?' grunted Olvar.

Haldin shook his head. 'The horses don't like it. But maybe sothran ones – or could they have dumped their booty in here, to hide it? To come back later?'

The captain shuddered. 'Back *here*?' He kicked free of his stirrups, took his long lance from its socket and poked around with the butt in the shallows. Strange bubbles rushed up, and an unpleasant smell tinged the air; but there was no sign of anything except pebbles. 'The centre's much deeper,' he reported. 'You'll not go riding across that. Better we go afoot and look for some other spoor.'

Glumly they plodded around that side of the slope, searching for another track, but there was nothing anyone could find. Olvar, though, stared uneasily at the opposite bank. 'Might be something there, see?'

Kunrad stared. 'A slip, you mean? But that must happen all the time in muck like that. Besides, you're not trying to tell me they went up there?'

They stared at each other a moment. Then they jumped. It was only a harsh bird-caw, but in that bleak place it echoed from wall to wall, harshly alive and urgent. Looking up, they watched black wings wheel above the valley an instant; then, as the call was answered from somewhere above, they vanished into the grey clouds. Kunrad saw with a sudden chill that these had been growing thicker even in the short time they searched. They were almost solid now, and the sun dwindled to a pale smoky disc, fluttering and fading like a blown candle. He could believe the birds were the fabled messengers of Raven, who had stolen the sun. Even as he looked, a wash of darker cloud came rushing up over the mountain crests and the towering wall of ice, and suddenly the very air seemed to turn grey.

'Enough!' he called out, though the words stuck like sharp bones in his throat. 'High time we turned for home!'

'High time and beyond!' shivered Gille, springing into his saddle. 'Come on, Olvar, you oaf, d'you want to lie the night here with an ice-block for your pillow and an Ice-witch for your bedmate?'

'There's still light enough,' said Haldin angrily. 'I mean, we've chased the bastards this far – and what's happened to Master Bold-Counsel? I never thought you the superstitious sort!'

'You think I like running away?' demanded Kunrad irritably. 'You don't have to believe in bogles and witches and spooks to feel there's something less than canny up there! I'll not have others face it on my account or anyone's!'

'He's right,' said Kennas flatly. 'To horse, my masters. We'll have to skirt the lake as is, to be away ere night.'

Then the rain came in earnest, a first great wave of it drumming down across their shoulders, and with it wafts of tiny stinging hailstones, spattering into the lake. Without a word the weary men clambered into the saddle, pulling their hoods down low; and, turning their faces from their first sight of the great Enemy, they set their horses to the east and south. Around the green lakelet they rode, still in silence, while the wind-driven rain whipped up its waters, as if to taunt them. Old Haldin took it hardest; Kunrad, riding beside him, saw his knuckles clench again and again on the shaft of the great axe, and understood why. Haldin had been as daunted as the rest of them by the Ice, perhaps more so; but like many men of little imagination and strong pride, he was afraid to admit his fear, most of all to himself. He had grown more and more eager in the chase, as if thirsting for revenge on those who had brought him to it; and now they had beaten him, they and the fear together.

Saying anything, though, would only worsen his shame. Kunrad decided he might give vent to his own feelings, when he could. That would make Haldin try to cheer him up, and lessen his own bitterness. As they passed the end of the lakelet, fording a sluggish outflow, the rain began to slacken, but the twilight was already deepening in around them, till all they saw were indistinct shadows and silhouettes against a grey sky, and the horses picked their way with difficulty.

Without warning Haldin's hand clamped down on Kunrad's arm, painfully. The older man half rose in his stirrups, and flung back his dripping hood. Kennas started to say something, but was silenced by Haldin's angry hiss. 'Up ahead there! Don't you hear something?'

'Sounds like . . .' Olvar hesitated. 'That's horses!'

'Just a few, by Hella!' hissed the captain. 'A ways ahead! And heading . . . aye, for the bloody passmouth! They must've been lurking in some fold of the slope all this time, to slink past us!'

'They've done it, too!' snapped Gille, as angry as the rest.

'By Ilmarinen's hot coulter, they haven't!' growled Haldin.

'We can't ride hard in this mirk!' protested Kennas. 'Over these bloody stones—'

'We can too, down the streambed!' was the older smith's furious response. 'Smoother there! Ride, if you're not afraid!'

He was away, spurring his weary horse, and Kunrad after him, his own blood suddenly roaring in his ears as the stream thrashed and spattered beneath him. For the sake of the others, he had sought to forget his driving rage; but he had only stifled it, and it erupted now with force redoubled. He plucked the sword, the cheap decent sword, from the saddle-scabbard; it felt like a feather in his hand. Ahead he saw the glint of Haldin's axe, swinging in the dark, a fearful weapon the master-smith, by all accounts, knew how to use. Even over the noise of their own charge Kunrad could still hear the horses ahead, trotting now but no more; the others couldn't have found a stream yet, or thought of it. The stones would not be slimy in this poisoned water, where not even that last lichen grew. They would overtake the sothrans fast, perhaps any moment, coming between them and the mouth of the pass; but it was growing truly dark now, and there could be a fearful game of hide-and-seek among the boulders.

But then, to his left, he heard a startled whinny, and a sudden triumphant roar of challenge from Haldin. At least the smith still had the sense to make sure whom he attacked. There was no answering voice, but a clash of metal. Kennas caught up with Kunrad and swept past him, out of the streambed and on to the gravel, lance lowering at the darkness ahead. Haldin shouted again; and this time he was answered.

Yet it was no voice, that answer, though it had shape and form of a kind. It was the high wailing shriek of a beast; but loud, dreadfully loud in that echoing bowl of a place, and heavy with jarring discords that stabbed the ears like steel spikes and froze even heated blood. It sparked sheer terror like struck iron, and Kunrad's horse reared and thrashed, almost spilling him from the saddle. But more terrible yet was the cry that vibrated beneath it, for that throat at least was human, and the agony of it plain. It was Haldin's; and when the other cry ended abruptly, it lasted a brief instant longer, before choking to nothing. Its echoes were lost in another, heavier noise, a thudding crash among scattering stones.

Horrified, ears ringing, Kunrad shouted Haldin's name, then ducked barely in time as something glinted in the darkness before his eyes. It sang by over his head, and he struck out at where he thought the swordwielder must be. Nothing; and the force of his blow almost toppled him from the saddle. Frantically he grabbed the pommel, tried to pull himself back up, and was horrified to see another, larger horse loom up, and the glint of its rider's breastplate. Nobody in their party wore one; this was an enemy, and his sword gleamed against it as it swung. Kunrad struck at it, frantically, and his sheer strength stopped the blow. Desperately he swung up, parried the horseman's next cut, and locked blades with him as their horses wheeled, hearing the other's furious breathing and half-mouthed curses. Furiously his enemy tried to disengage and thrust in one movement, but Kunrad had been taught the counter. Almost automatically his blade lifted, gave and whirled, sliding the other's sword past him and leaving his body undefended. It was so instinctive that Kunrad hesitated to complete the killing stroke; but nonetheless his sword ran under the other's armpit. A grind, a jar; a mouth a handsbreadth away yelled in utter incredulous agony. Horrified, he jerked his hand back, and the yell foundered in an inhuman gargling sound, a violent drowning cough. The shadow before him vanished, there was another dull crash, and the other horse bolted. Darkness reigned absolute.

Kunrad quietened his horse, hearing the heavy panting of others nearby, and further off the captain, swearing fearfully. Hoofbeats drummed now, near the pass-mouth, far and fading, hard to locate for ears still riven by that first awful howl, and minds still shaken. Then the moon rose.

Over the mountain wall its rim lifted, through the clouds that thinned once again as the rain died. And as its first rays struck the snowcaps of the peaks, they sprang to life, blossoming from faint grey shadows to white tongues of frozen flame, sparkling and shimmering to blind the few faint stars. Down the steep slopes the light cascaded, like an avalanche into the dismal valley; and at its head the Ice itself awoke in answer, a sweeping mantle of bitter white about the shoulders of the mountain. But not there alone. Around the distant peaks to the north and east the same majestic light arose, turning their craggy flanks to silver; and up against the grey clouds beyond, mirrored in stark beauty from the vast plains that stretched in silent dominion, unbroken, unchallenged, to the farther face of the world.

Even the pale pools glimmered in homage. Cloud shadows raced across the stones, and suddenly they could see the whole valley almost as clearly as by day. Close by Kunrad were Gille and Olvar, hefting their borrowed swords. Further ahead, trotting back from an evidently fruitless pursuit, was Kennas. Beneath Kunrad's feet a man sprawled, contorted around his right side, twitching slightly; a shining pool spreading beneath him. But some fifty yards further on lay a fallen horse, and beyond it a shapeless huddle. Kunrad swore, and with lead in his heart he spurred his horse across and sprang down.

Haldin lay there, still clutching the haft of his shattered axe; and there was no blood. Yet the moonlight glistened on his upturned eyes, already cloudy; they did not stir, and his mouth gaped below his bristling moustache.

Kunrad touched the Mastersmith's neck to seek a pulse, and recoiled at the chill of it. Behind him Gille squealed with sudden pain.

'What in Hella's name?' demanded Kunrad.

'It burns! With cold, I mean – the axe-shards! Covered in ice!'

Startled, Kunrad picked up the broken axe-head. His fingertips stuck, and he barely pulled them away without leaving skin. Fearfully he touched Haldin's dead face. It was hard, cold to the touch; the skin hardly moved over what felt like chill metal beneath. The captain, striding to Kunrad's side, reached out in fascinated horror, and touched the older smith's moustache. It snapped and crackled with a thin coating of ice. Even as they watched his eyes turned wholly opaque, and Kunrad could not shut them. The biting chill extended halfway back across the skull, down below the eyelids. The entire front of his head, and the brain behind it, seemed to have been frozen in one terrible instant.

'Frozen deep enough to shatter iron,' said Kunrad hollowly. 'Colder by far than . . . *that* could ever get.' He nodded up-valley.

'No man could do that – could they?' demanded Kennas.

'No. Not even any smith I've ever heard of. Vayde himself, maybe, who tethered demons in his creations. None other. This was . . . something. Some *thing*, from this place.'

'And they led us on to it, to cover their own filthy getaway,' spat Kennas in disgust. He glanced around anxiously, but the valley floor was clear for a mile around. 'Probably lured it out of its lair with that in mind. Like leading someone across the path of a bear-dog pack.'

'Worked, didn't it?' said Olvar sombrely. 'If he'd been a bit less headstrong . . . But he wasn't afraid of anything, old Haldin.'

'They didn't all get away, anyhow!' said Gille. 'Master Kunrad's taught this one a thing or two.'

'Pity he won't be telling us anything,' grunted the guard, bending over the still form. 'Learned him a lasting lesson, Master. Skewered him fair and pretty.'

Kunrad felt suddenly unsteady on his feet, and leaned against his horse, forehead down on the saddle. 'Wish I hadn't had to. Though when I heard Haldin – Powers, why did I ever embark on this accursed chase?'

''Cause you had to,' said the captain quietly. 'And so did he. Charging off like that, eh? Not your fault, my lad. You've done well enough. But we'd best be riding out now, and speedily. His nag's dead, poor brute, like himself.'

'I'll take him over mine,' said Kunrad. 'But the other?'

Gille and Olvar were already searching the man's body, Gille with squeamish shudders. 'A few gold coins – those sothran ones,' reported Olvar. 'Little else of interest, and his sword's bent. We've stuck him under his cloak and a few big stones, and that's as much as he deserves. Leave him to the Ice beasts, if they care to dig. Let's ride.'

'Aye, the clouds close in again,' said the captain. 'I'll not spend a moment more than needful here in the dark.'

There was an instant, silent accord on that. Within minutes the little party was trotting for the pass, with Haldin's body slung over Kunrad's mount. He was a widower, and without children living, so no kinsfolk were left bereft. But Kunrad knew that the whole town would mourn him; and some, at least, would blame Kunrad for having led him into danger. As they reached the lip of the pass he glared back a silent curse at the terrible light between the peaks, remembering the dream it had invaded. A warning, maybe; and yet, though there was menace in it, it did not feel like a foreboding.

A sudden cry broke into his gloomy thoughts. He looked to Gille; but it was Olvar, of all people, who had squealed. He was pointing to Haldin's body, tied behind his saddle. The hood of his cloak had fallen back, and now the face bobbed blankly up at the moon. Already it was thawing a little; the locked jaw had fallen closed, the eyelids sagged free. But it was not that Olvar pointed at. Across the features from chin to hairline, picked out in dark points where the violent freezing had broken blood vessels beneath the skin, was the shadow-outline of a huge, long-fingered but disturbingly human hand.

Their welcome back in town was much as he had feared. The guards had come home that morning, to be roundly scorned for leaving the smiths. When they themselves rode in, just as the gates were closing at sunset, the townspeople flocked to give them a hero's welcome. When they saw Haldin's body, though, all rejoicing ceased, and a gloom sank over the town. It was not long, either, before the first reproaches began to fly, and they were not all from people he could ignore. Kennas defended Kunrad, making it clear that Haldin's action was his own; but the guards who had fled now felt themselves justified, and said so. Metrye, whom he had known since his childhood, was coldly wrathful, and the Guildmaster, though more understanding, was sorely stricken by a death he saw as needless. The mastersmiths were kinder, understanding better what had driven Kunrad to such extremes. Many offered him lodging until his own house was repaired. But he preferred to go back to it, charred, gap-roofed and smoke-stinking as it was, and fall into his own rough bed. Gille and Olvar, wearied to silence, went back with him. Their weariness was in some part a mercy; they slept, and did not dream, nor did those awful voices return to haunt them. But nonetheless something must have turned over in Kunrad's mind; for when he awoke next morning, it was made up.

He sat and thought, as he sent the apprentices out to buy breakfast, and counted the little money left to him. They ate in near silence, the prentices sensing that he was coming to some decision; and when they were done he went to see the Guildmaster. He was already receiving the heads of guild and elders, but they summoned Kunrad in at once, the prentices trailing after.

'Ah, Mastersmith! Your name's been on our lips all morning!' The Guildmaster's tone was friendly, but it made Kunrad feel deeply uneasy.

'Yes, lad!' said Kolfe genially. 'You've been having yourself a hard time, no doubt about it. You'll have to rebuild your house, and no doubt your fortunes a wee bit. Well, the guild'll see you right on that, never fret! But it came to us, see, that since poor old Haldin's gone, you might find it good and profitable to step into his shoes as Town Smith, like as is – eh?'

'Oh, not for ever, maybe!' chimed in Tarkil. 'We know you've your fine armour to be working on – but just till you've the means to do yourself proud again, as you should.'

'But I don't have my armour, masters,' said Kunrad. 'I thank you, but that's the foremost problem. What are we to do about pursuing the thief – for my property, and justice, and the town's good name?'

Some looked at him, some would not. No smith spoke, and it was left to the head of the Bakers' Guild. 'Lad, what more can we do? That chase has cost us a heap of trouble, and one good man. Like it or not, the sothran bastard's beyond our reach now.'

'He can't be that far!' snapped Kunrad. 'One day's ride, maybe two. Barely out of our region, weeks of journeying before he's out of the North. He could still be overtaken and stopped – or you could send messengers!'

'Lad, lad, we're doing that,' sighed the Guildmaster. 'As many as we can manage, and some letters with folk going back from the fair. But what's a letter, or a messenger even, against the man himself? Him with his followers and his gold and his winning ways, in a far town that doesn't know us save as a name and maybe a trade rival? We've even hinted he's some kind of intelligencer for the South, and that may help, with times as they are. But nearer the Southland he'll be known by name, maybe, and his word carry more weight still. And once he's over that border, you may kiss him goodbye.'

'You could send a force!' said Kunrad angrily. 'Drag the bastard back, followers or no!'

'And at what cost?' demanded the baker. 'Mastersmith, think! We could pay you your losses twice over and still spend far less. I'm angry too, and I'll not see any man suffer that the Guilds can help. But can the town afford to send a huge riding so far from home for so long, and leave the town half defended?'

'You would if this stupid war comes about,' said Kunrad bitterly.

'Maybe, maybe!' muttered the Guildmaster. 'Though that's different. Men will volunteer, they won't have to be bribed – not so much, anyway. Lad, I'm all for justice – but when you're as old as I am, you'll know that it has its limits. You're angry now, and about poor old Haldin too, and small wonder. But don't let it eat you up! Where did it get Haldin, now?'

Galdred nodded. 'Vengeance is a fruit that rots in the mouth. Better settle down and be glad you're well friended here. That's worth all the vengeance in the world.'

'I thought you at least would understand, Mastersmith!' said Kunrad fiercely. 'It's not vengeance. Well, not foremost, not alone; though Merthian owes me a life now. But he owes me mine, too. There's too much of me in that suit. He might as well have cut off my right arm as take it – and by the Powers, I think he knew it! And there's that flaw – in the armour, and therefore in me. If I don't get it back, maybe I'll never find it. Even if I make another one, just the same as far as I know, it may not show it. Then it'll haunt me! Will it lurk in everything I make? Will it come back when I least expect it? I'll be incomplete in every sense. And I'll never be wholly a master.'

He hesitated, looking down at the waxed wood of the table. 'Guildmaster, Mastersmiths, masters – since you won't help me more, I must help myself. I must leave you, and my home, and go alone in search of what's been riven from me.'

'Metrye had the right of it!' exploded the Guildmaster. 'You're clean daft, boy!'

But none of the other masters protested, not even the baker. Galdred looked down at his boots. 'Yes, lad, I do understand. But that's not to say I think you're right. And as acting Head of Guild there's a question I'm bound to ask. What about your prentices, now? You're bound to them as they to you. I can't take 'em, and I don't know a Master in town who can. We're well served by ours, and yours, well, let's say they'll take some training up. Sorry.'

Kunrad looked around at the two young men. Gille was ashen, Olvar sitting like a piece of carven wood, but with a downward twist to his mouth. Kunrad knew him well enough to read the signs. 'You're right. And swift. I had been going to ask you to help. I won't, now. Lads, I'm truly sorry, but I'm going regardless. You must go back to your families and seek another indenture, or make what way you can with me. Maybe in another town there'll be places for you.'

He turned hastily away from their faces. 'I will ask you one thing, though, masters. To lend me some money.'

The Guildmaster snorted. 'As well toss it down the privy. Worse, for you might recover it even then. Nobody'll lend to a man who'll never come back!'

'Not even to a friend? Not even the Guild? What about those losses made good you promised? And there's the security of my house, my forge and all within it. That's worth something!'

Galdred shook his head sharply, and went on staring at his boots. Kolfe and the others avoided his eye. Kunrad said nothing, but nor did he move. It was the baker who finally spoke up. 'I'll lend what I can, Kunrad. Not much, but then I fear you're not going to need much. I doubt you'll do better.'

It was barely a quarter of what the house was worth, and Kunrad could hardly decide whether the baker was being generous or chiselling him. He suspected the baker was none too sure, either. With that in hand, he went to buy himself a horse from the town stable, and settled for the big bay that had borne him on the first day's hunt. But as he bargained, Gille and Olvar walked in.

'What about us? Expect us to run alongside, do you?'

'Or were you going to use us for baggage mounts?'

Kunrad shrugged. 'I didn't know you were coming. You haven't said a word about your choice.'

'*Choice?*' exploded Gille. 'To go back and rot as my father's youngest, and no good to him – as he'll be forever telling me? He'll blame me, whatever the truth of it. I'll be lucky if I'm set to sweep the floors and not banished to the stable, or worse. No gold and no future. Some choice!'

'And I'll be the deckhand for my brothers,' grunted Olvar. 'They don't care for smithcraft, not fishermen. They'll keep me half-starved and gutting fish, and laugh at it. You know that well enough! Choice!'

'So we're coming,' said Gille acidly. 'But not willingly! And at least we're going to be there when you admit this was all a fool's quest, and turn home with your tail between your legs – *Master!* And then maybe we'll be able to pick up the threads of our lives once again.'

'You may,' said Kunrad. 'I'll say it again, I'm sorry, lads. But I never could!'

So more of his money went on two more mounts. Packing what little gear remained to them did not take long, and it was only afternoon of that day when they led them down the main street to the gate. Metrye stood on the porch of her house, with its swirling sea-paintings leaping about her, and shook her head as they passed. 'A young fool in his folly. Men! If he'd stolen your balls, you couldn't be more frantic! But I say this to you, young Mastersmith – if you pass that gate now, on this wretched errand, then you will never *ever* return. Think upon that! And remember I have seen things true in my time, though I am not a smith to make a magic mirror.'

'I know of no smith who ever did, save in tales!' answered Kunrad. 'I'm sad to have offended you, as all my other friends. For that I blame Merthian all the more. But I say to you that you're wrong, Healer! I *will* have my justice. I *shall* succeed!'

Gille and Olvar looked at her sadly, and twirled their fingers about their temples.

'The more fools you, then!' she snorted, and went noisily inside and slammed the door.

The gate guards stood aside as they passed, as men did, sometimes, from the unlucky or accursed; and they too shook their heads. Kunrad held his high.

But Metrye saw truly; for as the Chronicles record, that day the Mastersmith Kunrad rode forth from his Northern home for the last time, and saw it never again.

CHAPTER THREE
Trail of Ashes

'WELL,' SAID OLVAR, 'WE can't say the bastard's making himself hard to follow!'

They surveyed the skeletal remains before them, nothing left to show what they had been save the great blackened anvil still standing by the shattered hearth. Pavi, weaponsmith of the little town of Folby, clutched his singed head in anguish. 'He's done this to you, too?'

Gille grimaced. 'This much, only to us – though our forge didn't catch so well. More clay in your walls and less wattle, next time, Mastersmith! But he's left a trail of everything from unpaid tallys to armed robbery along the road south these last few weeks. Like little piles of horse apples along the way.'

Kunrad nodded grimly. 'And with the weaponsmiths worst of all.'

In that short time they had ridden all the way down from their own corner of the North into the very heart of Nordeney, fully two-thirds the length of the land to its southern border; and with Merthian's ravages for stark signposts. At Aldreby, Athalby's first neighbour along the High Road, the Guild's messages had already arrived, but too late to prevent the taking of another weaponsmith's stock, this time by subterfuge. Merthian bought, then his men stole back the gold even as it was paid and swept out of town at speed, leaving the honest burghers still half-convinced there must be some mistake. Aldreby's guard had eventually ridden after the raiders, with even less success. When Kunrad pressed them to join him, they wished him well, called him a dreamer behind their hands and went back to their daily round once more.

Again Kunrad rode hard on the trail, and again nobody would join him. He found himself lagging further and further behind now, without spare mounts; desperate as he was, he would not kill or lame a horse.

At Karrborg, a fortified town, it was the same story, though here the weaponsmith's stocks had been quite calmly taken at swordpoint and in broad daylight, while Merthian passed the time of day with citizens in the street. By the time the smith and his journeyman escaped their bonds, the sothrans were hours away, bearing nights of fire and fear to the next towns along their way.

'But Merthian was so agreeable on his way north!' protested Pavi. 'A true sothran gentleman, I thought him. And so knowledgeable about the art of arms! I'll swear it was no pretence!'

'Sure!' said Olvar, with heavy cynicism. 'He saved his stealing for the homeward road!'

Kunrad shrugged. 'I felt the same, Pavi. But I guess there's more to it than that. Some change in him, that made all this possible.'

Gille looked around. 'You mean – once he'd raided us, that dropped all his barriers? He'd do anything after that?'

'Something like that. Not anything, perhaps; but anything he could find a good enough excuse for. Was it just weapons he took?'

Pavi groaned. 'My best! And almost all my ordinary stock, even my steel-shod bows the bow-wright shapes for me. That, and some horses from the inn. Maybe to bear the booty, for I had plenty. Had! And I sought to call out the town upon him – and that hog-headed captain of his ordered – *this!*'

'I know how you feel,' said Kunrad. 'None better. I'm going after him.'

The squat little smith blinked in popeyed surprise. 'You? *Just* you? But he's a lord and a sothran, he's got a whole following of men! And three good days start!'

Olvar and Gille exchanged looks. They were growing used to this reaction.

'He's still in our land,' said Kunrad. 'And if everyone he's robbed only got on his tracks, he'd stay here. And we'd get back most of what was stolen, maybe all. Will you help? Will you come along?'

'Me?' Pavi wagged his head sharply. 'Not for anything! I can't just go chasing off into the blue, I've a wife and children without a roof! I've got to rebuild here and earn my livelihood. The Guild'll help me, but I couldn't expect them to do anything if I went haring off to – to wherever! No, what can one or two men do against all this sothran arrogance? I wasn't going along with all this war talk – but now . . .' He shrugged. 'If you must fight, save it for that. I'm sorry I can't help. The Guildhall'll give you food and lodging – and listen, when you give up, we'll gladly find room for you here, I'm sure! But I'll be sticking to my anvil, thank you!'

'The same louseridden answer as always,' grunted Olvar, as the pretences strolled along to the Guildhall. 'How many towns is it, now? Nine? Ten?'

'And the villages he's stripped of provisions!' added Gille gloomily. 'At least Master Pavi didn't actually laugh in our faces. I'd swear some of 'em were ready to set the dogs on us.'

'I can understand that,' said Gille. 'The Mastersmith shows them up. No matter why, he's doing what they should have done, only they're too scared. They hate him for that. So they fob him off with a little charity, or laugh, or they get angry – anything they can share, and round on him with.'

Olvar was silent a moment. 'You're not telling me you're beginning to *agree* with him?'

'Should and ought don't always mean the same. There're times I hate him too. I want to go *home*, damn it! To a decent house and clean clothes and warm haylofts and girls who respect me, not treat me like some beggar off the wayside!'

'Me, I want regular meals and a comfortable bed, and regular work that leads somewhere, not slaving piecemeal in strange forges for someone of half the craft and a miserly hand with pay. Is that so very much to ask? And all these things we could have had by now. The town would've fallen over itself to help. All these other towns would jump to have someone of the Master's name. But we had to leave it all, and keep leaving it. What for? A dream, a daze. A lost soul. And Merthian gaining at every step. Three days ahead! Who knows where we'll be headed next?'

In town after town they found the pattern repeated. In the great community of Rasby, with more than half a million citizens and a huge indoor market that made Gille and Olvar gape, a whole series of swift thefts had been carried out in a single day.

'Becoming quite a practised felon!' was Kunrad's sour comment. 'And nobody even thought of following?'

Rasby's Guildmaster, himself a smith, spread his hands helplessly. 'To what profit? Could we have caught them, with such a start?'

'They have to camp sometime. They're far from home, they have to live on what they can carry from town to town. A little hard riding, and you could have had them. You still could.'

'Aye, with a force that would leave our town half undefended. You may sneer, Master Kunrad, but that is a real concern! Up there in your snug little backwater you don't know what's been happening down here!'

'The war talk? I've heard that. And if we can't band together to catch one thieving sothran, what chance have our armies?'

'A war's different. People swallow their pride and their differences, as they will for nothing less. But I didn't mean that!' The Guildmaster rapped the map of the Northlands richly inlaid in the top of the huge council table. 'I meant the raids and banditry that have brought us to this pass. They're on the increase, not just in numbers but in scale, by land and sea. All the stories we hear point to one band, a growing band that can strike at well-defended targets with an order little less than our own. Every bad character and outliver throughout the North seems to be flocking to join them, and in the South too, as I hear. Some say the South approves; certainly, with all its power, it does little enough to stop them! Did you know Thuneborg was attacked?'

Kunrad was taken aback. He had heard of Thuneborg as a rich castle town, one of the commanding points founded by the lord Vayde when he first scouted out the Northland for settlement. 'They surely didn't break through Vayde's fortifications?'

'They did not – but they tried. And not too badly, either. An assault upriver, from a sea landing, in some force. They were beaten back, but in good order and with few losses. It was almost as if they were trying themselves, or tempering their men. That was a week ago, and the word reached us yesterday. Men are still shaking and calling on the Powers.'

'A week ago . . .' mused Kunrad.

'So Lord Merthian didn't have anything to do with it, if that's what you're wondering. No, I've had word of him here before. He visited my brother Guildmaster in Dunmarhas a few years back, and made a fine impression. He's who he says he is, and a lord of renown in the Southlands, by all accounts. Why he's getting up to these little larks is beyond me. If he's robbed as many as you say, he must be gathering a mighty hoard of arms. Better made than any in his land, of course, but still . . . Maybe he just wants to have his men well equipped against these raids – or in case of war.'

'He seems to be doing his best to provoke it.'

'What, looting the odd shop? And with no backing from the Syndicacy of his land? Ill feeling, yes. A war, no. It's the great towns of the North that will decide for or against war, my lad. And that means their elected Guildmasters, and that means me, among others. That's the benefit of having no king any more, nor syndicacy of great lords, as the sothrans do. We're responsible to our folk. We won't go rushing in at such petty provocation. Nor will the Syndics, if my intelligencers are worth their fees.'

Kunrad tapped his winemug on the table. 'I'm glad to hear that, Guildmaster. Is Merthian a Syndic?'

'Has to be, lad! And not the least, though among the youngest.'

'And truly rich, too? So that he could afford to buy all these arms he's stealing?'

'Rich enough, aye. Though rich folk are no fonder of paying than you or I, when they don't have to.' Kunrad took in the Guildmaster's bejewelled fingers and gold chains, and smiled sourly to himself. 'In fact,' said the older man sagely, 'when I come to think about it – these sothran lords, lad, they may be decent enough to begin with, but they've too much power. Within their own lands they've the high justice, power of life and death, and nobody to so much as question. They're not in touch with everyday folk like you and I, not used to considering anyone's feelings, except on the surface. They're not used to being turned down. Could be they'd take it hard. Like insolence. Loss of dignity.'

'You mean – you think I offended Merthian enough to make *him* feel aggrieved?'

'Aye. Insulted. And maybe he could take against mastersmiths as a class, and be determined to teach 'em a lesson. Within limits, of course – and you'll notice he's killed nobody. He might think of that as restraint, a sothran aristo.'

That idea left Kunrad momentarily speechless, and gave the Guildmaster his opening. 'Well, lad, it's been grand to see you, though I wish it were in happier circumstance. You'll see, as things stand there's naught I can do to help, not truly. But you'll dine with me at the Guildhall tonight, you and your boys? Grand, grand. And if you ever give up this will-o'-the-wisp chase of yours, come make your fortune in a fine rich town. Your work's come of note down here, and I'll be glad to stand you sponsor. Fare you well now!'

The talk left Kunrad thoughtful, and the prentices also when he told them, that night in the Guildhall's guest-chambers. 'You know I've never taken much account of affairs of state, nor even of the town governance. But the way things are – well, the Guildmaster may be right, but I can't help wondering if Merthian has some purpose behind all this. Something deeper.'

Olvar, sprawled on the best bed he had slept in since leaving home, and full of the best food, was only up to a grunt. Gille, though, caught Kunrad's meaning. 'You mean – something for the Southlands against us?'

'Well – he might be testing our unity, the way we respond to a threat.'

'In which case he's got a pretty fair answer. He's robbed nine towns, stripped food from villages, and ended up with nobody on his trail but two abused apprentices and one mastersmith with a bent head. Proof conclusive, I'd say.'

'That's just the way Nordeney is,' Kunrad said. 'He didn't need to test that, it's well known. I knew it, I suppose. I just hoped some towns might be readier to react. Could he want war? Could he want people to hate the very name of Bryhaine?'

'He'd have killed, then, wouldn't he? War would be killing, so why hold back? He doesn't seem to do anything more than he needs to. Even the fire was largely accident, with us. Of course—' Gille looked blandly innocent. 'He may have done something worse by now. We're lagging pretty far behind. What is it now, two, three days? We've done well to keep that close!'

He did not miss the way his master's face fell at the reminder. 'He was headed southward still, the trackers say. Still on the Dunmarhas road. We'll be after him at first light tomorrow.'

'What if we lose him?' grunted Olvar. 'If he gets too far ahead, reaches his own land ahead of us? Which he surely might. It's a long haul, longer than we've come so far. As well you face that now, Mastersmith.'

Kunrad frowned. 'No! There's still Dunmarhas. It's a big town, bigger than Rasby or Thuneborg.'

'So you think he'll get up to his tricks there?'

Kunrad hesitated, visibly; the prentices exchanged

sharp glances. 'No; I'd guess not. Dunmarhas has links with the Southlands, that might make him wary. Beyond it there's nothing but the Debatable Lands and the Marshes, where he can't travel fast – unless he takes the long inland way, and that's little easier. Even if he steals more horses, he'll have a heavy load. And the Dunmarhas town guard is more like a small army these days, they tell me, and as used to the Marshes as anyone can be. He'd risk being overhauled and losing everything. More likely he'll rest his men a few days, and head south quite peacefully.'

Gille shuddered at the mention of the Marshes. 'What then? How far'll we be behind him? A week? We'll never overtake those big sothran warhorses with our breeds, they're too long in the hair and short in the leg. He'll hardly linger so long! Mastersmith, be reasonable – all that way, and you'll have to give up just the same. Unless you're proposing to follow him across the Marshes? Into Suderney itself?'

'In Niarad's name, don't suggest it!' groaned Olvar.

Kunrad was silent. Gille, looking at him, thought that his face had changed in these past weeks. It was leaner, slightly less vague in its look, but its frown graven deeper.

'If he escapes over the border . . .' The smith looked like a man whose teeth are being drawn. 'Then we'll see. Then, maybe – *maybe!* I'll have to call a halt. For now. Unless . . .' His gaze seemed to range out past the guest-room's painted walls. 'You'd better get some sleep. I need to think. We may be heading along unexpected ways – who knows?'

He blew out the smoky little lamp, and slumped gratefully back on his bolster.

'Unexpected?' said Gille's voice in the dark. 'You maybe think you've left me anything *to* expect?'

But at breakfast next morning he almost overset his bowl of cornmeal when a heavy hand clamped on his shoulder. Kunrad looked down at the prentices, and though his eyes were shadowed, there was a light in them that had not been there these last few weeks. 'Suppose we turn aside,' he said, sitting himself down beside them. 'Head for the coast. Will that hold your whingeing awhile?'

Gille looked stunned, then deeply suspicious. 'You mean . . . you'll quit the chase? Leave the armour?'

'Let the bastard go?' spluttered Olvar.

Kunrad was openly grinning now. 'You sound as if you're disappointed in me! No. I'll never give up, not wholly. I dreamt . . .' He shrugged. 'But you convinced me, you're right; we'll never catch him up in time. And believe me, I'm no more anxious to try the Marshes than you. There may be another way; I can't see it straight, not yet. Maybe I will, if I don't have the burden of the chase forever upon me, eating up my thoughts. And – well, Olvar, you've always been telling us that we should see the Sea. So here's your chance to show us.'

Olvar beamed, messily. 'That I will! Sink your worries in that sight awhile!'

Gille's eyes remained narrow. 'We could,' he suggested, 'always find a port – Saldenborg, say. Sell the horses, take ship for home.'

'That's one choice,' agreed Kunrad, pouring himself a mug of table-ale and breaking off a yellow-crumbed chunk of corncake from the steaming platter. 'Though there's little enough sea traffic, I hear, with this corsair business shrivelling the trade. It's not my choice, I'll allow, not for now. But maybe I'll come to feel differently, by then.'

Gille said nothing, but bent to his porridge.

The seaward road, winding westward down a wide river valley, was well made and well travelled, with villages and inns along its way. At first the smiths had little money to spare for these, and spent more time in stables and haystacks; but they rode in better spirits now, and in better harmony. Now that the immediate burden was off his shoulders, Kunrad became more his old self, and even took some heed of the world around him. Indeed, it was hard not to do so.

This was a mild, fruitful land compared to Athalby, its soils laid down deep and soft by long slow rivers, its vales wooded with trees they had never seen the like of. The ancient, high-crowned dawn redwoods that grew around their home had seemed tall; but here were their successors, giants of their kind, monsters seeded before even a rumour of the returning Ice was heard in the land. For many a thousand years they had grown undisturbed by beast or man; and not by ones and twos, but in vast shadowy ranks that dwarfed even the stands of bristlecone pine about them, to be felled only by the hand of wind or lightning, nothing less. Few men would ever dare, for the danger and the sheer awe of them, and perhaps also the lingering fear of the power that lay upon the vast gloomy forests at the land's heart, the hand of Tapiau.

So it was that farms and villages had grown up among them, sometimes between the very risings of their enormous roots, or in the wide jagged ring left by a fallen trunk, where its seedlings already formed a natural palisade. Such ruined majesty dwarfed mere human habitation, but these were wealthy communities, eager to pay well for the labour of three good smiths. And since Kunrad no longer counted every second, and seemed content to leave his purpose to work itself out, they were free to take more work, and live in greater comfort. Yet often, whether they lay among the hay of a stable or in the featherbeds of a homely inn, Gille, stealing off to seek out the serving girl he had winked at, would hear the mastersmith muttering to himself, half in and out of sleep. 'Not flank-rings!' came the words, in tones of quiet anguish. 'Not lame or leather, pauldron or tasset, staple or stop-rib! Not lining ... planishing ... not oil wanting or loose fastening, no! What, then? What? What ...'

It almost took the edge off Gille's appetite.

When the sun rose, though, Kunrad seemed as cheerful as ever, looking forward to the end of their road, and claiming to scent the sea in the warm west wind. Spring was shading into summer now, the early frost fading from the ground; and to men from the north of the land it already seemed warm. The bushes were glossy and green, and the first few flowers already spotting them with colour. In the ploughed fields the corn shoots were rising, and the hoes were hard at work, spades turning over the vegetable plots, rakes and forks spreading dung and clearing the orchards, axes and saws felling timber for seasoning and charcoal, metal-tyred wagon wheels bouncing along the roads. Spring was a busy time for smiths, too, and there was always work when they wanted it.

'We can buy some new clothes when we come to the coast!' said Gille cheerfully, shedding his cloak in the sunlight. 'Make a better impression. You can get rid of that dead sheep, for a start!'

'Leave it alone!' said Kunrad angrily, as he twitched the fleece on his jerkin back into place. 'I like it! It's comfortable in all weathers!'

'Makes him look tough!' rumbled Olvar. 'Huh!'

Kunrad snorted contemptuously, but there was more than a grain of truth in it. Against the belted black tunic and trousers that were a smith's garb, the bulky, old-fashioned jerkin sat rather oddly; still more so, with the gold-embroidered mastersmith's insignia around the collar. But it bulked out Kunrad's already broad chest and shoulders, and together with the plain sword tapping at his side made him a formidable figure, not one to trifle with. When local smiths felt inclined to whittle down his piecework rates, it was his look as much as his skill that dissuaded them.

'That's enough out of you!' he snapped at Olvar. 'Times were when a Mastersmith could expect decent respect from a prentice!'

Olvar knew exactly how serious Kunrad's anger was; and besides, he was almost as tall, and heavier. 'Times were when they didn't drag a prentice the length and breadth of the land after a wild goose!' he retorted. 'And clad like a mangy bellwether, at that!'

'Clad *in* a mangy bellwether!' added Gille, and then, quickly, lightly, 'And pressgang them off to sea, too!'

'One more word,' growled the smith, 'and I'll trade the pair of you for my passage! You may not be much use for rowers, but you'd make fine float-bladders!'

'Temper, temper!' said Gille cheerfully. 'So you do mean to take ship, then?'

'He's seen the light!' boomed Olvar.

Kunrad rounded on them, eyes suddenly not at all vague, so intense that Gille reined back in dismay.

'Yes,' said the Mastersmith slowly. 'Yes, Gille. I do. I always have. That was not the part of my plan I doubted.'

'Your plan?' grunted Olvar in surprise. 'But if you take ship—'

'You said I could sink my worries in the sight of the Sea,' Kunrad responded evenly. 'At the village back there they said—'

'I know, I know. *From the next rise!* I've heard that one before!' Gille waved a hand at the ridge ahead. 'And what'll we see? The next rise after that! At this rate we'll be old men before we reach this Ocean, for all you keep claiming you can smell it! Just the sweat-salt on our saddles, that's all!' He let an edge creep into his tone. 'And Merthian'll be back home and polishing up his armour for the front room, too!'

He did not miss the way Kunrad's hands clenched the reins. 'Front room or castle keep, I'll search it out. You can rely on that! And I won't do it by losing heart over one hillock more or less!'

'Then d'you mind telling us just how you do mean to find it – master?'

'Hate to lower the level of the dispute,' put in Olvar innocently, 'but I *know* what the sea smells like. And I think I smell it too.'

Kunrad was gone already, urging his horse to a canter up the steep road. The prentices, following more easily, saw him rein in at the top, and sit staring. 'What's got into him?' demanded Gille.

'Think I know,' said Olvar, and nothing more, to Gille's annoyance. But when they reached the ridge, he needed no explanation at all, but reined in at his master's side, rapt.

It was afternoon now, the sun westering low. No longer behind hills; there were none, for even the rise they stood on broke and dropped sheer and sudden to a grassy sward below. Towards an infinite hazy horizon the sun sank, and its long light traced a rippling track over the vast steely expanse of water, gilding the wave-crests that raced toward the wide shores far beneath their feet. Master and prentice alike were held close in thrall; infinity took their gaze. Olvar breathed deeper than he had for many a year, and rejoiced in the cool wind on his broad copper cheeks.

'So wide,' breathed Gille, wondering. 'Endless. As if it could swallow all the land. Is there another shore, Mastersmith?'

'So they say,' said Kunrad dreamily. 'Though it seems hard to believe, doesn't it? Yet that's the way Olvar's ancestors came, from a land over there beyond the curve of the world, where the Ice has a far worse grip. And our ancestors crossed over another ocean, far in the east behind us, for the same cause. As if this was the crucible of the world, and we the metals to be smelted and alloyed within it . . .'

'Coming over that!' shuddered Gille, contemplating the white-capped churning, and the relentless beat and break along the shore. 'Not through such waves, surely!'

'That?' laughed Olvar. 'That's but a light swell, an easy jog on a fine day. See, there's craft enough around the harbour down there – the wakes, see, and the sails, skipping over the crests?'

He stopped, startled. Even he had hardly noticed the sprawling stain along the far end of the bay, shapeless in the haze, as if it were no more than an extension of the sprawl of weed and debris along the tideline. Now the eye resolved it, stark against the low light, into spire and tower, turret and roof-peak, shadowed walls that stretched out to embrace a wide sea-pool, and calm it to blue glass that mirrored the sunset-reddened slopes above. Masts spiked out of the pool, like sea-thorns. 'A harbour! Some size! Why, that'd be Saldenborg, no less!'

'Saldenborg?' said Gille, in swift excitement. 'Then you do mean to head home after all, master?'

At that point, it is said, Kunrad came nearest to abandoning his pursuit, seeing it as a paltry concern amidst all the vastness and variety of the world. But in that, though he had no way of knowing it, he was gravely mistaken.

After a while, as the sea wind whipped his hair and plucked at his jerkin, his mood changed. Small he might be, before that great grey beast that breathed at the shore, or before the grim enormity of the Ice. But his life ran through them like a thread of warmth, swift and changing. A leaf that leaps up from the earth and is gone in a summer, perhaps; but for that time it was green and living, while the earth remained as still and grey as before. That life was all he had, and the part that was riven from him he must regain, or never fully live again. 'Come then, if you're coming!' he said, and urged his horse down the long slopes that led to the sea.

'Come? But come where?' shouted Gille, as he and Olvar cantered to catch up. 'There? And to what end? Where's this plan of yours to lead us?'

Kunrad glanced round. 'I thought you might have worked it out by now,' he said mildly. 'I mean to take ship: but not for home.'

Gille rose in his stirrups, and swore. 'I wondered! I wondered, the River swallow it! But I thought not even you – foolhardy, boneheaded son of a—' He choked with anger and disappointment. Olvar sat stolid and grim, but his eyes burned like coals under drooping lids.

Kunrad looked at them. 'I never promised you anything else. And I would not risk such a venture without a clear purpose. Merthian will be headed south now, no doubt – but suppose we come there before him?'

'Come where – in the Southlands?' gobbled Olvar. 'To do what, by Saithana's tits?'

'Lay charges against him, of course. Formal charges. All the way to Ker Bryhaine itself, and the Syndicacy.'

'Among his own fellows? Hold him, Gille, he'll start barking any bloody moment!'

'I'm ... not so sure,' said Gille, swaying in the saddle. 'Master, you may have something here!'

'The Guildmaster gave me the core of the idea, back at Rasby,' said Kunrad cheerfully. 'Talking about Merthian's dignity, and about the causes of war. I've turned it over and over, and it makes sense still. His fellow lordlings, they'd see this raiding as pretty petty stuff, wouldn't they? Jolly bad form. Beneath the dignity of a man who could pay for it.'

'Even of Northerners?'

'Especially of us, when there's a war brewing. And over accusations of brigandage. Something that petty, that silly; yet something that could spark off a bloody quarrel, because it's provable. They aren't going to like it much, those Syndic fellows. Some of them will be against war, I hear; and they'll be furious with Merthian. And the rest, well, in such a time it won't suit them to be openly unjust. They'd lose their dignity, and give the North a real grievance. At least—' Kunrad sucked his teeth uneasily. 'At least, I hope I can convince them of that.'

Olvar whistled. 'A bold stroke, Mastersmith – and a better one than just flapping forever after Merthian's shirt-tails. But it's a risky one. You could be putting your head between the bear's paws. You don't know these lordie fellows, after all.'

'No, but I've talked to some who do, the Guildmaster and others. They agree. And they tell me that although this corsair business has been shrivelling the trade, there are still captains making the passage. Since you say there are craft down there – I can't make them out, not against the sun. Any big boats?'

'Ships, you mean?' Olvar squinted. 'Now that's odd, Mastersmith, because there aren't. A few smaller sails, coasters and so on; there're some taller masts in the harbour, too many to pick 'em out clear. But round such a port I'd look to see one big merchantman, at least, bound south or north. Odd, indeed!'

Kunrad tossed his head. 'Well, we'll get our answers the sooner we come there. No Guildhall for us tonight, lads, but an inn, one where captains and seamasters lodge ashore. We may have some searching to do!'

Around every bend of the bay road the great port of Saldenborg grew clearer through the haze. The land was hilly to the sea's brink, so the town itself rose and fell across it in a wave, like some vast brown hank of storm-flung kelp. From afar off the smiths marvelled at the sprawl of it, the rising reek of its chimneys and the eccentric wavering line of its outer wall that, wide as it was, could not contain the life within. Here and there the crazy pattern of streets spilled over it into a scattered undertown, straggling out along the roads that led in from every direction.

As they drew closer, though, the brown stain resolved into a jagged jumble of rooftops, mostly wood-tiled as in their own town, but spattered here and there with richer cladding. The lowering light turned wood to copper, copper to glowing beryl and bronze to gold; and those tiles already gilded, for Saldenborg was rich, it ran with liquid flame. Towers they were, some of the roofs, and railed raised platforms where merchants could watch for their ships and captains their commands. Others, down towards the harbour, were lower but strong, hefty gable-ended houses for wares, fortresses against afflictions such as weather and thieves. And beyond them in the harbour itself gleamed summits of a different kind, the mastheads Olvar had seen. Masts naked of sail, unready to put to sea, great ships like basking seals cluttered the harbour, clustered along cramped moorings, rocking idle in the gentle swell.

'You'd think they'd moor some in those pools along the shore!' exclaimed Gille.

'No,' said Kunrad. 'See how much bluer they are! That's shallow water, over a white bed. Those must be the saltpans this place is named for, wider than the fields and richer. All the salt you've ever eaten comes from these parts, unless it were the expensive stuff ground from rock, or the cheapest from ashes. It's here that your food is flavoured and preserved; and it preserves us too, from the ills that strike inlanders prived of it.'

Olvar nodded. 'And stings your knuckles where the scales have skinned them, or the thumb you caught with the gutting knife. And come winter, the brine-meat gives you thirst enough to rush out and eat snow. But we used to watch for the salt-boats from here, nonetheless, for we could not pan enough on our own. That's what paid for those pretty rooftops.'

'That, and trade south,' agreed Kunrad. 'Now, though, I wonder. Are those masts commonly so crowded?'

'Wouldn't have thought so,' said Olvar.

They were coming in sight of the walls, and of the disorder beneath them. Saldenborg's undertown was well named, a dark ragged ribbon smeared back from the road, a demented clutter of little shanties built of anything to hand, from raw tree limbs to shattered boat timbers. More than once the whole boat was there, upturned with its mud and barnacles still encrusting the half-rotten keel turned rooftree. Windows flew open as they passed, mere hide or sacking flaps, or thin lath shutters. Men small and wiry peered out, beckoning them in for trade and drink. Bolder women sent other invitations, and hordes of children swarmed about their horses with mingled pleas, insults and threats. The noise and the stink were startling, and even Gille showed no urge to take up any invitation; he was too busy swatting small hands away from his saddlebags, his stirrups and even his boots.

'I'll sit on you!' roared Olvar, and the children scattered screaming in mock terror and promises to bite his backside.

'They'll be dead in a day if they do!' said Gille. 'Get off, you little horror! And no I don't want your sister – even if she's washed more recently than you!'

'Do you get the idea they're a mite desperate?' inquired Kunrad, fielding a small brown-skinned boy who was trying to manoeuvre his sword from his belt. He dangled him at arm's length. 'You, lad! Leave it! What's the fuss? Aren't there richer travellers than us to fleece?'

'No, Lord!' squeaked the infant. 'I mean, master! Mortal few, and they quiet and near with their pennies! There's folk here done die o' starving wi' all their bones stuck out, for true!'

'I believe you!' said Kunrad sombrely. 'And what's the cause? These corsair attacks?'

'Aye, L— Master! Scarce a ten-part o' the ships that were from here, they say, and they all huddled together like newborn pups for safety. Fewer yet t' Suderney way! Best linger here, master, till all's retted up again!'

Kunrad set the child down on his feet, and tucked a small coin in his palm. 'Wish I could spare more, boy! But leave my sword alone, or you'll slice your own fingers off! I've had grief enough with folk who covet shiny things.'

As they approached the city gate their tormentors fell behind. 'Lost anything?' asked Kunrad. 'Nothing? Good. We've little enough to pay our passage.'

'You were expecting that about the corsairs, Master-smith?' asked Gille.

'I'd heard, remember? This is still our best hope of overtaking Merthian. The Marshes won't slow him much, he has a large enough force to get through the margins safely enough. The troubles will make it harder for us to get a ship, of course – but there probably won't be much jostling for berths.' He looked up at the tall buildings of the town, clasping together like fingers over the narrow streets to make the most of the space. 'Even in a place such as this.'

The lodgings the guard directed them to overlooked the harbourside market, where the bustle and the smell were past the power of pane or shutter to keep out. The younger, hungrier captains favoured it because it was cheap, and because it was no more than a short distance from their craft if trouble threatened. By the time they reached the street the smiths had been nearly thrown from their horses a dozen times, and bumped and barged when they dismounted to lead them over the slippery cobbles. The tavern they came to was a strange, smoky deformity of a house, with a sideways list from subsidence and a crooked roof whose warped tiles seemed held in place only by a century of seagull droppings. Its sign, creaking rhythmically in the breeze, might have shown a luxuriantly female figure rising out of a stormcrest to shield a foundering barque, if all the flesh-coloured paint hadn't peeled. Only a dim, though striking, outline in the cloud was left.

'Saithana,' said Olvar, with a familiar salute. 'A Power of the sea. Watches over honest men adrift and in peril. So this'd be the *Sea Lady*.'

'Well, there's worse places to start,' said Gille. 'Might almost be worth a little danger, a sight of her!'

'Dunno about that. She only favours drowned men, they say. That's a long way to go for it.'

Gille swallowed. 'Too far for me. No insult, lady, but I'm not worthy.'

Inside the tavern was shabby and plain, but, after some of the roadside hovels, clean enough. There were rooms in plenty to choose from; and when they inquired after ships, the landlord clicked his tongue sadly. 'Were there more ships, Mastersmith, I'd have fewer beds. As you say, it's the corsairs, and nothing you hear about them's an exaggeration this year. They're out in force, and well manned, taking ships as it pleases them, and without let or mercy. A fair number of my regular skippers have miscarried so, good men too and brave drinkers, gone to feed the fishes. A bitter waste!' He tugged at his whiskers. 'So now the big ships huddle in harbour, and venture out only in convoys of force. Trade's becalmed, and what's left is mostly with the North.'

Kunrad nursed a small tankard of ale. 'And Suderney's doing nothing?'

'The sothrans? Oh, aye. They're sitting at home blaming us. And some of our lads are blaming them – though to be sure I know of ships taken and blood spilled on both sides. Every so often they send out a ship or two on patrol, but the sea-swine are never there. We did that at first, but now our warships guard only the big convoys. And there's none due out for many weeks yet.'

Kunrad frowned. 'Don't smaller ships try? I wouldn't think they'd miss the chance to grab back some profit from the bigger ones.'

'Well . . .' said the landlord reluctantly, as if weighing up Kunrad and the others. 'They do. That's no secret . . . but as to when, now, they're a mite cagey, you see? 'Cause it's as if those bastards *know* what vessels're sailing, and whither bound. Which'd mean, well—'

'They've eyes and ears here?'

'Guildmaster himself says so. So nobody trusts nobody else, outright. But you folks now, you being smiths and all, and you a master, sir, that'll be a whit different. There's one or two come in here still of a night; quiet, reliable men. And though I'm not saying nothing, mind, I could maybe lay you on a converging course, like . . .'

The first skipper Kunrad talked to, among the tavern company that night, was a solid, silent man who made it clear he didn't want to know. The landlord was apologetic. 'Could be he's no space left, or he already has passengers enough. But there's the sothran, Ceinor, there, has the *Ravenswing*, a neat little barque of fifteen oars a side, slick as spit off a stove even in light weather. Knows the runs like the backs of his hands, by day or night, as trustworthy as most. Being a sothran, he wants to get home, and he's a good cargo of fine Nordeney wool to make it worth his while. Now he—'

Ceinor was a cool, hard-faced man of about forty, with hair the colour of rust and level green eyes. When the landlord had spoken to him, he waited a while, sipping his drink and looking unhurriedly around. Then, passing the settle where the smith sat, he almost knocked over his alemug, apologised and fell into conversation in a natural-looking way. 'Truth is,' he said at last, in a lilting Southland accent, 'I'd as soon not carry passengers, for their sakes as well as mine. But you three, you're smiths, I understand, real Northland smiths.'

'This is a mastersmith!' said Olvar. 'And I'm a fisherman's son also, with time at sea.'

Ceinor nodded. 'Well, I might find places for a day or two hence, but not in comfort now, no pretty cabins nor nothing like. Bunk with the cargo, eat our scoff, lend a hand when's needed, pay in advance. You look like men who can stand that well enough. I could have uses for Northern smithcraft, and surely for smith's sinews at the oars. And you won't find cheaper on the Suderney run, not this summer.'

Kunrad contemplated the man a moment. From what the landlord had said, he was probably a smuggler in normal times, as ready to evade the corsairs as the seawatch in both South and North. Not a complete rogue, necessarily; but a man to be watched. 'Agreed,' he said. 'Except that we pay on shore, in Ker Bryhaine. Not before.'

'Bugger that,' said Ceinor calmly. 'How'll I know you've got it?'

'You won't,' said Kunrad. 'That's the point. So you won't decide halfway we can walk home.'

Ceinor chuckled. 'I'm not that much a villain, but you're right to have a care. We could take it from you anyway, if we wanted, but then I'd have to answer to mine host here. Half-and-half then – coming aboard, and at journey's end. Done? *Sleintje*, then, and a fair wind!'

'When do we sail?' demanded Olvar. 'With the dawn tide?'

Ceinor eyed him narrowly once more. 'We do not. Soon, but least said, safer we be. I'll send word to mine host, when and where we stand ready. We'll speak no more, till then!'

'D'you think we can trust him?' whispered Gille, as the captain ambled off towards the fire.

'Like enough,' said Kunrad. 'But I'll leave word with the Smith's Guild, and tell him so.' He drained his ale impatiently. 'May we sail soon!'

They had sold their horses, not without regret, to the landlord, who seemed to treat his beasts well enough; but that left little enough money to sit drinking, with things to buy for the voyage. Gille suggested the prentices take a turn out to get them, but Kunrad flatly forbade it. 'You'll be chasing skirts, and Olvar'll be eating, and there'll be money spent for nothing.'

Gille looked wistful. 'I wouldn't say that! But let's all go. We can at least see the town.'

It was a pleasant evening, and Kunrad himself was restless. 'Well enough! They say the castle's a sight to see, and the Guildhalls.'

Gille grinned at him as they went out. 'You should chase a skirt yourself now and again, Mastersmith. It'd do you good. Why, you can't have had any since – what, eight months back! Gretja from the mill, was it now?'

Kunrad raised his eyes to the Powers. 'Will you be quiet? Anyhow, I didn't get any, as you put it. Not from that quarter! I spent most of my time avoiding . . . any, if you must know.'

'Why?' grinned Olvar. 'Very nice girl. Healthy. Good cook. Make a change from banging on an anvil all the time.'

'Oh, go and find some fish to gut. Healthy, yes, but she was away ill the day the wits were handed out. And her hordes of relations too – would you have wanted them sponging around the smithy all day?'

'With the possible exception of her cousin Melle, no,' admitted Gille. 'There speaks age and wisdom, Olvar. I make a point of dodging relations.'

'Fathers especially,' said Kunrad. 'Enough of this, and admire the citadel up there. Founded by Vayde, they say, three hundred years back, the first in the Northlands, and the main fortifications built by him.'

The castle rose like a breaching whale above the waves of the town, built upon a black shelving cliff edge that glistened raw and iridescent in the evening sun. Tall trees clung to its ledges like mere twigs at this distance. 'Like to see any corsairs take *that* on,' whistled Gille. 'That rock face, and then the smooth stone on top – look at the size of the blocks! Couldn't get a grip on that with ladder or grapnel.'

'They say Vayde was a giant,' said Olvar. 'Shaped

stone as we shape metal.'

'Not quite,' said Kunrad. 'He planned amazing fortresses, yes, and greater ones in the South, I hear; but he didn't build them all with his own hands, as the legends have it. Big in body, a terrible-looking man, so the Chronicles say, wrathful, cruel even; but no monster. He was a giant in mind and craft; he devised clever engines, hoists and grinding wheels and so on, that let fewer men do the work. He was a smith above all smiths, and made all things material dance to his tune, steel and stone and stuff we hardly know of. It was people he couldn't handle. So when our folk came east after the fall of Morvan, he tried to get them accepted by the sothrans. When that didn't work, he set out to settle the North for us. But not in time to stop the fighting. When he came home from his last expedition, it was already happening, and he was old, old beyond any normal span. They say he died taking the last great settlement party north. In the Marshlands.'

'Glad we're not going that way,' said Gille softly.

'Nothing uncanny. He was holding off a band of sothran pursuers, nearly single-handed. But I'm pretty glad, too. That's no place for men.'

'Shouldn't think his ghost makes it any brighter,' said Olvar, and shuddered. Like most of the common folk, he believed in ghosts as a part of the natural cycle, ancestral ones especially. Kunrad was less sure; but even for him there was something disturbing about the thought of the mind that had shaped those sheer cliff walls still roaming the night somewhere.

'Let's do our buying,' he said. 'Weather gear, some extra foodstuffs, a book of the sothran dialect – though you should know enough, from your lessons.' All smiths learned both tongues, so they could read the ancient texts and tracts of their craft. 'And we'll learn something from the crew, no doubt.'

'But you two being landlubbers,' rumbled Olvar, 'they may be words you should be leery of using.'

The markets of Saldenborg were still busy at that hour,

alive with pushing and jostling and smells good and less so. To listen to the merchants, though, they might as well have been empty. 'You're getting these as a gift,' whined the man who sold them capes and trousers of coarse oiled cotton. 'Look at 'em – lovely, with a double flap at the shoulder, pitch-lined and all. Never feel a drop. And I can't afford to haggle, the way business is. Glad to shift 'em.'

Haggle he did, nonetheless, and by the time they escaped with their purchases it was growing dark. The streets were emptying, and though linkboys with their torches were escorting people all around them, there never seemed to be one free. 'Maybe we don't look rich enough!' grumbled Kunrad. 'Better make our way back while we can!'

They took the wider, lighter streets, and aimed for the harbour. That brought them out, in the end, along a narrow cobbled path by the shore, where the saltpans glimmered white in the deepening gloom. Kunrad stopped there again for a moment, leaning on the rickety fence, held by the sight and sound of the sea as it sluiced gently against the outer walls. The idea of going out on it both thrilled and alarmed him a little, of feeling a floor unsteady as a galloping horse beneath his feet. He drew a deep breath, and realised he was rather looking forward to it.

'Anything the matter, boss?' asked Olvar anxiously.

'No. Nothing. I was just thinking – but for that bastard Merthian, I might never have seen this. I might never have seen the citadel, or the Sea, or ships – or all the lands between. Or Suderney, when we get there. I might never have left home. I might have lived and died in that little nook of the world, and never pushed my nose outside.'

Gille made an extraordinary noise. 'Thanks, master. There was something I've been wondering, and I was angry with myself for even thinking it. Now I'm wondering all the harder. Are you running after Merthian, or away from yourself?'

Kunrad choked, and turned on him. Gille half cringed, but held his ground. Then his look changed, and he yelled, 'Master – *look out!*' He yelped in pain as Kunrad sprang back, and the blade that lunged past him pricked Gille's outthrust arm instead. Olvar bellowed like a bear, and smashed his fist down on the sword, striking it from the wielder's hand. His other fist came around, there was a soggy noise in the night, and the sound of a body falling under people's feet. Harsh oaths sizzled like kettles. Kunrad had the moment he needed to drop his bundle and draw his sword. 'Olvar! Gille! Here, back to back!'

Gille was whimpering with pain and fright, but his long dagger flashed in the gloom. Olvar's was in his left hand. He kicked down a length of fence and tore free a post. The prentices backed down the path. A high voice hissed in the shadows, long swords shimmered, and a knot of figures sprang forward in a fierce rush.

Kunrad parried the leader with a force that sent him staggering, then, with an effort of will as much as strength, struck him down. The second shot past, Gille struck out and was slashed at; but the prentice wasn't there any more, and the dagger ripped at cloth. A bellow of rage ended suddenly in the thud of Olvar's cudgel. Kunrad was trading swift slashing blows with the next attacker, a savage swordsman but no artist. Another thrust at his unprotected side, but Kunrad whirled, slashed out, then back to catch the first attacker's blow. The force of it drove him to his knees, but he held it – then gave way suddenly and ducked forward. The other's own lunge carried him half over Kunrad's shoulder, and the smith, gritting his teeth, stabbed upward, hard. He had been taught that defence. His attacker crashed to the ground with a groan, and Kunrad backed away after the prentices, along the path where it was hard for more than one at a time to come at him.

Another rush; another glinting blade. Somewhere in the darkness at his side Olvar's cudgel landed with a sound like squashing fruit. Kunrad parried, threw back his attacker and desperately struck again and again, hailing blows on the unseen shape in the darkness. There was the peculiar clink of poor metal breaking, a scream, and Kunrad felt his sword bite deep. Mail jangled as it struck the ground. He jerked his sword back as other feet rushed suddenly, winced and thrust it straight out before him, a classic lunge. Another blade knocked it aside, but Kunrad's swift disengage circled the point round to where it had been almost at once. A thudding impact jarred his arm to the shoulder. There was an awful, explosive wheeze, and coarse cloth folded over his fingers, with shuddering flesh beneath. He had run his attacker through the body, hilt-deep. A dull weight pulled down the blade, fingers clawed at his arm and suddenly flew open. The weight slid slowly away, and there was the sound of something rolling over. Kunrad tried to stifle his panting, lest it draw another attacker on him.

An instant's silence was broken by a sudden rustle on the cobbles, and Olvar shouted. 'There, another! Their ringleader! Stop you now, you bloody footpad—'

'Down there!' screamed Gille, his voice cracking. 'Get him! Flatten him!' And he too was haring down the dim bank in pursuit of the fleeing shadow, threshing through the dune grass barely ahead. To his own surprise, so was Kunrad, yelling and jeering in reaction to fright he hadn't had time to recognise. Ahead of him Gille's silhouette rose against the sky for an instant, then fell down flailing and cursing the seagrass.

Kunrad hauled him to his feet and they went slipping and skidding down the loose sand. Ahead of them feet splashed into the water, and they saw a silhouette threshing desperately away through the shallow pan, its thin limbs escaping its enveloping drapery, clearly visible against the pale saltbed. After it surged Olvar, a great black blot on the night, his cudgel raised like the hand of death. He had almost caught up to it, but the turgid half-evaporated salt was slowing him, and the shadow gained a breath or two. It whirled suddenly, a cloak flying wide, and seemed to crouch down, as if in terror. Olvar roared in triumph; and then he screamed.

Trail of Ashes

Kunrad and Gille, a footfall from the water's edge, saw it clearly in the dimness, as if a breath passed over the greenish face of the pan and changed it to glistening white. Even as their feet touched the brine, it no longer lapped but crunched and crackled, solid ice, and they skidded and fell across one another. Kunrad, winded, saw a ragged shape slide with skater's speed across the frozen pan. Gille was on his feet faster, and sliding almost as surefooted in its wake. Kunrad, unable to shout, prayed the boy wouldn't catch up; but it had already reached the far slope, and was scrambling spiderlike up the sandbank to the road. Gille poised a moment, still sliding, then sheathed his dagger and turned to the slumping figure of Olvar.

As a boy Kunrad, with his top-heavy build, had never been much use at ice-slides, and he took several falls before he reached them, more or less on all fours. Some ways away he heard Olvar groan, which eased his heart a little. 'I was feared we'd find you the fattest icicle this side of the mountains!' he panted. 'Frozen to glass with the rest!'

'We still might!' said Gille anxiously. 'The cold of this stuff! And it's fast around his boots! If we don't get him out quick, he'll lose toes. Or worse!' They were used to fierce Northland winters; they knew how fast flesh could succumb. Their own hands and feet were numbing by the second. Olvar, half fainting with the shock, couldn't help himself. Kunrad seized his cudgel and swung it at the ice, but it only splintered a little before the club skidded.

'This doesn't make sense!' protested Gille. 'Brine's hard to freeze, and this is the thickest I could imagine!'

'Everything freezes!' panted Kunrad. 'Eventually! We'll have to chop him free!'

Gille began hacking with his dagger, Kunrad with his sword. Now and again he turned it around and hammered with the heavy steel disc that balanced the hilt. The ice chipped and cracked, but too slowly. It was far too warm for the stuff naturally, and the surface was beginning to sweat; but it would not melt soon enough for Olvar. The big man had been shin-deep in the salty sludge when it froze, and his legs were held upright, but he was beginning to give at the knees. 'Hold fast, Olvar!' panted Gille. 'Things're bad enough without you falling on me!'

Olvar groaned. 'Can't feel anything – 'cept fire.'

Kunrad hacked away. 'Can't you move your feet, even a little?'

Olvar was evidently trying, but nothing gave. 'Might as well be set in crystal,' wheezed Gille, chipping away. 'Could we get help?'

Kunrad gave an unhappy laugh. 'In this town, at this hour, on such a cause? *Damn!*' The hilt skidded. He reversed the sword and began hewing again. 'And how would you know whom it was safe to ask?'

'Well – how about him?'

On the path that led along the sea wall separating the pans there was a figure walking with the slow gait of age, and leaning on a heavy staff. 'Hoi, old sir!' shouted Kunrad. 'Could you lend some help here?'

The walker turned, and came down off the path to the edge of the pan, tapping at it with his staff. 'Ice on a fine spring night? As soon see ripe fruit in midwinter! How did this come to be?' The voice was deep and stern, with a tone of command, and he wore a broad-brimmed hat, like a traveller. A retired captain, perhaps, or guard commander, thought Kunrad.

'I don't know any more than you! But this young man's caught and in pain. If you could spare your prop a moment—'

To their astonishment the watcher stepped easily on to the ice and came towards them with the same slow stride. 'You want my help, eh?'

'Mind you don't break your neck, sir!' said Gille, moving as if to help.

'I have been keeping my feet on the ice for many a year now, lad. Too many! But help, now, I do not often lend help. Help is something that must be paid for, in advance, perhaps.'

Kunrad looked at Olvar, and flushed with annoyance.

The staff was steel-shod, just what they needed. 'I haven't much money, but I'll spare you a little, if that's what you want!'

'Not at all,' said the old man evenly. Eyes glinted in the shadow of the broad brim. 'More than that is demanded, sometimes – a life, perhaps. Or a way of life. Sometimes more than the help is worth. Or the matter in which you seek it.'

Kunrad's temper blazed, and he stalked forward, fighting for balance. 'The matter is saving this lad from pain and maiming!'

'Is it?'

Kunrad stopped dead. He could see the old man's face clearly now, and it was an arresting one, an immense eagle nose set between eyes that shone like a young man's, belying the grey of the brows above and flowing beard beneath. The thin hard lips twisted in a strange ironic smile. 'Would he be here at all, if you had not brought him? Would he be in jeopardy now, if it were not for you? Is what you seek worth such a risk? In aiding you here, I aid that also. You ask a lot of me, and so it is only fair that I warn you of the price. Are you willing to pay?'

Gille tugged at his sleeve. 'Look, I was brought too. And I'd say to Hella with answers, till we do what's needful, and that's prising my friend loose! Then we can bloody well philosophise!'

'I would not trade this lad's life to succeed in my quest,' said Kunrad shakily. The old man's assurance had unnerved him. 'If that's what you mean.'

'Not precisely. He may still lose it. But you may lose also, even if you succeed – and gain even if you fail. Much depends on the manner.'

Kunrad drew a deep breath. 'You know more than any honest man ought to.'

'Do I? The name and face of Kunrad the Swordmaster are not wholly unknown throughout the North, nor the quest on which he has passed like a bushfire, leaving shame and anger in his wake. Such a determination is bound to attract attention, and interference. As it has here. That, at least, I may reverse.'

He lifted the heavy staff, and crashed its metal tip down against the frozen surface. Kunrad half expected it to turn to water again at the touch. It didn't. Ice chips flew up, and one caught him stinging on the cheek. Again the staff struck, and again; and suddenly there was a great moaning, yawning crack, and with a loud explosive pop a crack lanced right across the saltpan. Olvar's feet stirred suddenly and he fell, groaning, on to the protesting ice.

'Get him to shore!' said the old man. 'Get his boots off and his blood flowing. He will be well enough, for now. And you, Mastersmith – remember the price!'

The old man turned and strode calmly back towards the shore. Gille, assisting the helpless Olvar, turned a pale face after him, and eyes that stared wide in the gloom. 'Back then – when he talked about keeping his feet! Did he say ice – or *Ice?*'

'I don't know,' said Kunrad vaguely, watching the tall figure dwindle against the soft sky-glow. He could hardly bring his mind to bear on what had happened. It could only have been minutes, though it felt like endless hours. 'I feel . . . I don't know. Higher forces are in play here, maybe.'

He shivered. The ice-chill was numbing his feet even through his boots, but there was a deeper cold within him. Strange lights seemed to flicker a moment against the clouds, and he remembered the aurora crowning the Ice, the mountains and the valley, and Haldin. Resolve stiffened him, and practical common sense. 'But nothing he said changes anything. If I don't get back that armour, half my life is lost anyway. The better part. Come, let's heave our horse-whale home!'

By the time they came back to the town Olvar, though still steadying himself on their shoulders beside their other bundles, was walking again, his heavy boots unlaced. He looked like any ordinary drunk between taverns, and nobody on the street stirred a hair, save some underclad young whores who felt Kunrad's muscles and rumpled Gille's hair. But for tonight he was past even them, thinking how attractive were home, hay and the love of a good woman. By silent consent none of them spoke of what had happened, or why. Time enough for that behind barred doors, with a much-needed drink or two. But the *Sea Lady*'s landlord met them at the step in a great frenzy of excitement.

'Masters! Thank the Raven you're returned! Cap'n Ceinor's sent word his ship's been attacked! Aye, even in the dock as it lay, with but a watch-crew aboard, and the bastards drove off only along of some other ships took an interest! Now he's in a great passion and says he's sailing at the hour after midnight, come wind, tide or yourselves. He'll await you at the salt-jetty, down beside the pans – but not for long!'

'My lad's had a slight accident!' said Kunrad, and the host's eyes widened in shocked comprehension. 'But we'll be there! Mull him some wine, will you, while we make ready? My thanks!'

In the flurry of departure there was still no time for thinking. And maybe that was as well, Kunrad realised later; or they might never have gone at all.

And all things then, as the old tale makes plain, might have turned out very different. All then, and all that came after; even until the last withdrawing of the Great Ice – if withdrawn it truly is.

They hurried down the road to the jetty, reluctantly skirting the site of the attack, marked now only by the broken fence and a few smeared puddles, gleaming unpleasantly in the faint glow. The bodies of the attackers lay in the ditch on the other side, and probably would lie there till they stank too much to ignore. That he had slain three men of the five, and felled another, was yet another thought that Kunrad pushed aside for the present.

As he had hoped, there at the jetty's end rose a tall sleek mast, its heavy square sail gleaming dully in the light of the rising moon.

'Loose-furled, more like hanging from the yard!' Olvar pointed out. 'Ready to be let fall at a moment's notice, though there's little enough wind here inshore. In a fine haste, these lads!'

On the dock, barely visible among the rickety sheds, stood ten men with swords and axes, and Ceinor himself pacing back and forth on the encrusted planks. 'So!' he said between his teeth. 'You made the tryst. Thought you might not have. There's been dirty work on the path up yonder.'

'We know,' said Olvar. 'We did it.'

Ceinor's mouth lifted in a reptilian smile. 'The three of you? Not bad. Wish we'd had you aboard these three hours since. Now I'm short two good oarsmen, and we must row till we can pick up the sea breeze, so I'll have to trouble the larger of you gentlemen . . .'

'No, Olvar's been hardly used,' said Kunrad. 'Must needs be you and I for now, Gille! For all that sting in your arm!'

'I'll get blisters!' protested the young man, as he hurled his bag down among the woolsacks in the forward hold, and lurched down over the decking to the benches. 'I'll ruin my fine touch with incised work! You can't expect me to sit on that bench, I've got delicate skin!'

'Well, at least you know what to expect!' said Ceinor. 'As to the bench, think yourself lucky! On smaller craft you squat on your sea chest, and woe betide the man who's done fancy carvings on his! Hands on the sweep thusly, lean back on your stroke with straight arms like *that*, and keep time with the chant! *Ashore there! Get your arses aboard and to your places!* Bosun, pole 'er off and we're away!'

'*Poling away, skipper!*'

The rowers barely clattered into their seats. The sleek hull wallowed as it swung out from the jetty. '*Port side, pull!*' roared the bosun. '*And – pull! And – pull!*'

Kunrad's arms creaked at the first strain of the oar, but his shoulders flexed and took it, and his great strength came into play. He leaned back on the stroke as Ceinor had showed him, and the heavy sweep groaned in its socket. '*Starbr'd side, pull!*' yelled the captain. '*And – pull! And – pull! And – keep the frigging time, boy! Pull!*'

The landsmen felt the sudden lilt and lift as the *Ravenswing*'s bow turned into the waves, that instant of lurching instability in which it seems the boat will roll into the trough and capsize. Then there was the thump and slap as the crest passed beneath, and the bows swung up to ride the next one. It was exhilarating, in a way, but also very frightening for men who had never felt it before, and barely seen the great Sea. Only Olvar, sprawled in the stern with the helmsman, grinned and breathed deep. Gille was red in the face, while Kunrad was becoming uneasily aware that if he wasn't so busy he might have other troubles. He fought his gorge down, breathed deep and leaned back with an ease which his fellow rowers noted. 'Well run, smith!' said Ceinor approvingly. 'But hold the time now, that's the trick. Start the chant, somebody!'

A young man with strangely yellow hair, some rows up, began to sing in a clear high voice, and the others took up the rolling, liquid song. It was in the sothran speech, but when Kunrad caught the accent the words became clear, and to Gille almost at once.

> *Nights of love, of love and bliss,*
> *The southland breezes bearing,*
> *Soft and warm as sunlit kiss*
> *For shipmen homeward faring,*
> *For every stroke a girl's caress,*
> *   for every pain a pleasure,*
> *For every surge a softer yet, a*
> *   port with richer treasure,*
> *And a mooring sure –*
> *And a mooring sure*
> *By a sunwarm shore,*
> *By a sunwarm shore . . .*

* * *

It sounded a strangely gentle song for such a bunch of roughnecks. The man in front of Kunrad had a bristle-ridden chin raked by huge knife-scars, and teeth like ancient monuments, complete with lichen, but there were tears running down his cheeks as he sang. Kunrad remembered hearing that the sothrans had a sentimental, musical side, but he hadn't imagined it went this deep. Gille, once he got his breath and the drift of the subject matter, joined in with his own clear voice in elaborate harmonies, and improvised words when the chant faltered, though his images ran more to ripe fruit, deep valleys, and the scent of fresh-cut grasses. The crew seemed to like them.

In fact, Kunrad suspected, he was becoming the better rower. He had not half Kunrad's strength, of course, but he was still a smith, and though he took little exercise save one, it seemed to keep him fit. More, he had the sense of rhythm that helped him minimise his effort, and a younger, suppler back. All the same, he was beginning to wince at every stroke, and not only from the cut on his arm.

'We'll make a man o' you yet, young smith!' said Ceinor approvingly, as he rolled easily back from the bows.

'Hope not,' said Gille between clenched teeth. 'What would your sothran wives do for a change, then?'

Ceinor gave his cold chuckle. 'Wear out that tongue o' yours, for a start! They'll chew you up and spit you out, boy!'

'Not if I survive this! How much longer?'

'Till we're beyond the bay and in open sea. Maybe a half-hour, an hour.'

'Hour!'

'Sing, and you'll make it less!'

'Any minute now my arse is going to join in the chorus!'

'Well, then you can really serenade our ladies! Row on, laddie!'

It was only ten minutes later, as Ceinor must have expected, that the motion of the ship changed suddenly, to a wider, slower roll. Waves drummed against the hull, and little flashes of spray came over the gunwales and stung their faces. Ceinor gave a curt order, and the rowers shipped their oars. Gille slipped groaning from his bench, and Kunrad managed not to imitate him, just. They couldn't stand properly with the new corkscrewing action of the ship, and as the sailors rushed to let fall, barging and swearing at them, they crawled gratefully astern to where Olvar sat beaming by the deck-lantern like some smug sea-idol, joking with the helmsman at his oar.

The sail rustled down and thudded taut, its laced strands of tarred line fluttering. 'Watch the angle of them!' said Olvar as they arrived beside him. 'That's how these sothrans measure how close to the wind they can go. Fine sailors in their way, though less comfortable off-shore than we.'

'Oh, we're comfortable, are we?' said Kunrad. 'Glad you told me, lad.'

'How long's it going to go on rocking like this?'

Olvar shrugged. 'Till journey's end. Could blow livelier soon, mind you; there's promise of it in the air!'

'Swallow your prophecy and choke on it!' groaned Gille. In the yellow lantern-light the green pallor was climbing his cheeks as if filling a bottle. 'I've had enough shocks for one night!'

'I doubt Olvar'd disagree with you there!' said Kunrad feelingly.

There was a moment's silence. Everything they had been able to ignore in the flurry of their departure, all the implications of what had happened, came rushing back to them like the sharp cold splashes of spray.

'What . . .' Olvar glanced up at the helmsman, and lowered his voice. 'What *was* it?'

'What was the whole business about?' demanded Gille softly, easing his sore shoulder. 'I thought it was just footpads!'

Kunrad tapped one fist into another. 'Too many of 'em. And they all went straight for me. I don't think footpads would have done that. And there was somebody hanging back, giving orders – hissing them, maybe so the voice wouldn't be recognised. At a guess that was our quarry. But as to who, or why, or what they did . . . well, I'm baffled.'

'Cold again,' said Gille. 'Killing cold, like Haldin.'

'Too like,' agreed Kunrad unwillingly.

Olvar snorted. 'But that was a . . . a monster, in the wilderness! This was in a city, among men! And that was a man I was chasing, for all the cloak that muffled him. Normal number of arms and legs, a bit skinny. And a voice, though it was mostly panting.'

'Then maybe he had some trick given him, or somebody else was watching over him. I've never heard of smithcraft that could do such a thing, but who knows? And there are other forces in the world.' He shivered. 'That old man . . . But why us? Why should we come under their eyes, be they what they are?'

'Your bloody search,' said Gille bitterly. 'He said it was bound to attract attention.'

'I was thinking of that. So maybe – let's say, somebody important doesn't want it to succeed. Why? Because they want Merthian to? That just extends the question – why him? And while we're about it, how did they find us, when we're no longer on his heels? So, have you any of your quick answers to that, Gille my lad? Because I do not. And until I do, I'll go on searching.'

It was Olvar who spoke, then, over the wallow and splash of the rising swell. 'Maybe we're looking at the wrong end of things. This ship was raided, too, remember. Maybe we were jumped just 'cause we're the paying passengers.'

'Or maybe the ship was raided because of us. It cuts both ways. I'm baffled, I don't mind admitting it. And I can't think straight with this accursed hulk dancing about under me!'

'Dancing!' groaned Gille. 'More like corkscrewing!'

'Well, sirs?' demanded Ceinor cheerfully from the deck. 'We're running free now, nice and near the wind. A good speed for breakfast! No fires till we anchor at even, but there's a grand fresh cut of fat salt pork—'

Kunrad's face was turning as green as Gille's, and suddenly he sprang up and bent over the gunwale. The example was enough for Gille, who followed him, retching violently. The helmsman patted the young man's back kindly enough. 'That's it, lads! Not into the wind. Sure, it'll pass soon enough!'

Leaving Olvar to watch them, he leaned back on his oar. The two Northerners slid down the planks, groaning. 'Not the pork, then?' inquired Ceinor.

Their sickness buried their other concerns for that time. They were hardy men, though, and as the days passed and they grew more used to the motion and the labour, they talked over and over again of what befell them. They came no nearer an answer, nonetheless; and Kunrad, more than any of them, found himself staring out in anger at the grey infinity of ocean, as if somewhere along the hazy horizon he might make it out. He had seen many things there – the round heads of seals, so close he could look in their liquid brown eyes; the wide brown kelpbeds, swaying like forests; the low necks and blunt heads of the great seacows, fifty feet or more to their rounded tailtips, that browsed them, vanishing like panicked sheep as the rounded backs and knifing fins of orca packs parted the weed. He had seen greater whales breach, and been awed by their vast serpentine curves among banners of arcing spray, and the thunder of their flukes. Yet still, impatient, unsatisfied, he would turn to the low contours of the land off the larboard bow. He would imagine his suit of armour, and Merthian – he could not help thinking of them in that order, though he laughed at it himself – making their way southward.

Floundering, probably, in the Great Marshes; but the idea gave him no satisfaction. Strangely enough, he did not want to lose either armour or man, and it did not take him long to see why. He had liked Merthian, and he felt still that he had not been altogether mistaken, and that every villainy the man had done was somehow counter to his real self. The paradox caused Kunrad an almost physical pain, as unexpected hurt does to a child. As in all else in his life, he needed to understand, to see as complete a picture as he could. He desperately wanted to ask Merthian why, and close the gulf in his understanding; but still more, he wanted his armour. And to get that answer, he would forgo the other if he had to.

He gripped the gunwale, and felt the salt-hardened wood creak under the strength in his hands, still greater after long stints of rowing. It seemed like a twig he could snap without effort. He had never hurt anybody before he was forced out on this mad venture; now he had killed several, and hated the memory of it. Merthian had driven him to that. He baulked at the thought; but he knew now that, if he had to, he would kill again.

'My poor *Ravenswing*'ll get there no quicker for you tearing bits off it!' said Ceinor mildly at his side. 'Somewhere out there, is he?'

'Who might that be?' asked Kunrad guardedly.

'By your face, a walking dead man. Though dead he may be, if it's there – for see, yonder, where the line of the hills diminishes and gives way to the grey margins at sea level. Those are grass and reedbeds, swamps and dunes. There begin the Debatable Lands, and beyond them the Great Marshes. Making his way south, is he? Well, he may well be sunk without trace already, or spirited off by some marsh-demon. Best you contain yourself in patience. Our greatest danger begins here also.'

Kunrad stared at the harmless-looking grey line, and the tongues of dark sand that extended out into the turbulent sea, as if in challenge. In his first struggles with the sea, and the haunting terror of that last night ashore, he had quite forgotten the danger of the corsairs.

'Lurk in the rivermouths, they do,' said Ceinor, and spat generously over the side. 'Among the flies and the midges, being themselves greater bloodsuckers – aye, and the marsh-demons also, most like. Waiting for a sail to pass, standing into shore – and then they swarm out in all manner of craft and swarm aboard like lice. Look your fill upon the land, Mastersmith, for we must needs stand out as far as we can over the next few days.'

So they did, till the land was the barest thread distinguishing one horizon from another. It was quite far enough for Kunrad and Gille, though Olvar scoffed. 'Safer far to be out in the open sea and beyond sight of shore!'

Ceinor looked at him with hooded eyes. 'And if the corsairs are out there also, where'll you run to? Where hide? You Northerners in your little ships may skitter whither you will, but I'll stay within sight of land like any man of sense. Best save your breath for rowing, brown man!'

Yet as the days passed they did not have to. The winds grew lighter and the airs warmer, the sea that had seemed so grey and misty began to sparkle in the sun. The distant shore seemed to be a lighter shade of green, and less often overhung by rainclouds. Men's moods lightened as they claimed to smell the flowers of the Southlands on the landbreeze. The *Ravenswing* rode easily over the swell, and all their unease was forgotten. The sea seemed bluer here, though for Kunrad it never lost the feeling of fierce energy it had had. Porpoises came to race their bows, and fat fish leaped and glittered in the clear light as if daring anyone to catch them. Ceinor visibly relaxed, for they were past the last of the Marshes now, and would soon be entering the waters of the Southlands, where the corsairs did not dare to linger. A few days more, and they would be sighting the harbour towers of Ker Bryhaine itself. That gave Kunrad cause for thought, for then he would have to bring his plans into effect; and he spent more and more time in reflection.

Gille seemed to be enjoying himself as much as the sothrans, basking on the warm deck, but Olvar remained quietly watchful, even climbing to the masthead at times now that his feet had healed, although Kunrad half expected to see it bend under his bulk. Most of all Olvar took the watch at dawn and evening, when the low light threw long deceptive shadows like great seabeasts across the waves, and the shore faded in the sea mists.

So it was that his voice woke them, bringing the

sleepy deck-watch to their feet in the clammy cool of dawn, and rousing the others out of their oil-scented sleep among the warm wool bales below. *'Ahoy! A ship! Two ships, three, off the landward bow!'*

Ceinor was on deck ahead of all the rest, buckling his belt. 'Whither away, Northman?' he yelled, shading his eyes. 'I see nothing!'

'Landward ho!' boomed Olvar. 'Three hulls, no sails, low to the waves and rowing fast on our bearing!'

'Olvar has better eyes than most men,' said Kunrad at his side.

Ceinor stood an instant, breathing hard. 'Can you see how many oars a side?'

'I can not! Can you count a centipede's legs? For so they rise and fall!'

Ceinor beat on the steering oar. 'Corsairs, for sure! The luck, damn it, the luck! Longboats piled gunwale-high with hungry outlaws, rowing in relays! Well, they've left it too long! We'll sweat those starvelings close to the Southlands – and any that overhaul us, why, we'll send them home on the tide, to foul the beaches with their bony carrion! *To your sweeps, every man!'*

CHAPTER FOUR
The Light in the Marshes

THEY BENT THEIR BACKS and strained, pitting every fibre of their muscle to lighten the load on the sail, until the bows lifted and it seemed that the *Ravenswing* sought to live up to her name. But now those on the landward oars, Kunrad among them, could see the distant shapes in the mist, low dark arrow-streaks that sliced through the steely wavecrests with alarming speed. Ceinor stalked up and down the deck, alternately calling the stroke and cursing hoarsely. '*Pull*, now! And – *pull!* Asleep, are you, you lousy whoresons? Dreaming of your scabby port-girls? *Pull*, swine – and *pull!* Or they'll needs find better men to scratch their itches!'

He laid about him with his scabbard, landing stinging cracks on the rowers' backs, Kunrad's included; but no man had breath to yell or protest, not with those arrows driving in upon them.

'*Pull!* Till you break your backs – *pull!* Till you puke out your hearts – *pull!* Better that than a corsair pike!'

But very soon he ceased even to swear. For all they could do, the *Ravenswing*, much larger and heavily laden, was unmistakably being overhauled. Ceinor, clambering up to the quarterdeck, half drew his sword, then slammed it back in the scabbard. 'Well, then, sod it! If we can't slip them, we'll teach them a trick or two! *Ship your sweeps! Ready about!*' Rowers leaped from the benches to man the ropes. 'Helm! Put 'er over at my call! *Lee'o!*'

The heavy yard groaned around the flexing mast as the ship, suddenly baulked of her speed, swung broadside to the waves and then about, in a long listing arc upon the water. The sail sagged, the sheets dipped low into the wavecrests and rose dripping. Then the hull righted, the crew frantically hauled the sheets in around the cleats, the sail thumped taut again, and the *Ravenswing* bucked on to her new course, heeling low against the wind. Suddenly there was only sea in Kunrad's sight, at a crazy angle; but on the bench opposite, Olvar, craning over his shoulder, growled suddenly and bent to his oar, just as Ceinor shouted '*Out sweeps, and fast! Now, for your lives! We're going to ram them!*'

He stamped the time, screamed it, punched it in the air with his fists, an impossible pounding beat that somehow they kept up. Blood oozed along the leatherbound grips, the rowlocks creaked, the heeling ship topped the wavecrests and bounced along in great spouts of blinding spray. Still Kunrad saw nothing but the swaying horizon. Spray and sweat soaked him, pouring into his eyes; and then at Ceinor's warning cry he swung up his oar with the rest and braced himself against the thwart.

The impact was frightening, a boneshaking jar and crash. The mast juddered and twanged, the sail convulsed like a stricken animal, and a horrible medley of howls and screams burst out as if from Hella's gate. Then they were past, between long, narrow black bows and stern upthrust on either side, sinking swiftly among a flailing scatter of arms and bobbing heads. They had sliced the corsair longboat in two. A great howl of derision arose, and Ceinor, dancing on the quarterdeck, bayed like a hound.

The other boats were backing water frantically, turning faster than any sailing boat could to face them. They were readying something in the bows—

A flat heavy snap, a brief whistle and over the side a snake flew and struck clattering across the deck – a three-pronged grapnel. Ceinor, sword upraised, sprang to cut it free. Then the line jerked tight, the grapnel leaped from the deck and Ceinor screamed as it caught him by the chest and threw him back against the rail. The helmsman ran to help, but Ceinor was pulled over and into the sea. An arrow sang, and the helmsman staggered and slumped down. Kunrad, horrified, saw the heavy catapults in the longboats' bows and sterns swing around. More grapnels soared over the ship, with arrows hissing after them. A rower near Kunrad hacked at a grapnel's tail, but the first few feet were chain. He cut once, twice, and then Kunrad's sword smashed through the metal. An arrow hissed past him and caught the other man in the side. Then a line whipped dripping from the water, and another grapnel snapped tight.

Caught helmless and heeling by the sudden drag of the longboat, the *Ravenswing* jolted violently. The sail thrashed and bellied, the mast bucked out of its socket, and the forestay snapped. The rowers, no longer braced, were hurled headlong from their benches. The mast swung to one side, half overboard, the yard tilted and the sail slapped down into the sea. The *Ravenswing* lost all its way and wallowed in the swell, while the longboats slipped sharklike alongside. Kunrad, picking himself up, glimpsed a frieze of fierce faces, some pale, some dark, all with the same fixed hungry grin. In that boat alone there was twice the *Ravenswing*'s crew. Then the hulls bumped, the frieze broke and came spilling in a yelling tide over the rail.

The crew were already on their feet, Kunrad and Olvar among them. Gille ducked behind them only just in time, as boarding pikes bit into the rowers' benches. Kunrad hesitated, then, to his own surprise, shouted '*Now!*' and slashed out at the first aboard. They fell, and others with them as the crewmen hit out desperately, unable to miss. But those behind leaped over the men who fell, pressing in until there was little room to fight, slashing with dagger and boarding pike, tearing rings from ears and fingers even as they fought. Somebody somewhere was bellowing orders, but no voice Kunrad knew; it must be a corsair leader. The flat of a swinging pike-blade slapped at him, he staggered and was pushed back with the rest. Suddenly there was no deck beneath him, he was falling down among the benches. Feet caught him, then the benches and the sweepshafts, and he sprawled among them, bruised and breathless, while a wash of yelling and screaming passed over him, and sudden hot spatters of blood.

Then the noise faded, as suddenly as a blow, it seemed. He tried to sit up, failed and sank back with a groan. Something near by blotted out the glaring sunlight, and he was hoisted sharply to the deck, where he fell to his knees. He looked up, trying to see Olvar and Gille, but a hand in his hair turned his face to a tall man sitting on the quarterdeck's single step, a man with dirty ginger hair fastened in a gold-broidered band, and a blunt, ugly face made worse by a crisscross of old scars and bruises. His hair was wildly tousled, his gaudy patchwork jerkin splashed with blood, and he sat awkwardly, favouring one leg, but his face was expressionless as he looked at the cowed survivors. He picked up a short heavy cutlass and tapped it in the palm of one hand.

'Huh!' he said. 'Well, that's that.' His speech was sothran, heavily accented and hard to make out from the book dialect Kunrad had learned. 'Not bad, though, not at all. We might use you. Or a few, anyhow. We don't need you, mind, but you've sunk a few good lads today, and we could stand to replace them.' He jabbed the cutlass at one crewman, who was hustled forward. 'Nothing personal, friend—' Without a second's hesitation, the cutlass slashed at the sailor's neck, slicing it almost through.

The corsairs who held him flung the still flailing man over the side. 'That's just to show you how we do things,' grunted their commander, expressionless and calm. 'Might have been a good enough lad, but we've plenty. Sailors especially, so you don't much matter. You want to live, you take orders from this moment on, now and for ever. Answer when you're spoken to, shut up when you aren't, and you live and die when we say, like we're your pa and ma together. One word out of place, and I'll make half your number gut the other half.' He rattled out the speech as if from long habit. 'Now, answer me – anyone else on board with other skills 'side sailoring? Passengers, like?'

Kunrad couldn't blame the man who burst out, 'There're smiths! Three of them!'

The commander nodded. 'Smart lad. Learns quickly. Which three?'

It eased Kunrad's heart when Gille was pointed out, and Olvar, sitting nursing his head. At least they were alive; but then the whole burden of keeping them so fell back on his shoulders. The corsair jabbed the bloody cutlass at him. 'Northern smiths?'

Kunrad hesitated, and the cutlass jabbed him in the midriff, not hard enough to break the skin. 'I *said* Northern smiths? You get the second chance 'cause I saw you fight, and 'cause you might be some use. Make the best of it, big man.'

Kunrad nodded, though it hurt his head. 'Northern smiths, yes. I'm a master. These are my men.'

'Get 'em in the boat!' said the corsair. Kunrad's arms were seized, he was hauled to his feet and more or less bundled overside. He landed on an oarbench in the longship, and a length of chain was slapped around his legs. In front of him Olvar arrived with a crash that nearly broke the bench, and Gille was dumped ahead of him, chained like the others. After them corsairs came spilling, and Kunrad half expected to be kicked or taunted. But they filed to their benches without fuss, and settled themselves easily at the oars. Another man, burly and brown-haired, barked an order, and they seized the oars in almost perfect unison. A lash landed on his back, and he seized his. The longboat was shoved off from the *Ravenswing*, where he could see the crewmen hurriedly restepping the mast under corsair orders. Another order started his side rowing, swinging the longboat back towards the shore, into the light of the sunrise. It beat hotly on Kunrad's bruised back, and his mouth, cracked and dry already, but he knew he would have to row hard before he could rest or drink. There was no sign of provisions in the crowded boat, neither for corsair nor captive, only room for booty. These were not common outlaws. Their discipline was frightening, even in their brutality, and he was having his first lesson in it now. His head reeled from hard use, his heart welled up with dark despair, but he would endure. He had no choice.

So began the darkest time of Kunrad's searching, and certainly the farthest from any prospect of success. He had never seemed more foolish to himself, or cursed more thoroughly the day he had set out on a venture doomed from its beginning. Despair, true numbing despair, would almost have been welcome to him as he bent and strained and thirsted, a chill end to hope, because it would have stilled his feverish thoughts; despair, or madness. Yet he found that neither would come to him; and when he thought of courting death, of defying or attacking the corsairs, he could not bring himself to that, either. Not from cowardice, but from inner fires more compelling. One was the prentices; he could not leave them behind. Blind and ignorant, he had dragged them into this, to his shame, and them at least he must free, cost what it might. And the other, as always, was the armour; as soon abandon breathing as that. These thoughts burned deeper than mere despair could reach. But which burned stronger, to his fiercest shame, he did not dare to think.

The rowing shoreward was swifter than he expected, but even when the arms of the bay closed in behind them, and the sand of the shallows shone under the dark stern, the corsairs' pace neither stopped nor even slackened. There was a slight drumming lurch, a loud rustle, and then tall reeds hissed along the low flanks, tangling the oars, bending into a green arch overhead. They were passing through a wide reedbed in the mouth of a river, a stream almost. Kunrad guessed it was too slow and shallow to show up on any chart, and concealed from the sea among the reeds unless one walked right up to it, little likely in those bleak lands. Sand grated along the keel, weed snarled

The Light in the Marshes

about the bow, but soon they were through and rowing in deeper water, strings of tidal pools, salt-smelling and stagnant, with waving strings of green slime. Another grate over sand and through reedbeds, a long stretch in which the corsairs sprang out and hauled, and the longboat slid into a wide deep waterway.

Kunrad expected to rest soon, at least, to come upon some beach or cluster of rush huts where the corsairs would have their lair. But there was no such place, and not the slightest let-up in the rowing. Behind them, which was the only way Kunrad could see, the glimmer of the sea was fading, and the reeds closing in, level and featureless save for the occasional scrubby bushes and treelets that clung to scraps of solid ground. It threaded a glistening line across a different sea, a vast expanse of grey and brown, waving reed-blades, clumps of thin spiky grasses. They were on the margins of the Great Marshes.

Suddenly, as they passed a gap in the reeds, he saw a tall pale square sail some ways off, and stiffened in excitement; then he realised it was the *Ravenswing*, being sailed off down some wider, deeper channel, escorted by the other longboat. This boat seemed to be in a hurry, taking a faster route perhaps with some immensely valuable or important piece of booty. Then he almost missed his stroke, at the price of a warning kick, as he realised just what that booty must be.

As the sun climbed, the corsair rowers began sagging at their oars. Well before Gille, even, he was pleased to note, let alone Olvar or himself. The tall commander swore at them just once, then grudgingly ordered a halt and a meal. The boat did not land, but was made fast to an overhanging branch. The meal was twice-baked bread, rock hard and ridden with fat grubs, a few scraps of smoked meat, and water from overside strained through squares of sailcloth. The same portion was given to the smiths as the rest. The corsairs devoured it all ravenously, and so, after an initial hesitation, did the smiths, though they tapped out the grubs on the gunwale. Kunrad was able to exchange encouraging looks with Olvar, but no word; he caught Gille's eye, but he looked away.

The commander did not rest, but stood at the stern throughout, gnawing a single breadcake and scanning the featureless reed-fields in every direction. After only a few minutes he came stepping over the thwarts to the smiths, tugged back their hair to look into their eyes and examine their injuries. Then, with an approving grunt, he went leaping back to the tiller, the painter was untied and the rowing began again. At first it went more slowly, but the leader kept calling a faster pace, sometimes foolishly so; and Kunrad realised that he was getting nervous.

By late afternoon, with the low sun making the reeds a royal carpet of red and gold with ermine flecks, the corsairs were all visibly anxious, twisting about as they rowed, evidently looking for familiar landmarks. *Don't tell me he's lost us!* thought Kunrad, then grinned at himself. Smiths rarely got lost, and he was inclined to patronise sothrans. It occurred to him that his captors could be uneasy for other reasons, and he felt an urge to duck down, to hide himself beneath that great dome of sky. From end to end of it the Marshes stretched, and he was lost in the heart of them.

This was their form, a great delta plain that stretched all across the Debatable Lands between Nordeney and Ker Bryhaine, formed by an arm of the mighty river Gorlafros, also called Westflood. Out between a gap in the mountains of the Shield-Range it ran, from one of the many lakes along the path of the Gorlafros, from its dark and distant uprisings on the eastern side of the Northern Mountains, from the springs of the melting Ice. The Gorlafros was wholesome enough in itself, fed and diluted as it was by lesser streams that ran off the eastern slopes of the Shield-Range. By the time it flowed into the Southlands and to the sea at Bryhaine's southern border, a wide and sluggish desert flood, it carried nothing worse than a burden of rich silt. But in the North it was still

The Light in the Marshes 107

strangely influenced by the Ice, the greatest concentration of its influence beyond its own frozen boundaries, and carried many things dark and dangerous down into the lands of men. Where its waters flowed it was said that the Old Years lingered, when men had lived in caves, worn beastskins and worked nothing more than sharpened stones, and would have forgotten the very secret of fire if the kindlier Powers had not preserved it for them. And over that great delta, where those cold waters met and mingled with the inflowing tides of the sea, the hand of the Ice was strongest.

To the perils of any ordinary marsh, devouring bogs, straying paths, famine, insects and disease, were added rarer, darker terrors. Wild beasts were there, snakes, water-reptiles, bloodsucking bats and worse, but they were the least of it. Visions and phantoms haunted the night, some mere terrors of the mind alone, but others deceptive or predatory. Creatures more material laired there also, stalking the land with strange powers and purposes that legend made ghastly beyond comprehension. Men who would otherwise never be suffered to live sought desperate refuge among the mires, and found, often, that if only they too were fierce and cruel enough, they would be allowed to remain. Although not, perhaps, unchanged. Black tales were told of half-monstrous things that still showed some trace of human kinship, pathetic and sickening.

Yet men still sought to cross the Marshes, for there was no other way between North and South, save by sea – which had its own dire perils. At most times organised caravans could pass in reasonable safety, and armed escorts. In later years men were to build a massive causeway across them, a broad unbroken bed of stone from island to island, kept well defended at both ends for many centuries, and well valued.

In Kunrad's day this was not even dreamed of. There were only paths, winding and unreliable, with here and there a rickety bridge, small safeguard against such perils

– or, some said, a focus for them. If any were needed, added others. Children far off thrilled at tales of the Marshes, and sat up shivering in their beds thereafter. Kunrad had been such a child; and here he was, brutally driven deep into the heart of his nightmare. He might need to confront it still more closely yet.

Would they halt for the night, he wondered, as the twilight fell, and the mists rolled over the dimming sky? Make camp, set guard – that might give him some chance, however remote. Or would they just sit here in mid-channel and shiver, without light or fire? As it turned out, they did neither.

As the last light was fading on the reed-blades they slowed gradually, until the oars trailed in the calm black surface of the channel. The corsairs were silent, darting quick glances this way and that, sniffing the air. After a few minutes the leader gave a soft hiss, no more, and waved, and the steersman turned the nose in towards a tall stand of grasses that bowed over the channel, tall enough to hide the boat. There they sat in shadow, silent, while around them other voices grew, the thin song of stinging insects, the squeaks and snuffles of small creatures hunting among the reeds, the soft rustle of nightwings. Olvar swore and slapped at his neck, but a corsair caught his wrist and gestured for silence; the whites of the man's eyes glared in the gloom. At length the leader nodded, and the port oarsmen thrust off from the tangled grass clumps. Then, just as the nose was turning out into the open stream again, the leader jerked upright and clutched hard at the overhanging stems to hold them back. A distant rustle grew abruptly louder and a strange stench, musky, oily, rank as decaying fish, washed over the boat. The grasses bent low all of a sudden, and the corsairs ducked. With an explosive leathery clap a huge shadow swept overhead, and the acrid wind caught at Kunrad's throat and eyes. A confused impression of bronze and black, dully glittering, with a spark of glaring red; then it was past, and he saw it, long and thin against the cloud-shrouded moon, snaking through the air with the motion of a cracked whip, between two immense, slow-beating wings. Only then did the size of it come home to him, and the vision make chilling sense, black talons on legs held tightly back over an enamel-scaled flank, as large as the boat or larger. One deep rumbling cough echoed across the marsh, as alarmingly directionless as the cry of a hunting owl; another red spark flickered in the twilight. Then it was gone from sight, and every man in the boat sagged with escaping sighs. The leader gestured at them to wait, and it was only as the twilight deepened and the quiet continued that he at last let them row onward.

They set tall stands of iron at bow and stern, where there was less risk of sparks, and torches within them; but it was only at the last extremity of light that he ordered them lit. The crackling yellow flame was a comfort, spreading its warm glow across the cold water, colouring the grey rushes. But as they passed, the frontwall stirred here and there against the wind, and once or twice the light glittered on eyes that peered out, some small and timid, but some larger and gleaming pale. Kunrad imagined how the boat must look, two neat discs of gold gliding along in this vast, hazy blue-black expanse, where even the stars did not shine – how conspicuous, and how small.

He was rowing almost in a dream when he felt the stroke slacken, and his oar clatter against the one behind. Gille nodded with fatigue, Olvar sat like a wall, but all around him the corsairs were turning in their seats, half rising and staring eagerly, even the commander at the gunwales, clutching his wounded leg. Kunrad twisted around and saw, not too far ahead by the look of it, a welcome orange glow, a beacon maybe or a large campfire. The commander hissed angrily at his crew, and they sank back to their oars; the lash turned Kunrad's head again. The light would probably hold little good for him, he knew; but compared to being stranded out here, it seemed warm and encouraging. Whatever else, at least the corsairs were human.

An hour or so later, though, they were rowing yet, without sign of the light; and yet the corsairs were visibly taking heart. Wherever they were going, they must be nearly there. Kunrad was about to risk another glance around, when the leader saved him the trouble, snapping out an order and leaning hard on the helm. Kunrad's side shipped their oars and sagged over them as the longboat swung around. From somewhere ahead a single harsh trumpet sounded, and suddenly the boat was gliding into a pool of golden water. A reflection of what lay ahead; and as the swirls died it took sudden shape.

A shape that Kunrad could not believe. But he had to look up, all the same.

It was huge. It looked like the paw of some vast vanished beast-statue, a great island wedge of wind-scoured rock, some eight hundred paces long and little fewer in width, rising out of a wide dark pool. Its steep flanks, raw and jagged, deeply fissured, stripped of vegetation, reared full sixty feet above the marsh to a gently sloping table of stone; but they loomed higher yet, because all around that upper surface stood a wall of rough stone topped by a palisade of tall tree trunks, still bark-clad. Along its summit, behind galleries of wicker and wood, torches burned, their light glancing here and there off the helms of armoured sentinels. Behind the wall tall rooftops lifted, crude affairs of reed-thatch or rough-cut wooden scales, but stout and strong-looking, and light gleamed through shutters beneath. Other gleams of light broke from beneath the wall, from the rock itself, in cleft and channel, and from its base at the end of a long jetty, one of many that stretched out into the pool, like claws around the foot. Masts clustered around the jetties, more thickly even than in Saldenborg harbour, masts of all heights, some huge. Fat-bellied merchantmen and lean dragon-head warships huddled alongside little coasters and tiny fishing boats, silent witness to the terrible toll that had been levied upon the sea-trade of both lands, and to the savage strength that brooded above. A fortress for an army and a harbour for a fleet, all in one. Crude, maybe, and roughhewn, like the corsairs themselves; all made new and in haste, perhaps. And yet, in their image, frighteningly powerful.

Kunrad shivered. This place was not as strong as Vayde's ancient towers, but in this desolation it might as well be. In flat ground, he remembered, the horizon was only a league or so distant. This was what he had mistaken for a campfire, just as the two lands had mistaken the corsairs for a mere flare of nuisance, not a serious challenge to be reckoned with. How soon would they discover their mistake?

Slowly now, because the jetty was so crowded, they rowed in towards it, past the mouths of other channels. Their square-cut banks, and the tall stacks of marsh peat drying out along the margins of the pool, cordon and fuel in one, suggested that men had widened and deepened them. No doubt the *Ravenswing* would make its way here to join the lifeless array in the shadow of the jetties, swelling the wealth of the corsairs by a tiny fraction, and their numbers also. No doubt corsair captains had delivered that speech on every deck – and cut throats with the same casual will, to give it point.

Careful strategies; the relentless rowing, too, perhaps. As if they were watching and working on their captives, to single out the men who suited them best. What awaited the rest? Chains, certainly; mutilation perhaps, slow working to death. There were eyeless men among the starvling chain-gang on the dock, working the heavy capstain to reel in the longboat's lines. Its pawl clanked loudly across the pool, like a pendulum ticking away the last instants of life.

The bow bumped the jetty, lifting lightly, and the corsairs heaved themselves out, cramped and complaining. For the three smiths it was worse. The chains loosened from their legs were whipped around their arms and necks, and they were bundled ashore like so much livestock. At the end of the wharf a flight of wooden stairs, easy to cut loose, ran up the rock. Golden lantern-light picked it out momentarily, then was blotted out by a tall figure, with a knot of others at his heels, coming down at the easy trot of active men in no real hurry. The grousing corsairs fell silent and stood uneasily, and their captain hurried to the stairfoot.

As the man who led the way down strode under the light, Kunrad blinked; his clothes seemed to sparkle. The longboat commander made a great show of saluting him, and was greeted with a genial clap on the shoulder as the newcomer surged past, tossing curt questions back over his shoulder. 'Well, what's the cat dragged in now? Smiths, you say?' The voice was sothran, harsh but not uneducated.

'*Northland* smiths!' prompted the longboat commander, quietly smug. 'And the long one a mastersmith!'

The newcomer turned sharply. He was as tall as Kunrad, made more so by a tousled crown of dark brown hair, and the light of the wharf-lamps glistened on a gaunt, hard-lined face, long-nosed and lantern-jawed, with narrowed, frowning eyes. Between hair and beard his skin shone with a strange glossy pallor, yellowish and sickly-looking, as if he had been carved out of wax; but he moved with swaggering ease and strength, showing off the rich fur cloak that swept back from his shoulders, and the glitter of jewels at neck and belt and wrist, and scattered about his richly cut and trimmed clothes. The torch-light caught the earrings that dangled in his hair, and the heavy studs that pierced his nose and upper lip, shining among his moustache. He stopped before the three captives, looked them up and down a moment, then gave a slight snort and snapped out a question in heavily accented Northern speech. 'That true? All three?'

Kunrad nodded. No doubt who this was; and yet he was a little surprised.

'Heading south? Why?'

Kunrad shrugged, sullenly. 'I had a debt to collect. And there's more money to be made in the South, these days.' He sensed Olvar and Gille twitch with surprise, but nobody was looking at them.

The corsair's mouth twitched. 'You like money?'

'I could get attached to it, yes.'

The corsair's narrow eyes were unreadable. He looked around at the other men with him, and the commander, and went back to the sothran tongue. 'Any problems, Padrec?'

'He fought a bit,' said the commander. 'The boys too. Rows like a sonuvabitch, them too, less tired than we are. I'd say yea, skipper.'

The tall corsair nodded. 'Done any weaponsmithing?'

'Some. Of course.'

'Any good?'

Kunrad nodded, keeping his manner curt. 'I think one of your boys'll have my sword.'

The longboat commander glared at him, unsheathed his blade and tossed it. There was a rumble of amusement along the wharf. The tall corsair caught it easily, looked it over as if a touch disappointed by its plainness, hefted it, swiped it in the air with fierce grace, and gave a short laugh. One of his large front teeth was gold-capped, and what looked like a garnet gleamed in it.

'I've already got a Northland blade. But this one—' He drew his own sword and passed it to the commander, sheathing Kunrad's in its place. 'Not so bad. Not at all! Neat catch, Padrec!'

'I could make you a better yet,' said Kunrad. 'Far better, if you give me good makings. And our tool-kits and baggage, from our ship!'

The corsair raised his eyebrows a fraction. 'We'll see. Padrec, get your crew settled, and come drink. We'll see this your cargo well stowed! You three – follow!'

He led them up the narrow stair at the same long-limbed trot, never looking back to see whether they stumbled or faltered, being chained by the neck and weary. His followers drove them on with blows and curses through a small iron-bound door, into a rush-strewn courtyard milling with torch-lit life. Women washed clothes in steaming coppers, or piled peat-slabs to dry against the stone foundations; children shrilled and squalled and chased free-running goats and chickens. The tall man ignored them, or kicked beasts and children aside impartially, if the women didn't retrieve them first. Guards lounging in front of a heavy door snapped to attention as they saw him.

'Open!' he barked, without slackening his stride, and they flung back the door barely in time. A black stairwell opened into the rock, and he went clattering down, his cloak sweeping dustclouds from the steep stairs. They looked newly cut, and crude, with debris in the corners. They led only a little way down into a narrow corridor, like an extended cellar in the bare rock, shored here and there with rough timber. Low doors opened to either side, some heavily barred, but at its end stood a larger one, whose heavy outer bolts the chieftain unlocked with crude keys from his belt. He threw it booming back, unleashing a waft of hot dry air, and a dull glow that set Kunrad positively tingling with its familiarity. The room he was bundled into was long and low and by the look of it carved out of a cave in the stone, its roof, now rolling with smoke, finished off with patches of coarse brick and rough-cut rocks, crudely mortared in. The smoke rolled from under the brazen hood of a wide forge-hearth at the far wall, its heaped coals blazing in the fierce draught. The corsair chieftain roared at his followers, and the door was slammed to behind them. The coals dimmed, and the smoke went back into the chimney again. The air was heavy, for the room had no windows Kunrad could see, unless perhaps those narrow crevices high in the wall. Deep voices murmured, and squat figures scuttled back into the shadows at the tall man's bark.

'Our main forge. The shipwrights have another, but this is where you'll work, and bunk down for now. We're crowded in this forsaken hole, and there's no better. Think yourself lucky it's warm. We need weapons and armour made, when there's time, and refurbished when there isn't. Maybe we'll let you work on the ships and war-engines a little, in the open.' He snapped his fingers.

The smiths were suddenly seized and held fast. 'That's for later, when we can trust you. Work well and we'll see; but for now—' Even as he spoke, cold fetters snapped around their ankles, linking their feet with stiff rods and chains, too close to let them run. The tall man watched them struggle to control their expressions.

'Till you learn sense!' he said, answering their silent rage and humiliation. 'And realise what I'm telling you now is truth. You're here, you stay, and don't get ideas about making a bolt for it! Within the citadel, well, you're most likely safe enough, behind strong walls and weapons and ways clear to the sea for our supplies. Even so . . .' He trailed off for a moment, uneasily. 'Even so. Men, women, brats – we lose the odd one. They get careless, they stray. Maybe they get lured out. I don't know, nobody sees it happen – but they just seem to walk off, any time, no matter what. And they don't come walking back.'

'Some do!' said a short grey-haired man, with a venomous laugh. 'Hey, boss, remember the last of these icerat tinkers we had? He thought he could make it!'

The chieftain shot him a hard look. 'Ah yes, that one,' he mused. 'Just about to mention him, I was.' The look, thought Kunrad, suggested otherwise. 'A smith of Dunmarhas, as I remember. A clever little bugger, in his way. But he came back. A few nights lost on the Marshes were enough for him. In fact, I believe his tools are still around here, somewhere.'

'Not that he had any use for 'em!' sniggered the other, leering contemptuously at the captives. 'Or much else!' There was a nervous edge to his mockery, and the chieftain rounded on him.

'Will you be holding your lousy tongue, Palhe? They come back sick, that's all, deadly sick. Stands to reason – fall in the pools, drink the water unboiled. Marsh-blind, liver-rot, yellow vomit like I had, or worse. No mystery in that!' He shivered, and rubbed his waxy hands in the forge-warmth. 'No place for men, this boghole! And believe you me, we mean to be getting out very soon. Well out! And you—' He fixed his bleak eyes on Kunrad. 'Be you a help, you come too! There'll be money enough for a skilled man then, and a good fighter. But give us any sweat, seek to sling your hook, even, despite all I've said ...' He waved idly at the blank walls. 'Ach, I don't think you're that stupid. What's outside these? A sixty-foot dive, and then the Marshes. Afoot, in a boat supposing you could steal one – still, one way or another, the Marshes!'

There was a grim relish in the word. Gille looked sickly at Olvar.

The corsair chuckled. 'You're better off here, believe me. We'll even give you a couple of helping hands – *Hey, you two!*' He glared into the shadows, shading his eyes from the forge, and whistled sharply. 'Here! *Now!* Heel! Hop to it, savvy?'

Out of the glaring firelight two extraordinary figures came shuffling forward. Cripples, thought Kunrad, poor misshapen naturals; he was disgusted at the way the corsair whistled them up, like dogs. Then his jaw dropped like any callow child's; there was a proportion in them beyond all deformity, yet human it was not. They were short, the lesser no higher than his belt buckle, the taller than his chest, but that was more than made up for in breadth of body and the limbs that bowed under the tension of their massive muscles. Their rounded shoulders were broader even than Olvar's, their necks short and thick, their heads heavy and oddly long under tangled thatches of black hair. They looked down, away from the corsairs; but to the newcomers, suddenly, they raised their heads. The features were heavy and blunt, coarse and animalistic beneath dark slathers of furnace dirt; heavy brows overshadowed the deep-set eyes, wide and brown.

Gille stared, and swore. Olvar grunted with surprise. But something deeper than simple astonishment moved Kunrad, when he caught one flash of those eyes.

The corsairs chuckled, enjoying their shock. 'A facer, ain't it?' said the short man. '*Duergar* they be, to the life!

The Light in the Marshes

The Mountainfolk! Didn't think there was such things, eh?'

'Pretty brutes, to be sure!' said the chief. 'But fit to fetch and carry, tend the fire, pull the bellows. Even do some crude ironwork, if you can first hammer the idea through those thick skulls!'

Another corsair snorted his disgust. 'Fat chance! Sooner talk to a mutt! Copped those twain and an old 'un grubbing on a hillside, and never a clear word out of 'em, even when we headed the oldster!'

'Aye, an' that's truth!' spat the short man. 'A lash, smith, that's all they'll understand! You'll needs lay on, and hard, mind! They don't feel pain like proper folk!'

'Or a touch of a hot coulter! To the she, aye, an' then watch the buck jump!'

The tall corsair joined in the chuckles. 'Use them as you will, so long as the work is done! A shame you must share their stink, but there'll be more air for you soon enough, if you put your backs to it. You, Jaho, see our guests given rations and paliasses. In the morning you'll have swink enough! And, Mastersmith, we'll speak more of that sword!'

They trooped out noisily, awaiting no answer. The door banged open, then shut; the bolt clanged. Smoke swirled and boiled out of the hearth. Kunrad coughed, and then stood silently, looking at the half mythical creatures before him, and extended a tentative hand. They stood, squat, hard, unmoving and returned his gaze. He took a half step towards them, and his chains rattled. They did not respond. He sighed, and turned to the others. Olvar and Gille looked back at him, equally silent. Wind whistled in the wall slots and moaned in the chimney.

'All right!' he said, answering what he had not been spoken. 'It's my fault you're here, I know it. If it's humanly possible, I'll get you out. Out of here, out of the Marshes – and out of these fetters, first of all!' They looked back at him, and he knew they did not believe him. 'We can do it! We can always do it! You should already see some ways; I have.

But it'll take time. Meanwhile, we'll have to work.' Impulsively, he looked back at the duergar. Their chains were heavier, manacles that tethered wrist to ankle. 'And you! All that goes for you too!'

They lowered their gaze, and turned, and like bent old creatures they shuffled away without a word spoken. Kunrad heard Gille exhale, as if some tension were released.

'Talk about weird brutes!' whispered Olvar.

Gille shivered. 'And did you smell them? Like beasts. Those horrible faces . . .'

'Are they?' demanded Kunrad softly. 'Try looking at them. Look *properly*! Not like the corsairs! Look at them as people!'

It was him they looked at, both of them. 'Whatever you say . . . boss,' said Olvar. The hesitation was slight; and there was angry resentment in Gille's eyes. But Kunrad nodded. He was still the master, and the chains could have weighed no heavier.

Slumped on the rough straw mattresses, grateful for gulped-down bowls of fish stew and coarse bread, they did their best to rest. Even exhausted as they were, getting comfortable felt impossible, although they managed to slide the metal cuffs high enough to get their boots off. The duergar retreated to a cubbyhole behind the benches at the far end of the forge, and were silent still. Kunrad was the last to sleep, for the cares that lay upon him, cursing his folly that had brought them to this pass. Not that he yearned any the less for the armour; but it no longer seemed a wholly real thing. It was as if the cold metal he had shaped had come to stand for something else, something deeper he could not grasp, and yet had to.

The wind off the Marshes, moaning in the chimney, caught his mood only too well, and the strange night-cries it bore. Only the voices of bird and beast, perhaps; but to him, as he was, they were spirits astray out there among the reeds and rushes, lost and wandering beyond all redemption. Small wonder, he felt, that people might stray off from here. He battled hard with the blackness in his heart, and it says much for his strength that he slept at last. But in the heart of the night he was awoken by another sound, loud but brief, stifled so quickly he hardly knew whether he had heard or dreamed it. It was a woman's weeping.

They knew it was morning only by the thin rays that knifed down through the crevices across the smoky air. Before long, as the duergar tended the forge, the door banged open and the corsair chieftain came striding in, with armed guards at the door and a half-dozen leather-aproned followers bearing heavy baskets that clanked and clattered. 'Your little ship's in,' he said curtly, coughing at the smoke that swirled out from the hearth. 'Here are your tool kits and stuff, and your day's rations. Now be about some work! We've a mighty store of gear wants repairing, this isn't a hundredth of it! Bad mailshirts, worse blades – these lads of mine can't keep up. Fix what you can, salvage the rest and use it. Waste nothing, mind! Run up one mailshirt out of two, that wise. Got it?'

'That's not always the best way,' said Kunrad mildly. 'As often as not it's better to patch them together with new rings, if you've the wire. And other materials . . .'

The chief shrugged, and turned to a wizened creature who was eyeing the Northerners with deep suspicion. 'Well?'

'Some,' the sothran smith admitted unwillingly. 'There's a wire drawer there on the end bench to size it, with your swage blocks and such, or to make more – if you can! But naught else, for all things are costly to obtain out here, save spooks and stinks! You Northerners can all read and write, can't you? Well, I want a close tally kept—'

The chief waved impatiently. 'Back to your own forges, for what little bloody use you are!' The little man scuttled off, looking back with wide frightened eyes, and his followers with him. The chief leaned back against a bench. 'How you manage is your business, Mastersmith, so long as it's swift. And no idling, if you want bread, and a whole gullet to swallow it! Now, set your lads to work, and come talk. For you I've a task more demanding.' He drew Kunrad's sword, and leaned close. 'Tell me what you can craft that's better than this!'

The chieftain listened, turning the blade in a shaft of light, as Kunrad described the various kinds and shapes he could make, all the refinements and improvements he could add, the strength and richness of the decoration. The corsair's eyes were as yellow and dull as his complexion, but they gleamed with greedy anticipation. 'How soon?' he interrupted. 'A fine straight blade of this pattern, with the blood-channel like you said, but to fit me – the best you can make, the mingled metal with the gold inlay? And the fancy pattern-work hilt, the jewels on the grip, all the trimmings?'

Kunrad made a great show of considering, as he had seen his father do. 'Well, let me see now . . . If I'm let work upon it all my time . . . let me see, let me see, two or three trial pieces first, pick the best and so on . . . blade first, hilt second – a plain one to test it . . . but drawing the wire especially . . . Mmm? Maybe two weeks? Say three to be safe. Once I have the makings in hand, of course.'

'Nothing's safe, Mastersmith!' said the corsair sardonically. 'Two weeks. Leave the rest to the boys and the beastfolk. List all that you'll need, and you'll have it. But you'll be a damned wise man to deliver all that you promise!'

Kunrad watched him go, hearing the door boom shut again and the massive bolts slide home. The strongest sword or axe he could shape wouldn't cut through those nearly quickly enough. And there was that gaggle of guards, as no doubt there would be every time the door opened. They had crossbows, some of them; no fighting your way past those. At anything to do with fighting, as he had expected, the corsairs were able and disciplined to a fault. Their weaknesses would lie elsewhere. Another kind of craft would have to serve him here.

He smiled slowly to himself. Then the hair bristled on the back of his neck. He looked around quickly, and saw that one of the duergar was watching him, through the slowly settling forge-smoke. There was no more expression on the face, but something was different – in the stance, perhaps, less lumpish, more eager. And there was something about that face, now he saw it raised and in the light. Look past the hair dirt-tangled around it, the perpetual slather of grease and soot . . .

The she. He hadn't taken that in, at the time. It was a woman. He could see the shape of her now, though the duergar build and the hunched stance concealed it. Quite a young woman, too, if human standards applied; most of the apparent age on that face was dirt. Dirt deftly applied – cleverly, even.

His scrutiny must have been too obvious, for she turned sharply away, hunching more than ever. But he had not missed the sudden widening of those large eyes, the quick flash of fear. He looked hard at the other duergh, laboriously beating out a dented helmet-hoop under Olvar's direction. That one was male – no. A man. A husband, perhaps, if they had such things, or a kinsman.

Something caught his eye, by the bench where the woman had been crouching. He stooped to pick it up. It was a book, small but thick, well bound but better worn, and much stained with soot and strange substances. He thought better of trying to talk to her, and carefully opened it. It was in the Northern speech, and it looked like a tract on smithcraft, handwritten as they often were. Keeping one eye on the strange creatures, he began to read, slowly at first and then faster, as he grew used to the old-fashioned script. It was about smithcraft, all right; a basic enough tract, of the kind prepared by some Masters with many prentices to teach. This one was more advanced, for journeymen, and it had passed through many hands, that was obvious from the thickly clustered marginal notes. Some of these were in more modern scripts, one in particular in new-looking rough black ink, a neat hand but so cramped and abbreviated only another smith could easily read it. This writer was evidently an advanced journeyman, nearing his mastership; but there was a tone of suppressed excitement about the notes, as if he had suddenly tapped a whole new fount of knowledge. As Kunrad, master that he was, read on, he began to feel the same growing thrill.

Throughout that afternoon they brought the materials he had listed for the sword, with armed guards as always watching the door. When it closed Kunrad spoke to the duergar, though they gave no sign of even hearing. 'I'm going to need a lot of wire. Strong wire, but finer than the stuff from the mailshirts. The wire drawer is set, and the sword-makings—' He paused. 'All the metals you need should be there. I'm going to ask you to help with other matters, but in any time you can spare, it'll answer well to your strength. Remember what I said.'

He turned away without waiting for an answer, while the prentices elaborately tapped their heads at him. 'Good to see you're keeping your sense of humour,' Kunrad said flatly, waving away the forge-smoke. 'How're those chain-shirts coming along?'

'Badly. Especially the patch-up jobs. Why didn't you tell the man they won't last like that? You said to give the new rings a virtue against rust, but we'd need a lot more phosphoric corrosives. Without those the new could feed on the old, and not hold.'

'Do you want them to? Anyhow, I warned him in some wise. He seemed more concerned about his sword, and that's what I'll be about.'

So they laboured through that day, ate the food that was doled out to them, and at last sank exhausted on their rough bedding. The duergar, tirelessly strong, still laboured away quietly on what they had been given, and nobody felt inclined to stop them. Kunrad had spent the day making moulds in heavy boxes with the forge's supply of sand and clay, and made a start on preparing the great heaps of materials he had been given, weighing out scraps of metal and piles of filings, together with other stuffs such as scraps of hide and pure twice-burnt charcoal, setting them aside in separate crucibles. It was easy work that had left him time enough to think, and this night he lay down in better heart. The pottering sounds that still came from the forge, the soft creaking of taut metal, he found positively familiar and comforting, an antidote to the marshland cries, and he slept deeply despite them.

Next morning he was up with the sun and twice as eager, chivvying up the prentices to stoke the forge fire high and strong, the duergar to work the great bellows. The moment it was ready he set within it the largest crucible he had prepared, containing fine cast iron. Others he ranged along the hearth-side, and as the cast iron began to melt in the strong, steady bellows-blast he would set them to liquefy, too, or add them as they were, solid, to the growing pool of red in the main crucible. He chose his time, carefully watching as the crucibles hissed and spat, doling out his materials with a cold, considering eye. And as he watched and added he sang over them, slow words of unity and strength, of flowing together into something greater; and he turned to Gille again. 'I need more words! Fresh words, that haven't been staled with use, words that will wake every virtue a great sword must have!'

Gille snorted. 'What, for that bloody pirate? Better any blade of his should fold like tin, as you say! Why wear yourself out for him?'

Kunrad seized him by the shoulders. 'You won't be near mastery till you understand why! Until you make every work, large or small, with the same inner fire. Fixing mailshirts, that's different, that's just . . . labour. Not creation! But whatever you make yourself, it has to be true to yourself, the best you can make of its kind. If it's a cheap sword, it mustn't be a mean one. It has to be the *best* cheap sword you can come up with! Or you make yourself that much meaner!'

The prentices retreated, startled, before his tirade, though he never raised his voice. 'And who it's for – well, can you ever tell? Could I foresee my best blades would end up in Merthian's hands? But I'm still not sorry I made them so fine. Nor even the armour.' He grinned suddenly, and cuffed Gille gently about his head. 'After all, they may end up in better hands than his one day. Who's to say this blade won't, too? So bend your wordsmithing to it, for that's the best of your art so far. And you, Olvar, come help me with my alloying and learn a precision to match your patience! I'll have you both masters yet, if it's the death of me!'

'Well – all right!' said Olvar doubtfully. 'But all this repair? Best we keep the corsairs happy.'

'I guess you can leave a lot of that to our friends,' Kunrad told him. 'They know what they're doing. They know, all right!'

The duergar turned their heads to him. Their expressions did not alter a jot; but then the woman quietly picked up the mailrings Olvar had been welding, and began tapping them into perfect shape.

In Kunrad's day the fashion was to make a sword in two pieces, adding a cutting edge of harder steel to a softer, more springy centre, that would absorb the weight of the blows without snapping; but he had perfected a subtler technique. 'Devouring more hours!' he told prentices, as they heaved the glowing crucible out of the furnace, on winch-chains that smoked as their oil burned in the withering airs. 'And more minute care – but infinitely better!'

He leaned over the first of his blade-moulds, lying couched among the forge-coals, and the pale-glowing strip of metal at its heart. 'So to this core, rich in essence of charcoal, we add the first of my alloyings, *so*, with less, and a touch more nickel, in a thin stream, *thus—*'

His hand, bound in cloth and leather, tilted the crucible and swung it in a quick but controlled double arc around the glowing mould, as if sewing in the fine thread of metal it trickled. He waited, watching it ooze across the glowing surface of the steel already there, ignoring the smoke that was rising between his fingers. Then he grunted with satisfaction and gestured to the male duergh, who swung the great bellows-lever as if it were a twig, rocking it back and forth with slow sure strokes, one leather lung gasping full as the other emptied. 'Now we blow air through it, across it, to blend it and burn out that last brittleness!' coughed Kunrad, ducking the fine ashcloud that puffed up through the coals. Squinting painfully in the frizzling dragon's-breath he swung the crucible back again, his hand-guards smoking. 'And thus! Heat it again, with force!' He coughed. 'Blast this chimney! So that the steel alloys unite at the edges, flow just enough, and mingle as one! Or they'll crack at the first tempering, like lesser trash. There now!'

His hand burst into flames. With speedy calm he steadied the crucible and scraped back the flow, then turned to the cooling-trough and thrust his hand in. Smoke arose, and a stink of charred leather. 'But if it mingles when you heat the mould again—' put in Gille.

'It doesn't. Not completely. The alloy remains where it's laid within the mould. Only the meeting faces mingle completely, stronger than a mere weld, because you heat them to just the right viscosity. It takes a smith's eye to gauge that finely, looking for the virtues we've sung into the metal. One reason we imbue them so early and strong, into the very cohesion of the alloy. When they begin to blur – in the mould, see? – then it's growing too hot. So we let the forge subside a moment, shift the mould and turn again to the metal. The small crucible laid out with the nickel, the copper and those rare earths, heat it now! And sing, damn it – sing!'

Gille shifted the crucible in the flame, watching as its flanks began to glow and the filings heaped within smoked, spat and sagged inward; and in his clear tenor, to the panting pulse of the bellows, he sang to the metals they were working.

When first from stone fire set you free,
From sleep to new life waking,
You took on purer, firmer form
Through smelting fierce and slaking!
Now sweat again to be refined,
By word and smithfire glowing,
To mingle with a nobler kind
To sterner purpose growing!
Within the walls of clay take shape,
Obey the hands that pour you,
Flow straight and true to edge and point
Drive air and dross before you!

Kunrad, hunched at the fireside, tapped and shook the metal gently, watching the rhythm of the ripples across its surface. Suddenly he seized the tongs and lifted it, and just as easily Gille shifted the rhythm.

Be confined, that you may spring free!
Be silent, to ring valiantly!
Be still, to win your liberty!
Be mastered, and find mastery!

It was an illusion, perhaps, that as he sang the words over the trickling thread of steel it somehow poured more smoothly, and the erupting bubbles grew smaller and finer. In low voices the others joined in the chant, catching its beat. The duergh's hand on the bellows never slackened, rocking easily, rocking long, while the men's strength lasted.

That was the pattern for the days to come. Sometimes Kunrad sent the prentices to rest, or to lighter work away from the stifling, stinging forge, but he himself hardly left it from waking to sleep. And yet, every so often he would turn away to the far end of the hearth, where he had set other, much smaller crucibles deep in the coals, and tipped in needle-thin threads of molten silver, mumbling deep words of his own in a hoarse monotone over the earthenware mouths. And when he could do nothing more at the forge he would hunch over his workbench, working away with grip and plier and hammer at finer, smaller things. When the great door creaked open for the arrival of food, or the taking away of their repairing, he hardly so much as looked up. Yet at one sudden roar in the chimney he rose suddenly, and met the chieftain's cold eye as he swept in with the same careless vigour, scattering the duergar from his path. He stopped by the benches, glaring at the loom of fine wires that Kunrad had been twisting together, and snatched up the small ring-moulds that lay half uncased beside them. 'What's this? Pissing about with trinkets?'

Kunrad caught the larger mould as he tossed it in the air. 'That's a ring to support the wire-work on the guard. The other's a form to shape the end of the grip. Hold a moment, and look at these, though they're barely cool yet, and in the rough. This one's the best.'

The chieftain peered dubiously at the dull length of metal Kunrad selected from the sheaf. 'Looks like the rest, to me.' He took it gingerly by the broad tang, frowning at the furnace-bloom and hammer scars that marred it.

'Not tempered as yet,' Kunrad told him. 'Not hammered out, or trimmed, or ground to exact length, or fined off, or balanced. And then we'll pickle it a day or two in corrosive, and only then inlay it and polish it properly, put an edge on. And a plain hilt, to check the action and the shape. The real one, the ornate one, last of all.'

The corsair nodded abstractedly, swinging the rough sword this way and that. He tapped it against the metal bench-strap and at the soft clear ring a smile grew on his face. Kunrad nodded confidently. 'Like the feel of it? Wait till the right hilt's on it, with the proper balance, the wirework and gems and everything. We'll need you in for that, to measure your reach and cut and so on. A sword can be tailored as close as fine clothes.'

The corsair's thin lips twisted, and he stroked his well-cut woollen tunic. He kicked something under the bench, that clattered softly. 'And that's the wire for it, eh? Looks rich. Padrec never made a better sweep than you lads! And I hear the repairs are coming on apace, too. Well, keep at it, my smith. Events are marching on. A few months more and we'll be ready to make our move. That'll end our need to skulk here in secret, and to keep you enchained. Go on serving us so well and there'll be rewards for you beyond your dreams!'

'I don't doubt it!' said Kunrad evenly, as the chieftain stalked out again. As the door closed he shook his head. The more he saw of the man, the more surprised he was, and the less impressed. Hard, certainly, bold and brutal, probably, with a taste for show and dash that would impress his followers; but to his mind the bejewelled corsair showed little of the wits or vision that could create and hold together such a formidable place as this. He hefted the ring thoughtfully, and turned back to his loom. 'Trinkets? He should talk!'

Then he remembered something, and looked beneath the bench. Wire? Had he dropped some? He stared. It was a big coil, and he did not remember it being there the last time he looked. He picked it up and hefted it. Very light and flexible, nothing he recognised. He shrugged, and was about to put it aside when he caught the woman looking at him. He grinned. He was rewarded by a sudden flash of teeth among the grime, large white teeth; and then she glanced back at the cubbyhole, and turned away even more sharply than before.

He looked at the wire. It was thicker than the gauges he had asked for. He peered more closely, and saw that it was not solid; it had been twined, braided almost, out of finer wires. He strode over to the wire drawer. Sliding out of their cubbyhole with startling speed, the male duergh was there before him. Dropping the wire, Kunrad lunged, and their hands closed together on the book.

'I've read it,' he said. 'All of it. Don't be angry with her, she was right to give it me. This; this was the other smith's, wasn't it? It was you who helped him, wasn't it?

Yes!' Again he felt like a hound on a fresh scent. 'He had the same idea as me. Only you added . . . something, that made it a whole lot easier. And, damn it, you didn't escape with him. Why—' He stopped suddenly. 'Well,' he said slowly. 'I keep *my* promises, whatever. But you must help me, as you helped him.'

The male duergh looked at him, expressionless as a statue, then passed him the coil of wire. 'Yes, yes!' muttered Kunrad impatiently. 'Very pretty, yes! But what I really need is—' He stopped, stared more closely at the wire, and sucked in his breath sharply. The duergh snapped his huge teeth with a loud crack, and ducked back into his cubby. Kunrad peered at the wire, and then snipped a piece from it, and held it to the flame with the pincers.

He dropped it in sudden alarm.

He scrabbled through the materials he had been given for the sword, trying to work out what had been used. Copper, magnesium, all the things the book had mentioned, but they couldn't all account for this. A set of thin bar-moulds by the hearth still held some scraps of fresh sprue, of a glinting green-gold alloy he didn't recognise, and filings of it lay by the wire drawer. He stood a moment, thinking; and then he laughed aloud. 'I see! Then it's high time I was about my part!'

Laying the wire aside, he turned to the anvil, and picked up the sword he had singled out for the corsair. 'Olvar, see the forge is charged, if you please, and the trough filled. Gille, would you set in the soaked hides, and measure out the ground minerals as I showed you? And then we'll hear how your words sound to a new beat!'

All through that long day the sentinels on the walls above found themselves marching involuntarily to the relentless rhythm that came juddering and clanging up from the hidden forges, and late into the night they glanced down apprehensively at the red glares that blossomed from the crevices in the rock. They shivered, for the whole community of the rock was talking about the strange Northern mages, enslaved to perform their savage magics within the stone dens. It was talk their leaders encouraged, knowing it provided a distraction from the Marshland perils and a heartening sense of strength. All the same, the ceaseless hammering disturbed the sentinels, wondering how any man or even men could keep up such labour for so long; and hearing the chanted words, so archaic and poetic in form that even those who spoke the Northern tongue could make out only a few dark words. It was whispered then that the mages hammered steel by the force of their voices alone; and so, it seems, they made it sound.

> *Now sweat within the breaths that burn!*
> *I strike you, that you strike in turn,*
> *I temper, that you temper may,*
> *I grind you, that you're sharp to slay!*
> *Be hot as wrath can make you!*
> *Be quenched as blood can slake you!*
> *Be strong, so none shall harm you!*
> *Be cold, that flesh shall warm you!*
> *A lesson grim for warrior kind,*
> *You son of steel and burning,*
> *On anvil learn beneath our blows*
> *That blows are for returning!*

Over the next few days Kunrad was more intent than ever, carefully chiselling fine channels in the steel and flattening gold wire into them, wire he had had drawn anew by the duergar. He seemed barely to notice his prentices, save when he had a task for them. 'Like the Weaver of Destinies with that wire, and as enigmatic!' complained Olvar at last. 'Must have enough there for a hundred hilts!'

'Or a prettier birdcage, if you're not content with this one!' put in Gille.

Kunrad looked at them, and his face was as blank as the duergar's. 'You'll see the uses of wire soon enough. And pay good heed, I think.'

The Light in the Marshes

They stiffened. They too had heard the bolts rattle back, felt the air change about the forge. The chieftain strode in, impatience in every line of his sallow features, his officers lounging along behind him with carefully neutral faces. They coughed in the sudden smoke.

Kunrad, rising from his work, smiled grimly. 'With the winds across these open lands you'd have done better to build a draught-furnace!'

'To Hella with that—' snapped the chieftain, but had to break off and spit on the floor. Before he got his voice back Kunrad waved casually at the workbench, and he fell silent, mouth wide.

There, resting alongside plain black scabbards, lay three formidable swords. Two were fine solid affairs, but between them, as in an honour guard, was one that shone out like a hawk among grey pigeons, shimmering as the forge-flame flickered briefly in the sudden draught. The corsair stalked over to it, eyes gleaming, seized the smooth steel and leather hilt, and held it high in the air. The corsair commanders shouted in surprise. The afternoon outside was grey, the gleam of the narrow slots was dimmed; but the polished steel caught it and turned it to a sullen flame, and the gold beaten into the fine incised lines throbbed like living veins.

To the eyes of the smiths there was another, deeper light that blazed within, and Gille read in it the echo of his own words, cold and biting, yet clear as a Northland winter's dawn. It seemed a profanity that such a fair thing should lend that ruthless hand a still greater strength and terror. He stole a look at Kunrad's face, but saw there only the smug satisfaction of a craftsman with a pleased customer.

'It's a bloody marvel!' exclaimed the corsair. 'It feels like part of my arm. And that edge—' He tested it with a thumb, and whistled.

'Try a feather!' suggested one of the officers. They clustered around it like children. 'You know, toss it in the air and—'

'I will if you're growing any, you little tit!' The chieftain looked around for something, then reached out and plucked a hank of sheepskin out of Kunrad's jerkin. Kunrad's expression did not change in the least. The corsair flicked it in the air, and as it fell slashed at it with vicious precision, back and forth. Three wisps of wool floated to the dirty floor. The chieftain hefted it, looked to his officers and grinned evilly. 'Anyone else got any smart saws? We'll needs be taking those tales our Northern lads tell a bit more seriously! This is your plain hilt, eh? I'd just about settle for that—'

'No, you wouldn't,' said Kunrad. 'Not with all those gauds of yours.'

The corsair looked nonplussed, and then decided he could laugh off the insolence. 'Well, a leader must needs appear impressive, Mastersmith!'

'So I've heard,' said Kunrad, 'from another. Anyhow, that's just a temporary hilt there – don't want it cracking on you, do you? The sword'll be ready by the time I said. You can see I have matters in hand.'

'Seems you do. Well, you've proved yourself thus far, smith.'

'I've yet to do so, I think.'

The corsair shrugged, and put down the blade. 'Go ahead, then. Have you all you need?'

'I think so. But we could use some better food, to keep our strength up. Some more of it, anyway.'

The corsair grimaced. 'Couldn't we all? So much has to be brought in from outside. Not all that runs or swims around here is fit to eat. But you're earning your keep, I'll give you that, you and your lads. Very well! But you must cook for yourselves, from now on, and save us the labour. An extra sack of biscuit, a side of smoke-meat, some salt-fish, some wine – see he has it, Frasten! Come along, all, time for the noon inspections!'

When he heard the bolts shoot home, Kunrad leaned over the workbench and breathed hard. It was only then the others saw how nervous he had been. 'You see why

I don't want to spill my words at every move?' he demanded quietly. 'Suppose they'd been listening?' He pulled the bellows, and the half-open door of the furnace below the hearth roared like a dragon, sucking away the smoke. 'That'll baulk any unfriendly ears for a moment. And do you see why I put up with these things?' He clanked his manacles. 'When we're dealing with the kind of mind that assumes iron fetters will hold a smith, best we don't disabuse them. Or they might start thinking what else we might be capable of, beyond the ordinary. I'd rather they found out for themselves. Wouldn't you?'

Neither prentice could answer. Kunrad grinned evilly. He nodded at the duergar. 'I got the idea from them. They had no way to make the corsairs trust them. So they became as dull and dirty as they were expected to be – and just useful enough. There's no better security for a slave than meeting a master's expectations – just! They couldn't do more. But that strutting peacock handed me a way to win some trust, up to a point, anyhow. The food was the missing ingredient. Not enough, I expect, but as good as we'll get. So be ready now – what for?' Kunrad grinned. 'Anything! I'm going to keep my promises. All of them!'

Nothing woke Kunrad that night; for he never slept.

In the early hours, as the sounds of the citadel faded, he shook Gille, and together they managed to rouse Olvar. That took time, but when his eyes finally opened they flew wide. The duergar were watching them, eyes wider yet in the darkness of the forge; and Kunrad realised how such eyes might serve them, in ways beneath the stone. But there was more; for these were no longer hunched and crabbed creatures, dull and stooping. They stood straight-backed and alert, with the deadly stillness of snakes.

Kunrad nodded calmly. 'All right, lads. And here, don't forget those swords!'

'The trial pieces?' blinked Gille sleepily. 'Why?'

Kunrad passed them across, but lastly he reached for

the beautiful one, hefted it, and slid the scabbard into his belt. 'Well, I and our bejewelled host are much of a size. So what I tailor to myself feels well enough to him – better than aught else he's handled, anyhow. But *me* it fits! And I thought you two might appreciate a decent blade or two, instead of that tinker's stuff you've been patching up. If we were thinking of escaping, that is.'

'You mean – *now*?' demanded Olvar in a sleepy whisper.

'Find me a better time! Master Peacock's going to want his sword soon, and he may start wondering just what's become of the leftover materials. So wake now – and come here!'

From the anvil he picked up one of the great hammers he had wielded, with beside it a heavy chisel muffled in rags. 'Now, if you'll just swing your legs up here, Gille my lad . . .'

There was a gentle touch on his arm. It was the duergar woman, staying his blow. She reached past him, clasped Gille's ankles, and seemed to be sliding something. Then the fetters collapsed to the floor with a gentle clunking sound, and Gille stumbled free. The three smiths stared at them, the metal that had felt so solid split open along bevels of bright metal that had lain concealed below the corroded surface. Kunrad became aware of delicate fingers around his own ankles, and a sudden lightness. Olvar was tugging at his and swearing softly, but only when the woman touched them did the cuffs fall free. He noticed as if in a dream that her own manacles had gone, and the man's; and though their countenances could still be carven out of rough bark, something lurked there as potent as any laughter.

'Well,' said Gille, in the ensuing silence. 'I see some legends are true, anyhow. I'm not sure I'd be able to make anything like those!'

'I know damn well I couldn't!' said Kunrad grimly. 'I've been just as dense as the corsairs, it seems. Legends? Lad, you haven't seen the half of it yet! But first we have to pack – quietly! Take only what you must, leave all the room you can for food. Gille, portion out the biscuit, cut up the meat and fish into lots, as much as we can carry. Five lots! Olvar, pick us each a crossbow out of the repaired stock, and a good store of bolts! Tie 'em well, we've a climb ahead!'

Gille hesitated. 'A climb? Where—' He stared disbelievingly at the narrow crevices, and then slowly followed Kunrad's gaze. His mouth sagged. Kunrad nodded. 'But how did you *know*, master?' hissed Gille. 'Did *they* tell you, the Mountainfolk?'

Kunrad chuckled. 'Not them! They wouldn't tell their left hand what the right was doing. No, it was our jibing hosts themselves who set me on the track. Letting slip that a smith had escaped from here already! And that they either didn't know how, or wanted to conceal it. Cardinal error. It started me looking around; and with a smith's eye. You should have noticed, too. What happened in this hole every time somebody opens that bloody door.'

'Well . . . it set the forge smoking,' said Olvar, rummaging among the arrows.

Gille slapped his brow with annoyance. 'Hella's curlies! Of course!'

'Indeed,' nodded Kunrad. 'It changed the weight of the air in here, ruined the flow, and sucked out all the smoke. Not even a sothran smith would build a chimney that stupidly! It means the flue's bigger than it ought to be, at the mouth especially, and too exposed. And consider – this whole place has been freshly carved out of the rock, with clefts for light and air. So would the corsairs have bothered to cut a whole long chimney, or simply chosen another cleft? Well, when you take the trouble to look, it's obvious. Down here it's a channel of stone, but you can see masonry further up. They just stopped up the cleft till the flow was right. So, a man might climb up and chip away at it. A fairly skinny human might find it easier than duergar. Only when it was all ready, he started to think of the risk they were running, and finding himself alone in the Marsh with the strange creatures, and how he could just slip away on his own—'

'Taking the wire they'd made for a rope!' exploded Gille. 'The bastard!' The duergar swung around suddenly, and looked at him.

'That's it!' said Kunrad quietly. 'But there's more! Now, go pack, and swiftly!'

The corsairs had left them little enough; but though Kunrad had said nothing for or against, each prentice still carried a roll of their most precious tools. He had not had the heart to forbid it, for he carried his own also. A Northern smith might sooner lose the odd finger than the implements shaped by his hand and spirit. It sent a slight shock down his spine, nonetheless, to see that the duergar also carried them, man and woman both.

'Then we're ready?' he said quietly. 'Well, Gille, you guessed about the chimney – but how did you think we were to climb it?'

'I'd been trying my best not to! The wire for climbing down, of course. But I see no footholds . . .'

Kunrad unhooked a small grapnel from the thick coil he carried, visibly cannibalised from bent spearheads and swords. 'Then see instead what the craft of the Mountain-folk can achieve!'

Springing up on the stones of the hearth, he peered up the chimney into the smoky dark. 'Shouldn't we put the fire out?' suggested Olvar.

'No!' said Kunrad, and his voice echoed eerily into the blackness. 'If my eyes would only answer . . .'

The male duergh's hard fingers plucked the grapnel out of his hand and hurled it, all in one fluid motion. Kunrad barely managed to pay out the knotted wire fast enough, as it went whistling up into the dark. A clank, a thud, and the line went slack. Hastily Kunrad jerked it tight, and leaned his weight on it. It held. Kunrad was uneasily aware that he had expected to try several times. The duergh's accuracy was unnerving.

The Light in the Marshes

'Well shot!' exclaimed Gille. 'But it sounds like a hard climb!'

'Wait and see!' said Kunrad, and he prodded the bar at his end of the line into the hearthfire.

'What, you mean you think we'll climb faster with our fingers singeing?'

Kunrad looked at the duergh, the duergh at him. He shrugged, seized his rolled pack, and caught hold of the wire above two convenient knots. It felt warm already, but he did not expect it to get too hot; the heat had other things to do. Something was happening already. He felt it under his hands, just as in the sample that had writhed so shockingly in his grippers.

Abruptly he was jerked off his feet, hard. He had read once of snakes in the far southern forests that dropped their coils around you and whisked you, choking, off among the branches. He was sorry he had.

Then he was hurling upwards towards the edge of a great steel axe-blade.

He shut his eyes tight and tried not to scream. There was an impact, but not a hard one, save where his elbows scraped the rock. He opened his eyes, and found himself sliding back down out of the wedge of grey light. It was a cleft, and he was heading back out into the void. He jammed his elbows and knees painfully against the rock, and clutched at the writhing tangle of wire beneath him, knitted up into a contracting mass. Somewhere below the bar bounced and clanked, losing heat rapidly, relaxing the wire. He began to scrabble up towards the grapnel, caught in the notch of light at the summit.

He hesitated. It was the first free sky he had seen for a fortnight, but there was nothing in it except heavy cloud turned to pearl here and there by a dying moon. Nor could he make out anything below except flatness and greyness, an ocean without movement, an awful hazy shadow on which the mind could shine its shapeless fears. He glanced quickly around. There were the hammer and chisel marks, where the cleft had been carefully widened, probably over many nights. He understood the other smith all too well, up here. So easy to just haul up that strange wire and go sliding down towards freedom, forgetting everything behind you. There would be dangers enough in these marshes without encumbering yourself with those strange beings, who seemed part and parcel of the unnatural life you were escaping from . . .

But Kunrad was not the other smith. The wire was relaxing behind him as it cooled, and he paid it off down into the sooty blackness, jamming the grapnel more firmly with his boot. After a few minutes the wire went taut. There was a slithering from below, and a startled oath as Gille's dishevelled head popped up in the cleft. 'What *is* this stuff? It's bloody well alive!'

'Quiet! You'll have to ask the duergar about that,' said Kunrad, as he hauled Gille up into the face of the rock. 'There was the outline of it in the smith's book, though he didn't understand all they told him. I don't either, but it seems to work like the strings of our sinews, expanding and contracting like all metals when it's heated or cooled. And yet with this tremendous force! Keep your head in, damn it! There're probably sentries on the wall up there!'

Next came the duergh woman, and the face that appeared was grinning widely, as if she had enjoyed the ride. When Gille hauled her up, by whatever handholds he could find, she gave him a light and sooty tap across the face, a playful gesture wholly unlike the grim, bestial appearance these people had assumed. The man was still dour when he emerged, but as he sniffed the air he gave a wry twist of his mouth which was wholly human. The wire was extending more slowly now, and Kunrad began to wonder if they should have sent Olvar up earlier. It would not carry him all the way; but the duergar, without hesitation, seized the wire and hauled the hefty young man in with no more effort than one might a trout.

Now they and their baggage were all crammed into the narrow space, making it hard to coil up the wire.

They bided their time, nonetheless, looking out over the marsh, listening for footsteps, voices, anything that would give away the presence of watchers. Finally Kunrad inched out a small mirror from his kit, mounted on a thin stalk, used for looking into complex work. It showed him the wall with its torches still blowing, but no sign of any watchers; and he remembered about the people who had mysteriously vanished. Perhaps the sentries kept well back from the rampart in the darkest hours, lest they be tempted or ensnared. The thought made him shudder, but better such risks than linger here. Below them was a jetty, where also nothing stirred. He looked to the male duergh, and nodded.

The grapnel was made fast against the stone now, but they could not simply pay out the wire. It would rattle against the rock face, and betray them. Kunrad braced his boots against the bar, took tight hold with one hand and, trusting in duergar strength, swung himself out into the night.

For a moment he thought the creature had let go, so fast did he fall, and very nearly cried out. But it was simply the confidence of inhuman strength, and hands too hard for even the wire to cut. Fending off the rock face with his left hand and his hip, Kunrad plummeted easily towards the jetty, and fetched up smoothly a few inches short of the boards. Quickly he stepped off, and tugged the wire taut and fast around an outcrop. Down came Gille, almost too quickly as his boots slipped over the knots. The woman next, with swift ease, carrying Gille's pack as well as her own.

Never fails! thought Kunrad sourly.

Olvar was next, clumsily. In one heart-stopping moment his boots left the wire completely, and he dangled by his hands high overhead; but he kept his wits, and regained his footing. The duergh came after them with an apelike grasp, hand over hand, hardly using his feet at all. He touched down lightly, though, and immediately cut the wire free with a gripper from his tool-roll. The earlier smith had had enough wire to double over, and pull after him; this they would have to leave. Kunrad touched one of the jetty torches to the end. In that cool flame, its potency nearly ended, the wire contracted only slowly. Without the bar it made hardly a sound as it crept up the rock, winding around crevices. Nobody down here would notice it – at least until it cooled again.

And it took that long to dawn on Kunrad that for now, at least, he was free.

'Too easy!' whispered Gille, glancing anxiously about. 'It can't be this easy!'

'Remember the chieftain? They're scared, stone-blind scared.'

'And we aren't?'

'You can always slip back up. They'll be glad to have you.'

'Save it. But what *are* we going to do?'

Kunrad grinned. He was feeling a lot better. 'Trust to luck, and cold iron. That's more of a defence than you might think, iron, and silver too. But they say the human spirit's better than all else together. And leaving philosophy for a moment, we're going to find out if they leave sentries on these ships.'

Down through the misty shadows to the jetties they slunk, stopping for an instant as the duergar spotted helms and pikes patrolling above. They stood like stone, feeling horribly exposed; but movement would be more visible still. But the sentries did not linger. After a moment the pikes bobbed quickly away.

'Looks like you were right!' whispered Gille.

The craft were moored in twos and threes alongside the jetty, so rich was the corsair harvest, little smacks and coasters alongside the high-curved bows of huge warships. The dark stains and scars that still streaked their planking told a nightmarish tale that lent an extra unease to the clammy night air and the faint creaking of the hulls.

'Like a sort of echo,' said Olvar unhappily. The whites of his eyes showed in the shadow of the rock wall.

'Stop it!' said Kunrad sharply. 'Any ghosts around here ought to be on our side, right? And I for one can use all the help I can get. What we need is something small and fast—'

'How about that?' whispered Gille. He was pointing out a small narrow craft moored below the stern of the largest warship, low, black and sleek like the corsair longboats.

'A mast!' said Kunrad anxiously. 'Can you handle it, Olvar?'

'With help, maybe. But the wind's westward, by my reckoning. Inland. And you can't tack properly on these narrow channels.'

'Doesn't matter. Any way, as long as it's away from here.'

Still watching the ramparts, they scuttled swiftly aboard the nearest craft, a fat-bellied merchantman, and across its deck into the looming shadow of the warship, the biggest craft Kunrad had ever seen, with its dragon-head gaping impotently at the moon. If the corsairs could dispose of something like this, no wonder they dominated the sea. The corsair chieftain was probably some kind of renegade sothran ship-captain, but even so, how could he have managed not only to achieve such things, but to find a purpose for them? It made Kunrad horribly uneasy. He wished he could kindle fire among these ships; but there were too many, too far apart, and it would only call the corsairs down on him.

The warship, like the merchantman, was deserted, its hatches and every other opening battened and bolted shut with iron, presumably so nothing off the Marshes could creep into the bilges. There was no one to challenge the little group as they swung down the stern chains into the little craft behind.

It ducked and wallowed under their weight, but settled easily enough. Kunrad, at the bow chain, reached for a saw, but the duergar woman simply took a hammer from her pack, rang one iron link gently, chose a point carefully and hit it. With a dull clank the welded ends opened, and were easily levered free. Olvar found a pair of oars padlocked to the thwart, and Gille picked the lock with ease. 'I'll take them!' said Kunrad. 'You ready the sail for when we're clear of here. Gille, take the tiller!'

'All right!' he said uneasily. 'Which channel shall we take?'

'The nearest! D'you want to risk circling this hellhole?'

Kunrad found paired oars harder to handle than he had expected, nearly ramming the warship's flank once or twice, causing Olvar and the duergar to hand off frantically. Olvar's urgent whispers gave him the idea, though, and he smiled to see the boat's bow swing outwards into the channel, between the faintly bobbing reed-walls. That, of course, brought the citadel into his view astern, and he strained at the oars, expecting more helmeted heads at the wall, trumpet alarms and showers of arrows. But the boat surged forward, and as the minutes passed there was nothing, nothing at all save the reeds closing in behind them. Kunrad rowed harder now than any lash could have made him, bending and straightening with a wild bubbling relief that swelled at every stroke gained. He could see it in Gille's face, hear it in Olvar's cheerful curses as he readied the sail.

'Would you believe it, our friends are good seamen also?' came Olvar's hoarse whisper. 'Boatmen, anyhow. Now where'd they ever learn such a skill, I wonder? They might be handier on these channels than I!'

At length they came to a sandy spit that marked the junction with another channel, wider but more winding, and Gille promptly grounded them. 'No matter!' said Olvar, glancing back to the citadel, still clearly in sight. 'She'll pull off easy, and it's about time we set sail, I reckon. More use running than laying low, now!'

Kunrad, exhausted, agreed. The duergar were already raising the narrow yard, angling it to the mast in a way that Olvar marvelled at. 'Heard of this, but it's mortally hard. Lets you sail a lot closer to the wind, if you've the knack. Well, overside, all, and let's float her.'

But as the men clambered overside the little craft rose free of the sand by herself. Olvar caught the stern – and then stumbled forward as the duergar man hauled hard on the sheet. The coarse canvas filled, and the gunwale was pulled from their fingers. Olvar was towed a yard or so, then lost his grip and floundered. 'Hey!' shouted Gille. 'Hey, you little b—'

Kunrad slapped a hand across his mouth, though he wanted to yell himself. He sprang up on the soft bank and tried to run after the boat, but caught his foot in a tangle and fell heavily. It swayed out into the glittering centre of the new channel, and as he scrambled up the long moonlight showed him the duergh settling himself at the tiller, holding the sheet with easy strength. The man met his eye with a look of grim indifference, and waved the woman to the thwart. She too met Kunrad's eye, and hesitated, and for the first time he read a clear expression on that strange face, regret and shame. Suddenly she ducked down, and began hurling things at the bank.

The man moved as if to stop her, but he could not do so and control the boat. Instead he sat back and laughed, a deep quiet laugh that boomed back against the tittering rustle of the reeds. The little craft swung away around the first wide bend, and was hidden from their sight. Only the taut sail glided across the rushlands, like some disembodied wing under the moon.

CHAPTER FIVE
Faces in the Reeds

OLVAR WAS CLIMBING OUT of the water, shaking his head. Gille still stood ankle-deep, weeping openly, like a child. The shock, and Kunrad's powerful slap, had been too much for him.

'I'm sorry, lad!' he said, helping the young man ashore, and meant it. 'But look back! I had to shut you up fast. We're barely a league away, and sound'll carry that far in this open land.'

Gille slumped down on the bank, wiping a split lip. 'What difference does it make? Fuck it, fuck them, and you too! We're lost!'

'Might as well stroll on back!' said Olvar miserably. 'Hope they don't hamstring us or something this time. And if you've any more bright ideas, *boss*, you can keep them to yourself. And your fists too! Or I might just feel like trying who's the stronger, all right?'

Kunrad said nothing, but turned and walked away along the bank, more careful where he put his feet this time. He knew he ought to feel the sting of their despair, but he could not. It simply was not in him to writhe with guilt. He felt airy, liberated, not hopeful exactly, but in hope of hope, as the sky might feel before the dawn. He found he was not even angry with the duergar, not when he came across their packs, all of them, their bows and bolts, and another food-bag.

'The woman's portion,' he said, as he showed it them. 'Kind of her – yes, kind! I don't blame them, not really – not after the way they were betrayed before. Even the man; he could have ditched us any number of ways, much sooner. He had the woman to worry about. That'd make him ruthless, think of us as a burden, a bigger risk to her; and maybe he was right, at that. But he saw us safe out, all the same. Gave us our chance and then took his.'

Gille shrugged listlessly. 'Maybe you're right. So what? Some bloody chance! We're stuck here in this horrible place, we haven't got a boat, and we've no idea where we're going. We'll end up wandering round in circles, if something doesn't get us first. Best we head back to the citadel while we can still see it!'

'*No!*' said Kunrad, and the force of his denial was better than a shout.

'Got something else up your sleeve, have you?' sneered Olvar.

'As it happens,' said Kunrad, 'yes.'

He shook it down over his hand, to dangle by its chain, twisting and turning in the long low moonbeams – a wide ring, perforated and inscribed with strange patterns. Gille blinked at it, his eyes chasing the deeper gleams that darted beneath the moonglow, like fish in a gleaming pool, letting them waken echoes in his mind. 'That casting you told them was for the hilt? A – a direction bracelet?'

Kunrad nodded. 'I made one or two useful things that way, since they kindly supplied the wherewithal. They won't have these, or at best the weak ones the cheap-jack peddlers sell. I'd have liked a lodestone, too, but even sothrans would have fathomed that. At least we've some idea where we're heading now. I could be more worried about the boat, I meant to ditch it soon enough – not this close, agreed! So unless you're so set on going back—'

The prentices exchanged glances. 'Gulled again, my lad!' grunted Olvar.

'He's preparing something really foul for us this time!' agreed Gille.

'I'm not,' said Kunrad, 'but the marshwater might, if you don't get something drier on, Olvar. Then let's hop!'

Almost at once the reeds closed in around them, and sail, citadel and all else were hidden in the dark. Even the moonlight only touched the tips of the tall leaf-blades, barely glittering on the dark waters of the half-hidden channel. In a way Kunrad was heartened. He had not expected the reed fronds to be so tall, ten feet high in some stands and rarely lower than his head. He had imagined an open plain on which fleeing figures would stand out for leagues; instead they could lurk like mice among grasses, invisible even from a few feet away. But he had also expected to be able to see, and he could not. He and the prentices were trapped in a tiny cell that opened and closed behind them, but otherwise varied little, no larger than the span of their arms. Without the bracelet . . .

His blood ran cold at the thought. A man could wander forever within the same small space. That blank grey-green curtain, softly swaying with a sound like slow breathing, the mind could people with all the lurking horrors of its own dark corners. The Marshes needed no greater terrors; and yet they were there.

Their feet sank noisily into the spongy peat, squeezing out strange and stinking airs. Gille stumbled constantly. 'Hop, the man said!' he complained. 'Stagger, yes; swim, any moment! But hop? All well enough for you half-trolls, you just trail this muck along after you. I get snared every third step!'

'Missing your nice fetters?' demanded Kunrad cheerfully. 'Anyhow, the land's rising a little, maybe.'

'Oh yes! About a finger's breadth!'

Kunrad held up a hand for silence. Gille flinched; then, as he too looked back, he ducked down behind the stems, shivering. Along the channel, still faintly skylit, dark shapes were approaching, narrow, foreshortened darts, low and black. They came at a shocking speed, and in an eerie silence. The smiths lifted their arms to cover their pale faces. In no more than minutes they heard the water-rush, the harsh creak of rowlocks and the soft gasping breaths of the straining oarsmen. Suddenly a black lance streaked past the reeds, and another behind it, with bowmen crouching in

Faces in the Reeds

the bows, drawn swords gleaming at the stern. In the space of a few thudding heartbeats they were come and gone, their wash lapping against the reeds and disturbing small night creatures.

'Good job we weren't still sat there!' said Olvar shakily. 'Though we almost could have, they were paying so little heed to the shore! More as if they were chasing ...'

'Yes,' said Kunrad. 'The sailboat. Easier to see from high up, across this expanse. That's why I meant to leave it. I hope for their sakes the duergar do too. But you can bet the corsairs'll be combing the shores as well, when it's light. Maybe with trackers or dogs. We're a danger to them. When folk hear about this place they may just be alarmed enough to persuade an army in and smoke it out.'

'Sooner them than me!' said Gille. 'But you're right, Mastersmith. As usual. And you kept your promise – thus far.'

'Might even end up owing the bugger an apology,' grumbled Olvar.

'Never that!' said Kunrad. 'I should never have dragged you both along.'

'Shouldn't have come yourself.'

Kunrad did not bother to reply. He had argued that out with himself often enough. He turned and walked on, with the peat sucking at his boots, and the prentices trudged on after him. Home and livelihood this had already cost him, and might all too easily claim his life also; but it was only these other lives he regretted casting into the balance. He thought of childhood stories, of bleached bones under the sky. If they found his, they would be pointing towards that suit of armour. He shivered. Much good it would do him!

'Well,' said Olvar some time later, as they rested for a bite of breakfast. 'Sun's well-nigh up, and nothing's eaten us yet! Reckon we should be safe till tonight now!' Then he swore and slapped, as a cloud of small shifting spots danced about his face.

'Nothing's eaten us?' inquired Gille politely, and spat violently as they invaded his mouth, along with his biscuit. 'And what about drink? Breaded bloodsucker, that's thirsty meat!'

'We'll have to risk drinking this boggy horsepiss,' sighed Olvar. 'And there was me clamping my lips tight!'

'Well,' said Kunrad, producing a flat leather bottle from his pack, 'we have some answer to that, at least.' He held up a metal circlet crowning a maze of wire, stuck it in the neck and dipped it in the nearby channel. 'Silver's signal against evils in more ways than one. I said this was a form for wire, remember? And so it is – but with strong virtues woven in to filter and purify the water passing through. I thought of using forge-charcoal, but that needs renewing.' He stared dubiously into the bottle, and sipped gingerly. 'Well, I wouldn't risk this in just any puddle, but it seems to cleanse running water well enough. Tastes strange, though . . . brackish. All right, the horse is unfit for work. But better than naught.'

He passed the bottle to the silent prentices. Gille toasted Olvar, held his nose and drank. Olvar was nervously sampling it when he spluttered and pointed. Through the reeds, just beyond arm's length, a face was peering at them. It was not a frightening face, save as any other face here was disconcerting; and this was a small boy. A white weasel-faced thing of at most eight, maybe, with a malicious glint in the narrow eyes peeping out below the thick round thatch of hair, as coarse and black as Olvar's. 'Well, what have we here?' boomed Olvar cheerfully. 'First meat and drink, then company! You hungry, then, laddie?' He held out half a biscuit, but the face vanished back among the reeds. Kunrad glimpsed one skinny white hand, there was a flurry in the reeds, then nothing to be seen.

'Kiddies loose in a place like this!' said Olvar anxiously. 'Look, we should go after him!'

'Should we?' demanded Gille. 'We're still only a league or two from the citadel. Maybe there are outlivers nearby.'

'He seems able to look after himself, anyhow,' said Kunrad firmly. 'Leave him, Olvar, and let's walk!'

But he looked out at them again, when next they halted, and vanished when a somewhat conscience-ridden Kunrad tried to talk to him. 'Could a child wander off and live wild here?' he wondered, peering uselessly through the reeds.

'Doesn't bear thinking about,' said Olvar, his cheeks heavy with paternal concern. 'Poor little bugger!'

'A poor little bugger who's kept pace with us!' Gille pointed out. 'Don't suppose *he'd* like to rescue *us*, do you?'

He was there again when they next stopped, and by common consent they ignored him, hoping he would creep closer. He stayed where he was, though, and his gaze made them acutely uncomfortable. He appeared at their next halt also, in the early afternoon, only to vanish when Gille tried to talk to him. 'Well, that's one way!' said the prentice cheerfully.

'No soul, that's your problem,' said Olvar sourly. 'Just as well you haven't whelped yet!'

'Not for want of trying, though,' was Kunrad's comment. 'Still, he was getting on my nerves a shade, that lad. I plod leagues through squelching mire, unable to see beyond the end of my nose, and up pops a little squit who isn't tired of this game yet. It depresses me.' He dangled the direction bracelet, and watched it turn the same way as before – inland, to where there must be higher and drier ground.

He swore and sprang up. Cold water had suddenly invaded his breeches, and the marsh, if anything stank more strongly than before. Gille too was exclaiming with disgust and alarm. 'What's happening? I Knew it, we're sinking!'

Olvar chuckled. 'It's high tide, you lubbers! Backing the water up the channels for a good way inland, mingling with it even. Remember you said it tasted brackish?'

Gille had a fair amount to say on the point, as usual. Kunrad gave up, and led them on. Movement caught his eye above the reeds and the eternal dance of insects, and he pointed. A small flight of seagulls wheeled overhead, their sickle wings glowing against the great rolling cloud-swathes. An instant, and they were gone; but Olvar gestured for silence. 'Nothing,' he said at last. 'Did you hear it – or not, rather? Not a cry, not so much as a squawk before or after. Powers, I miss that! Did you ever hear of a silent gull?'

'I don't know,' said Kunrad. 'But it squares with all else here. Move on, lads! It's high time!'

Their next halt was a rock, one of the many small outcrops in the mire. Kunrad suspected they were the tips of large boulders, and wondered if the corsairs' citadel was built on an immense one. The duergar would have known, probably. He tapped the smith's book, in his pack. There was so much he would have liked to ask them . . .

'There again!' said Olvar, unbelievingly. Kunrad stood up, and walked carefully down the rock towards the reed curtain. He held out a hand, and this time the face did not disappear.

'Just what do you want from us?' he demanded quietly, in his best sothran. Again he stretched out a piece of biscuit, within inches of the face. 'Is it food, or just – *hey!*'

The small features contorted, the little boy chittered and snapped at him like a furious weasel. Kunrad barely jerked his hand away in time. 'Thank *you!*' he said shakily as the face vanished, still chittering and clicking its teeth.

'Just what we should have done, years ago!' said Gille. Kunrad glared at him.

Light faded among the reedbeds quite early, as the cloud-hidden sun sank too low to pierce them. A dull red glow shone for a moment through gaps here and there, and then the gloom returned. The escapees looked around uneasily as they trudged on. 'My legs are aching!' complained Olvar. 'Isn't there any dry ground we can kip on round here?'

'Doesn't look promising,' said Kunrad unhappily. 'More mud-pools than usual, I'd say, so watch your step.'

Faces in the Reeds

There was a loud obscene bubble. 'Now he tells us!' said Gille, shaking one ankle free of slime. 'Nearly sucked my boot off, that stuff! Though wait a minute—'

Kunrad was stamping around the thinner patch of reeds ahead. 'Yes! This is real ground just here, a sort of hummock – maybe another boulder. Draining to cause the quags, maybe. Well, it's still pretty damp, but if we cut a few reeds—'

'Can't imagine where we'll find those!' wheezed Olvar. 'Listen, this is the land where good smiths go, right? We'll take it!'

They slashed great handfuls of stalks and strewed them down before collapsing on them, groaning. 'How far've we come?' asked Gille after a while. 'A league and a half, you reckon?'

'Maybe two, by the bracelet's reckoning,' Kunrad said. 'Better than I'd hoped, over such ground.'

Gille opened one eye hopefully. 'Any chance of a fire, then?'

'A small one, maybe. We're still in sight of the citadel, but the reeds should hide it – provided we wait till after dark, to hide the smoke. Don't know if we'll find any dry kindling, though – *You again!*'

The reeds riffled apart, and the familiar face peered beadily out at them. In that light the boy looked less than reassuring. Then he suddenly tossed something through the reeds, that spilled at their feet. A pale flash among the twilit reeds, and he was gone. 'Well! What's this muck he's left us?'

'It's dry stalks!' said Gille enthusiastically. '*Kindling!* He must've heard us! C'mon, let's build a fire—'

Kunrad was staring at the reed curtain. 'Yes,' he said slowly. 'We'll do that, in my fashion. But after that, I think, we'll keep watch by turns. Close watch.'

The fire that rose among the reedbeds as dark descended was not very large, but it shone like a red stone on dark velvet. Kunrad, on the midnight watch, hunched uneasily into his jerkin, and hoped it wasn't going mouldy.

Suddenly he sat up, and shook the young men snoring at his side. Olvar was up in the space of a breath, Gille, panting, reaching for his sword. 'Not much like at home, is it?' whispered Kunrad. 'Listen – d'you hear something?'

They listened a moment, then turned anxious faces towards him. He nodded. 'Not too loud, but getting closer! Keep down!' They slithered on their bellies to the reed wall overlooking the rock, parting the stems just enough to peer through. At first there was nothing; then a small shape pattered past, its pale skin catching the faint fireglow. Another, and another, dancing, hopping, and then a whole crowd of them. Something else moved slowly and heavily in their midst.

The silence of it all was the terrible thing, like a dream. Kunrad swallowed nervously, and it sounded thunderous in his ears. The thing came level with him, and he held his breath. He could feel Gille shivering at his side. The faint light of the hidden moon glinted upon its back, also pale but bunched and knobbed and carunculated, a huge mound of warty greyish hide. Its head was another mound in front, high-crowned and wrinkled, with great heavy ears that flapped this way and that, not unlike the mammut they knew lived in Northland forests. The head lifted a moment, and large eyes gleamed momentarily. It was bald, but a fringe of dark hairs straggled here and there behind the ears. It snuffled softly, and the small figures shivered and clustered against its flanks; long blade-like incisor teeth were bared, and shining saliva welled out in strings. The thing moved ponderously forward on heavy fore and hindlimbs, splayed out to either side, and a clawed foot, foul and slimy, fell so close to the watchers it almost tore down their screening reeds.

Kunrad realised he was trembling too. He could see it all too clearly now. Bulging haunches, ending in a pointed, tailless stump, waddled slowly past with frightful strength; and the tiny things that capered two-legged around it were the same inhuman shape. Seeing them so openly, their proportions were wrong, their feet and hands too large, their limbs too spindly, their haunches pointing in the same manner. All their human traits were accidental, that was clear, mere growing stages of the huge four-legged beast that inched slowly forward now, each foot hovering and twitching before being slowly lowered, lest it make a sound. They were its young, its scouts and decoys, its acolytes and parasites, and the sudden tension in their bodies mirrored the bunching of its muscles.

With a horrible chittering hiss it sprang, straight at the dying glow and the faint plume of smoke that still lifted from it. The glow vanished, in a huge sucking splash, a barely liquid sound, and a horrible threshing. The little creatures shrilled in wild alarm, and the great bald head reared up out of the quaggy hole over which the fire was burning, on a floating mat of half-dried peat. It bucked and roared, a curious whistling bellow, but with such bulk it was having trouble fighting free. The little creatures scrabbled frantically around it, and were crushed or scattered heedlessly under those flailing paws. Kunrad sprang up, and the others behind him, still half-hidden in the reeds, raising the crossbows they had laid ready. At a range of seven or eight paces it was no shot, even in that light. Three bolts sang home, Gille's in one massive eye, and the thing shrieked horribly. Still threshing, it rolled over, clawing at its eye, and sank back. The smaller creatures squalled and chittered, some sprang and snapped insanely at their assailants. Kunrad kicked one off his boot into the reeds, Olvar trod on another, with unpleasant results, and the rest scattered and fled.

The smiths snatched up their gear and sidled off through the high reeds, as silently as they could; not that anyone wanted to speak, just then. It was another mile before they found another patch dry enough to slump down on, and they sat in silence, constantly looking over their shoulders. It was one thing to hear about this awful place, and another to come up against some manifestation of it. To know that all day long they had been stalked, with uncanny care and intelligence . . . What else might be stalking them, now? The silence was more than Kunrad could stand.

'Worth shifting the fire for, eh, Gille?' he whispered. 'A good idea of yours, that peat!'

Gille could only wheeze. 'Your nasty suspicious nature! Look a gift fire in the mouth, eh?'

Olvar was looking back. 'I suppose . . . they weren't human at all, really, were they?'

'I don't know – no! Just some monstrous flesh-hungry thing – those teeth! Like a bear, maybe. And yet . . .'

'The shape,' shivered Gille. 'And the gift of the kindling . . . You hear stories, you know. Listen, shouldn't we be pressing on?'

Kunrad bit off the obvious comment. 'If you say so, lad,' he answered quietly. 'Don't overtax yourself.'

'I'll be ready again the moment it's light!'

'Me too!' rumbled Olvar. 'Sooner we're out of here, the better.'

Kunrad nodded fiercely; but he was glad neither prentice had asked him how long that might be.

The next day passed, and the next, without any change, and the days after with little more. The sing and stab of insects became a constant monotonous undercurrent they hardly noticed. Here and there, away from the channels, the reeds seemed to become more varied, with patches of a shorter kind, no higher than their knees, that allowed them a brief glimpse of light and air. But soon enough all there was to see before or behind were the taller reed walls. 'Torture by hope!' groaned Gille, as they plunged into them yet again. 'Like letting a man out of the condemned cell just long enough to see the gallows!'

Kunrad growled impatiently. Gille had a miserable knack of putting his own feelings into words, and making them more intense. Which was exactly what Kunrad had taken him on to do, but that didn't make him any less irritating. Lack of sleep, too, was sapping Kunrad's tolerance. Their last few nights had been spent, at best, curled up on some drier patch; at worst, huddled back to back under mist or drizzle, heads to knees, feeling the damp wick up through their clothes and boots. Fires were out of the question, and hot food. If they had not been Northerners, hardened to far worse cold, they would have died. Little wonder that the corsairs, mostly sothrans, succumbed more easily.

As it was, it seemed like an age since Kunrad had had dry feet. His skin was becoming blighted in places, soggy, sore and peeling off with his boots when he tried to dry them. Beneath the leather they were wrapped in a mass of rags now, torn-off strips of clothing held on by dried blood. The young men were beginning to suffer the same way. But worse, far worse, was the shadow that forever invaded their sleep, filling it with visions that jerked them awake, quivering with shock. What these were exactly, they never could remember, but they constantly hung over their dreams, and their minds during the days following. They took watches; but it was so common now for the watchers to doze off that it seemed hardly worth the trouble. When one rainy night, Olvar, on the dawn watch, sprang up with a shout, they were on their feet in a moment, swords in hand; but when there was nothing, they sagged and sat, groaning softly, without questions or reproaches. Any of them could have done the same.

Dawn came without further incident, but as they woke the light showed them the big prentice twitchy and uneasy, and with an odd hue to his face. 'If it was me,' said Gille judiciously, 'I'd be green. Your copper's developing a touch of verdigris.'

'My guts aren't too happy,' admitted Olvar. 'Maybe I did swallow a drop of that channel. And – well, the shapes, they were just mist catching the breeze, I know that. Up above the reed-tops . . . But I did hear something, something heavy, moving. Thataway, a long way off, or I'd have woken you earlier.' He pointed.

Kunrad held up his bracelet. 'That's the way we're going. My turn for the dawn watch tomorrow, isn't it?'

They all flinched at a sudden flurry of wings, but it was more gulls, higher this time. 'Why don't they cry?' muttered Olvar. 'It's not natural! I wish they'd cry!'

Even as he said it, one of them broke and wheeled, screeching raucously. Others answered. 'Now why didn't they do that a few days back? They can't shut up for a minute, normally. Worse than Gille.'

Gille didn't rise to the bait. He stared around. 'Maybe because we had – company, then. Maybe they sensed what was following us.'

'Well,' said Kunrad, 'they're noisy enough, now, aren't they? That's a good sign. Maybe we should watch out for it. Now, on your feet!'

The march that day, as on the days ahead, was a longer one, for they were moving away from the rivers and channels now. The waters seemed to be growing less brackish, the tide-swell less apparent, but the ground ahead was becoming still more soggy and treacherous. The reedlands were cut across by larger pools and stagnant ponds that they had to skirt, at endless trouble and annoyance, slipping and stumbling in shallow streams choked half solid with green slimy strings and tangles of coarse weed. Even waterlilies looked bleak and colourless in this green monotony, and the few other flowering plants appeared weak and overborne by the reeds, whose endless shadow cut out so much of the light, grey and overcast as it was. Here and there among them grew wide stands of black rushes, and these were the worst of all, sharp-edged and pointed as if the marsh had teeth. The first unwary foray through them left the three smiths bleeding and cursing. The smell was worse here than it was in the channels, and sometimes great bubbles of bad air came gurgling up under their feet, and made them feel breathless and giddy.

It had not always been this way, this levelled sink of corruption. The fallen trunks of great trees, half rotted or shrivelled and mummified by the peat, thrust out here and there like vainly clutching hands from a foundered world. Dripping creepers choked them, bloated fungi sprang from them, mosses encrusted them and living slime, dully phosphorescent in the dark hours, made them one with the dank pools around about; but there were often no better places to sit and seize a moment's heartsick rest. Olvar in particular needed it. He seemed as tireless as ever, but moved as if his bulk was become a burden to him; he was sweating heavily, more silent than usual, and from time to time his guts rebelled violently. Kunrad would hold back unobtrusively to help him, but that left Gille, who trod lightest, leaping impatiently ahead. His fears seemed rather to spur him on than teach him caution, and often Kunrad had to call him sharply back before they lost sight of him altogether. When late one afternoon, two days later, they heard a sudden rustle and thump, and then silence, Kunrad sprang forward, fearing the worst, and Olvar floundered after him. But almost at once Gille reappeared, clambering over a wide tree-bole, arms flailing to wave them down. He clapped his hand over his mouth and pointed frantically. They sidled up more quietly then.

There was a gap visible through the reeds ahead, a wide gap that led off in two directions, around sharp bends. 'A path, by the Powers!' wheezed Olvar.

'Paths don't just make themselves!' whispered Gille. Kunrad nodded, and lowered himself gingerly off the crumbling wood. A couple of small brown birds flew up from a puddle, but nothing else moved. His feet touched ground, solid ground, only slightly spongy and carpeted with grass and small flat-growing weeds, not reeds or rushes. Here and there the earth was torn up, tarry-black and oozing. The gap looked about ten feet wide, and at either side the eternal reeds were flattened and broken. 'What you heard the other morn, I think, Olvar. Some things went this way all right – heavy things.' He held up the bracelet thoughtfully. 'You know, this almost looks as if it follows the solid ground, what of it there is. That'd make sense. It could lead our way, for a while anyhow. I think it's worth trying, as long as we keep an eye open. And ear.'

The prentices jumped down after him, almost unsteady on land that didn't subside. 'Not much worse than anywhere else here!' said Olvar fretfully. 'Powers, what a place! What an awful bloody place! And there's a nice new smell of some sort. How much longer do you reckon, boss?'

Kunrad looked around, as they trudged carefully off down the cleared space. The waders had settled to their puddle again, darting only the occasional beady glance at the newcomers. 'Peaceful enough, for now. I don't know, lad. Days, for sure. As I remember the maps, the Marshes narrow as you get further inland, but that's about the only thing certain. I'm hoping we can strike south-east in a while – along one of the trade-trails, hopefully, or one of the river channels. More than that I can't say.'

'Could this be a trade-trail?' demanded Olvar hopefully.

Kunrad looked up at the rushes curving in over them. 'Doesn't look like it, not a wagon-trail. Too narrow. Those leaves close over at the top, almost. More like . . . a tunnel. As if feet had passed here, and compacted it. And it looks to run east–west, not north–south.'

Gille looked around warily. 'Don't go forgetting the corsairs. They raid inland and vanish, don't they? Maybe along hidden routes like this. That something Olvar heard the other morn – couldn't have been a search party, could it?'

Olvar thumbed his chin. 'No. It was – one noise, not many. And not loud, but solid.'

Gille looked around. 'Could it have been a boat dragged along? Could this be a portage between channels?'

'You know, it sounded a lot like that. And I've heard such things.'

Silence. 'Well,' said Kunrad. 'We'll just have to hear them coming, that's all.'

Faces in the Reeds

That night they spent on the strange path. As Kunrad had suspected, its winding course took them from one solid spot to the next, with as little interruption as possible. The going was far easier for Olvar, and they made much better time before they stopped for some of their dwindling provisions. 'Leagues further, and with less effort!' sighed Gille, washing down the last dry scrap of his portion of biscuit and jerked meat. 'And it's almost dry enough to sleep on, even – o noble mosses! Whom should we thank, I wonder?'

'You might get a chance to find out!' said Kunrad grimly. 'You're on first watch, remember? Better let Olvar sleep unbroken, we'll split the dark hours between us. Wake me at moon's height!' And he rolled himself in the ragged blanket which was all his bedding, and snored almost at once.

When he released a yawning Gille to his sleep, the moon was high, and the clouds racing across it, more broken than by day. It ruffled the fronds above, so that the few stars visible flickered between them. Nothing else moved. Kunrad lost himself in thoughts of the past, and of other starlit nights when he had been Gille's age, making the first painful essays at what that wretched brat seemed to find so easy and casual. He had become more at ease with women since then, of course. Things were sweet while they lasted; but they never had. When the first eager excitement waned, and he had begun to know the girls as people, they had seemed more ordinary, less interesting. He had been fond of them; he still was, mostly. But he had never wanted to share his life with them. His craft seemed more important, then, more exciting. Far away now, those nights, impossibly far, washed away on the vast River that men looked to in the heavens, from which they believed human life fell to earth, and to which it returned after death. Perhaps it too had perilous marshes along its course; and perhaps he was lost in those also. As well no woman waited for him at home; and yet he could not be glad of it. Adrift in this green hissing ocean, a man came to know the face of loneliness too well.

Some of the cloud seemed to be drifting lower. He looked up as it passed overhead. Too low to be cloud; mist, then. There was no shortage of that. He felt its chill settle upon him, and longed for day. Even Northerners could not survive here for ever. He was worried about Olvar.

He looked up again. The mist was thickening. Then shock stiffened him. He had seen a face in it, clearly. A boy's face, maybe, eyes closed, mouth wide; a sleeping face, or a dead one. He rubbed his eyes, though he did not doubt them; any excuse not to look up again. But he had to, hoping it would have drifted by. It had; but there were others. Each face in its own little flow or flurry of the mist, defined in its grey hues yet somehow more distinct, utterly unmistakable. Men, women, children, all a few feet above his head, all placidly asleep and nonetheless horribly disturbing. How was he even seeing them, in this light? Instinctively he stood up.

The moment his head rose above the reeds, instantly a face was staring into his, wide-eyed, snarling, while fingers icy but all too solid grappled at his throat. He clawed back the grasp, but saw nothing save the face, eyes narrowed and alight with malice and hungry intent. Teeth gaped, and misty breath numbed his cheek. Stinging revulsion lent him strength, and he flung the thing free as he might a stinging insect. At once it was a creamy wisp of mist scattered a foot from his face; and equally swiftly its loose tendrils twined together again, coalescing into that furious gaping mask. He had gained the moment to spring back, reaching for the hilt at his side. The new sword slid from the scabbard with a soft clear ring. The unstained edge slashed the air and struck the mist in two, without resistance; but something solid tumbled down the night, with a thin, high-pitched shriek, and splashed into a nearby pool. Kunrad sank down, blade upraised; but the mist drifted calmly by overhead, and to see faces in it was entirely fanciful.

Faces in the Reeds

Olvar, feverish and uneasy, lifted on one elbow. 'Anything the matter?'

'Tell you in the morning,' coughed Kunrad, shaking his head. His mouth was dry, a stream only yards away through the deep rushes. He could wait until the light.

It came, with its fragment of extra warmth; but Kunrad was chilled more deeply. He had wished for company, and like a macabre joke it had come. Was the mist-thing some horrible human relict, or only the semblance of a mocking ice-spirit? The cold lingered, and left him no stomach for the bleak scraps of breakfast. He told the prentices as he walked, enough to warn them; but Olvar needed none. 'I saw them too! Though never so clearly. I thought it was just the edge of sleep! But then – that was when this sickness of mine—'

'The water, more likely. Don't worry about it. But keep your head down near dawn!'

Gille took his share of helping Olvar, but still tended to bound ahead, although he made great play of looking around every corner. Once he scared a huge pair of herons from the reeds, and ran most of the way back to the others before he realised what caused all the thrashing and screeching. That dimmed his impatience for perhaps half an hour; then he was off again. 'Take care!' said Kunrad grimly. 'I don't think this can be any kind of portage now, not miles long.'

'Might be, if they used skids,' objected Olvar. 'I've heard of longer, in the old days of the North, when the settlers were desperate. The marks would soon grow out, in this stuff. So—' He stopped. Gille was up at the next bend, as usual, but he was skipping up and down and waving like an eight-year-old. 'Now what's the pillock found? You go, I don't feel like hurrying.'

'No. Getting strung out's all we need. Take your time.'

Gille was still dancing around when they reached him, with a weird look on his face. 'I've found what made this track!' he hissed.

'*What?*' Kunrad's sword was in his hand at once, and Olvar was drawing his bow.

'No, no!' insisted Gille. 'It's all right! It's dead, long dead! Can't you smell it? See?'

There was an unsavoury smell on the air, all right, more acrid than the usual boggy stinks, with a sweetish, musky undertone. Olvar sagged, but Kunrad looked cautiously around the corner at what lay in the path through the reeds. 'I've smelt something like that along the way . . .'

'Dead and decayed!' interrupted Gille. 'Wouldn't like to meet something that size alive, but this is just a rotten old bag of skin!'

Despite his words he was keeping well back. Kunrad stepped forward and prodded the thing with his sword. It stank, and it was ragged and pale. 'Like it was a giant slug or something—' shuddered Gille. Then he saw Kunrad's face.

'Not a slug! You young idiot, keep your voice down! Not dead, either! At least, not the rest of it! Gille, you lackwit – haven't you ever seen a snake before?'

Gille gaped. 'A snake?'

'Yes! This is its shed skin!'

Gille looked around at the almost circular tunnel, ten feet wide, with its crushed curved sides. Kunrad hooked the pale mouldering mass on his swordpoint, and they saw the girth of it, higher than his shoulder, or his head even, and the diamond pattern of scales the size of his body. 'And you know why they shed them? Because they've grown! Olvar – where's Olvar?'

'Olvar!' cried out Gille, then clapped a hand to his mouth. He was nowhere to be seen; and there was a sudden rustle among the reeds. Gille drew his bow; but next moment Olvar clambered out, doing up his belt.

'More notches tighter—' he began, and then saw the skin. 'Hand of Ilmarinen! You mean this—'

The image was clear in their minds. The bulk crushing through the reeds, winding across the solider land, where it could move fast without needing to swim, the tongue flickering as it sensed its prey.

'Yes. They shed, they get hungry, they hunt. We've got to get off this run.'

Olvar shook his head. 'There's just swamp here. Hardly even a spot to take a quiet – Maybe that's why. Maybe it's in there.'

'Then,' said Kunrad. 'We move, and fast. And Gille, we stay together. Close. You never know what's waiting.'

They spent one more night on the trail, in the shelter of more ancient uprooted trunks, and the young men slept. Olvar lay calmer, but still looked sick and sweaty. Kunrad's was the first watch, and his eyes were heavy. After last night he was determined to keep to neutral thoughts, but that was no help, or worse. The musky snake-smell seemed still to hang around the path. Bats flitted across the reeds, sweeping up the last late insects, and every time they swooped into the pathway they made him jump, remembering those immense hunting wings. He was feeling feverish; but was it mere exhaustion, or would it swell into horrible delirium? He leaned back against a stump, and hung his head. This whole trek felt like a fevered dream. Some day, soon, he was going to have to cease dodging the point, and confess to the prentices.

He held up his bracelet. The direction it swung was still right, but it was scanty comfort. As he remembered the maps, the Marshlands stretched back from the coast some seventy leagues, in some places more, flanked nearer the coast by the desolate Debatable Lands. He had done his best to reckon how far inland the corsair citadel was, but in the end it was little more than a guess. By that reckoning they should be far from the sea by now; but it was still with them. Twice a day the water swelled up, though less visibly than before, and twice a day it sank; and for all his filter could do, it was still tinged with salt. There might be a day's journey left, or a hundred. And the Marsh, and all within it, was still their master.

He looked up suddenly, and thought his nightmares had taken shape. There was a woman looking at him – a girl, rather. The face was not at all like his misty vision. It was awake, aware, but calm and clear-eyed. She was there, she was material; the rushes brushed about her ragged gown, and her dark hair stirred in the breeze. She was good to look at, peering shyly through the fronds; but her calm was eerie. Kunrad stood up, slowly, and put hand to sword. He was not going to be fooled this time. He would have to wake the boys, but not too urgently. She made no move; she was just standing there, as if to hold his attention. He wasn't having any of it. He looked around quickly, but the tangle of trunks was so thick that nothing material could sneak up from behind unheard. He propped himself against a trunk for reassurance, and smiled at her, cynically. If he had to have visions, this he could stand; he was short of entertainment. What next? Would she shed her gown, or something? He fought down the urge to cheer and jeer as men did at fairground dancing-girls. 'Getting a touch light-headed, aren't we, boy?' he told himself, and remembered to prod Olvar with his toe. Gille he couldn't reach, and he didn't want to shout. It might break the spell.

She straightened up, slowly. The gown was a fair touch, ragged enough to look pathetic, revealing enough to tempt a man's curiosity. Probably a few corsairs had gone that way, and good riddance. She took a quick step back, which startled him; but he chuckled again. All right, maybe she was human, maybe she was some kind of refugee on the marsh; too bad. If she came to him, she'd stay a sword's-length away until daylight; and if she went, well, too bad. He wasn't going to follow, not if there were a hundred out there like her. There she was, beckoning. Now that was the limit. What normal women would behave like that? It lifted the shreds of her gown in a very interesting way. He almost burst out laughing. She could go on all night, for all he cared. All this fun for free! He leaned back against the trunk again, relaxing.

It wasn't there. He toppled over backwards, just as his feet shot out from under him. He screamed. He was sliding down a slope into deeper darkness, and he clutched frantically at the soggy peat beneath him, digging his heels in hard. They whipped out into emptiness, and he heard things fall away, a long way, into water below; but his fingers tangled in root-fibre, clutched and held him. He kicked, got a purchase and shoved himself back up. There was a sudden rush behind him, and huge hands caught at his shoulders. He struggled, but heard Olvar shouting 'It's me, boss, it's me! I got you!'

Kunrad let himself be hauled back up. 'You all right?' demanded Gille. 'What got into you, wandering off like that? As well Olvar woke!'

'I didn't know,' he muttered. 'It ... held my attention. Quite well. Just false enough to make me feel safe and superior. I could give it up, any time. And all the time, my legs were walking ... Like a dream.'

'A nightmare!' rumbled Olvar. 'Look at your destination!' They stood on a low island, and by the side of the track opened a muddy pit, like a well.

'Ever seen an ant-lion?' inquired Gille. He kicked a stone half sunk in the moss, and it bounced down the slope. As it tumbled out into the blackness he let out a low wail. It was a human skull.

It fell in silence. Then suddenly from below there was a musical note, a splash and a yelp, echoing in the pit. 'Bullseye!' chuckled Olvar nervously, backing away. 'Would've pleased the late owner, I'm sure! Stop a moment!' He pulled his flint and steel from his pocket, and dry kindling and bulrush stalks from his pack. It flared, and the smiths yelled and sprang back, reaching for their swords. The place was thick with bones, floored with them, and not just bones. Almost at their feet lay a man's corpse, shrunken to little more than a skeleton, yet still clad in a mud-encrusted mailshirt and shreds of clothing, the bright colours absurdly fresh. 'All twisted and ... wrung like that!' moaned Gille.

'Like everything'd been sucked out of him!' said Olvar, nauseously. '*Everything!* Aagh!' In a paroxysm he hurled the bulrush. Falling, it lit the pit sides. They were lined with rough-laid stones, like any ordinary well. But as it reached the bottom, the bulrush flared with an explosive pop. Flame belched in the depths, and there was a frenzied shrieking that died away in a wail. They turned away, shaken. That flash had shown them the bottom, the ribcages like rotting ships upon the black water, the bobbing fragments green with decay.

'Bad airs,' said Kunrad. 'They'll do that, sometimes.'

'The voice . . .' said Gille. 'Sounded human enough, didn't it?'

Kunrad nodded.

'Did it say anything to you?'

'No. But the body did.'

'What?'

'Didn't you see? Mail. Mangled, but not rusty; and those wide breeches, like the corsairs wore. Probably he was one. And not long ago, or the clothes would have been rotten. And the skin.'

'Gah,' said Gille, then looked at him sharply. 'Not long? How long?'

Kunrad voiced the thought. 'A day or two. At most.'

Gille hissed an obscenity, and looked wildly around at the reed walls. Olvar put his hand to his forehead. Nobody said anything more; they were sharing the same thought, the same feeling. The marshland was closing in around them. They had come this far, for this many days, and seen nothing at all of their captors beyond that one swift pursuit. Yet all this time, for all their efforts, and the terrors they had evaded, the corsairs had been on their heels, and they had never so much as noticed. Maybe they were closing in even now.

'He could have been here for some other reason,' suggested Olvar.

'Such as?' demanded Gille. 'You know how they feel about the place, and I for one don't blame them, if they've got to make their way around with just lodestones. No, if he ventured out here, it was after us.'

'Well, maybe losing him will scare them off. But yes, they could be still about. We'd better up stakes at once. After that flash . . .'

'Yes. Too visible. And it's almost mist time, remember?'

They shuffled along in the half-light, stumbling frequently, looking back anxiously at the spot where they had lain. The sky should have lightened, but it did not, and there was no mist drifting. Instead they heard a pattering in the blackness, loud and drawing closer, like the fresh breeze that chilled their necks; and a curtain of drizzle swept across them. That was enough; they huddled down under the reeds for protection. But somehow they did not stop this breeze, and the waters wept down on them as the light reluctantly grew. Birds were crying, more birds than they had ever heard here; and as the drizzle thinned a little to let the late dawn through, they saw why.

Small wonder they had had no shelter; for the long trail opened out at last, on to the reedy slopes of a small mere, dotted with islands. Some bore a tree or two, little things bent and distorted by the prevailing winds, but trees nonetheless. Birds nested there, and waterfowl of all kinds and sizes flocked and squabbled about the grey waters. It seemed almost impossibly airy and alive after the dead green world of the reeds and the decaying swamp. Kunrad rose to his feet, shivering, lips working.

'What is it?' demanded Gille.

'Don't you see?' Kunrad felt as if he would explode like the well.

'What's to see?' groaned Olvar. 'More reeds, more water, more marsh as far as the eye can see! Is there never an end to this place?'

Kunrad laughed. 'Reeds, yes! True reeds, broad-bladed, not like the great frondy grasses we've been caught in. And shorter! So you can see past them! With those and those birds, I'll wager that's fresh water out there! This isn't saltmarsh any more. This is sweetmarsh, river-fed, beyond the tide-reach!'

'What difference does that make? Better class of monster? Still can't see a bloody way out!'

'But you only see a league or so! Look at the horizon – aren't those trees there, real trees? More than here. It could be that near. It needn't be much further. A day, two days. The edge. The Southlands, damn it! The way *out*!'

They gaped at him, as if hope hurt like the blood returning to a limb constricted. That was how he felt. Over the days past – how many days? – this awful world had become theirs, their horizons limited to the reed-beds. Open space and a hint of freedom was almost frightening. He slumped down on the green slope, and for a minute or two they rested, and watched the birds.

'And that's something else,' said Gille after a while. 'That smoked meat's all but gone. I've seen nothing in the reeds I felt like eating.' He reached for his crossbow and bolts.

Olvar looked troubled. 'D'you have to? I just like watching the little buggers. Nice to see something cheerful and colourful for a change.'

Kunrad nodded. 'There's some meat left, yet, and plenty of biscuit.'

'The meat's maggot-fodder,' said Gille; 'and you, my lad, need some better food to help your guts heal. We're weak enough, but you could be brewing something really serious.'

That was true enough, and they watched Gille as he wormed his way to the water's edge. The birds were not especially concerned here, far from human haunts, though they did avoid the mouth of the trackway. There were ducks skidding about in plenty, but Gille had his eye on a flock of geese, brown-backed with dark heads, that bobbed on the open mere some ways off. Kunrad wondered how they would get anything that far out without a dog, but Gille had his own ideas. From behind a black-reed clutch he sprang up suddenly, and the whole face of the mere seemed to take off with a deafening rustle, a fluttering curtain of white bellies and underwings across the grey sky. The heavy geese rose more slowly, and Gille waited as they crossed the shoreline, then aimed his bow and fired. A snap, a hiss, a dull crack and one of the bright birds was a limp shape dropping groundward. Its fellows broke and wheeled in panic, and came skimming across the reeds over the watchers' heads, honking loudly.

All three of them saw it. Not far away, some half a mile maybe, a huge arrowhead struck upwards, out of the reeds, straight into the panicky flock. Jaws parted, eyes gleamed, scales shimmered a fresh gold-green; then half the flock was gone, the jaws snapped and the shining bulk dropped back with a heavy thud. Gille came running back, the goose dangling forgotten in his hand.

'Did you see it? Did you frigging *see* it?'

'The pathmaker,' said Olvar glassily. 'Headed – in this direction, wouldn't you say?'

Kunrad sprang up. 'Nice shot, lad, but time to leave! A thing that size, just half a dozen geese aren't going to keep it happy long.'

They scrambled down the slope, and along the banks of the mere where it was driest, looking back over their shoulders when they dared in case that huge pointed snout was emerging from the reedbeds, tongue flickering for their trail.

'Across running water the first chance we get!' ordered Kunrad. 'It'll help break the scent!'

'*Across* it?' panted Gille. 'If I see that thing again I'll provide it!'

They did not, fortunately. They leaped one small stream and skidded and splashed across the stones of a wider one, and out into the open fen.

This was a bleak place even on the edges of summer, but after the reeds it seemed like a paradise, so much more open and alive. Here and there real grass grew in tussocks around the pools, and among it heathers and other flowers. Moths and butterflies flitted among them, and now and again bees; even the occasional questing hornet seemed almost normal. There were the same clouds of stinging insects, but also breezes to carry them off now and again. Fish stirred in the slow brown pools, some of them startlingly large, and it almost seemed worth trying to catch them. Kunrad would not allow it. 'The corsairs! Forgotten them, have you? And in this open land we're far more visible.' He read the exhaustion in their faces, felt it run lead in his bones also, and relented a little. 'When we've a day between us and the reeds, then we can stop. Maybe even risk a fire, if we're careful.'

'Cook your goose, Gille!' said Olvar dreamily.

'Provided,' said Kunrad, 'our late hosts don't do it first.'

That night they reached a small island without any sign of pursuit, and behind a screen of bushes they managed to kindle a small and nearly smokeless fire. Strengthened by goose dripping, it dried their boots as they ate, and heated a little water to cook some roots of marsh samphire and other herbs. The residue served to bathe their afflicted feet. Kunrad lay back with an exhausted sigh. 'Let it die now. I thought of smoking some goose-meat, but we'll finish what's there tomorrow.' He rubbed his bristly chin. 'I've enough fat in my beard to shave, almost.'

'Leave it,' said Gille sleepily. 'Keeps the flies off.'

They slept that night better than for some time, and did not remember their dreams. Morning saw them weary and stiff, and their boots stiffer still, but they were in better heart than for many a day. The Marshes had been only another kind of prison; but now freedom, real freedom, might be within a day's march. For Kunrad in particular it made a difference. His promise would be kept, his way open if he wished it. He could forget the armour, return to his old life or seek a new one; or he could follow the way he was driven, still. Neither choice pleased him; but they had to be better than this. And as he eased on his boots with painful grunts and the aid of

Faces in the Reeds

goose-grease, he reminded himself that he did not have to decide, not yet.

As it turned out, the Marshes were wider than they thought; and beyond the line of trees there was only more of the same, and a wide horizon. But the disappointment was made up for by a change in the weather. The mists dispersed, the clouds showed some sign of breaking, the weather grew warmer and the wind fresher. And best of all, throughout all the flat land they could see, there was no sign of pursuit. Another day, and they found the land changing beneath them as they walked, from morn to evening. The streamlets spread less, and ran in clearer channels; the pools ran deeper, and the reeds and sedges grew chiefly around their margins. The bushes became thicker, and the trees taller, the stands thicker and less windswept. Patches of blue sky appeared, and a bright sun eased their aches and pains, as warm as a gentle Northland summer. Breezes brought them strange scents and odours, and the flowers that grew up around their feet were often new to them, bigger and brighter. Here and there berries grew, and Gille brought down another goose. They roasted it over a real wood fire that evening, among a stand of strange trees, and used the fat on their feet once again. They were almost out of bread, but that hardly worried them now. This looked like a kindly land, and they could surely make shift to live until they found some help. Their news about the corsairs should ensure them a welcome, at least.

They dozed off around the fire, exhausted as they were; nobody could blame another. But it was nearly the end of them, for that. It was Kunrad who rose first the next morning at first light, and found the fire still alight but low, and the smoke from an over-green branch coiling up through the leaves to catch the first sun. Biting his lip, he turned and stared back along the way they had come. Then he prodded Olvar awake, and pointed; and Olvar's face confirmed his own fears. Gille rose sleepily, then sprang up in his turn, kicking out the fire and trampling the embers. With hardly a word spoken they gathered up their ragged gear. The specks on the horizon looked remote and tiny, but they were hardly a league distant, and they were moving with a purpose. They would have seen that smoke. They were coming.

The three smiths did not bother to look back again. They shouldered their gear and limped on, for the last stage of the race they thought to have won. They turned away under the trees, and towards the sunrise.

CHAPTER SIX
The Hill of the Winds

BEFORE LONG, THOUGH, THEY realised that the reeds were growing thicker again, yet only to the left side. The ground to the right was firmer. Trees grew in taller, closer thickets, and between them wide grass-meadows that no beast grazed. Towards the middle of the day, Olvar pointed towards the horizon, where Kunrad could make out only a blue line, and Gille little at all. 'Mountains!' he said. 'Hills, anyway, but with peaks behind them, or I'm a bat!'

'I can just see you hanging in the eaves!' said Gille. 'All right, they're mountains. The Shield-Range?'

'I'd guess so, from the maps,' said Kunrad. 'And that fits the lie of the land. We're a long way inland, lads. Somewhere off to our left over there must be the great river that feeds the Marshes. But we're out of them.' He drew a deep breath of the clean air, and half laughed, unable to quite believe it. 'Really out, at long last. This is the Southlands! And out of the corsairs' grip.'

'Splendid!' said Gille heavily. 'But don't tell me – tell them!'

The figures were coming on less swiftly than he had feared, but they moved like hunters close on the trail. Probably they had not seen the fugitives yet, but they would have found their tracks even without the smoke, for there had been no way to hide them in the marsh. 'Any more than there is in this soft ground!' said Kunrad irritably. He looked around. 'If we make for the trees over there, we might lose 'em in the brush. Or find enough cover to let us thin out the odds a bit with our bows.'

Olvar looked at him quizzically. 'Getting good at this kind of thing, aren't you?'

Kunrad glared at him. 'Just trying to keep my promises, that's all! Are you feeling strong enough to run a bit?'

Olvar grinned. 'Those geese didn't die in vain. All I have to do is imagine a loaf of fresh-baked bread out there, and—'

He was off at his stumping trot. Gille grinned as they fell in behind him. 'Now, I – well, you can guess, I suppose. But what makes *you* run, revered Mastersmith?'

Kunrad was taken aback. 'I . . . Well, the armour – I suppose – yes, of course, the armour! Surely!'

'You don't sound too sure!' puffed Gille, grabbing his bouncing pack. 'And I don't think so! Sure, Olvar wants his dinner, I want anyone female, under thirty and still alive, and I'll stretch a point or two! But that armour's just an obsession, you'd be rid of it if you could!' The young man's intelligent eyes scanned Kunrad intently. 'So what do you really *want*?'

'I *want*?' Kunrad's feet pounded the meadow stalks, and clouds of weed seeds flew about his boots, like his thoughts flying out on the wind. 'I want my home back, my forge, my town! The green, and the gate, and the tower, and the sun over my bed in the morning, the starry evenings, the young folk walking out and the old women gossiping, the Guildhall, the pale roads and the mountains at the edge of the world! I want my old life, my old certainties – *Damn you, boy!*'

'Sorry, master!' muttered Gille, astonished at the strength of the reaction. Kunrad sped on ahead, past him, past Olvar, fleeing for the forest's rim. It was not only the hunt he ran from.

When they caught up with him he was pale and composed, already scouting out likely paths. It was an old oak-wood of a kind they had never seen in the North, its trunks so huge and gnarled they might have stood here since before the Ice came. Over their heads the leaves spread in one great interlacing canopy, and little enough grew beneath its shadow save light bushes and low

The Hill of the Winds

groundweeds. A rich leafmould carpet, still light brown in patches from the previous autumn, whispered and rustled where small things ran, and the living leaves sighed like the sea.

'Less shelter than I hoped!' he said. 'We've got to get deeper in!' He glanced back, and was shocked. 'Are they really that much closer, Olvar?'

The big man squinted. ''Fraid so! Looks like they've got horses, a couple of them! Maybe eighteen, twenty of the bastards, all told!'

Gille groaned. 'Well, what're we waiting for?'

They ran, and the leafmould muffled their footsteps; but it soon became clear that Olvar was weakening. Gille was already weary, and Kunrad, though he still had strength, knew he would soon falter. And it seemed to him that through the roaring in his ears he already heard hooves, and a horse whinnying. 'Just through that brake ahead there!' he panted. 'We'll make a stand in the next bushes and pick 'em off as they come through!'

It was the best he could think of; but against twenty men, two mounted, it was hardly likely to be enough. Two shots each, at best, before it was hand-to-hand. Death, probably, or killing slavery; almost as bad if they did somehow survive. Blood, either way. Getting good at such things? He couldn't think of a word foul enough. He'd never wanted anything less.

'They're not moving too fast, either!' wheezed Olvar, fighting to talk. 'Look as ragged as we!'

That was something; but Kunrad did not bother to look for himself. Here was the brake, a leap would carry him through.

He stopped dead; and as the others came through, they too stared at what they saw. A hundred strides ahead of them the forest opened to the sun once again, a wide clearing framed for them by two old oaks. Through its centre ran a wide open space where grass and brush were trodden low. Not a well-used road, maybe, but a road nonetheless. And it was in use now, for horses were pacing slowly along it, huge ridden horses, ten or fifteen maybe, gathered around two heavy carts of some kind, drawn by even larger teams. Armour gleamed in the sunshine, on horse and rider, mail and tall helms of a kind they knew only from books, an old Southland pattern. The spear-points above their heads flashed a warning as they sank quickly to the defence.

'Help!' Kunrad shouted, and stumbled down towards the road. No reason to hesitate. Whatever these sothrans were like, they had to be better than what was on their heels.

'Help us!' added Gille. 'We've escaped from corsairs! And they're chasing us!'

A tall rider wheeled his horse, staring down at them. His face looked hard and weathered as the old oaks around, his nose badly broken and his chin jutting. White eyebrows bushed out beneath the coif of his mail, shadowing cold grey eyes. 'Northerners, anyway, by your tongues! Escaped, you say?'

'Yes,' panted Kunrad, falling to his knees. 'Across the Marshes!'

'Across the Marshes?' Another horse turned to them; but this was a woman's voice, very clear and very doubtful. 'On foot?'

Gille, of course, responded. 'Yes! They kept us, we're smiths, and we escaped!'

The older man frowned, and his mouth twisted. 'That's as may be. But if they're on your heels, I can't help you!'

'*Captain!*' exclaimed the woman. She was wearing some kind of breeches, Kunrad saw, and riding like a man.

The captain shook his head firmly. 'No, my lady! I'll not risk my care and duty for any man. More than my honour's worth, and my head too! Ride on, fast!'

'*Stay!*' snapped the woman. 'Is it honourable to run?'

'My lady, my lady!' croaked a voice from one of the carts – or carriages, rather, Kunrad realised, such as rich merchants and their wives used sometimes in the North.

These, though, looked a good deal heavier and richer. The voice was an old woman's. 'Never be risking yourself, my dear! What would the poor Lord Warden say? And your father?'

'Never you worry, Nanny!' The woman's voice softened considerably, but the next moment it was steel again. 'Captain, I place these men under my protection and I *order* you to defend us and them!'

The older man drew a deep breath. But just then, with a loud crashing and a shout that faltered, the corsairs burst through the trees.

They looked haggard and fell, hardly used by the Marshes, perhaps; but they were fresher and fiercer, and their faces twisted with savage satisfaction as they saw their quarry. Kunrad recognised the mounted leader from the crew that had captured them, and the man also gave a fierce half-laugh, half-gasp of recognition.

'Well! There's neatly taken for you!' He weighed up the other party, the carriages, the woman. 'No need you should fear for yourselves, good folk! We've no quarrel with you – only with these here runagate slaves! Leave 'em to us, and you may go your way in peace!'

He had chosen the wrong line with the captain. The older man's face seemed to swell, and purple rose in his cheeks. 'And just who in Raven's name d'you think *you* are to be telling us what we may and may not do? Who're you to give us leave?'

'A stronger bunch than yours, Grandpa!' rapped the corsair. 'So you just fuck along off and look to your precious lordlings! Or we'll add them to the bag and your head for a makeweight, savvy?'

'My lady!' came the creaking voice from within the cart. 'Take care! Take care, leave these awful people while you can!'

The corsairs laughed. 'Better listen!' they jeered. 'While you've ears!'

'Only one hand rules here, and one justice!' rasped the captain. He jerked his head, and the escort wheeled over to his side, forming a line in front of the carriages. 'I command you, lay down your arms and submit, in the name of the Lord Kermorvan!'

That name made Kunrad look around, and startled the corsairs also, momentarily. But the leader angrily waved his men forward. 'Take 'em!'

The captain drew his sword. Kunrad sprang up and drew his also, and the captain shot him a surprised glance. The inlaid metals flamed in the southern sun. Olvar drew his, the spears dipped and as the corsairs sprang forward Gille's bow leaped to his shoulder. The first man saw it and tried to duck. The bolt sang and took him in the throat, the two behind fell over him, and then the line was upon them.

Gille fired again and missed, then parried a corsair sword with the stock, slammed the man in the face and jumped back to draw his own sword. Olvar felled another with a great slash, and found himself hewing at a man his own size. Kunrad crossed blades with a first-comer, but as he parried one of the spearmen thrust over his shoulder and stabbed the corsair in the breast. The man behind closed with Kunrad, the other corsairs were among the horses, slashing wildly about to make them scatter, and a fearful mill developed. There was no room for proper swordplay; Kunrad knocked down his man by main force and drove his sword down through the corsair's mail with both hands and killing weight. Olvar bounded by him, slashing wildly, scattering friend and foe alike as he backed off from his opponent. Kunrad ducked and glimpsed Gille briefly, rolling in the dust with his adversary among the steel-shod hooves; then one of the horses collided with him as it wheeled, sending him staggering. Its rider, dragged from his saddle, crashed down on the other side, and two corsairs fell upon him, their slashes landing with harsh dull thumps.

Kunrad had been thrown back out of the ruck; and the mounted corsairs, circling it, saw him and spurred forward. The leader was on top of him, waving a great clumsy sabre overarm, like a mill-sail. Kunrad dived aside, only to find himself sprawling helpless in the path of the other, who jabbed down a short heavy hunting spear as if sticking a pig. Kunrad had scarcely enough time to panic; the moment the spear struck the earth at his side was the same that the other spear, with a sickening thump, took the corsair in the stomach. The shaft bent, snapped, and he lolled in the saddle a moment, then, as his horse bolted, toppled sideways into a bush. The other rider threw the bloody truncheon after him, then checked as Kunrad scrambled up. He stared, startled. It was the woman. Her eyes widened, and she yelled, 'Look out!'

The corsair leader had reined in and was wheeling back, swinging that sword again. Kunrad jumped into his path.

Years before a customer had shown him a trick he had thought he would never need in earnest. He held his place, braced lightly on his toes, and as the corsair bore down on him he shifted his balance suddenly, and pivoted aside on one foot. A searing cramp in his tired legs almost betrayed him, but he was swift enough to escape the cut and aim his own blow as the horseman plunged by. There was a thump, heat sprayed his hand and the corsair screamed shrilly. His great sword wheeled into the bushes, still held in half his lower arm. Then the scream was cut off as the captain, riding to the woman's side, hewed him from his saddle. The other corsair, clutching the spearshaft, staggered to his feet. Another rider slashed at his back, a sickening sight Kunrad turned from, only to see that all was already over. Most of the corsairs lay stretched out across the road in streaks of dusty blood, while the mailed riders cantered this way and that, cutting off the last few wounded stragglers. Screams, groans, frantic pleas they ignored; the spearheads pinned them to earth, lifted and passed on.

Two riders also lay still; and Kunrad looked anxiously around for the prentices. They were seeking him, Olvar with a few cuts and Gille with a nosebleed and a chewed ear – literally, he said. 'One of the spearmen got him, lifted him up six feet with the thump. No more trouble. Olvar wounded his man, and then they got that one too.'

'Two spears as he stood, left and right. Dead before he fell – catmeat!' grunted the prentice. 'Strong lad, too. But these sothrans don't mess about, eh?'

'No,' said Kunrad thoughtfully, 'they don't. They're formidable warriors. If they're all like these, it's one more reason not to have a war. If we needed one!'

The captain reined in before the woman. 'Your orders are carried out, lady. All eighteen dead, and two of my men. Are you satisfied, then? You should not have exposed yourself to danger, and endangered my trust when your orders prevented me—'

She cut him off. 'Yes, captain! I'm sorry, but there was nothing else to be done. There was a gap, and one of the fugitives in danger. You've done very well, all of you. Two dead, you said?'

'Two, alas; and one slashed in the leg, so he may never ride again.'

'He and their families will be taken care of,' said the woman wearily. She turned and smiled at the Northerners. Kunrad saw in some surprise that she was quite young – no! Really young, and quite striking, if you liked this sothran pale skin and flame-coloured hair. He rather felt he did. 'And these men did bravely enough, also, for their weakness.'

The captain nodded. 'That they did. They're finely armed, too. Did you take those blades from the corsairs, man?'

Kunrad laughed, a little hysterically. 'No! We made them – for the corsairs, as they thought, who greedily supplied us the makings.' That raised a general chuckle, and he gathered his wits. 'I should present myself, captain and lady, and offer my thanks to you all. I am Kunrad of Athalby, Mastersmith of the Northlands, and these my prentices Olvar and Gille. I apologise for setting you all at risk, but there was naught else we could do.

You have saved our lives, and we are under great obligation to you.'

'Mastersmith, eh?' commented the captain. 'You fight well, for tradesmen. But as to obligation, you'll needs account for your presence here—'

'Later, captain!' said the woman. 'They need rest, and we have a road ahead. They have a tale to tell, I think, and they can explain to the Marchwarden when they are recovered.'

Kunrad bowed deeply. 'Happily, lady. And I have some tidings which may save lives, to compensate for those spent in defending ours. The presence of a really powerful corsair fortress deep in the Marshes, and its ambitions to move against the world beyond.'

The captain was suddenly alert. 'And that you've escaped from? So your father was right, lady! That'll be news for the Lord Warden, and a half!'

She nodded. 'You could lead a force there? Excellent! Bravely done!' She sounded so pompous that Kunrad had trouble keeping a straight face. No more than a slip of a girl, really, Gille's age or less, probably, but determined to be taken seriously. Despite her fine features and delicate tip-tilted nose, no doubt. Well, she deserved it. He gave her a very grave bow, hand on heart in the Merthian manner, and she looked surprised.

'Well, Mastersmith K-Kunrad, I am the Lady Alais Kermorvan, daughter of Lord Ieran Kermorvan of Morvan that was. This is my father's captain-in-chief, Ferlias. I think it best we take you to our destination, another few days' journey, and you can present your information to the Lord Warden there.' Nose still in air, she turned to the captain. 'Please see they are tended with your man, while we rest briefly. Then they can all lie in the rear carriage on top of the baggage—' There was a brief squawk from the front carriage. 'No, Nanny dear, I shall see they do not bleed into it! On blankets, of course. That can be done? Then see to it, please. I –' she glanced back at the carriage with an air of resignation, ' – had better ride inside for a little.'

The captain was practically chuckling. 'Very good, highness! I'm sure you'll reassure her. Very well, my lads, take your ease in the sun a few moments, and I'll send you a man with some healing skills. And some food and drink you could use, I guess!'

'Captain,' rumbled Olvar, 'you could just leave the horse.'

The captain glanced at him a little suspiciously, and then at the others, as if Olvar had less right to speak; then allowed himself a stern smile and turned away.

'Did you see that?' demanded Gille, amazed, as they waited for their wounds to be tended. 'As if Olvar was a servant or something!'

Olvar chuckled dismissively. 'Let 'em!'

'I guess,' said Kunrad, painfully easing off his boots, 'that they're not too used to his looks down here. Think it sets him apart, maybe; I've heard that. But they're amiable enough, in their way – even Little Lady Bountiful there!'

'I just wonder how amiable they'll stay!' said Gille darkly.

'I, too. So not a word about our quest, until I say otherwise. I have a debt to collect, and that's all you know. Later I may tell them more.'

Their hurts were well tended. The Lady Alais, it seemed, had provided salves and bandages from her own travel-chest, and an old sergeant applied them with a skilled hand. They clambered wearily into the carriage, and helped make the injured soldier comfortable there, slung hammock-fashion from the roof. He was cheerful enough about his wounded leg.

'Luck o' the draw, isn't it? Twelve years a trooper, never a scratch and now this!'

'I'm sorry it was on our account!' Kunrad told him. 'And grateful!'

'Ah, don't mention it! Got to stick together 'gainst those lousy bandit bastards, haven't we? Old man Kermorvan'll see me right! A good lord, even if – well, we all grow old. And the Lord Warden, too. They don't forget a man! Soft job in the castle guard, most like, or the stores or armoury if I'm really hobbled. No worries . . .'

Weak with loss of blood, the soldier soon drifted off as the coach rumbled on its way, and the smiths settled down among the blanket-topped chests. The road was scarcely even, and the coach-springs were small answer. Swaying and cramped as they were, though, it was a better bed than they had slept in for some weeks, and with fewer fears and forebodings. Soon they too were deeply asleep.

All the rest of that day they slept, through halts and starts, unmoved, and through the night as well. Morning sunlight, slanting through the carriage window, travelled on to Kunrad's face, and he awoke, blinking in the warmth and staring at a roof he did not recognise at first. The air seemed impossibly warm and full of strange scents, and from somewhere near by came the sound of running water, soft but massive. There was no sense of movement. Grudgingly and by degrees it all came back to him, and he tried to sit up, winced and stretched. That woke Gille, and he Olvar; the soldier's hammock hung empty above. They peered out of the window, and saw him stretched out on a grassy slope, noisily eating from a bowl. He waved. 'Back to life, are we? Thought we'd have to have you stuffed! Morning's halt to let the ladies rest, an' you too. There's breakfast at the fire there. Or you could take a dip first – wish I could!'

There was the sound of splashing from down the slope, and Kunrad suddenly felt the grime of the Marshes encrusted deep into his skin. 'I stink,' said Olvar.

'I agree,' said Gille. 'But I'm not exactly rose essence, either. Come on!'

They were halted in a wide meadow beside the banks of the Marsh river, and though it ran black and cold even in this bright sunshine, it was a fairer prospect than its lower reaches. The soldiers, leaping and horsing around at the edge, were startled to see how vigorously the former fugitives raced down to join them.

'If I'd been weeks a-starving in them hag-bound marshes I'd'a been half way to a frog meself!' grinned one.

'Don't remind me!' laughed Kunrad, sinking into the chilly shallows with a delicious shudder. 'I feel like I'm bearing half the muck around with me now!'

Another man jerked a thumb at a rock. 'Er, there's a cake o' soap there, if you use that stuff in the North, like—'

'Oh, yes!' said Gille, rolling into a lazy backstroke. 'All the civilised comforts. We've even learned how to wipe our arses, you know – in polite society, that is!'

The soldier grinned weakly. 'No offence, friend – but I just don't *know*, you know? We don't hear much about you, how you live, like – 'cept tales about, well, good lads an' all that, stout stuff but a mite – you know?'

'Barbarians, you mean?' smiled Kunrad, sitting up to his chest on the grey sand.

'Well, didn't mean that exactly—'

'Don't blame you in the least,' Kunrad laughed, 'especially as we looked when we leapt out at you. We've been a shade short of such comforts this last month. Your soap should bring back some of our civilised gloss. We'll gladly submit to inspection afterwards!'

It had not occurred to Kunrad, weary and desperate as he was, what kind of a figure he must have cut at first, wild-haired, filthy and unshaven. No wonder they had been talking down to him! The soldiers were ignorant, but their attitudes would reflect what most sothrans expected from the North. He would have to spruce himself up to make any kind of good impression, let alone get his story taken seriously, and now was a good time to start.

'That look a bit more human?' he asked a while later, tossing the soap to Gille.

'Well, it's not muster fashion!' grinned the soldiers. 'But you'll do!'

'Give the girls a fright, mind!' added another archly. 'With them muscles, I mean!'

'Yeah, should've been watching my tongue!' laughed the soap's owner. 'Could tie me in little knots, any of 'em!'

'Ah well, they're smiths, see, aren't they? Keeps 'em in training, all that banging away! Powers, I see what you mean – them poor Northern girls!'

They seemed fascinated by Olvar; even the ones who had left the water sat on the bank to watch him. It turned out they were laying bets to see if he was the same shade all over. Gille bristled, but Olvar himself only laughed mightily, and swapped dubious jokes with them. Kunrad hoisted himself out on the bank and, retrieving their swords, thrust Gille's upright in the ground as a mirror and began to shave with the edge of his own. This too collected a horrified audience. 'Either he's made of saddle-leather or that's some flamin' sword!' was one comment.

'I'd cut my friggin' throat if I tried that!'

Kunrad smiled as he felt his skin clean and smooth once again. 'I wouldn't do this normally, but my razor's buried deep in my pack somewhere, if I've still got it. Now – where in Hella's name are my clothes?'

'Thought you could use 'em washing and that,' the soldiers laughed. 'We'll lend a couple of spare tunics for now. Top-quality sackcloth, same's our issue.'

All that long morning they ate and lazed in the hot sun, and it was only at midday that their clothes reappeared, to their great surprise very neatly mended of the worst tears and snags they had suffered.

'That was the ladies done that,' said the soldier who brought them.

'The ladies? That was . . . very kind of them! I wouldn't have expected—'

'She's a peach,' grinned the soldier. 'Goes all grand on you, but underneath she really cares! There's some treat you fine, but – no touch, know what I'm saying? And there's one or two treat you . . . well, maybe you've got 'em too.'

'Not so many,' said Kunrad. 'And in the North we don't let 'em lord it so much. A rich merchant's a man you hearken to, if you've any sense, but a man nonetheless like any other.'

'Sounds better all the time, friend!' He eyed the black tunic Kunrad was pulling on, and the gold embroidery around its neck. 'Seems to me you might be one of the better ones yourself, though. You a big bug up there?'

'Any mastersmith counts for something, yes. We're respected. But nothing like a lord, and I wouldn't want to be!'

'Dunno why not!' said the soldier a little ruefully. 'You might make a better stab at it than most!'

'Stabbing's not my strong point, I suppose.'

'And that might be why. It's often the best lords as like it least, say I! Well, there's my sergeant's sweet voice a-callin'! I'll take the tunics for you, sir. Good day!'

'*Sir!*' said Gille. 'That's new!'

'Yes, I noticed. I wish he hadn't, somehow. I – never mind!' Kunrad pulled on his sheepskin jerkin and stretched luxuriously. The heavy cloth of the tunic was still a little damp, but after the Marshes he hardly noticed.

'Can't blame him, though!' said Olvar.

'That's so,' agreed Gille. 'You're beginning to look the part again, Mastersmith. More than ever, maybe.'

He held up his sword, and Kunrad blinked with surprise. He had changed, though he would not have noticed until now. It was partly the hair, grown longer so it had to be pulled back. But the amiable roundness had been worn from his face, and some, at least, of the vagueness from his eyes. The shape of his bones showed through his cheeks now, and it was a squarer-looking chin he tilted to the reflection. The lines were deeper, too, graven marks of experience on a countenance grown stronger and more alert.

'Suits him, I'd say,' remarked Gille. 'Goes with that commanding air he's come by – man who keeps his promises, that kind of thing!'

'Well, I did, didn't I?'

'Oh sure,' said Olvar. 'But we can't be having you

getting all swell-headed about it, can we? Our duty to look after you, o mighty master, hand and foot and – well, there's thanks for you!'

'Didn't think he even knew what that gesture meant!' agreed Gille. 'Hold hard, here comes our host!'

The captain greeted them as he strode down the hill, mopping his brow. Evidently he had not been swimming, and regretted it. He stared at Kunrad as he rose to greet him. 'They told me you were recovered, but I hardly guessed – a tough-fibred race, you *nordinneichs* must be. Well it is, then, for my lady sends me to ask if any of you would rather ride today, we having spare mounts.'

Olvar preferred the carriage, but Gille and Kunrad chose horses, and Kunrad attracted more attention as he mounted. The horses were huge compared to the short-legged Northland breeds, leaving Gille at some disadvantage, but Kunrad's long limbs suited his very well. The captain gave an order, and the column formed itself around the coaches once again. 'Where shall I ride?' Kunrad asked him.

'Why, wherever it likes you, sir,' said the captain, 'front or rear, so you don't get in the way of the carriage teams. If trouble threatens, take post by me and let the spears take the first of it, as is sound tactics. You and I and your lad there, we'll back 'em up. But I don't expect more, not now.'

'I'm told the corsairs have been striking inland in the South here as well, though.'

'That they have, sir, this deep inland and further, even to the hills. But chiefly using the river to bring their bloody reivers in through the Marshes, and we're turning south from the river now. They don't normally cross the Marshes, not them!'

'Yes, and I can give you about a hundred good reasons why!' Kunrad shivered. 'I wondered. Of course they had to send out foot parties after us.'

'That's so. And by what you say, it looks like we'll be boating back the other way now!' The captain rubbed his hands. 'So it be that my Lord Warden can make the Syndics stir down there in Ker Bryhaine. They never take enough heed of what happens so far north. I would you were bound that way yourself. You might put the fear on them properly!'

'Well, captain, as it happens, I may be. I was on my way south when we were taken, so—'

The captain nudged him gently, and tipped his head to one side. Kunrad looked that way, and saw the Lady Alais come riding out from behind the carriage. He did his best to bow on horseback, and again it seemed to surprise her.

'Well, Master K-Kunrad, you seem in good health already!' She had a pleasant smile, when she wasn't acting a part, thought Kunrad.

'Thanks to your care, lady. We were never more lucky in our lives than to happen upon you!'

She nodded. 'As well you did, for that road is not used so much these days. The corsairs have raided the fords where it crosses the river, further north, and plundered so many of the villages and farms—' She shook her head furiously. 'Something must be done. Maybe you'll be the key! I was happy to help you, and I'm richly rewarded if that's so!'

Kunrad bowed again. 'But what reason brought you on such a perilous path, lady?'

She laughed, and then hastily assumed a haughty face again. 'The very best! I'm going to be married!'

'Oh,' said Kunrad. 'My . . . compliments, lady. And best wishes! May I ask who the lucky man is?' He suddenly felt a complete loathing for whoever it was.

She smiled, warmly, looking past him to the south. 'The Lord Warden. And I'm the lucky one, I'm sure! He's such a man. So powerful, but . . . well, you'll meet him. He'll like you, I'm sure!'

'The Marchwarden, is this? So his realm is around here somewhere?'

She smiled again. 'All around here, everywhere. He

rules the whole north of our land, as a viceroy almost. All this is his realm, you know, from the mountains to the sea. Even my father holds his land and castle from him. Of course he's not a young man any more, but he's wise and good and kind . . .' She prattled on, while Kunrad tried to formulate tactfully a question that had to be asked.

'Forgive me, lady,' he put in, when he could, 'but do you know of a place called Anlaithann?'

She stared. 'Of course. It's in the far south, near the edges of the desert. They grow a lot of fruit there. Why do you ask?'

Kunrad felt deeply relieved. 'I . . . well, I have my own reasons for coming south. I was travelling to collect a debt there. A debt, and justice.'

She nodded. 'Then again, you had best ask the Lord Warden, than leave it to the Syndics. He is a just man, and will smooth your path, where the Syndics would be unlikely to lift a finger. So few people are troubled these days.'

'I think there were always few. It's a matter of how many of them are in power at any one time. It changes from one generation to the next. You now, you care, and I'm grateful! You stopped that charge, you risked yourself at our side . . . And you've even turned needlesmith for us!'

She laughed at the Northern nickname for a tailor. 'It was no trouble, believe me. I was bored, I don't get enough to do with my hands. And I learned a little about you. That's gold bullion thread around your collar, isn't it? And those characters mean something, that's clear. I should have known you were a man of consequence, even before you were cleaned up.'

'Of no consequence to equal yours, lady!' he answered, a little irritably. 'A mastersmith is much less than a lord. We don't have lords, I'm afraid.'

'So I've heard,' she said, with mouth slightly pursed. 'All men equal and rule by the people, that's it, isn't it? Except that some people rule more than others, don't they? A lot more. Those with the money, the family, the connections – or, I suppose, the talent. Just like ours, really; for if you have those, then you will become a lord in our land these days, or a Syndic, which is worse. So why do Northerners pretend their ways are any better? It is a pretence, isn't it? A sham, a . . . a semblance of rudery and wildness you insist on keeping up!' She snorted. 'Like this jerkin of yours! So rough and wild it looks, as if you'd just stuck a half-tanned sheepskin over your shoulders. But it isn't, is it? It's made to look that way, very carefully made. Lots of little diamond-shapes of sheepskin, all carefully laid together on some very soft leather lining—'

'Doeskin. They've some special way of tanning it—'

'It's beautiful, yes! But if you can make stuff like that, or that tunic of yours, why dress up as a barbarian?'

'Look, that's not the point! The jerkin's made like that so it can be repaired easily – when a piece of fleece gets torn or old, you replace it. It's tough and it's comfortable and it lasts. And it's warm, it keeps the wind out; and that's important in the North. We've made jerkins like that for hundreds of years, since Morvan or before.'

'And you go on wearing them, just to be obstinate! Pretending, just as with all that beautiful jewellery and stuff you people make. And swords and things too – it's all marvellously made, you're very clever at handicrafts, so why make yourselves out to be superstitious savages? You don't need to go on pretending you put all kinds of magical powers into it.'

'We do,' said Kunrad, so simply and baldly that she stared. 'Put them in, I mean. Though I've never thought of them as magical, at least the way you mean it. It's just part of our skill, our unity with the things we make.'

'Oh,' she said, slightly bewildered. 'You mean in a poetic sort of way! Even so—'

He shook his head, chuckling. 'Pardon, lady, but no! Poetry comes into it, poetry is to our minds what the hammer is to our hands – but what it expresses is real. A true smith can hardly help putting himself into his work, though it's better done deliberately – more focused, you might say.'

She stared again, half laughing. 'Oh, come! You're not one of these superstitious peddlers, I can see that! I always wondered why Northerners ever believed in all that – mumbo-jumbo! I hoped I'd meet an intelligent one some day, a man of some, well, wisdom, some learning, and hear what he thought! And now – really, you're just playacting like the rest of them!'

'Lady, whether I'm wise or learned's not for me to say. But I wouldn't lie to you.'

She bridled. 'Well, if you believe it all yourself, then, you can't be very wise, can you? Such nonsense!' She stared moodily at the horizon, screwing up her eyes. 'It's not as if you can actually see it working, can you? These charms and spells and things, there's no proof they actually do anything, is there? You can't watch them in action, striking sparks like a tinderbox or something, can you?'

'As a matter of fact . . .' said Kunrad, and grinned at her expression. He slid the bracelet down his wrist, and passed it over to her. 'Did you not wonder how we came through the Marshlands, where even the corsairs could barely follow? I made this, as my father taught me; and I have always made them well.'

She held the bracelet by its short chain, as if it was going to bite her. 'It's quite beautiful, in its way. I've heard of these. They're just lodestones, aren't they?'

'They are not, lady. The poorly made ones that reach the South may behave no better, perhaps, for they will point north if that's what's expected of them. Hold it steady, and think of a place, a direction – your home, perhaps, that you have left. Think hard, to make up for your lack of belief!'

The bracelet was swinging as she rode, in a kind of gentle half-spin; but as she lifted it to her face and glared dubiously at it, brows furrowing, its swing changed. The spin grew slightly, and then lessened; the swinging did not stop, but the bias was obviously different. 'The spearhead slot, see the way it faces – back there to the mountain-roots? Is that where your home lies?'

She would not look at him. 'Somewhere that way, yes! Though it is not our true home, that castle. My father only holds it from the Lord Warden; we no longer have any estates. Our true home is our old house in Ker Bryhaine itself, though—'

She caught her breath. The swing had changed again. The face she turned on him was wide-eyed, hovering on the edge of anger because it was easier to admit than fright. 'Are you doing this? You're laughing at me, aren't you? It's a trick, I suppose—'

'A poor return for your kindness if it was, lady! But you challenged a truth that runs deep in my blood. Try a true test, that can be no trick. Hold your horse a moment, steady the bracelet, think of where your true love lies, his home, your destination. For that I could have no way of knowing.'

Moving apart from the caravan a moment, she steadied the bracelet in her hands, closed her eyes, frowned hard. Then her eyes flew open. The bracelet was spinning wildly, unnaturally, this way and that. Maybe it favoured a direction one moment, another the next; it was too fast to be sure. 'Oh!' she breathed, outraged. 'Why . . . You *are* laughing at me! Here! Take it! Take the horrible thing!' She tossed it up as violently as if it were a poisonous snake. Kunrad's large hand scooped it deftly out of the air. Her cheeks flamed the shade of her flowing hair. She pulled on her reins and dug in her heels. 'Thank you, Mastersmith! I think I'll ride inside again, for today! All day! Thank you very much!'

She spurred hastily back to the carriage. Gille came cantering up, alive with questions; but none of them found answers. But deep inside, Kunrad, rather to his own surprise, was chuckling.

The ride was a leisurely one, as befitted the ladies, and when early in the evening they came to a pleasant grassy dell by a clear swift streamlet, they made camp at once. Fires were kindled and cauldrons set out. The smiths were about to join the soldiers when the captain appeared, wearing a very straight face and bringing Kunrad a courteous invitation from the Lady Alais. 'Wups! Nanny fancies 'im!' chortled one of the soldiers, earning an appalled glare from the captain. And certainly when he approached the other fire, the figure that rose to greet him was not Alais.

A rather tall, lean, stooping figure held out long wrinkled fingers to be kissed, with a tremendous air of courtly delicacy and a waft of faded flower scent. 'The Mastersmith Kunrad, is it not? Do be seated – no, here on the cushions, I insist! My lady will be with us presently! There!' She beamed at him in a rather short-sighted way, while he marvelled at how this old grey mare had managed to suggest by the sheer tone of her voice that to be a mastersmith was both something remarkable, hopelessly inferior and nothing to be ashamed of all the same. 'I am Mistress Nolys, but I cannot remember the last time anyone called me that. The present Lord Warden's father, possibly. Otherwise everyone calls me Nanny, so you may also, if you wish.' She beamed again, with an intensity that lit up her wrinkled horsy face.

He found himself warming to her, though he suspected there was a considerable wit behind the dim green eyes, like weathered glass.

'I'm greatly honoured, er – Nanny,' he said gravely.

'And now – but ah! Here comes my darling duckie now!' Alais ruined what would have been a grand entrance by putting her hands to her eyes.

'Nanny darling, *must* you?' She drew breath, and swept her skirts around to face Kunrad as he rose. Her dress was a vivid green that set the grass to shame, yet made something immensely pleasing out of her hair and creamy skin. It even suited her freckles, and it caught the flashing brilliance of her eyes. 'You are very welcome, Master Kunrad.'

'I'm honoured. 'Truly.' Her fingers were cool, and the flowers she bore were in their first bloom. She sat again, and motioned him to do the same. 'Nanny will fetch our food – no, stay! I want to talk to you.' She looked at him very gravely. 'I was rude to you this afternoon. Suppose there were some truth to your clever little device, what would you think it told you?'

He shrugged. 'That you were uncertain, perhaps; unsure of yourself. I wouldn't make anything of that. Very normal and usual for a gi— young lady about to marry, I'm sure.'

She looked immensely relieved. 'Yes. Almost a joke, really. And a little upsetting to find oneself so . . . predictable. I keep telling myself I shouldn't be. Something I want more than anything else on earth, that I've always wanted, yet I hesitate . . .'

Kunrad nodded. 'Perhaps because you want it so much? It comes almost too soon?'

'Yes!' she said, startled and grateful. 'Yes! I didn't think anyone would understand that. I hardly do myself!' She gave him a sudden arch smile. 'You must know a lot about the way we think!'

It was Kunrad's turn to look startled. 'Women? I? Hardly a thing. Anyone from my town'd fall about laughing. About wanting, maybe. I've had a few lessons in that lately. It's my prentice Gille who's the expert on women, I suppose. A flaming nuisance with them, too.'

She chuckled earthily. 'Yes, I can see he might be. He's going to be very popular in Bryhaine, with that swarthy sort of face and the dark eyes. Just wait till all the old Syndics' wives get a sight of him! They'll all want to mother him! *Aoh, my deah deah boyyy*—' Kunrad chortled at her mimicry. 'Who knows, it might help your cause! But I think he's the wrong kind of authority. Mostly, mmm, horizontal, and that has its limits – I'm told, I mean. But you – he doesn't bother your wife, does he?'

'Mine? He'd have a job. I haven't got one.'

'Now that lowers my opinion of Northern women

right away. I suppose they couldn't compete with a really nice large sooty anvil, or something?'

'Something like that. Anvils don't talk back.'

'Nonsense!' she said briskly. 'You want someone who can talk back. They just have to say something sensible, that's all – oh, thank you, Nanny!'

The bowls were silver, and work fine enough to please even Kunrad, but the food in them was the same stew as the soldiers had. There was a fine wine, though, white and green-tasting, in goblets that really did startle him. They were of cut crystal, age-worn and cloudy, set in a holder of a strange gold-and-silver alloy called orichalcum, and deeply and magnificently carven. The design was a landscape of some kind, a deep valley and a high tower beneath which a tall waterfall flowed, its waters sculpted so that the low light of an afternoon sun seemed to play gold across the ripples, and the foam at the falls-foot glittered silver. Above the tower, in pure gold, rose an applied emblem in antique style of Raven, Friend of Men, carrying off the sun.

He became aware that the women were watching him as he turned the piece this way and that; and the firelight shone in their eyes with something of the same glitter. 'I wondered if you would see something about the goblets,' said Alais. 'Are there these – these *virtues* in them, then?'

'Are there—' He almost choked. The design itself ran and coursed with glittering threads of virtues, but the golden emblem blazed and pulsed with a single brilliant force, so powerful that it seemed to pain his eyes like hot needles. It spoke to him of strength in adversity, of loyalty in trial, of gallantry in defeat and victory alike, of feelings of love and hate so strong he could hardly contain them, let alone speak of them. 'This . . . whoever made this was a smith of power. Far greater than I will ever be, but also . . . not mad, perhaps, but very far from ordinary in his mind. It almost challenges me to go on holding this.'

She nodded gravely, and the old woman raised a hand. 'I feel the same. You see truly, for these were made some three hundred years since, far in the East that is lost to us, for my lady's line. For, know you, she is a Kermorvan, and that, that is—'

'The ancient royal line, the house that once ruled both Northern and Southern folk in the East-kingdoms of old. Yes, the name's not forgotten in our land – far from it! I knew it at once. So did the corsairs, mind you. And this is an heirloom of yours?'

'It is,' she said softly, 'it and the others like it, for they were made for my forebears by Lord Vayde himself. The design is the great Gate of Kerys itself.'

'Vayde!' Kunrad raised the glass above the level of his eyes, in the respectful gesture with which smiths seek out the maker's mark on some fine work. There it was, large and forceful, the two characters entwined which stood for *VK*, Vayde of Kerys, last latecomer from that legendary land. To his eyes they burned a dull ember-red, He lowered the goblet, a little shakily, pledged the women with all the ceremony he knew, and sipped the wine. Cold seemed to sear his veins, but it was cold fire, strengthening.

'No wonder you're a remarkable family,' he managed, 'if you drink from these all the time. This is like . . . I don't know, a thunderstorm captured in metal.'

She smiled regretfully. 'I've never felt anything, not that I could be sure of. Nanny won't touch them, though, not without a cloth. And as to remarkable, well, we're not what we were. Our estates have gone – our enemies' doing, partly, but our own, as well. Too much living in past glories, too much . . . Well, now my father holds a position of honour, but only a minor one, and by my Lord Warden's kindness, in truth. My brothers hold offices of some weight in Ker Bryhaine, but under the Syndicacy, not by right. My Lord Warden is nearer a king than any man alive today, and he deserves it more, I must admit.'

'Well,' said Kunrad, 'you're uniting his right and yours, aren't you? Maybe your children will have the best of both!'

She blushed quickly. The old woman chuckled. 'Now, my dear, this bluff Northerner is indulging you too much, to talk of yourself all the time. We must hear of him, what brings him so far from his homeland and into so much peril? A quest of honour, perhaps? It cannot merely be to gather up a debt, to be worth so great an expense of effort.'

Kunrad flushed, in his turn. He was still exhausted, and the strong wine was working on him. 'Honour is part of it, yes. And other concerns it is hard to explain. There was a work, that in a sense I have been labouring on all my life . . .'

He meant to tell only a part of his tale, for he feared that these sothran lordlings would tend to stick together, however just they might be. He named no names, but still he knew he was saying more than he meant, by the tone of his voice and the words he chose.

'. . . and so, to make a long story short, I came south by sea, and the corsairs took us. I am a fool, perhaps, to pursue a thief with so little hope of success. But I have never had anything but my work, and that was taken away from me. And my land was insulted, a slug's bright trail of theft and arson stretched down it, and at least one death also. That I will have him answer for! Before a fair court if I can; but if not, before my own hand.'

He felt the words fall like lead, and was surprised at the indignation in Alais's voice. 'And so you should! It does you credit! I hear your injury in everything you say! Do you not agree, Nanny?'

'A dangerous quest, my dear!' said the old woman reflectively. 'But then honour is always hung about with danger, is it not? Danger for oneself and others, who may be whirled along in its path. A man of Anlaithann, you say?'

'Merthian, he called himself,' said Kunrad tonelessly, wishing he had never heard the name. The old woman had unerringly put her finger on what bothered him most.

Nonetheless he noticed the quick exchange of glances between her and the girl.

'So,' said Alais, 'the Lord of Anlaithann. Then you had certainly better appeal to the Lord Warden.'

'You know this man, then?'

'A little,' she said. 'My Lord Warden knows him better, I think. I cannot believe – but never mind about that! He will hear your plea, and I will see that he does!' She smiled, radiantly he thought. 'He is a just man, of that I can assure you. Perhaps this can be settled peacefully. But, yes, Nanny, we're in danger of talking about me again. And I want to hear about the Marshes, and the corsairs. For it was partly to get me away from a land become so dangerous that my father let me come south to the Warden so early. Our marriage was not due for another six months yet, whereas now it will only be a few weeks hence! Oh dear – myself again! In the name of the Powers, Master Kunrad, say something! How ever did they catch you?'

Kunrad was not over-eager to bring back the darkness, even in memory; but he was glad enough to change the subject. He talked, the strange ancient goblet fast in his hand, and it seemed to give him strength. The women listened in silence as he told his tale. When she heard of the fortress, the girl's eyes blazed. 'My father said there must be such a lair! Ten years ago he said it, and my Lord Warden agrees now, too – but will those slugabed cynics of Syndics listen? The reports we've sent, the accounts of the raids, and what answer have we had, what action? *The Marchwarden's forces should be amply sufficient to suppress mere sporadic local raiding* – but how in the name of Amicac do you *find* the raiders in time, without spreading yourself so thin you cannot meet any threat adequately?' Her excited eyes caught the firelight as she leaned forward, and the flame danced upon her ruddy hair and finely freckled cheeks, so that she looked like some primal firespirit of the younger world. 'And now you bring us this news!'

'I will tell it to anyone you wish, lady!' he said, setting

down the goblet with exaggerated care. 'And in such a way as they'll hearken to. But for now . . .'

'Yes, of course!' she said. 'Go sleep, for tomorrow's a longer ride! And Mastersmith – if you would share it with me, I'd be greatly honoured!'

Even Olvar was mildly curious when he returned to their fire, and Gille practically beside himself. But Kunrad said little, wrapped himself in his blanket, and lay looking at the Southland stars till he drifted off into sleep.

The sun woke him, rising into a sky of cloudless blue, and a day that promised to be even warmer than the ones before. Olvar felt restored enough to ride; the soldiers found him their stoutest horse, and pretended to bet on who would end up carrying who. Him they had treated almost like some sort of pet or talking animal at first, but he was now well accepted, not least by association with Kunrad. Gille joined him; they had made friends, with the younger men especially, although at Kunrad's dire warning they had been careful to keep their counsel. Kunrad rode ahead to the leading coach, to find Alais practising mounting from its footboard, to the old woman's great distress.

'Master Kunrad!' she called out, in the middle of one such dangerous manoeuvre. 'Isn't it an absolutely glorious sky?'

'It is,' he said, bowing to the old woman, and carefully shepherding Alais into her saddle, 'and a fair country beneath. Mine's bleak and barren by comparison. And cold. You know, I never realised it before, but I think I've been cold all my life? Maybe it was living so near the Great Ice. I can feel the sun warming my bones here. And the trees and the grasses and the flowers, the birds – so rich, so open. And soon it'll all be yours.'

'Mine?' She laughed. 'Say rather, I'll belong to it, or that we'll belong to the same lord. It's his to hold, not mine. If I had any lands, he'd have those as well. Why're you looking so stuffed?'

Kunrad blinked. 'You don't mind that?'

'No – why should I?'

Kunrad scratched his head. 'We, well, we think of things a bit differently in the North. A wife has rights in her husband's goods and so on, as he hers – a partnership. She's a person, an equal, not a possession.'

She smiled lazily up at him. 'An equal, eh? Very well, Mastersmith – how many equals have *you* got? How many women smiths are there?'

Kunrad was taken aback. He was no good whatever at humming and hawing. 'Well . . . there have been some, I know . . .'

'How many do *you* know? Don't tell me, I have this mysterious power that lets me guess what you're thinking. *A feitschac!*'

'If that means what I think it means, you should be ashamed of yourself.'

'But it's right?'

'F— I mean, none. Well, yes, none I know personally, but then it's not a talent women often possess very strongly.'

'Or don't get a chance to develop?'

'Look, you need strength too, you know! How many women want muscles like Olvar's, or like mine, even?'

'It depends where and how, exactly,' she said demurely, and ruined it with an explosive giggle. He raised his eyes to the Powers.

'After all,' she added apologetically, 'I really do want to marry him, you know. He's handsome, he's rich, he's kind, the most marvellous man I've ever met, and I've known him so long, I know he loves me too. He's a bit serious-minded, but maybe I need a touch of that – or would you disagree?'

'Sounds perfect to me. But he's much older, isn't he?'

She chuckled. 'He'll do. Oh, marriage, children – I'm looking forward to all that. I don't mind it at all. It's not a prison. I shall be a great lady, and such a one can even exercise some power on her own here, if she has the wits. And I think I might, don't you? He does. He's promised me as much.'

'And that's enough?'

'*Feitanallac!*' she spat suddenly. 'Sorry. It ought to be. It is. Only it isn't – and if you repeat that I will personally give that tattle-tale bracelet of yours a whole new direction! I shouldn't want more. Only I do – but what? What else is there? Except dreams, and those I can still have, can't I?'

'Maybe you want what you're getting, only not quite so overwhelmingly, and so soon.'

'Maybe,' she said morosely, hunching in on herself. 'Thank you for letting me say it to you, Master Kunrad. There's nobody else in the world I dare to – only you, because you're so far from my everyday world, so remote. Wish me well when you're back in your lonely glen or wherever, surrounded by all those beefy blacksmith ladies.'

'I wish you well now. And I can keep silent. But not even Nanny?'

She cringed at the thought. 'Oh Powers, her least of all! She thinks I'm still a babe in arms.'

Kunrad nodded sympathetically. 'I don't like being babied, either. Women always seem to . . .'

She stared. '*You?* I'd as soon baby the Sea Devourer! It must be your fault. You're really inviting it, probably. All men do.'

Kunrad did not like being compared to the monstrous Amicac. 'Well, aren't you any better? Stepping right into the open cage door. Suppose this power turns out not to be so very meaningful? I don't know much about how noble ladies live here, but I've seen the wives of wealthy guildmasters and such made trophies or dolls. Or simply dull gossips with nothing to do but badger servants and so on.'

She pulled her horse closer, and jabbed a long finger into his arm. 'Got you! So that's how you do things better in the North, is it?'

He waved a hand irritably. 'No, really, that's rare. Most men treat women better – equals, as I said, not servants. None of this—' he almost added *nobility nonsense*, but caught himself just in time.

'Equals, is it? Get the privilege of the hard work, more like. I'm not that fond of this nonsense about nobility and privilege, little though you may credit it; but at least it'll save me being thrust into a kitchen or a nursery and left to get on with it.'

'Or a bed?' suggested Kunrad, and was rewarded by a flood of spectacular red in her face. He found himself enjoying her high colour, so unlike any Northern beauty's.

'Right!' she said, with venomous force. 'You say you've heard of some women smiths – how many was that, exactly? And how easy did they find it? Testify, smith, or something awful is going to happen to you!'

He drew a deep breath. 'Well – they're most of them jewellers, you see, and I've never really ... The older men in the profession are often a shade conservative ...'

Some way behind, Gille and Olvar exchanged looks. It was perfectly obvious to both of them how much these two were enjoying one another's company. 'And to the old nurse or whatever she is,' whispered Olvar. 'Look at the sour face on her!'

'Oh, just intent, I think,' chuckled Gille. 'Seeing they don't accidentally ride off into the bushes or something. Little does she know! If the mastersmith did that, he'd just –' He became aware that the old woman was looking at him now, although mercifully too far away to hear. He bowed politely, with his most sincere look, and she gave him a smile as fragile as ancient parchment.

'She doesn't seem to mind overmuch,' he whispered to Olvar. 'It's the captain I'm not so sure of. He's taken to the master, I think, but he's not looking too happy now!'

Olvar glanced across, and shrugged. 'Let him! Another day or two and we reach this Warden's castle, and then our ways part. He'll let 'em be for now!'

He did indeed, though even Kunrad noticed his disquiet eventually. But the captain remained polite and amiable, the old nurse smiled benignly, and the two rode together all that long day, and never ceased their disputations. They ate together again that night, under the nurse's kindly eye, and Kunrad returned to his blanket under the stars, with the cool wine coursing moonlight in his veins. For once in his life he had managed to forget the future, forget his plans and projects and simply live for what was, here and now. In part it was the stark contrast with the nightmare of the Marshes, now an age away as it seemed; but it was also sheer enjoyment of a kind he had never before known. He suspected Alais was enjoying it just as much.

The very impossibility of it all was a help. Neither need worry about entanglements, appearances, outcomes; it was impossible, and that was all there was to it. The gulf between them was already open, the end to their time together was set, and curiously that made them free. They spoke more openly, each to another, than they would have to some more lasting acquaintance, and revealed their hearts more freely; although they both found a curious reticence in themselves about the impending marriage.

The ground was rising again now, and they rode over low hills and along paths in deep pinewood that reminded Kunrad of the North, drinking in the moist resinous air and listening to the cries of birds among the trunks, darting this way and that in such scattered shafts of hazy sunlight as could pierce the cool green gloom. Their talk had left the place of women, by now, to their mutual relief, and gone on to the arts of men. He extolled the carving and modelling of the North, she the limning of the South, making him promise he would seek out the vast painted murals of Ker Bryhaine. He tried to show her something of the same love of shape in the less realistic style of the North, with the swooping energy of its lines and the symbolic shadings based on human features; she found that crude but fascinating. She read him the great epics of the South, in sonorous, lilting phrases that her voice turned to music by the subtlety of metre and inflection. He told her the romances and sagas of the North, in language that rolled and beat on the shores of the mind, and stirred the heart like a sea breeze. His was all from memory, which greatly impressed her, even when he pointed out the subtle storyteller's trick by which forgetfulness might be concealed and missing lines padded out. It seemed to him he had never enjoyed his own heritage so much as when she took delight in it, and he guessed she felt the same. Disputation filled the air again when they talked of state and the affairs of state, and of the meaning of freedom; yet it was a dispute neither would gladly have cut short.

As the riverside oakwoods had given way to the pines and the hills, so the hills in their turn passed by to lower slopes, and the woods changed again. Great stands of white birch appeared, of a taller and whiter kind than Kunrad knew in the North, and elsewhere hazels and tall maples tossing in the wind, and other trees he did not recognise. These woods were not as solid as the pines; they opened out here and there, in small patches of blue sky at first, and later in wide clearings, some dotted with stumps that were clearly sawn, the first work of man he had seen in all this wide land. 'Nature still holds its sway here,' said Alais, 'and we are only the latecomers. In the great unbroken forests elsewhere in the land Tapiau still rules, so men believe, whom they say loves humans little better than does the Ice. That may be why this old road curves so far and roundabout, through the lesser woods for the most part and avoiding when it can the greater tracts of pines and redwoods.' She shivered. 'Mile upon mile through that green shadow! Pleasant enough at first, but after a few hours one might imagine anything!'

He looked at her. 'You say *men believe*, as if you didn't.'

She shrugged. 'I do not disbelieve, not as such. The forces you see in metal, the evils you saw in the Great Marshes – I would no longer deny that there is something to those, and to many other things we cannot explain. The Ice destroyed Morvan the Great – perhaps ancient Kerys also, since we have heard nothing for so long. Perhaps that was merely mindless nature in action, perhaps something more. There may well be powers in the world, even the Powers men believe in; but they may not be all men believe. More benign, even – who knows?'

'Who indeed?' he said. 'But I have looked upon the Ice at its merest edge, and I never wish to more. And I have seen the face of a friend struck to solid ice, all in an instant. I have little room for doubts. And again, when we were attacked, and Olvar entrapped in ice as in a wolf-snare—'

A shadow fell across his eyes, and he looked up sharply. The gap in the tree-roof was wider; and above it, dwarfing the highest of the swaying trees, a mighty mountain-crest rose purple, far nearer than he had imagined it could be in so short a time. It was what whirled against it that caught his eye, wings wide and black, two pairs, larger than any bird he had seen in these parts. A single croaking cry drifted back down the wind. 'Those? Eagles, maybe,' said the girl, narrowing her eyes against the blue brightness. 'Or the great scavenger condors. I have seen them above my father's walls, gliding like clouds made solid. Never so far into the open lands, though. And the cry sounded different. Like a raven's.'

'Very like a raven's,' said Kunrad.

They rode on later that evening, and camped at dark in what again looked like a man-made clearing around a small clear spring, naturally sheltered by low rises and a tall screen of wind-bent oak and ash. The scars of other fires still showed here and there, though none were new. Again Kunrad guested with the ladies, and talked long with Alais, so that the prentices wondered if he would come back to them. Back he came, though; and did not sleep at once, but tossed and turned, although the grass was soft and the night-breezes mild.

The next day, though, he rose at first light full of vigour, and strode up to the highest rise. Alais saw him there, and came running to join him. 'Well?' he inquired. 'I'm here as you asked!'

'I didn't want you to see it for the first time without me!' she said, and led him out of the screen of trees on to the rounded crest of a long sloping hill.

To the east, beyond the mountains, the sky was still red; but between the sawtoothed peaks, still young and unworn by wind and weather, its beams fell through air far clearer than mere crystal, across a wide land of green and blue, in many shades and hues. Very dark green were the gently waving forests, whose vastness he could only guess at, lying like fallen cloaks around the mountain-roots, fading away into hazy distances to the south. Blue shone the rivers that threaded out between them, fed by the mighty mountain torrents, into a lower, wider land, rolling and open. Lighter green were the trees here, and lighter still the wide open spaces between them, the hue of sunlit grass and ripening grain. Even at this remove Kunrad could see the ripples pass across them, like a golden sea; he guessed they must be divided into fields, widespread ones such as might surround large homesteads or small villages. Bluer still, and shimmering silver, were wider expanses, little lakes scattered here and there about the land, swallowing many small fast streams and giving birth to still more, wider and meandering. Here and there he made out wisps of duller yellow that threaded from clearing to clearing; wide roads, maybe, but barely significant among the expanse of wood and field around them. But then, as he turned from the mountains westward, the perspective changed; and he saw the hand of man set firm upon the land, turning all its richness, with a grim artistry a smith could only admire, into the mere setting of a single stone.

This was his first sight of Ker an Aruel, the Castle of the Winds. Its fashion is known as he saw it, set upon many works and designs; for save the Citadel of Ker Bryhaine itself, the Seven-Crowned, there was no greater stronghold in all the Southlands, or all the lands he knew of. Only in Morvan had it been surpassed, ground to dust beneath the Ice, and in the Old Lands of the East and

Kerys; and who knew what had befallen their strength?

The lake that held it lay in a wide circle of low hills, capped by the one on whose brow he stood. Its dark waters glinted like cut glass in the breezes that blew constantly about it, blowing off the sea over marsh and forest, warmed by the sun and turned back by the mountain-slopes to swirl around its shores. There rose at its heart a broad island of grey-brown rock, in great slanted striations that formed low but savage crags. Yet these could hardly be seen save from very close, for the island had been levelled to the water as though by the sweep of a giant's hand, and from end to end a massive fortress raised upon it, so that scarcely a sure foothold was left beyond the base of its long walls, and the lake lapped deep beneath.

Immensely thick were those walls, twice the measure of a man, taller than a house of many storeys and topped by thick battlements; save at their corners, where sturdy red-roofed towers, round and massive, rose as high again. Between these towers the walls ran straight and angular, following the edges of the rock; and its white stone was smooth and flat and sheer, featureless as sawn alabaster, without so much as a window to be seen. At one inset angle, where the rocks surfaced for a moment, opened what must have been a mighty gate; but beneath those overlooking battlements it seemed diminished, and it opened on to nothing but what looked like a narrow jetty, and the lake.

Ker an Aruel shone defiantly over the waters, quite alone and apart from the land. A bridgehead was built across two little rocky islets by the shore, but beyond that the lake lay wide and open, with nothing at all between it and the long pier. Long banners were the only sign of life, green and gold, whipping in the wind. As Kunrad first looked upon that great stronghold from the heights, it seemed to him as bright and faceted as a cut jewel, as fair and precious, and as hard.

'I haven't seen this view for *years*!' panted Alais, leaning a hand on his shoulder. 'This is Yn Aruel, the Hill of the Winds! I grew up here when my father was castellan to the last Warden, I used to ramble all over these lands! I wanted to be the one to show you!'

'Thank you!' said Kunrad abstractedly. He was wondering how the art of either North or South could ever capture this. This one was too abstract, the other too literal. Work of man as it was, jewel and setting together defied man and became something greater.

For once she did not seem inclined to argue, when he said this. 'This was Lord Vayde's work, after all. The first great fortress he built, to claim this land for the South-kingdom, and to be a base for his exploration of the North.'

'He had some foresight, that man,' agreed Kunrad. 'He saw the coming quarrels, and that the Northern kind must have their own land. A shame he could not use his wisdom to quell those quarrels. They have never seemed more foolish to me than now!'

She smiled at him, but before she could say anything the old nurse was calling to her, and with a light laugh she went capering away down the hill as eagerly as she had come. He stayed a little longer, rejoicing in the fresh breeze that swept the hill so constantly that it had shaped the trees, shaking his head in wonder; but the camp was packing up below him, and he came unwillingly down.

They could have ridden down the long slopes to the shore directly; but the road was made for cart and carriage, and led them around the hill towards the south, through vale well shrouded in trees, so that even from sunlit clearings they saw nothing of the wide lands and hardly even the mountain-peaks. Kunrad rode with the Lady Alais, and in greater harmony at first; for he was as deeply impressed by Ker an Aruel as she could wish. 'You could fit many a Northland village between those walls, whole and entire. I have to admit it, though you sothrans may have less skill in metal, yet your mastery with stone is well-nigh as great!'

'And,' she said innocently, 'we don't even need to chant hocus-pocus over it . . .'

Kunrad was too serious to be drawn thus. He shook his head. 'I am less sure, lady. It's said on good authority that the duergar, the Mountain-people, can imbue stone with powerful virtues, as well as they can metal.'

She laughed. 'The duergar? The little people? Come now, that's too much! Only our simplest peasants and children will credit those. Oh, perhaps some tribe of mountain-lurking savages gave rise to the legends, that I'll gladly allow you. They say some peasants still slay outlivers and wild men whom they catch, taking them for duergar; a cruel custom I'd see forbidden. But magic-workers, fairytale folk! Why, you'll be telling me next the Forest People exist, or the Ageless Ones, or the Sea People!'

Kunrad had never mentioned the duergar in his tales, and he was wondering how he might deliver this revelation without endless teasing when he was saved the trouble. Without their noticing, the forest around them had been changing, growing thinner; and they found themselves riding into yet another sunny clearing, and its floor was almost level. Its far side was scarcely more than a screen, through which they could easily see the glitter of water, and within it something mirrored.

There was a cheer from the riders, and the captain rode up to the fore. He saluted the Lady Alais, and bowed to Kunrad, not without something a little puzzling in his face. 'Your leave to be your herald, my lady?'

'You have earned that and more, dear Ferlias. Go and call!'

He bowed again, and cantered his huge horse forward through the few trees ahead, drawing a great horn from his saddlebags. Beyond the trees they saw him halt, and sound the horn. Its note, clear and strong, echoed out across the lake; and a second later it was answered. They rode on after the captain, hearing him sound again, and at last, as they emerged from the trees, call out. Another trumpet answered; then, suddenly, a whole fanfare. And it seemed to Gille and Olvar, seeing for the first time what lay before them, that the sound was merely the expression of the sight.

To Kunrad it had looked like a jewel; but here it rose before them in all its power, and the blue mountains beyond shrank to a backdrop for its towers. This close he could see there were windows in them, a few high under the eaves and facing mostly inwards. Below them were mere arrowslots; but in the walls themselves there were none. The gate itself was puzzling. A drawbridge fronted it; but that opened only on to the rocks below, and the jetty. To one side of the gate the wooden quay stretched out, wider than it had seemed from the hill, with an arched gateway at either end and a string of small boats moored beneath; but of any other bridge he could see none. Without one the castle could be assailed only by water; and the fate of any but the largest boats beneath those lowering white walls was in little doubt.

They might have been made in mockery of the Ice itself, sheer, smooth, baffling the eye and daunting the mind. Yet the sunlight on them was joyous, and the old red tiles of the round tower rooftops glowed mellow, and the banners that streamed from tall white masts at their summits waved a welcome in the winds. For sheer strength this stronghold made even the corsair fortress look crude and feeble, yet there was a sweeping, airy grace on its lines, so that it seemed like a bright ship sailing on the constant breeze.

'Why,' exclaimed Gille suddenly, riding up behind them, 'it *is* the corsair fortress! They must have seen it and sought to copy it as best they could, in that fell place!'

'A flattery, I suppose!' said Alais, and Gille bowed, a little stiffly, for it was the first word she had spoken directly to him.

'A weak one!' said Olvar. 'These sothrans are a mighty folk!' He bowed also.

She inclined her head gracefully to them both. 'You must not think of me as altogether a sothran!' she said, with a seriousness that caught their attention. 'My line ruled over the ancestors of both peoples once, and I am blood kin to both. I always believed the North must be of great worth. Now I know how far short even my belief fell; and I shall see the South knows it also.'

Her smile, calm as it was, left them both speechless. Then another fanfare from the castle caught their attention. At the gate the drawbridge was winding slowly downward; but something else was moving. The construction they had taken for a pier was rocking gently in the waves as it swung outward from the base of the rock. The boats were not moored beneath it, they were part of it, a massive pontoon bridge that was being hauled into position by a complex system of chains and cables and pulleys running out from the rocks beneath the wall.

'What of our skills with metal now, Mastersmith?' teased Alais.

'What indeed?' Kunrad answered absently, studying the mechanism with a critical wag of the head; and she shot him a smouldering glare.

'Now, now, my duck!' announced the nurse firmly from beside her. 'here's the gate away opening, and you still playing around in your riding habit! Off with you now and into your best as is fitting, while I comb out your poor hair! Come along now and don't be all-a-pout like that! Mustn't spoil your face for your poor Lord Warden!'

The prentices watched her led back to the carriage, with barely concealed chuckles. *'Mustn't spoil your face!'* cackled Olvar.

'Into your best now!' squeaked Gille, and nudged his master heavily in the ribs.

Kunrad turned on him furiously. 'Leave me in peace, you young idiots! As if I haven't had enough prattling and pontificating! Stars and Powers, these women, never a minute's peace they give you! And the kind they breed here most of all! Lady this, lady that – excellent! Bravely done! All that silly pretence! Never set foot out of the South and hardly credits the Ice that it's cold! By Glaiscav's bow, I pity her poor husband to be!'

The procession was moving past, and he goaded his horse to the fore. The prentices stared at each other a moment, then collapsed, whooping with laughter. 'They say it's the sun!' crowed Gille, urging his astonished horse after Kunrad.

'No, something in the water, definitely the water!' boomed Olvar. 'It's finally happened!'

'He's woken up! All those nice town girls wasting their time billing and cooing, when they should have been treating him like muck—'

'Kicking him about a bit!'

Gille gurgled. 'Shall we tell them he likes it rough?

> *Legends tell each Power and Hero*
> *Learned a better half to fear, oh!*
> *Come in drunk from wandering, Raven*
> *From his angry wife turns craven!*
> *Hunter Glaiscav drops his arrows,*
> *When his fair one scolds and harrows!*
> *When he wants his jollies, Artes*
> *Licks Saithana's nether partes!*
> *Who's to doubt that Mistress Vayde*
> *Beat her husband every Friday,*
> *When he . . .'*

Kunrad's large fist, clenched tight in Gille's tunic, all but lifted him bodily out of his saddle. 'Now hear me, you brainless little worm! We are presently escorting a great lady of a land in which we're guests, and to whom we're indebted for our lives, to greet an even greater lord whom she's going to marry! And there's a fair chance some folk here understand our tongue about as well as we do theirs. *Do I make myself clear?* Then get to the rear, the pair of you! And don't so much as show your faces till I tell you!'

The chastened prentices dropped back at once, to sympathetic mutters from the soldiers – which probably meant they hadn't understood the song. Kunrad was deeply relieved. More woman trouble!

The cavalcade reached the bridgehead and the planked

walkway which led across the little islands. Beyond it they could see the gate on the end of the bridge swinging smoothly in. An arch at the end met and married with the one on the end of the bridge to make a solid gateway, and soldiers in armour snapped home wooden bars to steady it. They wore decent mail, Kunrad noted, with black surcoats bearing an image of the castle itself. They saluted captain Ferlias, who led the way, while the other soldiers and Kunrad with them pulled aside to let the carriages rumble across. The guards knelt as they passed. The bridge rocked gently, but took the weight well; clearly you could march an army across it. Then the soldiers waved Kunrad on, and fell in behind, in pairs, sitting very straight in their saddles and carrying their spears high.

The drawbridge was down and a black portcullis rising before gates that were already opening. Beyond a wide stone arch, so deep it was almost a tunnel, Kunrad could see trees, tall ones growing, he realised, at the centre of a wide courtyard, out of flags and cobbles, with stone benches around their ancient trunks. Flowers blazed in deep troughs around the sides, or trailed in long locks like hair from the boxes at the inner windows of the tall buildings round about. Guards were drawn up on parade order in the courtyard, and trumpeters sounded, scaring doves out of the dovecotes among the trees. It was more like a small town square than a place of war, and Kunrad found himself warming to it, as he reined in his horse behind the carriages.

Alais was already leaping out of the door, running to greet a tall man in the black castle livery who strode down through the crowd. She established his identity by springing up to embrace him with a force that made Kunrad smile wryly. An older man? He might well be a lot older soon. Then her hair came away from his face, and their eyes met.

And, strange as it may seem, all Kunrad could think in that moment was, if she believes he is so very old, what must she think of me?

He stared in utter unbelief, and the other stared back, no whit less stunned. The girl looked from one to another, and almost doubled up in whoops of undignified laughter.

'Your *faces* . . .' she spluttered. 'I had to see your *faces!*'

Kunrad's voice came only in starts. 'Y-you said you were t-taking me t-to s-see the M-Marchwarden . . . Yes. Of course!'

'And so I have!' she said happily. 'Permit me to introduce you. Merthian, by birth Lord of Anlaithann, by merit Lord Warden of the Northern Marches, Governor of the Northern Provinces, Lord Commander of the realm of Bryhaine. Darling, meet the Mastersmith Kunrad of Athalby, a very brave and clever Northerner who *never* stops arguing, and has come all this way to settle some claim of honour with you. So, since he seemed to want to meet you so much, I felt I could do nothing better than bring him along. I told him he would get justice from the Marchwarden – and he will, won't he, my lord?'

Merthian's voice was in better condition than Kunrad's, and he managed one of his impressive bows. 'My darling, I'm more than delighted to welcome you here! You've often surprised me, but never more than turning up for your wedding with an angry debt collector in tow! But you're right; no amount of haggling ever satisfies these Northerners. Still, since you promised, my dear, I am bound to attend to his complaint – in due course.'

She beamed up at him, and at Kunrad. 'I knew I could depend on you!'

'Always,' said Merthian fervently. 'And now, you must be utterly exhausted after your journey. And you, my dear Nanny, and you, captain – join us for rest and refreshment, while my men will play host to yours in the finest style they can. And to our Northern guest especially,' added Merthian, 'until I am ready to attend to him. At such a happy time you will excuse the wait, Mastersmith, I'm sure?'

He swept Alais off towards the wide steps of the

tallest tower, with such engaging energy she had barely time to waggle her fingers at Kunrad as he sat there, more stunned than he could have believed possible. Merthian, as he went by, turned to the grizzled soldier who had accompanied him in the North. 'Look to him well, Erlan! Till I'm ready for him!'

Kunrad did not move. He was surrounded by the Marchwarden's men, and Alais's soldiers, without their captain, were already dismounting and greeting old acquaintances with heavy hints about wine and meat. The red-haired captain bowed to Kunrad, and, evidently unsure he spoke the language, gestured to him to dismount. No weapons were drawn; but then, they did not need to be. The gate was not closed, but that too was not necessary. It was far behind him, and the way full of men and horses.

Slowly, dully, Kunrad swung down from his horse, automatically taking his scanty roll of baggage. The captain bowed courteously, handed his horse to a groom, and led him through the confusion to a side-door of another building. A discreet enough door; a roundabout way, probably, to an inevitable end.

But as he was led away, Kunrad looked back to the end of the possession, and his heart thrilled. At the very rear of the procession he saw only two horses. Their saddles stood empty; but the gate, at last, was swinging shut.

CHAPTER SEVEN
Light Airs, Dark Waters

He heard the gate boom shut behind him, saw the door open ahead, and they seemed like happenings in another world. The door closed silently, the courtyard light was cut off, and he was not at all surprised to find his arms seized and pinioned. The shrug with which he threw his captors off was almost unthinking, and he looked without emotion at the sword against his throat. 'That's one of mine,' was all he said.

Merthian's officer relaxed. Swift hands plucked the sword from his belt, searched him lightly, taking his eating knife and his tool-roll, but nothing else. Hands prodded him forward, rather than sword-points, and in his detached thoughts he guessed the captain was taking care with a prisoner who might be valuable. There was a long corridor, shadowy and echoing, a single shaft of sun striking through a slot window somewhere high above. There was a door, a chamber, another door, double this time, and a long stairway leading to yet another corridor, low-roofed but clean-swept, like all the rest, lined along one side with heavy iron-bound doors, with numbers and spyholes. It all seemed too familiar, and too closed in. Light manacles were thrust on to his wrists and locked with a linking chain. He might have made some cold jest about the corsairs, but he felt too weary and heartsick to speak. A door was unlocked, he was thrust in, not at all brutally, and it closed quietly behind him.

He stood there a moment, dumb; until a sound unexpected called him to himself, and he looked around in growing surprise. He was certainly in a cell, but the like of which he had never seen. Its builder had made use of a portion of the island where the layers of bedrock had been separated, perhaps by the weathering out of softer intruded stone. This had created a deep notch – a whole line of them, probably – shaped like a canted arrowhead. Rubble had been packed in with some kind of hardened earth to make a slightly sloping floor, and the end and roof sealed off with massive stone blocks – that awesome outer wall, he realised, and shrank momentarily at the thought of the weight above his head. There was light from somewhere, but no window, only water washing at the far wall, gentle wavelets lapping some way up the floor. He made out a narrow slot there that must open on to the lake, at water level; and each wave that washed against the outside wall revealed the deepset bars that sealed it. Air could get in, and more light than he expected, mirrored in the water; but for anything else to pass seemed impossible. It was clean, humane, impassable, and from the outside must be all but invisible, a brilliant means of both airing and concealing a dungeon without windows to weaken the outer wall.

On the natural shelf created by the lower edge of the notch lay a large hay bale with a coarse blanket draped over it. There was nothing else at all. Kunrad sat slowly down on it, eyes fixed on the narrow line of light at the water-line, and abandoned himself to his thoughts.

When the clack of the bolts brought him back to himself, he realised by the change in the light that some hours must have passed. A dim sunset glow reddened the water, and it matched his state of mind. The door swung back, and a man stepped in. He looked at Kunrad a moment, then tossed a swift word to somebody behind the door and elbowed it shut. Kunrad stood up and strode towards the man, who stood and waited calmly enough. It was Merthian.

'I looked at you through the spyhole,' he said, almost apologetically. He was dressed in quiet richness, some stuff of gold-laced green, though it was hard to be sure in this light. 'You seemed to be lost in thought, Mastersmith. About what, may I ask?'

'Renewing my curses on womankind and sothrans,' said Kunrad. 'Are you surprised?'

Merthian ducked his head slightly. 'You should understand, my Lady Alais meant no harm in the world.'

Kunrad sighed. 'I acknowledge that. She's besotted with you; so however it appeared, I had to be the one in the wrong. She just can't conceive you'd do anything so ill.'

'No more can I,' said Merthian heavily; and Kunrad drew a breath in surprise. 'In normal times I would never, *never* have done such a thing. But I had to have that armour, *had to!* It was more than a foible. It is more important than your feelings or mine—'

He reeled backwards, clutching his mouth. Kunrad himself stood aghast at the speed with which he had moved, the broken chains swinging from his skinned wrists. The manacles had taken almost all the force of his blow, or it might well have laid Merthian witless on the spot. By his eyes, the Warden knew it. He dabbed at his cut lip.

'I suppose,' he said thickly, 'that I owe you that, at the least.'

'You're forgetting,' said Kunrad icily. 'I saw the other towns. Until I turned off to Saldenborg, anyhow. The money, the weapons, all else – did you *have* to have them also? Spare me your little pieties. What you owe, you would not survive.'

Merthian's face twisted in pain that did not come from Kunrad; at the least, not from his hand. His voice trembled, and yet he seemed not at all humbled. 'All – *all!* – I will faithfully repay, with money for use, with generous compensation too. All, and soon. That is the best I can say. But meanwhile—'

'And the life of my friend? Shall I see you repay that?'

Merthian stood his ground; but he seemed to writhe faintly. 'I had no hand in that!'

'You'd not be human if you had. But you knew of it.'

The Marchwarden hunched his shoulders. 'That, and other things I wish I could have prevented. Worse, too, that I may yet prevent!'

'A fine beggar's tale, to cadge a copper!' snorted Kunrad, but not as scornfully as he felt he should. In part it was the way the man stood there before him, unarmed, unafraid. Of course he had men within call, but he had not done so. It was more the calm intensity behind that voice, like the arrow quivering faintly on the taut string.

'Whatever you may say, it is true! I will show you, smith, one day. One day soon.'

'Is that all you came here to say?'

Merthian smiled lopsidedly. 'I came to ask you something, but I can see you are in no mood for a calm answer.' He turned and knocked commandingly at the door. 'I'll return tomorrow, when you are grown cooler.'

'Ask me now.'

'Very well,' said Merthian, as it opened. 'Whether you would agree to work for me, Mastersmith. I would value that.'

The door closed swiftly and solidly before Kunrad could think of an answer. He glared at it a moment, and returned to his thoughts. What he had said to Merthian was less than the truth. He had been brooding indeed, but on nothing so petty as curses; at least, not all the time.

He had been stunned, at first, at his own stupidity in allowing himself to walk from one captivity into another. He had been worrying about the prentices, hoping they would try nothing so stupid as a rescue. He was not sure that they would not. He could do nothing to stop them, or to redeem his folly; nothing that was, save free himself. So he had been turning his mind to the problem, like a man flexing his arms after long labour, and finding he had grown strong.

It was so with Kunrad, as he himself knew, that his mind would follow a direction as a cart follows ruts. It had always been thus, a part of what had made him so fine a smith, but also so narrow and unfulfilled a man. That singleness of purpose would drive his thoughts farther and deeper than most, if he could only manage to direct it. Sometimes, though, it would carve those ruts for itself, and be a burden to him. Only of late had he begun to see how it had hindered him so long from looking beyond his craft; sometimes he blamed it for his obsessive need of the armour. Now, though, that same need was forcing him to learn to apply this fierce concentration to other concerns. It had shown him the clues he needed to escape the corsairs; and so, almost unconsciously, he was looking about at this cell also.

One thing forced itself on him. The lake water would serve for thirst and other needs, that was clear. But there was no food; and if there was going to be, it would probably have appeared by now. That could mean all manner of things, none good; but for now he might as well make the best of it. Fasting made for clearer thinking, it was said.

He knelt at the water's edge and drank his fill, considering the bars. Like all the sothran work he knew of, they had no special virtues set upon them, but were mere lifeless metal, clumsily forged – and extremely solid, set in the living rock with stuff like tough mortar. In a window one might try to chip away at this; but under water it was not to be thought of. He stretched out on his prickly couch, wrapping the blanket around him. He would conserve strength thus, and be stronger on the morrow. He might have need to be.

He lay abed for most of that day, resting his body, easing his mind. Famine did indeed clear his thoughts, but it was the terrible clarity of nightmare. He began to twitch nervously at every shadow. His hunger was fading, now, and that, he knew, was precisely when you began to starve. Towards evening he drifted off, but woke almost at once sharply, sweating despite the cool air. Not a nightmare, not exactly; but a very fierce, direct dream in which the door stood straining to open if he could only find the key somebody had dropped about the cell. Somewhere close, almost at his fingertips; somewhere he had already seen it, without realising it . . .

He plucked a straw-shaft out of his ear and sat up. At least the stuff wasn't damp or lice-ridden. He sank his head in his hands, and groaned. Then he looked at the floor more closely. He stretched out, idly it seemed, plucked up one of the loose stones and struck it once or twice against his manacles. The noise of the loose chains brought a guard to the spyhole, but Kunrad was lying back by then, hands behind his head, staring at the great slab of a ceiling.

At some point he must have drifted into uneasy sleep, for at first light the next morning he was awoken, thick-tongued and heavy of heart, by Merthian. The Marchwarden seemed impatient, standing over him as he went to splash his face in the surging little pool. 'Well? Have you thought over what I ask?'

Kunrad blinked up at him with little goodwill. He felt cold, and his belly was growling to itself like an old dog dreaming. 'My heart says, to Hella with you and all around you! But in reason, I'd need to know more, much more. All I know of you is as a thief. What am I to do, open the windows you slip into? Distract the infants while you snatch their pennies?'

'Don't be stupid!' said Merthian sharply. 'There is of course a moral difference! If I have turned thief, it was in no small cause, believe me!' He kicked savagely at the water's edge, so that it sprayed out across the stone. 'There is something afoot – something of moment, so great, so vital ... I would like to tell you, but I dare not. Enough, that the cost of it will be huge, the gains immeasurable! So huge that every least coin I have and can or will raise on my great credit is already committed to it. So that every saving, even the very least trifle, is a great gain. I'll not hang men for stealing, like my cruel forefathers; but I hate it as bitterly as you! I had hoped I could avoid it, buying in the North – but hate it as I do, I was always ready to. Does that tell you something of my need?'

'Only of your duplicity. Is that any reason I should serve you?'

Merthian rounded on Kunrad, so suddenly the smith, still kneeling, ducked his head from a blow; but there were only words. 'Reasons! I should not tell you this, but you, you who have gone through so much to hunt me down ... you shame me. So hear! The realm of the Southlands, the state of Ker Bryhaine, is governed ill. Ill, and it grows weaker by the day!' He shrugged. 'I speak no treason. All know it, none will act lest their own selfish interest be put at risk! The Syndics are grown too fat and complacent, too corrupt – a self-chosen band that robs the commons to no purpose beyond their own gain and their families. They cast out the old nobility for its arrogance, yet their own is swollen far greater! Another rule is needed.'

He looked the smith in the face, and Kunrad almost sought to stop his mouth; for in what he was being told, he read his own death-warrant.

'I see you take my meaning,' said Merthian quietly. 'A king such as they had of old, yes. And yes, also, I see myself as the one. In the years since I was given this great office, so young, I have ruled firmly but fairly, as nowhere else in Bryhaine, and with vision. My hand is light, I encourage freedom and free thought. Even my enemies concede as much. I am proven. I can do the same for the whole land, perhaps even reunite the two peoples—'

'What,' asked Kunrad, holding up a blunt hand to stem the flow, 'if some wish to be ruled by no king save themselves? And what of the true royal line, the Kermorvannen ... oh.'

'Exactly!' smiled Merthian, a little sadly. 'They are not in contention. When I wed Alais I shall *be* a Kermorvan. That is how they have remained hale and strong for so long – always ready to take in new blood, so long as it is tried and proven. Alais is the flower of her generation, and her line will mingle with mine. I will give her power in the land, so the people will follow us, and our children will be kings beyond question.' He smacked one hand into the other. 'That is for the future. For now – much remains to be done! And there is nobody more capable of it than I. Believe me, if there were, they would have been created Lord Warden in my stead! All the others are too old, or slight men, meriting little, or too jealously bound to one faction or another, unable to command enough respect.'

'And you can? Without starting a bloody kinstrife?'

'So I believe, on good foundation. From the majority of the people, certainly. Many of the Syndics, also. The Lord Bryheren, who sits as Chief Syndic, he is a good man in his way, unlike many of that line, but narrow and cold, a mind that draws lines and balances pennies and can look no further. He thinks well of me, but he might contest my claim, perhaps, and some others; so I must gather all the force I can. The more I have, the less likely they will be to unleash so destructive a war. But if they are so foolish, then the more easily I shall limit the chaos, and the sooner they will tire. Then they will accept me.'

He spoke quietly, without heat or boasting, a reasonable man sure of reasonable things. And to his own great annoyance Kunrad found himself carried along by the man's sincerity, forced to turn and battle against it like a headwind. 'There'll still be a lot of harm done. People will die, and those who live won't forget, any more than I could. If you're so bloody confident, why not stake your claim out in the open?'

'Without first taking every precaution?' Merthian gave a bitter laugh. 'I would not last half a day. And there is no time for endless argument. Would you wait to cast ballots upon who is to stop runaway horses? There are chances I cannot yet speak of that may be lost. I must let some ill be done, in the pursuit of good – but what I can, I'll amend, as I've already said. And more, to those who help me. You can, Mastersmith. Now d'you see why your armour so impressed me? To become a king, I must *look* a king, every inch of me—'

'You do. For what that's worth.'

'Not truly. Not a potent figure out of ancient time and times to come, both. A being more than human, one favoured by the Powers, a figure to rally to in battle—'

'And to aim at, I'd have thought!'

Merthian laughed. 'And that is why it has to be armour! And good armour, not mere jewellery! I sought it for a long time, something I could trust. I begged the Powers to send me what I needed – and by your humble hearth one day it blazed out at me. You have achieved that much already. You can do more, much more, with your art – and beyond it, if I am any judge of men. And I am. You, you hard-handed Northerner from a little corner of the Wild, you are nonetheless a man of great worth. You are a man I could trust with offices and employments, with land and people both. Help me, work with me, and you shall rise higher in the world than you can imagine, that I promise you!'

'I don't doubt it.' Kunrad stared at him, a long while, and sighed. 'No. No, you still can't see it, can you, my lord? A fact every smith knows. It's *where* the blow falls that shapes the steel – not why. Think upon that, my Lord Merthian. You'll have no other answer from me today.'

Merthian stared at him a moment, and his face was as unreadable as the moon's. At last he said, quietly, 'Then I shall return tomorrow.'

Kunrad watched the door shut once again, heard the bars drop home. So that was the prize! As it had been through all the years of sothran history, if he had heard true. Long years of squabble and discord, while the North sat back in its isolation and felt superior. Now it would all happen again – and who knows, with some result this time. Merthian King, riding in triumph – in Kunrad's armour! He could see it now, the young man, his hair flying, parading his warhorse in the bright sun, a dazzling vision almost too bright to look upon . . .

He shook his head angrily, and slumped down by the water, watching the play of invisible clouds in the luminous surface. It must be a fine morning out there, fine and warm; the lake would be glowing blue instead of this dank green. How were the prentices faring out there?

He could easily end this, give Merthian an answer, as he had the corsairs; but Merthian was no man's fool. The Marchwarden would release him, but under conditions; and he would be carefully watched. Every hold that could be kept upon him, would be. Merthian had not ordered Kunrad's chain replaced; but liberty would load him with invisible restraints, much harder to break. Better to be mewed up in here and out of the way, out of thought, so that he could do his own thinking at will.

The door was no hope, not with so many other doors behind it, and so many guards. The rock was steel-hard, above and below. That left the slot, and those bars. No virtues – and yet they had been there a long time, perhaps since Ker an Aruel was built. He glanced at the spyhole, but it was shut, and his ear caught nothing from beyond it but low snores. Hastily he stripped down and slipped into the water, feeling the strong undertow that kept it circulating and clean. He tugged at the bars, really tugged, but not the faintest hint of give or movement came to him.

They rasped at his fingers. Without the benefits of a virtue against rusting, the water had eaten away at them somewhat, but only on the outside; they were rough and jagged there, but of course that formed a coating that protected the rest. The rust would be softer, yet even scratching that away would take too long, and achieve little. Merthian was not a stupid corsair, to leave a smith his tools. There was nothing here except a few sharp stones in the floor. Nothing he might bring his craft to bear on. If he could only have brought in a few small things with him . . .

Perhaps he had.

Kunrad clambered up, towelled himself roughly with the blanket, and began to search through his pockets. At least Alais in her mending had left them as they were. In his breeches pockets there were always odd bits and pieces of things, but he was surprised to find just how much. A small coin or two, a nail, two thin slivers of gold rod; how long since he'd worked with that gauge? Years, it had to be. There were cuts and clippings, tiny triangular snippets and sharp-edged shavings, some old and air-dulled, some new and sharp. The very dust and fluff glinted with small heavy particles. His jerkin pockets, chiefly for thrusting cold hands into, yielded a twist of one kind of wire from the contracting rope – useless now, but wire was always useful. They had missed his belt pocket, too; he vaguely remembered thrusting some useful things into that when he left home, a long age past. He searched hurriedly, in case there was a box of picklocks or a small sturdy file. What tumbled out was some waxed paper packets of salt, now caked solid, a few more of spices, and another containing unlovely brown shrivels he remembered were dried mushrooms used for flavouring stews. He allowed himself a quiet laugh over what he had thought was important, once. The mushrooms only reminded him how hungry he was. If his guts had been a wolf, somebody would have taken a spear to it.

All in all, it was a discouraging haul; and yet it was something more than nothing. He lay back on his bed, and stared at the shadowy rock overhead. Craft did not always lie in the wielding of vast powers, like Vayde's. Sometimes you could achieve powerful effects with weaker forces by placing them cleverly, as you might roll a round pebble under the foot of a charging berserk. Somehow or other he must make such a pebble of what he had here, something that could affect some aspect of his cell. He turned over and contemplated his bed. Could he pack all that straw against the door and ignite it, somehow? Not without alerting the guards, and suffocating himself, most likely. He might make a loose rope of it, but not thin enough to trip or snare anyone . . .

He snorted impatiently. He was starting at the wrong end of things. The pebble was all very well; but first

Light Airs, Dark Waters

find your berserk, the force you can turn to your own advantage. He lay back, and searched now for something that would serve, something quite simple, probably. It would need to be.

And then, when the lapping lake water had turned dim and cold and blue, he sat up again, ignoring the faint dizziness and the roaring in his ears, and tore at his bedding. Then, stumbling in the dark, he hauled a flat stone out of the floor, and in the hardened hollow it had left he coiled the long twisted hank of straw he had made, and with it a little heap of fluff, dry grass that had caught in his boot, and more straw. Then he struck the stone against his manacle again, and sparks sprang from the flint and steel to settle glowing in the little heap. Again, and the glows grew. He blew on them, whisper-soft, and they wavered, mingled, merged. A shaky yellow flame awoke at the end of the hank, and grew steadily, setting shadows leaping about the stone roof. He sat back and drew a tremulous breath. He had been reduced to nothing, yet out of nothing he now had kindled fire. Its faint warmth brought home to him how chill he felt. He must move quickly before he wakened too far, and that meant going down into the water. Quickly he examined and sorted his scanty ingredients by the wavering light. It would be enough; it had to be.

He came back numbed and dripping to find the hank already nine-tenths burned, and fed it swiftly with more of his bedding, until a small fire crackled in the hollow and the thin smoke rolled down the sloping ceiling. He stifled a cough. Not even if he burned all his straw and blanket also could he make a fire hot enough for true metalwork; but all he needed was its semblance. The metal fragments were already heating among the ashes, and the stuff he had garnered was drying out. The iron of the bars was formed already, and he could not sing any virtue into that; but into the scraps before him, he could. He added more straw, keeping more ready to hand. And, as the fire grew and crackled, he urged the dry ingredients together on the stone, tapping them slowly with the nail as they began to merge, and singing softly to the rhythm of the tapping. A stone for an anvil, a nailhead for a hammer – and yet the forces were the same, conduits through which the strength he could summon up could flow.

> *Strip the rust and shield the iron,*
> *Ward the moisture from the metal,*
> *Blend the eater with the eaten,*
> *Set the enemy as sentry!*

He felt that strength grow as the song swelled, simple as it was, an easy thing a child in his first prenticeship might commit to memory, a deliberately mild and elementary virtue to set in a metal. He thought a moment, and added a few lines that might direct the chant closer to what he had in mind.

> *Draw from water what is wanting,*
> *Suck the salt and breathe the lifesbreath,*
> *Break the wave against the ironwork,*
> *Free the light airs to their wandering!*

Over and over again, to the dull beat of the hammer shaping a simple bar or rudderpin into rustless form; or the rings of a corroded mailshirt, as he had set the prentices to do. Only from him there was nothing simple about it. Into those discarded twists and flakes he poured the full force of his mastery, the carefully nurtured source that made his swords hold their edge and his armour its shape beyond the mere strength of the metal. And behind it rode a black tide of anger that till now he had been careful to stem.

There was a suspicion in him, a foreboding of what Merthian was about. All he could pin down of it was the havoc a king-making war might create; but there was something worse, something the young Marchwarden had glanced over. Something worse. The nailhead tapped, the words fell and the stone clinked dull wrath through the smoke. Even Olvar and Gille had sung richer, more entangled versions, over the corsair mailshirts; but it was directness, not complexity, that was needed here, a sheer focusing of force. Kunrad heaped the fire, though even his leathern fingers were shrivelling from the heat. He must finish before the dawn.

He was tired, so tired that he found himself sagging over the fire, yet without slackening the beat in the slightest, or faltering on a single syllable, so much was smithcraft a part of him. He stared stupidly at the tiny heap of metal he was tapping, seeing it choking in the embers. Hastily he blew them back and snatched up the fragments, burning his fingers on the hot stone. Keenly he stared at them, and even as the fire faltered he felt a fierce inner glow that stirred his heart and filled his empty stomach; for tiny glints awoke there, brighter far than the embers, bright as the stars that faded in the sky beyond. Stumbling on stiffened legs he hurried back to the water and in, untwining the wire as he went, crouching, shivering, in the sunken notch to wrap it around and around the bars, and with each a tiny particle of the metal. It took most of his strength, and he stumbled back up. But before he allowed himself to collapse, he built up the fire, and brushed the stone clean, and wrang water into its hollow surface. Into that he put the dried mushrooms; and only then sank back on his decimated bed, more stone than otherwise, and curled up shivering in his blanket.

He did not notice falling asleep; but he was awoken, some time later, by a strange sound. He looked toward the water, turning steel-grey now with the dawn, and saw a few bubbles rise there and burst, along the line of the bars. He smiled to himself, and reached over to the stone. The fire had died, but the stone was still hot, and in it lay a thick warm gummy liquid, with a savour that set his mouth watering. He scooped it up almost in one mouthful, chewing at the mess beneath, licking the wrapper of his salt packets, for he had used the rest. Then he lay back, feeling immeasurably better. Now there was nothing but to wait, and listen to wind and water.

A minute later, it seemed, Merthian was shaking him again. 'What've you been up to? It stinks of smoke in here!' He stared at the barren rock. 'Burning your bedding? I'm surprised a Northerner would feel the cold.' He glanced alertly around the cell. 'No! It was something else – wasn't it? You were trying to escape, as you did from those idiot corsairs. Alais was very impressed. But not this time, I suspect.'

'I'm still here,' said Kunrad, rolling away from him.

'Yes. Are you surprised? This fortress was begun by Vayde, though he died before it was completed. It was one of my ancestors who finished it off, the second Lord Warden, in fact. I don't imagine smiths' tricks would avail you much against solid stone. Well,' he added mildly, 'I'm sorry. You have, as it were, unmade your bed and must lie on it. I can't offer you any more bedding for now. Or breakfast, for that matter. Genuinely sorry.'

'Didn't know you were that poor,' grunted Kunrad. 'Even poor folk are hospitable, up north – remember?'

'It's not a matter of being poor,' said Merthian patiently. 'I feed my guests, always. But I did not invite you here. If you wish food, you must work for it, and there is little or nothing you can do in here.'

'Chalk it up against what you owe me,' mumbled Kunrad. 'I'll have a side of beef to start with, and a banquet for two hundred.'

'I am not yet able to pay that debt. If you will work for me, though, I shall make the extra effort to advance you an earnest of my good will. Come, agree! Let us waste no more time!'

Kunrad rolled over and looked hard at Merthian. He did not seem to enjoy the game he was playing, yet he played it to the hilt nonetheless. Something more than ambition drove him.

'Time!' said Kunrad. 'Time ... You're in haste, Merthian, black haste. So what's the hurry? Desperate to be king before the winter comes?'

That was it! The flash of expression in Merthian's controlled features was unmistakable; and a truth dangled before him, almost within his grasp. 'Yes!' grated Kunrad, sitting up. 'You want to succeed, and succeed now! That's when the foot slips, though, isn't it? Take time to think, for your own sake if no other. Mind what I told you! What counts in the end is what you do, not why!'

Merthian shrugged elegantly. 'In the South we are perhaps a little less ... simple? Unsophisticated? Straightforward? Let's say straightforward. The art of rule lies in compromise and negotiation. We recognise that you cannot always forward a cause by the purest means. But when the cause is good ...'

'I know! We've that saying in the North also! You're telling me your end will justify your means. And I say to you, whatever the end you start out with, the means dictate how it turns out! Man, look, it's happening already! With all your machinations you've neglected this corsair presence. You've set the North in full cry with your little shopping spree. While you're getting fitted for your throne, the two lands are hovering on the brink of war. Now you'll risk adding civil strife in your own land to that? A fine start to give your new subjects, my lord! And a fine gift for their real enemies! To leave us scuffling, weakened, growing poorer and fewer in number! So the Old Wild may draw in around us once more, and the grip of Winter. A pretty present for the Ice!'

Merthian stamped the floor, and rounded on him with a rare note of anger in his word. 'Ah yes – the Ice! Since you bring it up, let us talk of means and ends there! Since you are so keen to judge matters of which you know little! Reason me this then – what has standing out against such a mighty enemy ever brought us? The loss and destruction of our lands, sundering from our kin across the Oceans, generations of flight and misery. How can we fight it? What use are even your swords and spears swung against the advancing walls of Winter? Neither weapons nor courage will slow the glaciers a finger's breadth, or bite upon the wills that lie behind them! So, when you have an enemy you cannot overcome, should you not then seek some accommodation with them? That I shall do – at least until we are stronger again, and united.'

Kunrad blinked suspiciously. 'Funny kind of sothran you are. Alais doesn't even believe there's mind behind the Ice; or at least she isn't sure. She's half inclined to laugh, and it's obvious that's how most of your folk think. They don't know any better. You do, though – don't you?' And then he boiled over with sudden understanding, and sprang to his feet and shouted, 'That's why you turned north from Athalby! You were going to the bloody Ice all along! You, you're talking to them already!'

Horror seethed behind his eyes, and his stomach felt like chilled lead. He had heard evil tales of men who had dared to confront the Powers of the Ice. And after that coldly murderous dusk in that far valley, he found believing them no trouble at all. Merthian turned away sharply, and stalked down to the water. The lake seemed to be more disturbed; thin foam washed back and forth along the bars, and big bubbles rose and burst. Kunrad stiffened, and his fists clenched at his side. As before, Merthian wore a well-worn sword-hanger on his belt, but neither blade nor scabbard. A display of courage, or of caution? In case Kunrad should overpower him and seize them? He still might manage to tip Merthian into the water, hold his head under, maybe. But he would still be locked in, at the mercy of the guards; and by now he was unsure of his strength.

The Warden peered absent-mindedly at the bubbles for a moment and when he turned back his voice was calm and conciliatory again. He looked up at the spyhole before he answered. 'Yes. Yes, though I would not say it to many beyond this door, I have. To talk, that was all. To consult a few among them who are not as hostile to mankind as most, who do not return its indiscriminate hatred, who might be willing to compromise, if we can make it possible for them. It was their world first, remember, before ever life stirred upon its crust. Life displaced them, and they fight only to regain what was their own.' He gave a slight laugh. 'They know little of humans, in some ways. They actually counselled me to seize you yourself, as well as your armour, to have your skills to hand. I told them that would be too dishonourable, and it struck them greatly that humans had any notion of honour. Perhaps that helped to bridge a gap, who can tell? But one must always try.'

He looked at Kunrad, and there was something different in his eye now. 'And here you are, Mastersmith, in any case; and what am I to do with you? Again I ask you – I beg you! Lend me your mind, your skills, and I will tax them to their utmost, challenge you, exhaust you – and reward you a thousandfold! Kunrad, they were right, in their way, those voices of the Ice. I should have engaged you at our first meeting, I should have asked only for the use of that armour, have offered to leave it as your property for ever. To pay you and your boys for the use of it and to work all you wished upon it, if only I could wear it meanwhile.' He laughed. 'I would have been your trial-piece! But I was not so sure of you then as I am now. I will be, still. I make you this offer now, along with all else. And I bitterly regret I did not make it then!'

Kunrad smiled slowly. 'I do not, Merthian. Or I might well have accepted! Not now.'

He stretched his shoulders beneath that bleak roof, clinking the loose chains, and in a strange way he felt free. 'You talk of compromise. You compromise too easily already, with honesty for the sake of expediency, with common sense for the sake of ambition. You might have been a good ruler, but you never will be, not now. You're too ready to let today go to ruin for the sake of some brighter tomorrow. And you are ten times over a fool, that you are so ready to meddle with the Ice. You have lived too far from it, sothran. You cannot judge it, as you can a man. It is one voice and many, it is a mind not ruled by human constraints. You cannot treat with it, or temporise, or trust any single word that comes from it, whatever the mouth that shapes it. It looks to a struggle that lasts beyond lives, beyond generations; why should it make peace with one? Only one outcome will satisfy it, in the long run; and its voices will agree only to what will advance that, eventually. Even to us in the North it was no more than a sleeping menace; but at least we knew!'

Kunrad was ready for Merthian to fly into a rage; but he seemed no worse than exasperated and earnest. 'I beg you, smith, don't be so ready to judge! Maybe I know more of the Ice than you think! But for now, you *will* work for me, and that's it, long and short. I could hardly let you go, after all, to draw attention to me. Still less now I have told you so much.'

'I wondered why you were so free. I expected you meant to kill me.'

Merthian shook his head, horrified. 'As soon shatter a priceless artwork! No, smith. But then what am I to do? If you won't earn, I cannot very well feed you. You won't die of thirst in here, with the lake water to serve you for drink and –' he paused delicately – 'bodily needs. And before you can starve to death, my plans should have advanced so far your knowledge cannot stop them; and I shall have some leisure to review your case. You will, however, have a needlessly uncomfortable time, lose the chance of honours you truly deserve. And, if matters should take too long, and I am kept unable to attend to your case . . .' There was a moment's silence, broken only by the bubbling note of the wavelets. Merthian glanced down at the pool a moment, puzzled, then swiftly back to Kunrad, who might have been about to step between him and the door.

'Well, the decision is yours. I shall be busy now, and must leave you alone to your brooding. Call the guard if you have anything more to say to me.'

The door slammed. Kunrad heard it with a great feeling of relief. He watched the door carefully, but the spyhole did not reopen. He squatted down by the water, watching the play of light. He brooded indeed; but it was on how far wrong a man may go, even on the best of intentions. All Merthian said about being the only possible candidate for kingship might even be true – probably was. A manner commanding yet genial, courage, strength, clear wits, a fair and open face – oh yes, no wonder the wretched girl was so besotted with him! No wonder Kunrad had warmed to the man himself, on first acquaintance. Yet this fine fellow found it possible to threaten a man with slow starvation, simply to command his services. He would see that as he had seen all the rest, a brief regrettable diversion from a long straight road. He did not understand that this was the result of an earlier straying, and that from this still another would spring, until the road itself was forever lost to view. Many a well-meaning ruler had begun so, only to find himself at the end a helpless tyrant trapped between retribution and still greater outrage. Merthian managed to turn his very virtue back upon itself, to serve a base end.

And Merthian had been talking to the Ice, to some of the Powers that ruled it. How that had come about Kunrad could not imagine. What had been said, and how much truth there was in it, he could not guess. But when he turned the force of his mind upon it, one thing he saw for sure. The Ice was nowhere near the South, save perhaps in the impotent snows of the mountain-summits. It had few meeting-points with men, at all. So whatever was supposed to happen, would happen in the North. Where Merthian's word counted for nothing – now. But later? That was what must lie behind his talk of uniting the peoples. Whatever he hoped to achieve with the Ice, wisdom or folly, he would have to control the Northlands to do it.

But then, thought Kunrad, what was meaningful to the Ice? There was no tribute one could make, no damages one could exact. It had no cause of strife with man or beast or tree save one, and that was existence itself. So what accommodation could it possibly reach with anyone, even if it wished to?

There was only one ground, whatever its terms. It was human settlement the Ice hated, the bright fires that sprang up in the dark night, that drove off the chill and stayed defiantly alive where all else must bow to the walls of Winter, or perish. Vayde had brought the fires, and with his awesome powers had cleared the Northern lands of their terrors and settled men at the very feet of their foes. What the Ice would demand, implicitly or openly, must be an end to that – the emptying of settled land, the withdrawing of men beyond their cold sight. There was nothing the South could offer them, no wealth, no wine, no wise books or rich pastures. Merthian was planning to buy the Ice's favour with the lands of the North.

The thought set outraged flame in Kunrad's blood. There might be some selfish logic in such a compromise, for the South. They might demand something major in return – the clearing of the Great Marshes, perhaps, so that they could be drained for cultivation. That would suit the new king! He would become the lord of a vast realm, one that could even take in the ousted Northerners – upon terms, no doubt, of labour and duty to their new overlords. And the redheads would applaud him for it! But logic or not, it was an enormous gamble; and Merthian had taken care to gamble with what did not belong to him. What if those lands were lost for nothing, and no Vayde to settle them anew? Still it was only the North.

Kunrad drew breath, though the air had an evil tinge to it. He felt his cheeks flaming. He was going too far, perhaps; on slender evidence. The trouble was, it fitted what he knew only too well. He looked again at the seething water. The foam was spreading now, washing in under the wall. He went impatiently back to his blanket. He had been ready to murder Merthian there, though it cost his own life. He was almost sorry he had not, now. Still, there were the prentices to think of. And he would thwart him yet.

Light Airs, Dark Waters

He woke again, swiftly. It was no hand on his shoulder this time, and it was dark. In his weakened state he had slept the day away. But something had awoken him. He sat, ignoring the rushing sensation in his head; the mushrooms were a long-forgotten feast, and he had little interest in food. He looked around, but everything was dark; even the line of the slot was a darker blue, as if the moon was behind clouds, and the bars stood out only as strange-looking shadows. He rubbed his eyes. His head felt heavy, and somebody seemed to have been sitting on his chest, but the strangeness wasn't merely a trick of the light. He had a hank or two of straw left, and he kindled fire on the stone again, lit them and held them high to see more clearly.

He very nearly never saw anything again. Only the fact that he rose a little stiffly, so his arm went high above his eyes, saved his sight. Above his head the entire sloping rock-vault seemed to light with one great flaring cough, not loud or destructive, but a blast of flame that rolled across the roof right down to the wall and down, with a force that blew the lake-wash backwards out of the slot. Kunrad fell flat on his face, only to be drenched by the incoming wave as the lake reasserted itself and washed almost to the door. That, as he realised a moment later, put out the small flames smouldering in his jerkin and hair, and woke him up with a vengeance.

He wasted a precious moment damning himself for his stupidity; then he realised that he must have been growing thick-headed with the bad airs already. The light airs wandering, as the words put it, had had nowhere to escape to, and built up beneath the roof. He listened, but the soft flare had not attracted any attention. The question was, had it done anything else? Only one way to find out, Kunrad reminded himself. Swiftly, while he was still drenched, the Mastersmith stepped into the still-slapping water and squatted down with a painful whimper. He tugged at the bars. It was like grasping at an illusion. They were still there, solid as ever at water level; but what he felt in his hands was more like thin irregular sticks of rough coral, pitted and crumbling. He knew then that he had done what he hoped; he had turned the virtues that guarded against rust back upon themselves. These, properly imbued into the metal, could prevent the interaction of substances that created rust. But where rust was already, with the right admixture of other substances, phosphoric corrosives among them, they could also throw it off, and alter the very rusting process itself to form a protective surface. In salt water, such as he had briefly created, this was particularly powerful; but the salt had been washed away almost at once, and there were none of the other substances needed. Rust formed, and was crumbled away, for no coating took its place over the bare metal beneath; and so there was more rust, and always more, a process that had only one end. But had it gone far enough?

He heaved, and almost fell over in the shallows as the bars bent and shattered in his fingers. Another two went the same way, and he had a gap the width of his shoulders. Excitedly he plucked two more away like dry twigs, not noticing till he saw the faint bloom in the water that he was cutting his fingers. Even being more careful he broke loose the three remaining in a moment. He looked around quickly. He was wet already; there was nothing to go back for. He ducked, shivered with sudden hunger, then took a deep breath and plunged his head beneath the surface.

Kunrad did not like being under water, especially his face. He had not mastered the knack of keeping air in his nostrils to balance the water, and he winced as they flooded. The slot was narrow for any man, let alone of his size, and there were still stumps of bar sticking up. He kicked one of the rotten teeth loose, tore another, squeezed mightily, stuck, panicked, almost breathed in but had the sense to breathe out, flattening his chest. Suddenly he was sliding over slimy stone – and through.

He was drifting upward. Was this what being born was like?

Light Airs, Dark Waters

Laughing and coughing, he broke surface, and the wind-swell gently lifted him and banged his head against the rock. The stars wheeled above him as he clung, scrabbling for a hold on the sloping layers of rock. He was free! Dazed, but free.

The next realisation, though, was instantly sobering. He was in the middle of a very deep lake, with black gulfs beneath him. And Kunrad could not swim.

Northland rivers were seldom icier than those around Kunrad's town, where they ran mountain meltwater and sometimes that of the Ice itself. Most children never learned to swim properly. Gille had, apparently because he had found it a good way to sneak up on girls; and Olvar, brought up on the warmer coast, swam before he could walk. Kunrad, heavily built and with little buoyancy, had never learned to do more than dabble about in the shallows.

He looked down anxiously. The water was warmer here, but weakened and weary as he was, he would have been in trouble if he were not a Northerner. The manacles were bands of ice around his wrists. The rocks he struggled to hold on to sloped away steeply into unknown depths. He had just enough buoyancy to be bounced by every ripple. And there was a current trying to pull him loose. Above him, against the shifting moonlight, the rocks went nowhere, a mere outcrop against the castle wall. Some way beyond them he could just make out the bridge, as he had expected. He had hoped to cross beneath it, hand over hand if need be; but it was folded back. No matter; he could hide beneath, and wait. Only now, with the current, and without better handholds, he did not think he could reach it. Behind him, at the other side of the slot, the rock might be a little easier. He had no choice. He reached out, caught the bar stumps once again and let the current swing him along.

He hit the rock harder than he expected, scrabbled for holds and got them, for a moment, on rock high and dry overhead. The current pulled him loose before he could heave himself out. He was swung around the point, over scraping rock edges, managed to catch himself on one and swing into the shelter of the other side. The eddy there was almost as powerful, but it sent him bobbing and gasping along the wall, where deep growths of weed and slime broke his handholds, but shielded him against the bruising blows. Slowly, painfully, fighting for every hold, keeping low so that water welled into his nose and mouth, he worked his way along. He found only more shallow outcrops, nothing large enough even to stand on. The mighty masonry above was cut so close that not even weeds could gain a footing in the seams, let alone Kunrad's numbed and puffy fingers. It was all obviously deliberate. No siege engine could approach this place; even siege ladders and grapnels would have to be mounted from a boat, and be horribly vulnerable. The water whirled him under the shadow of a tower; soon he would be flung out the other side, into the current again.

Then, looking up, he felt a faint thrill. In the corner between wall and tower there was a buttress leading down into the water; it looked newer than the rest, and ill situated, spoiling the smoothness of the line. He pulled himself closer, and saw why. The faint moonlight revealed brickwork rather than stone, crumbling in patches. Within them he saw exposed pipework – running down either side, concealed by the bricks.

Again, he had no choice. He swung himself over to its base, clutched the coarse mortar with his fingertips, secured a better foothold and heaved himself free of the water's grasp. His weight returned, and he hung there a moment, dripping, before he was able to reach for the brickwork above, and clamber slowly up. After the deadly whirl of the water it seemed almost comfortable. From where he hung he could make out the pipes above the buttress, running parallel straight up the tower's flank and painted to match it, entering it below high windows that gleamed warmly in the night – real leaded windows, not arrowslots, on this side

Light Airs, Dark Waters

away from shore. By the look of the scars in the masonry they were later additions, luxuries for living quarters, no doubt. The pipes, too, probably, a device for raising water by handpump, and flushing it away down the other pipe, into the current presumably; he had heard of such things. In emergency the upper pipes could be knocked loose in a moment, providing no purchase for any invader; but it looked as if they would bear his weight. He might just be able to jump on to the wall; from there he might just be able to slink around to the gate or the bridge, somehow. It was not an alluring prospect, but it was better than the depths below.

It was no easy climb, nonetheless. The constant wind dried him a little, but also chilled him. Gaps and broken bricks gave him handholds, but cracked or crumbled all too easily, sending little showers of debris down into the water. Once or twice he almost went with them. The pipes were little better; he felt their soldered seams giving under his fingers. Fortunately there was nothing in them just then, but he swore at sothran smithcraft. And the higher he got, the more hopeless it looked. Whoever built the buttress had not been that careless. The rounded flank of the tower made a leap to the wall-head unthinkable. He could only keep on going up. The windows might serve, if he could only hold on for so long.

There was a window ledge of sorts, little more than a hand's breadth deep, and sloping. The pipes vanished into the stonework a few feet below. With his feet wedged as firmly as he could between them, Kunrad leaned out, clamped his hands on the ledge and peered at the near window. It was an ornate wooden casement set with little leaded lozenges of glass. There was no light behind them, and the frame seemed to be locked. Cursing, Kunrad thought of knocking the glass in with a manacle. He reached up, stretched too far and his foot slipped. He swung into emptiness, supported by one hand and one foot, neither too secure, looking down into the face of the dim moon dancing over the lake far below.

He could not even scream. He was more than ten times his own height in the air, his other hand was slipping, and not even when his father took him prospecting in the mountains had he ever looked into a deeper gulf. Angrily he grabbed at the ledge again and pulled himself upright, taking a second to risk wiping his palms dry. He could not make out the other window; but as he pulled himself around the ledge from one side of the pipes to the other he saw the casement was open a little, and that yellow light flickered on the panes. He felt faint with exhaustion and relief. Again, no choices – and probably only one try. He lashed out a hand, and felt the other slip, even as his fingers clamped over the firm edge of a sill. He knocked the casement wide, grabbed with his other hand and hauled himself up as his feet skidded off the pipes. A brief impression of light and colour met his eyes as he jackknifed over the sill, caught his balance and sat up, with one leg still out on the ledge.

It was a bedroom, richly adorned with hangings of many colours that took the light and seemed to blaze. The bed in the centre was huge, and richly carven. And on the end of it, frozen in the act of climbing in, was the Lady Alais.

She was wearing a light robe of something sky-blue and shiny over a nightgown trimmed with fine lace. What he could see of it suggested there was more lace than gown. To Kunrad's great surprise she did not scream. She simply sat there looking at him. He looked back.

'Well,' she said at last, 'since you don't have a rose in your teeth . . .'

'If I had, I'd eat it.'

She sighed in a businesslike way. 'Definitely not a romantic call, then. You look too scruffy, anyhow. Can't care for your clothes, that's clear. Why so hungry, anyhow? Is the cooking not what a sensitive Northerner's used to? Too much oil and garlic?'

Kunrad shut his eyes briefly. 'I'll tell you when I've tried it. For the last three days I've had nothing but the hospitality of your nice fresh lake.'

Her expression changed. 'What are you talking about?'

'A dungeon, and nothing to eat is what I'm talking about. Except helpings of cold tongue pie from your beloved Merthian.'

'Oh.' For the first time she looked away. 'Well, young man, you will be letting your mouth off the reins, won't you? You and your silly rant about stealing!' She chuckled. 'But you must have said something pretty potent! He doesn't usually react so harshly, even to insults. Would I'd been a fly on the wall, to hear—'

Kunrad slid down from the sill, dripping all over an elaborate window-seat figured with quails. He felt curiously safe and at peace. 'He didn't give me a chance to say anything. I've been in fetters since the door closed behind you.'

Colour flared in her cheeks, then drained away. She sat there an instant, then sprang up, almost tripping on the long robe, and strode into the corner. On a low chest stood a covered tray, which she snatched up and held out to him. 'It's just chicken and bread and wine,' she said, with an almost defiant note in her voice. 'I never eat it, but they always leave it anyway. Probably so they can polish it off themselves later, on the sly. When I'm chatelaine here we'll have that sort of thing given to the poor.'

'Huh!' said Kunrad. 'Better it isn't taken from them in the first place . . .' But then the smell of the chicken struck him, and he took off the lid with over-elaborate care, afraid he would worry the meat like a dog. It was a large bird, and he cut himself a slice of breast with the knife that lay there. He noted how sharp it was, but somehow he could not bring himself to believe he would need it.

'What do you mean, taken from . . .' She gave an exasperated sigh. 'Oh, I see. I swear you're obsessed with that kind of thing. Typical Northerner! They pay taxes up there, don't they? Even if it is in salt herrings or something! Well, it's the same down here. Nobody pays more than they can afford – at least,' she added with a slight toss of the hair, 'mostly – and they get fair value for it.'

Kunrad's temper had not been improved by the last three days, and still less by the last hour. Mentally his Northern heels dug in. 'Oh aye! Tower rooms, private plumbing, servants chasing each other up and down all those stairs, chicken on a silver tray—' The smith was arguing with his mouth full. He nearly choked at the noise from the sill.

'Defence, justice, a place in the commonwealth, a secure life from cradle to grave—' she broke off with a startled squeak. Kunrad barely shifted in time, clutching the chicken in an iron grasp, as the bulk crashed down where he had been sitting a moment before, and slid to the floor.

'Heard someone arguing,' said a breathless voice at the casement, 'so we decided you had to be in here.'

'*Gille?*' squeaked Alais.

'Uh – 'lo, m'lady!' said the heap on the floor, trying to knuckle his forelock. 'Saw your signal, Mastersmith . . . Hey, is that chicken?'

'Eh?' was all Kunrad could manage.

'The flare, right?' demanded Gille, swinging one well-shaped but waterlogged leg in. 'We were keeping cavey from the hill-top opposite, but we'd no idea where you might be till then. Knew that must be you all right, so we swam over to try and get you out, but then we saw you were out already and shinning up the drain. Couldn't call out of course, so we followed. That flare –' he shook his head, spraying Kunrad with more lake water ' – Master, that was fine thinking. How on earth did you manage it?'

Kunrad made an impressively mystical gesture with the chicken. 'Oh – well – a flash of inspiration,' he said modestly. 'Tell you all about it sometime – er, want some chicken?'

'Shall I send for some more?' inquired Alais sweetly. 'And maybe some wine and sweetmeats, since we're holding festival in my bedchamber? Or should I just call out the guard?'

'Don't suppose you could manage a steak while

you're about it?' mumbled Olvar, from the belly of the chicken.

'Well, yes, you could call the guard,' admitted Kunrad, absent-mindedly cuffing Olvar about the ear, and retrieving the remains. 'Except that you could have done that the moment I appeared, my lady, instead of wasting your true love's chicken. I have a better suggestion. Why don't you escort us out of here?'

She stared. 'And just why on earth should I?'

She flinched at Kunrad's stony look. 'Because your light-o'-love tells me that if I don't swink for him, I'll be left to starve. Until, that is, he's got his honourable paws on the whole of the South *and* Northlands. If that takes him a little too long, too bad for me. Oh yes, and I'm to throw in that armour, the damages and all else, against his note – falling due on your joint enthronement. Or thereafter.'

For a beautiful young woman, she looked momentarily very much like a chicken herself. 'My – what in Amicac's name are you *talking* about?'

'Not me. He's been doing all the talking. And he's *your* sweetheart. You may be a part of this if you will, but let us out of it. And, my lady, if I'm not wrong about you, you will.'

'If . . .' She had turned very pale, her breasts heaved in a manner Kunrad found mildly distracting, but she said nothing more. Nor, as he noted, did she call out the guard. He could almost see the fierce struggle going on beneath, like the currents swirling beneath the black lake water, and he admired and pitied her for that. Many women would have made less of an effort, and taken the easier path.

'My lady,' he said, more gently. 'All I ask is that you take us to the gate, next time you go out—' he hesitated. He had seen her look change. 'You do go out, don't you?'

'Oh yes!' She threw it away lightly, but the hair on his neck bristled. 'Any time, at my pleasure – only, well, there's been no reason to go. Everything's in here. And, well, you wouldn't expect them to let me go without an escort, would you?'

'Well, you've got your own, haven't you? Old Ferlias would do anything for—'

She shook her head, looking more troubled by the moment. 'He's gone. They were my father's men, they went back to him yesterday. Kunrad, I'm alone here.'

He thought that a strange way to put it, but he smiled. 'Surely you've still got your old Nanny, at least?'

She smiled affectionately. 'Well, yes, she's always here. But didn't you know? She's not my old nurse, she's Merthian's. Though she often looked after us both as children, so naturally he sent her to escort me here.'

Kunrad nodded. 'You said you'd known Merthian all your life. It can't be easy to believe unpleasant things about him. I find it hard myself. Even he seems to; but it doesn't stop him.'

The girl looked up sharply, and he thought he had lost. But her face appeared flushed and hunted. 'That . . . No. Not if he genuinely believed it was for the best. I can't imagine anything stopping him, then. He's so strong, so dedicated. Not like me; I've never found anything to believe in that strongly, that clearly. It was one of the things I liked . . . like about him.'

Even Olvar looked up at that, and at Kunrad. Kunrad looked back. Olvar flinched and subsided, Gille hunched up and gnawed at a chicken wing. Kunrad relaxed his frown. 'Well, the old woman's loyalty will be to him, then. And it seems you're as much a prisoner as I was.'

'I am not!' she spat at him, and bounced off the bed. 'A fine bold courtesy you have in you! The cheek of the man, to say that a lady of the Kermorvannen is held prisoner! He just wishes to protect me, that's all! Still thinks of me as half a child, maybe!'

'*The Maiden in the Tower!*' chipped in Gille, mockingly. It was the name of an old romance, and it was evidently known in the Southlands also, because she flushed scarlet this time.

'Gille, how dare you!' she snapped. '*I'm* not being forced into wedlock like that stupid simpering girlie.

I'd like to see anyone try!'

'But you have felt imprisoned,' Kunrad persisted softly. 'Haven't you, my lady?'

She shut her eyes and pursed her mouth angrily. 'By the idea of wedlock, aye, just maybe! Do you expect me to be proud of that? It's what I've dreamed of since I was a little girl, only—'

'Only you wish it might not come so soon,' said Kunrad. 'As you said on the road.'

Her eyes met his; and for a moment they were back in the sunlit glades, in the easy companionship of the road. She snorted in sudden outrage. 'You should be free! He should never have penned you like a beast, not after the corsairs did as much. And I'll tell him so to his face!' She gave a sudden half-giggle, half-tremor. 'I can't wait to see it! After I've got you all out and away!'

She whirled around, threw off her outer robe and went bounding barefoot across the bed to the far side. Gille's eyes bulged. She flung back the hangings and threw open the small door they revealed, to a chamber that appeared to be lined with chests and robes on tall racks. A strong scent of herbs and aromatics drifted out. Kunrad recognised the odours of cedar and bay oils traders had brought back from the South, and wondered if there were whole sun-warmed forests that smelt like that. 'Now where has Nanny put – ah!'

The lace nightgown came flying out of the door in a shameful ball, to crumple across the bed. A flash of pink crossed and recrossed the open door, and Kunrad gulped. A sudden ripple of heat washed the lake-chill out of him and set his cheeks aflame, and he hastily twisted the prentices' heads away.

'Owww!' protested Gille softly. 'How 'bout you, *master?*'

Kunrad scorned to answer, sitting there rigid as a steel rod. He had seen a fair number of women naked, even some he had found deeply attractive; but there were aspects of creamy skin, freckles and rich red hair that had never entered his imagination, not to mention unusually lithe and healthy limbs, and he would have a hard time getting rid of them now. He hastily unhanded the squirming prentices as she thrust a dishevelled head around the door, holding a garment to her front and leaving her shoulders bare. 'I'll take you down this minute! Soon, anyway! There's a lot going on down there, and they've had the bridge open once already this afternoon; that usually means it'll open again. They don't know you've escaped yet, clearly, or the place would be in an uproar. May assume you've swum ashore, probably. But then they may not, either. So, best we move swiftly! Get you out on some pretext—' She snapped her fingers. 'In the gold! We'll hide you!'

She whirled around, giving Kunrad a glimpse of some kind of brown riding breeches, and nothing above them but hair cascading down between bare silky shoulder blades. He hoped she would take a little longer than a second. By then he might be safe to stand up.

She stormed out of her dressing chamber without even looking at them, clad in a shapeless brown tunic, tucking her hair into a loose woollen hood. It shadowed her face and made her surprisingly hard to recognise. 'Wait here!' she rapped out. 'I'll be a while!' But as she reached the door she turned to look at them again, weighing up all three from head to toe with an unnerving intensity. 'I'm going to get you some brave disguises!'

The door seemed about to slam, but closed quietly, and then reopened again. 'If anyone should knock, out the window, understand? *Not* under the bed or anything witty. I'm compromised enough as it is!'

The door clicked to again. Olvar paid her the ultimate tribute by putting down the last shreds of the chicken carcass, and swallowing. 'Some wild little biddy, is that one!'

'Can we trust her?' muttered Gille. 'After the last time? Little bitch! We nearly went into the bag with you.'

Kunrad cuffed him on the back of the head, but very gently. 'I was never more glad than when I saw those empty saddles. That was quick thinking. As to trusting her, who else exactly had you in mind?'

'We could get you back across that pond,' said Olvar. 'No problem. Smooth as seal's milk out there.'

'No,' said Kunrad. 'Getting down those pipes would be a lot worse than getting up. And we'd most likely be seen. You could dive, but not supporting me.'

'Who needs you to dive?' demanded Olvar cheerfully. 'Just let you sink a bit.'

Kunrad shivered. The room was warm, but he could still feel the lake-chill. 'No. Not unless there's no other way. We'll trust her. She's a determined one, this, and she keeps her word – after a fashion.'

'Hella take fashion,' said Gille, with surprising grimness. 'Let's see how she keeps it now.'

It was almost an hour before she returned. Gille was biting his nails and looking to the window, although Kunrad pointed out she would have betrayed them at once, if at all. 'Maybe, but I don't trust this one. Who knows what folly she's cooking up now?'

'Something new,' grunted Olvar. 'Skirt Gille doesn't take to.'

'I know 'em,' said the young man sullenly. 'Jokers. Teases. They want to see yours, run screaming to Mummy when you show 'em. Get you to climb in their bedroom window, only it's Grandma's, and Grandma still chops down trees. Lure you into the woods where their real fancyman's waiting with a big stick. Get you by the—'

Kunrad and Olvar were holding their sides. 'No idea you lived so dangerously, lad! These are the ones you don't boast about, eh?'

'They're the ones I've learned to avoid. You want this bit of fluff, Mastersmith, you have her, and the Powers protect you!'

Kunrad stared. '*I* want?'

The door opened. A bulky bundle swayed in, with two slender arms around it, and fell heavily on the bed. Alais straightened up from the pile, face scarlet, hair straggled, heaving for breath and grinning like a puppy. 'Got them!' she wheezed, as Kunrad sprang to shut the door.

'Guard uniforms, mail, leggings, surcoats, the lot. One long cloak to wrap 'em in. Your sizes, close enough. Chose lightest mail. Fit over those black things you wear. Boots, too, though I can't guarantee the fit. Swords, as well.'

Kunrad hefted a mailshirt. 'Northern work – my old friend Galdred's worst, in fact! Or you'd never have managed to carry four. I'm still impressed. A princess with thews! But where'd you get them?'

She puffed. 'My father couldn't afford a teacher for me. Wouldn't send me to common school, and he was right, too; they'd have run me ragged. Taught me himself, like a boy. Said I did better than my big brothers. Only when Nanny took me in hand . . . Oh, you mean the hauberks? Out of a storeroom.'

'Fine,' said Kunrad, who had had visions of four naked guards cowering in a corner somewhere. Then he thought again. 'Our sizes? You had a good choice, then – there were a lot of armours there?'

'Woof, thousands!' laughed the girl. 'No idea he'd need so many . . . Oh.'

'He's been building up his stocks,' said Kunrad, as he and the prentices sorted out their gear. 'Wonder why, don't you? And the men to fill them – where'll he get those . . .' He broke off. The girl was unfolding the fourth mailshirt. 'I thought you brought that as a spare ! You're not—'

'My father,' she said. 'You've made me sure now. Not convinced me, but – I want to get word to him about this idea of yours. You may be lying in your teeth, or Merthian's playing little tricks, but – well, this could be dangerous, and I'm taking no chances. If anyone's going to be kings in this land, it'll be the rightful lords of Morvan!' For a moment her mouth was a pale twisted line; then she relaxed. 'Not that he can do much, poor old dear, but my brothers are officials under the Chief Syndic, that cold salt stockfish Bryheren. He can at least get word to them.'

'Look,' protested Kunrad helplessly, 'we can manage so much, you need never do a thing. Give us directions, and you can sit here safe and, and—'

'Marry Merthian? Yes.'

'Well, you were concerned about working against him!'

'If he's innocent, I'll saw your head off myself! If . . . there's some other explanation for all those weapons and uniforms . . . oh, I don't know! I don't! But I've got to!' She saw the sympathy in his eyes, and stiffened. 'There's no other way to be sure, and I won't have any argument about it! I know the way across country to my father's, better than most. All the shortcuts and safe paths! I can get you there ahead of any hunt.'

Kunrad gestured to her writing table. 'Take a moment to write down the directions, anyhow. Just in case.'

She nodded, and quickly pulled the mailshirt over her head.

'How do I look?' said Kunrad, buckling his belt, while she was still scratching away with a silvered quill. 'Feels well fitted, my lady . . .'

The prentices, settling their mail over their own clothes, stared. 'You'd look fine if you hadn't put that bloody sheep on!' said Gille.

'Well, what'm I supposed to do with it?'

'Tell him, somebody!' said Olvar despondently.

'Try rolling it up at your belt – no, you'd be arrested for sheep-stealing. Or worse. On your back, like a pack? No, don't think they hire many snowtrolls down here – though I wouldn't put it past Merthian. Sorry, lady. Look, master, put it back on, unlaced, and drape the cloak over it, so . . .'

They surveyed the result. Alais stifled a giggle. 'A touch monstrous,' admitted Gille. 'Still trollish about the shoulders. But they had some awful thugs in the courtyard here. I suppose you'll do.'

'At least it's dark,' agreed Alais.

Four guards, two of them huge and two somewhat undersized, strolled confidently down the lower steps of the tower; or did their best to. Kunrad was luxuriating in new boots that fitted him better than his own battered pair. Olvar's sword was sticking in his scabbard, and he kept fidgeting to find the maker's mark. Gille was still eyeing Alais suspiciously, and doing his best not to bite his nails. Alais was doing her best to copy their walks. 'Glaiscav's arrows! Not like *that*!' hissed Kunrad. 'You're strutting like a randy pine-grouse! You walk like a man already, just open your stride a bit . . . that's better!'

'I do not walk like a man!' she smouldered. 'How would you know, anyway? You've hardly looked at a woman in your life!'

'Let me tell you—'

'*Shut up!*' hissed Gille. 'There's people down there! Our accents will give us away! Or Olvar's face!'

A door stood half open on to the battlements, and rather than plunge into the brightly lit hall below, they paced out with the heavy tread of bored guards. 'Shouldn't we keep in step?' hissed Gille.

Alais kicked him. 'No! They'll know there's no patrol listed. We're just lounging about off-duty, right? What you do naturally, remember?'

Gille glared. 'Now listen—'

Olvar's mailed fists knocked their helmets together, and he laughed raucously. After a moment Kunrad joined him, slapping him on the back. The watchers who had begun to notice them saw only skylarking soldiers, not afraid to draw attention to themselves, and turned away again.

Alais straightened her helmet, which had tipped over her eyes, and glared. Kunrad only grinned. 'Well done, Olvar! Stop looking so conspiratorial, everyone! There are more people about than I expected this late, princess.'

She leaned back on the battlements, looking at the wide courtyard below, and then turned to gaze out at the black lake and the softly mirrored moon. 'I love this aspect . . . Yes. That's unusual, I think. They're pulling stuff out of store and piling it up. Food, I guess, from the sacks. Preserved stuff.'

'Are they indeed?' grinned Kunrad. 'Well, I think we might give them a hand, don't you? Olvar, you'd better keep in the shadows—'

'No need, boss!' answered the big prentice. 'Three or four of those guys down there are Northerner colour, see? And there's a couple more whiteskins I'd wager were Northern. Hark to the voices.'

Alais peered into the flickering torchlight. 'Why ... that's right. Recruiting Northerners? I've never heard of that, even here.' She rubbed a little dust from the wall across her face. 'There goes the princess. Let's lend that hand.'

The four guards lumbered cheerfully down among the lines of hurrying men, casually plucking the bags from their shoulders and heaving them on to the growing stacks. 'For wagons,' grunted Olvar, heaving a sack so hard it slid across the pile, and bending down to retrieve it.

'Why not load it straight, then?' argued Gille. 'Must be coming in from somewhere, and in a hurry too – ah, twice-baked bread in this one. Fresher than that corsair stuff.' He was stowing bags under his belt.

'I've got a couple of bags of salted smoke-meat,' said Kunrad, deftly turning over the sack he had slit.

'Sausages,' contributed Alais. 'Nice big ones!'

'Well, lucky old you!' said Gille archly. 'More meat, in this. Must be enough here to stand a siege!'

'I wonder when they're going to take it away,' murmured Kunrad, heaving another sack on to the pile. 'That might be our chance. The gate-guards look alert enough, more's the pity. But sooner or later—'

His fingers clenched hard on the sacking. A trumpet sounded, harsh and cold, from the tower above, and others from the walls joined it in a jarring discord which seemed to echo across the lake.

'They're on to us, lady!' he hissed. 'Found me gone! There's no more you can do now! We'll need shift for ourselves, and best you get away!'

She shook her head. 'I'm safe enough, believe me. I'll stay as long as I can! Besides, I don't think you're right ...'

'*Hoi!*' blasted a voice behind them. 'You four beauties! Enough lounging around those sacks! To the gate, and snappy!'

They needed no excuse for jumping; the voice could only belong to a sergeant, and he sent blistering words after them as they scuttled to obey. 'Get your 'ands on that there winch! Can't be worse 'n where you keep 'em most times, can it now? Well, what're you waiting for? Mustn't keep our precious flamin' guests waitin'!'

To the side of the gate stood a huge and complex affair of wheels and capstans and counterweights, enough to make anyone hesitate. The fugitives gathered around it in momentary disarray, and Alais looked up at Kunrad in blank horror. 'Get on with it!' bellowed their tormentor, landing a blow with his stick across Olvar's huge shoulders. 'I dunno, we've got to put up with you half-trained bloody marshrats! The wheel, shithead – know what a wheel is? The one with little 'andles what you put your 'ands on like they showed you all—'

Anyone else might have been discovered then; but it was not a mechanism to baffle three smiths of Nordeney, still less a master. Before the sergeant finished his tirade Kunrad had already seen which way the wheel should turn, and how to slip the pawl that held it. He threw his weight on it, and Olvar after him, and the sergeant's tone changed as the others joined them. 'That's it! Got some thews on yer, that's something! Handsomely, now! We'll have that bridge across like spit off a stove! Maybe make a wager or two on you lads one day soon, what d'you say? Against the reg'lars, like?'

The wheel turned, the chains clanked, the counterweights descended, and a fine spray of black oil improved their disguises. Something seemed to be worrying Alais more than the labour. 'Marshrats,' she muttered. 'Regulars . . .'

'Cease hauling!' called the sergeant. 'Take a breather! You up there, gate open! Come on, jump to it!'

The fugitives leaned on the locked wheel, pretending

to pant. 'Heads down!' whispered Olvar. 'Enter the guests!'

'Not much ceremony about it!' whispered Alais as they heard the drum of hooves from the drawbridge, and the rumble of wagon-wheels. 'No flares, no flags – no Merthian, and he's such a stickler! And those were alarm trumpets. Curious . . . Who's this?'

Riders were coming into the gate, into the centre of the courtyard, and behind them the wagons, big crude-looking things drawn by heavy horses. The riders halted so suddenly that the wagons almost collided in the gate, and they heard the sergeant swearing fearfully as he ran to sort them out. 'Time to sling the hook, I think!' muttered Olvar delightedly. Then he froze as Kunrad's hand clamped down on his arm.

The riders were dismounting in the open square, under the dim light of the braziers that flanked the great door. It opened, and Merthian strode out, casually and without ceremony, with the sleepy-looking captain Erlan at his heels. Alais shrank behind Kunrad, though she was by now barely recognisable. The light flamed scarlet on the robe of the man who stepped up to meet Merthian, and on the jewels that spangled his body from his ears to his boots. The parchment face with its deep lines looked even sallower in the firelight.

'You know him?' hissed Alais. 'Who is that?'

Kunrad turned to her with a horrible weight on his heart. 'My lady . . . that's the chieftain of the corsairs, as I described him to you. None other.' He turned back, quickly, so he need not recognise the sound behind him. He felt sick himself.

'I'd never . . .' began Gille, and stopped, unable to form the words.

'It makes sense, as always,' whispered Kunrad. 'Fine sense, if you know no limits. All that well-made war-gear, and where the bodies to wear it? I thought he'd raise a force from his own loyal peasantry, or other lords, or something. But this way he'll have, what? Two thousand hardened fighters, not very well trained maybe but tough and rapacious. And desperate to get out of that marsh and that hole of a fortress.'

Gille ground his teeth. 'And we know now why that place looked so much like this one. They hadn't just seen it . . .'

The corsair chieftain halted on the lower step before Merthian, and bent his knee to the stone.

Merthian's voice cut across the silent courtyard. 'Well, sealord? To what do I owe this honour? I was expecting only your supply train. What brings you in person? Come to count the sacks or the mailsuits?'

The corsair rose uneasily. 'Hardly, my Lord Warden. Your generosity needs no accounting. No, I came to warn you of a danger to your, uh, precious person.'

The flattery seemed to stick on the chieftain's tongue. 'My lord, if we could consult in private . . .'

Merthian's auburn tresses shook slightly. 'By no means. Say what you have to before me and mine, openly.'

The chieftain clutched at his beard. 'Not long since, we took some handy prisoners, as we thought. Smiths of Nordeney. One of them claimed to have some grievance against you, my lord, but we left his head on his shoulders because we're in so dire a need of such craft, and he seemed of no common skill. We chained him in our deepest smithy and set him to work.'

Merthian nodded calmly. 'Very well. That does not concern me, then.'

The corsair winced. 'Except that . . . Lord Warden, he has escaped from us, by arcane means we could never have guarded against. Most probably they are lost in the Marshes, and he was scarcely a serious threat, anyhow. But nonetheless we thought it best to come and warn you in person . . .'

Merthian's nod was imperceptible. 'Of course. After, equally of course, wasting precious days, and no doubt precious lives, in fruitless searching – rather than admit such paramount stupidity to me. You locked up a Northern smith with iron? As soon douse a fire with twice-burnt wine! Hear this, my ambitious friend! This smith of yours did indeed escape the Marshes! But no thanks to you, I have him safe under my lock and my key, and they—' He stopped dead, expressionless. 'They, did you say?'

The corsair's face was expressionless in the gusty light. 'Why yes, Lord Warden. He had two boys who escaped with him. And two of those duergar vermin, who stole a boat, and—'

Merthian paid him no heed. 'Two! Lost in the Marshes, most likely, but—' He rounded on the captain with curt command. 'Go, man, see that the fellow's safe in his cell! I doubt it not, but – *run!*'

A guard clattered across to the side door, and Kunrad heard the word being passed down those echoing corridors, faster than any feet. The fugitives were penned in, unable to make a move away from the bridge winches without drawing attention. Kunrad looked for something to block the mechanism, but could see nothing save their swords; and those they might need. Then the voices began again, and the guard came running back. 'My Lord Warden! His door's locked and barred fast, but – the Northerner's gone!'

Merthian's face did not change, but he took a swift step forward as if to strike at something that was not there. The corsair stroked his beard with deliberate lack of expression. Another guard came rushing out. 'Lord Warden, Lord Warden! He's out into the lake! The bars have rotted away like old wood, and there's scuffings all over the wall's foot!'

'The bars have . . .' Merthian could hardly speak.

'Arcane means, as I said, Lord Warden,' intoned the corsair with grim satisfaction. 'It seems there is something to these old tales, after all; and you have a most powerful mage for your enemy!'

Merthian's face still showed no emotion. 'Well, if the signs are so fresh he must still be around here somewhere. Captain! Muster a search, from stone to tower-top—'

'My Lord Warden! My Lord Warden!' Kunrad heard Alais catch her breath.

'Yes, Nanny?' said Merthian, startled. 'What's the matter?'

'It's my dear Lady Alais! Her room's empty, the window open and all's soaking wet beneath! She's disappeared!'

Merthian's face suddenly darkened to the hue of the torchlight, and there was genuine horror in his voice. 'That sorceror! He's kidnapped her! Search, damn you all! Find her, find the Lady Alais! Every man jack of you, search!'

The same image appeared in everyone's mind, even Kunrad's; though he had to stifle an insane giggle. The girl sitting innocently by the window; the scrawny shape, dripping with weed, clinging inhumanly to the bare face of the tower, and reaching up a clawlike hand . . .

It seemed that all the imps of the Ice were let loose in the courtyard then, men milling and shouting, women screaming, horses whinnying. 'The gate!' roared somebody, starting a rush of guards to shift the wagons, others to the winches. In a moment it would close and shut the fugitives firmly in. It was then Gille had an inspiration, and began to shout, 'The shore! From the lake! Search the shore!'

His clear voice cut through the confusion, and others took it up, starting a rush out towards the gate. Kunrad shot one glance at the others and they ran to join it, barging and jostling through the narrow tunnel. Suddenly the drawbridge boomed beneath their feet, and the lake wind rushed into their faces. On to the pontoon bridge, its planks rocking beneath so many running treads; water rushed and gurgled at every step. From the wall overhead Merthian's clear voice carried. *'Find me them! Slay any intruders you find, but bring back the Lady Alais, whatever the cost! The man who harms her dies by my hand!'*

She stopped dead on the bridge a moment, turned back, looking up at the wall. Then Kunrad's hand jerked her round and she ran on as swiftly as before. He wondered if she was weeping, but in the dull moonlight he could not see.

Across the smaller islands and up on to the shore they ran, soldiers among the rest; but as the others fanned out they took their chance to slip in among the trees. 'Don't run!' gasped Kunrad. 'Look like the hunters, remember, not the quarry!' The others nodded, panting, and drew their swords, scouting around for the road. It was there; but soldiers were already lugging fallen trees across it to form a barrier, and shining lanterns on all who passed.

'Well-trained bunch!' said Kunrad. 'We must get past that first cordon somehow. Maybe we could strike over the hill that way, see if we could find a path . . .'

'No!' said Alais, puffing with the effort of keeping up in her heavy mailshirt. 'There's none clear enough. But there's one down yonder, through that stand of tall birches, an old drover's trail, I think. It goes up beside the streambed there, and northwestward to our first way through the pinewoods, about an hour on foot.' She giggled softly at the others' silence. 'I told you. I played here as a little girl, and rode and walked everywhere. Even when I wasn't supposed to. It's just like old times, this!'

'Somehow I believe you,' said Kunrad. They were already turning the way she chose, being careful to poke swords into clumps of bushes and peer around suspicious rocks, as if searching. The birches made an excellent landmark in the waning moonlight, and they passed swiftly by other little knots of searchers, who gave them no second glance. They came in among the birches, and saw the stream gleaming below them, emerging from its hillside notch in a series of small pools. The path ran across it, through a narrow ford just beyond the birches. They were passing through these, and had it in sight, when suddenly yellow lantern-light painted their outlines on the pale bark, and a harsh voice commanded them to halt. Six or seven men were trotting up the path, their manner anything but casual.

'No fooling this lot!' said Olvar tensely.

'Keep them guessing!' said Kunrad, and waved to them, and to the path.

'Hold you there!' came the reply. 'We'll see to that together – when I've got your names and numbers!'

'And won't he be surprised!' said Gille softly. The men were almost on them now, when by bad luck the bouncing light fell full on Alais. In the rush a great lock of her red hair had come free of her mailcap, and was straggling down her temple.

'Be damned!' shouted her leader. 'It's the princess! Take 'em boys, and watch those bloody wizards!' He charged on Kunrad, his heavy sword swinging. Kunrad's met it with a clang, threw the man back. He recovered instantly, slashed at Kunrad's head, then ducked under the parry to thrust at Kunrad's stomach. Barely in time Kunrad's sword came down and stretched him flat on the path. The others, armed with long spears, were less rash, trying to pin the fugitives in while they called for help. Alais slashed out, shattering a spear that jabbed at Kunrad, and sprang forward to wound its wielder in the arm. The soldiers held back, momentarily confused.

'Go!' she yelled at the others. 'Get word to . . . to him! I'll hold the way!'

'Don't be daft!' hissed Kunrad. 'Come on while we still can!'

'They'll hunt you!' she hissed. 'If you don't get a start! I'll be fine, they don't dare hurt me!' She sprang out of the trees again, smashed another spear, and the soldiers bunched nervously back. 'See? And Merthian neither, he needs me! You'll go faster cross-country without me! Go, fool, or they'll have us all!'

Lights and torches were coming across the slope, drawn by the noise; and, out on the lake, riders were cantering across the bridge.

'We can't leave her!' protested Gille.

'*Run!*' she screeched at them. '*Run for your lives, you stupid Nordeney bastards!*'

Kunrad looked at the others. His face was as blank as Merthian's. 'You heard her ladyship. She's right. *Run!*'

CHAPTER EIGHT
A Lord and a Lady

'YOU SEE 'EM NOW?' demanded Olvar

Kunrad, sprawled among berry bushes at the crest of the ridge, looked up from the ruddy pebbles he had been examining, lifting his head as high as he dared on what might be someone's skyline. Even the Shield-Range behind might not shadow him enough. 'I've not got your eyes, but . . . yes, I think so. By that big broken redwood, clambering down the far slope?'

'Slipping down it, you mean. There goes another now, arsy-versy into the thorns! Wouldn't waste skin that way if they knew about Alais's path, would they?'

Kunrad frowned, and spilled the pebbles. 'No. But they'll still know the lie of the land, probably. That would put them about a day behind us.'

'Maybe two,' suggested Gille. 'They can't know they're following anyone. That path we took could have led a dozen ways, and we covered our tracks. They're just searching. That'll slow them.'

Kunrad slid down, and sat unhappily, chin on hand. 'That's what worries me, boy. Merthian might know!'

Gille ducked down beside him. 'Hey, surely not! How would he find out . . . Oh, come, Mastersmith! He wouldn't hurt her!'

'Wouldn't dare!' added Olvar.

Kunrad sighed. 'I begin to think that bastard would do anything – *anything!* – if he felt it was important enough to his great mission. He has some kind of trick of thinking, something truly strange, a kind of dam in the head. All that passes through is the odd trickle of remorse, and he mops that up quick with apologies.'

Olvar laughed quietly. 'Then he goes right on pissing over the other side, you mean? Could be.' He plucked a berry off the bush, and chewed it. 'Not bad. Enough like our hedgeberries so I could risk it. But some of these bright green things might be all right, too. Wish I knew more Southland fruit.'

'Better be going,' grumbled Gille, 'if you don't want to be pushing it up. And keep an eye open for more of those fat ground birds. We've hardly any dried food left, and no fat to spare after the Marshes – and no woodcraft for these Suderney forests.'

Kunrad heaved himself to his feet, scratching under his mail. 'Shouldn't be long now. By Alais's directions we should hove in sight of the tower tonight or tomorrow morning, and then our problems will be at an end. One way or another.'

'Nice if we could sight a farm or two along the way,' sighed Olvar. 'Farms have chickens, or whatever the poor folk here raise instead.'

'Lizards, probably,' suggested Gille.

They had come a long way swiftly since leaving Alais in the wood. Kunrad had had trouble following his own command. More than once on that first slope he had practically to be dragged along because he kept stopping to look back. Olvar said he had seen Alais being set on a horse and led away, but Kunrad couldn't be sure he was telling the truth – and even if he was, what had awaited her? He knew well enough he could have done nothing more, but it stuck in his throat nonetheless, and he pressed on across country at a killing pace, the more so as he insisted they keep their cumbersome mailshirts. Alais's scribbled directions had got them through the land around the lake, which she evidently knew better than did Merthian's men, but out here in the wild land she could do no more than indicate paths and landmarks. And here there were searchers out.

'But if you're right, Gille,' mused Kunrad, as they scrambled down a thin sheep trail to the next ridge, 'and they are just searching, it can't be this region alone.

Merthian must be combing the whole country around!'

Olvar whistled. 'That'll take a mort of his men!'

'Maybe just the most likely places,' suggested Gille, then shook his head. 'No! Not him. We can bring his whole scheme down around his ears. He wants us, badly!'

'Just what I was thinking,' said Kunrad grimly. 'So he'll have to spread his searchers thinner, and that's to our advantage. If I read Alais's words aright, we'll be among the mountain-roots soon, and into the settled lands again; and we'll get ahead of them there also!'

So it proved; for beyond the next ridge a valley opened before them, wide green country carved by the mountain rivers and fed by them. In many places among the plain fabric of the trees, wide patchwork fields opened, and orderly orchards still splashed with colour, and on the lower mountain slopes the long yellowish scars of vineyards, in the fertile ashen soil belched up by ancient earthfires. On the far side of the vale the mountains thrust out another spur, its end raised like the head of a sleeping lion; and Kunrad breathed deep satisfaction, for Alais had drawn it as the last of her directions.

'There! Beyond that, on the far slopes, her father's castle stands. It will be our landmark among the trees, if only we can get beneath them unseen!'

'Provided they aren't already full of trackers!' snorted Gille.

'Dunno about that,' said Olvar soberly. 'Worst comes to worst, we could always eat one.'

Below them the slope was open and grassy, yellowing already in the early summer sun; but across it a trail ran like the thin trace of an old scar. Where other trails crossed it, the meeting point was marked by man-high stakes, most smeared with something black and greasy. Here and there rocks stood out among the grass, and as they came lower, so the country became stonier, the soil yellower and drier. To Northerners it seemed unnaturally hot; sweat poured down their necks and pooled at the base of their spines till their garments chafed and sagged. Stripping off their mailshirts helped little. Kunrad licked cracking lips, and did his best to think of nothing save the road, the end, the pursuit; but he was as glad as the prentices when eventually they saw a trail cross theirs ahead, leading down from the mountainside above to the valley floor. Hard by the crossroads a stand of gnarly trees promised shade, and beyond them four solid marker stakes stood among a circle of great stones.

'Might be a spring!' muttered Gille, and hurried on. A cloud of crows lifted with a startled rush. His wild yell brought the others running. Sweat blurred Kunrad's eyes as he approached. The stakes bore paint-splashed signboards, and . . .

He had little warning. The shrivelled forms dangling beneath the boards became suddenly and sickeningly recognisable. He stopped dead and swore, hoarsely. Olvar whistled, but the tone failed. 'What do those boards say?' he mumbled anxiously.

Kunrad's face was as stony as the soil. '*Vermin,*' he translated the crude characters. '*Keep out!*'

'But these are people!' protested Gille, in horrified fascination. 'Old people – or is it the sun . . . These bloody sothrans!' he burst out suddenly. 'What kind of folk . . .'

Kunrad shook his head. 'Look again, boy!'

'Why . . . So small . . . They're *duergar*!' He licked his dry lips and swallowed hard, as if forcing back vomit. 'All of them – Powers, that one's a woman. Isn't it? Strung out like this, and tarred, like rats or something . . . Scarecrows!' Then he went even paler than usual. 'Hey, you don't think . . .'

'No. Not ours. At least I hope not. With the men it's hard to tell; but she has – had white hair. They've all been here a while. And the teeth are worn . . .'

Olvar looked quickly away from the gaping grin. 'Take your word for it. Ilmarinen's arse! Those little buggers – wouldn't have blamed them if they'd just sunk us in the mire and left us.'

'They did, practically,' sighed Kunrad. 'Not much love lost on either side. But I think they may be a touch more civilised. I feel sick.'

A Lord and a Lady

'Me too,' said Gille faintly.

'We can't just leave 'em!' protested Olvar. They all followed his gaze, back to the hills.

'If we're going to do anything,' said Kunrad, 'it had better be damn quick.' But even as he spoke he was gingerly putting his hands to the nearest pole. It was dug shallowly into the hard red-brown soil, and stayed with stones; they tumbled, and it slowly sagged with its blackened occupant. Olvar toppled the rest, while Kunrad tried to cut the bodies free. Their tarry coating stuck them firmly to the poles, though; and in the end all the Northerners could do was drag them some way up the trail into a little crevice, and pile heavy stones around the end, like a cairn. The crows, balked of their food, circled overhead with protesting squawks. Gille could hardly bring himself to touch the poles; but when all was done he smashed a signboard to flinders on the cairn. Kunrad hurled the others away into the brush.

'There! That's the best we can do! Now, for the trees, and fast!'

As the cool wood-shadow closed over them at last, they paused, panting, and looked back. Even to Olvar's eyes there was no sign of any movement on all the barren slopes above. Only the crows still wheeled and croaked.

'We're still ahead, then!' said Kunrad with satisfaction. 'And our trail will be less easy to follow in here, even for hounds.'

'What's hound taste like, I wonder?' muttered Olvar.

The only dog they heard, though, was the tethered watchdog at one of the valley farms, who got wind of Gille as he went slithering up to the chicken run. By the time a shouting man appeared and loosed it, the Northerners were deep in the woods again and splashing down a small stream. The dog, and the man's great dung-fork, put some extra spring in their stride.

'I'm none too proud of this,' said Kunrad some time later, licking his fingers. 'These folk aren't rich. They look poorer than any Northern farmer with so much land.'

'Chalk it all up to Merthian's bill,' suggested Gille, gnawing at a drumstick. 'Pay 'em back two for one, when he coughs up for the armour.'

Kunrad shook his head. 'I don't know. This has all grown a lot larger than the armour now. And yet, yes, I've got to have it. That hasn't changed. You know I still dream about it?'

'Wonder if these sothrans live on chicken,' said Olvar placidly. 'Couldn't manage a shoat next time, could you, Gille me lad? What was that, boss – still dreaming about it? Not surprised. Bad grub makes you dream about anything.'

The next time Gille surpassed himself by stealing two loaves and a pie that stood cooling on a windowsill. Kunrad shrivelled with shame; but he also ate his share of pie. 'Poor people! Hardly richer than the last. Is it this red soil, or what?'

'Don't think so,' said Gille, whose family owned farmland. 'Good as ours for all I can see, though it's drier. Must be a long growing season, too. They don't work it so well; but maybe they've no cause to. Maybe any more they grow'd just be taxed.'

'Ours pay taxes. But I think you're right.'

'I'd like to do something for 'em,' rumbled Olvar.

'Better they do something for themselves,' was Kunrad's immediate response. 'It's the only way to learn. The way a baby walks – falling flat on its nose half the time. Still, I know what you mean. I'll repay them if I humanly can.'

Gille stretched out under a shady linden. 'You're doing something for them now. Keeping them from under the corsairs' thumb. And other bits.'

'True. And that means we'd best press on, and swiftly. If there is a pursuit, we're leaving a trail, and one that'll soon betray our destination. We could be there tomorrow morning, if we don't laze around under trees. Maybe even late tonight.'

So it was; and great haste they made. They skirted the foot of the tall ridge, and saw more of the dreadful posts around every crossroads on the slopes. The lonelier villages in these parts had guarded palisades, many new-looking, and it became hard to find food. Soon the woods themselves began to thin out, and they found themselves crossing large areas of streams and soft banks, the precursor to marshland. This was the extreme north of the Southlands, and little valued except for pride and as a natural barrier. That could have been guessed from the castle that overlooked it.

High on the farther flank of the spur it stood, a bleak, bare place, even to Northern eyes. In contrast to the Castle of the Winds, this was a single square tower, topped with a strong but crumbling battlement, an outer wall encircling a few outbuildings huddled around its foot. Its sentinels, too, looked battered and unimpressive, leaning against the wall in the late evening sun, staring at the newcomers without curiosity or concern.

'I feared they might have had word!' whispered Kunrad as they drew nearer. 'Seems I needn't have. I can't believe that girl grew up in this flyblown hole!'

'So we needn't have stopped to put these bloody mailshirts on?'

'I didn't say that! There's more than one kind of armour. Come on!'

Only one of the sentries stepped out to challenge them, but his spear trailed casually under his arm. 'What's your concern, soldiers—' He saw the surcoats, and hesitated. 'My Lord Warden's men, and afoot?'

'For speed's sake, overland!' rapped Kunrad truthfully, trying to sound as clipped and sothran as he could. 'There's trouble afoot! I bear an important message to Lord Kermorvan. Take me to him, please!'

'Trouble?' said the guard sharply. 'Not more of those bloody bastard corsairs?'

Kunrad's heart rejoiced. They seemed to know nothing of the plot. 'Could be,' he said grimly. 'But my word's for his lordship only. He's within?'

'Well . . . yes,' began the sentry slowly, 'but, well, s'not for me to say, but . . . All right! Porry, take these lads in t'see the Castellan! Announce 'em proper, remember – good an' loud!'

Porry, looking distinctly uneasy, led them into the tower, through a hall populated only by some very shabby servants, who stared at Olvar in particular. Waving aside the protests of one elderly flunkey, the sentinel went clumping up the main stair, steep and open, to pause before a curtained arch and bellow out *'My Lord Ieran! Messengers from his lordship the Marchwarden!'*

'The voice that called a million hogs!' muttered Gille.

A pewter mug whizzed past the sentry's ear, and he scuttled off downstairs, muttering, 'Lord K'm'n see you now!'

They looked at one another, then they stepped to the threshold, and bowed. But the bow froze halfway, when they saw the figure stretched out in the armchair before them. All of them had been curious to see this lord of a royal line, the man who in principle was still a king in their land. They had all seen images of his ancestors, tall, fair-skinned, hard-featured but handsome, and for the most part with a kindly twist to their features. The chamber before them was lined – littered, almost – with such images; but the man in the great threadbare chair resembled them hardly at all.

Lord Ieran Kermorvan must once have been solid and strong, though never especially tall. Now, though, he sprawled in his chair, hands crossed over a bulging belly, and the hair that fell around his shoulders was white and shaggy. 'Like a waterfall of cares!' thought Gille; for care was graven on his face, a hundred lines deep-chiselled by experience. His nose might once have been aquiline, but it was bulbous now, tipped with red veins, and with a purple-stained moustache beneath; a strong chin was barely visible among folds of stubbled skin. If there was outward nobility anywhere, it was in the sudden flash of the red-rimmed eyes, startlingly clear blue-grey, like a glimpse of sky among dreary raincloud. But the lids sank over them, guarded, wary; and they closed again, and he belched slightly. He was quite drunk.

A Lord and a Lady

'Well?' he barked suddenly, without opening an eye. 'Why does my young lord and master the Warden honour me with such a sorry pack of ragamuffin messengers? What more does he demand of me now?'

Kunrad dropped hastily to one knee, which seemed to startle the old man. 'My Lord Kermorvan, we are come from Merthian, but we are not his men. We are Northerners whom your daughter befriended, and we bring you urgent news of her!'

'My daughter?' The eyes flashed at him again, then dimmed. 'Well, I am glad to hear she has not forgotten me already. But if it's as to the wedding, spare me that! I still will not come, and that you may tell her—'

'My lord! It's nothing to do with that! Let me speak—'

'Well, well, go on, go on! What's the little vixen want now? What promises can't her precious betrothed keep, all of a sudden?'

Kunrad felt a flush of excitement. There was no love lost for Merthian here. 'My lord – he has ways of keeping his promises.'

He told his tale quickly, giving the old man no chance to interrupt, leaving out only how smithcraft had helped them, lest it awaken a sothran's disbelief. The blue eyes remained fixed on him, but they seemed to lose focus as he talked, as if their gaze were somehow turning away, perhaps inward. When Kunrad finished, the lids fluttered closed a moment.

'Well?' he grumbled. 'A long enough tale. What earnest have I that any of it's true? That you come from my daughter at all?'

'These directions she wrote!' said Kunrad, showing him the scrap of paper. 'And your captain, Ferlias. He was with us on the way, saw how your daughter befriended us, saw how Merthian greeted us at the castle—'

Kermorvan waved him silent. 'Ferlias – uh? He's off mopping up after another damned corsair raid. Flocks driven off, barns emptied, men cut down or captured for slavery . . . What d'you want to come bothering me for with your wild tales? What could I do, even if there was any truth in 'em? Go see the Syndics. Go see that bastard Bryheren who's made my sons into bellwethers – *Wine!*'

The roar was so sudden Kunrad almost fell over, but the servants had evidently been expecting it. The shrivelled little servant came scurrying in with a lidded earthenware jug and the dented mug, cast a fearful look at the Northerners, and scuttled out. Kermorvan seized the flagon, and gestured with it. 'Go on, get out. Out! Not have you prigging round me with stories, tales . . .'

Angrily Kunrad sprang up and seized the jug. Gille and Olvar winced, then blinked as Lord Kermorvan, without much effort, pulled it back, rocking Kunrad on his feet. Kunrad braced himself, and with an appalling effort he snatched it away again, sending a great spatter of red across the worn floorcloth. 'Now will you listen, damn you?' he grated.

The old man flexed his arm, and grunted something. The prentices were ready to draw sword or run, but when he looked up there was more amusement than fury in the slack face. 'Well, if you're that thirsty, pour yourself a drink! And for the boys! Ho, three more goblets, there!' He turned to the young men. 'Northern laddies, uh? Not met many! You all of you that strong?'

'Not quite, my lord,' said Gille nervously. 'Working on it, though.'

'Me,' said the old man, leaning confidingly over the arm of his chair, 'I'm the strongest arm in this castle, see? Wrestled men half my age. Not as fast as I was, though. Wine slows you; and I haven't the heart any more. My sons are strong enough, but not in the head, see? No independence. This friend of yours – what's yer name? Kunrad? He's got that.' He leaned back. 'Also a damned bloody load of Northern cheek!'

Kunrad was diplomatically pouring the wine into the cups the servant brought. He offered the pewter one to Kermorvan. 'I had to make you hear me, lord.'

Kermorvan beckoned him closer. 'Word of advice.

That's an old trick from the romances, standing up to yer superior. Bloody risky. Works with me, but that's 'cause I've read the romances too. Try it with Bryheren and he'll have you chained arse-upward on a dungeon wall in two short breaths.' Kermorvan grinned, and years fell away. 'Or Merthian, if I read him aright. Little prick! Known him since he was a brat. Never took to him. Too goody-goody perfect! Always the ones who go wrong – although,' he added, sipping easily at his wine, 'I'll admit something might've been made of him. All in the upbringing. Knock the corners off 'em a bit, never too hard, never too hard, never try an' make 'em what you want – just the best of what they're meant to be. Missed that with my boys. Not with little Alais, though! Now what is it *you* are, my lad?'

'A mastersmith, as I said. And Gille and Olvar here are my prentices.'

'Smiths? *Smiths?* Powers around us! Real Northern mastersmiths?' Kermorvan's eyes glittered. 'Never met any before! Always wanted to! Tales in my family 'bout the court mastersmiths we had, right down to old Badgerbeard Vayde who was the last of 'em! Things they could do, things they could make . . .' Kunrad was alarmed to see the lids flutters, the clear eyes dim again, looking out into emptiness. 'Used to dream of having one, when I was a little lad. Huh! Some hope. What am I come to instead? No court. Just a broken-down command I hold only for the favour of my daughter. And now she's not here any more, off half-crazy to hop 'tween the sheets with that little prick with ears . . . Well, if she's happy, let her, let her . . .'

Kunrad was about to say something when the eyes suddenly went wide. 'Smiths! That how you got out of that dungeon? And the corsairs? Hah! Main reason your story didn't stick! So that's how! You tell me more about that, boy – but then . . .'

For a moment they were looking at a different man, as if the light in those eyes had somehow transformed the face. 'Then she is in danger, isn't she? It's true. Alais. In durance, or worse . . . *If he's harmed her I'll leave nothing worth burying!'*

He sagged again. 'Hark at me! Words! What can they change? What can I?

> *A warrior bold, a free lance am I,*
> *Over the blood-red Marches riding,*
> *Waving my freedom's golden pennons . . .*

Hear that? Merthian wouldn't know that – not 'less you were going to set him a test on it! He'd know it then, backward – but not what it meant. Me stop him? Huh.'

'Alais knew,' said Kunrad, and wondered why he put her in the past. 'That was her message – get word to her brothers, and through them to the Chief Syndic, this Bryheren man. That you can do, if you're quick enough!'

'Uh,' said Kermorvan. 'Fact is, they and I . . . Good lads, really; but when they took service under the Lord Bryheren . . . Ancient family enemies, the Herens; right back to Kerys. Unmitigated bastards, most of 'em, and worse, sometimes; traitors, serving the Ice, even.'

Kunrad nodded. 'We've heard the old tales in the North. But this one?'

Kermorvan shrugged, grudgingly. 'Oh, he's not that bad. Well enough in his way, perhaps, one of the best of 'em. But a chill narrow sort of a mind, no spirit to bring things back to life. Everything as his daddy had it, and don't disturb the dust! Makes me want to sneeze every time I see him! And hard, hard, unyielding. My lads – well, they're bright enough. But we quarrelled. They think I'm an old souse; they may not take me seriously. And Bryheren? Wouldn't credit me if I said the sun came up i' the morning!'

'That doesn't matter!' said Kunrad, leaning over the chair. 'Believe it or not, they'll mount guard, won't they? And then they'll send a force north to investigate. Maybe not a big one – but even a small force will spoil my Lord Warden's plans. If only it's quick enough!'

Kermorvan's stained moustache twitched. '*Guards!*'

he roared, almost overturning Kunrad again. '*Guards!* Pass the word for my clerk, and find volunteers to bear messages for me. Southward!' He grimaced. 'No shortage, I'll wager. Any chance to get out of this arse-end posting!'

'But my lord,' pleaded Gille, 'won't they go straight to the Marchwarden? They're his men!'

Kermorvan snorted. 'Laddie, they may wear his livery 'cause I can't afford one, but they're my own housetroops for the most part, and men off my own lands, as were. Only way I could keep 'em. The Marchwarden may have a spy or two here, almost certainly does; but the men I'll send, I'll pick myself, men I can trust. And send several, by different ways. That'll pin his ears back! And Bryheren, by the Powers, who was so hot in appointing him!'

He was half out of his chair, but he slumped back. 'Bryheren! There's a stumbling block, still. You don't know him. Merthian was his man for the Warden's office, and if he's rotten, Bryheren's a long way out. He'll investigate, you say; but will he make known what he finds, or simply bury it? Seek to draw Merthian's teeth and keep quiet about it? Suppress those who know? If there's the least error, any lie, any misunderstanding even he can make use of, then I'm humiliated. Ruined. Oh yes, he'll see to that.'

'But there is no error!' protested Kunrad. 'He's only to ask Alais . . . Yes. I see.'

The old man nodded grimly. 'Puts her in danger, doesn't it? Her, the chief witness, because she's of our folk, and my stock – and one even Bryheren could never silence. Not Merthian's betrothed! Her word'll carry far more weight than any Northerner's.'

Kunrad bit his lip angrily. 'Merthian's in love with her.'

Kermorvan leaned forward. His eyes were very cold. 'Yes – and if all you say's true, she's betrayed him. What's he going to feel then? Ever heard of a thing called jealousy? And with a couple of companies marching to his doorstep, and her the only witness worth the name – what might that make him do?'

Kunrad was pacing around the room like a caged animal, looking at the rows of stern faces, seeing sudden flashes of Alais's bright, impulsive features everywhere. 'My lord, I don't know. I hadn't been thinking much beyond getting out the warning. I urge you, send that, whatever else. If Merthian and his ambitions are not reined in, there could be so many lives lost. Here, and in the North; and we were your people once, also. Your daughter knew that, when she stayed behind. And I left her only because I knew it, and because it was the only chance of getting through. She's important to you, obviously. I, well ... My Lord Kermorvan, just send that warning, and –' Kunrad stopped almost in midstride '– and you can clap me in chains and trade me back to Merthian for her!'

Olvar groaned. Kermorvan stared. 'You think he'll agree?'

Kunrad shrugged, desperately. 'He might not! Or he might try some treachery, more like. Either one of us is a threat to him. But he might just be desperate enough to do it, for now.'

'But Lord Kermorvan,' said Gille into the silence, 'even if he lets Lady Alais go against our master for now, he's never going to feel secure. Not while she lives – or you, now. Even hearing our tale like this places you in peril. He might agree, and then descend on this place.'

'He can try!' snorted Kermorvan. 'That at least's no concern! We're not as strong as his great fastness, but this old burg has stood a good few sieges in its day. Doubt the Warden could take it by storm, even with all his garrison! Not in time, anyway!'

'He wouldn't have to!' said Gille. 'He'd use corsairs. They have men enough, and he's been training them, remember? It'd look like one more bold raid. He could even use it to extract more money from the Syndics.'

'Getting her out!' cut in Kunrad emphatically. 'That's what matters! Then she can make a run for the south! You all can! He won't be able to harm you openly down there!'

'I don't know,' mused Kermorvan. The wine-cup hung unnoticed in his hand. 'Don't know . . .'

It was then they heard the sounds of a horse hard-ridden, not far off in the still afternoon; and even as they listened the hoofbeats echoed in the courtyard below.

'Courier from the Lord Marchwarden!' came the cry. 'Utmost importance!'

Kermorvan stood suddenly, with an effortful wheeze. He looked much more impressive thus, the ruins of a sturdy frame and strong face more apparent, like old walls suddenly glimpsed through ivy and overgrowth. Snorting wine fumes, he rolled over to the stairs and roared down. 'From my Lord Warden? Send up the scrip, then – no, my lad, spare the ceremony, you look hot and hungry! You there, see him looked to at the buttery. Just toss me up his message!'

Kunrad shot an excited glance at the prentices. Kermorvan wasn't giving them away – yet.

The old man deftly snatched a small bag out of the air, grunting with satisfaction, and glared at the red wax seals which dangled from it. 'Never misses a chance for the formalities, the twerp!' He crumbled them impatiently in his stubby fingers and tore out a neat roll of red-ribboned vellum. 'Let's see, now . . . *Merthian Anlaithannen, by the grace of the Powers and appointment of the Syndicacy and people of Ker Bryhaine Lord Warden of the Northern Marches, Governor of the Provinces Northern, Protector of the Frontiers, Lord Commander of the Realm of Bryhaine, Holder of the Castle of the Winds, High Steward of . . . Defender of the* . . . um, um, and little prick with ears . . . Ah! *Does make known to you the escape from due custody of three condemned outlaws and pirates of Svarhath extraction, and mongrel Northern birth, claiming to be smiths, their leader of the description following . . .* hmmn, hah, not very flattering! *They are to be immediately recaptured, alive or dead, upon suspicion of involvement with recent outlaw incursions into our domain and the robbery, rapine and . . .* so on and so on. *If alive, they are to be held without interrogation, strictly apart, firmly gagged and without free movement; and to have no communication with anyone of whatever standing, to forestall their treasonous links with the outlawry, and to prevent any possible transmission of intelligences detrimental to our preparations for the defence of the region. They or their corpses are to be returned under heavy guard and in conditions of strict secrecy with immediate effect, upon pain of* . . . cheeky little bugger! *It is to be noted that the security of the state depends upon prompt and efficient action, and will take precedence over* . . . *all* . . . *other* . . . *considerations* . . .'

The bleak blue eyes looked at them over the edge of the tanned skin. 'Well!' said Kermorvan gustily. 'Well, well, well!' He turned to the stairs. 'You below! See to it that the man waits. I may have word to send back, very shortly!'

'Merthian didn't know we had Alais's guidance!' said Gille. 'He couldn't imagine we might get here before a fast horseman!'

Kermorvan appeared to ignore him. His eyes were more alert than Kunrad had yet seen them. 'My time for wavering is ended! These orders leave me no option but to send you back. To disobey's treason and ruin in itself.'

Kunrad smiled suddenly. 'Then that is what you must do, my lord. Obey.'

It was sunrise five days later when the column of horsemen with the Marchwarden's banner at their head wound their way down out of the hills, and through the open woods along the shore of the great Lake of the Winds. There were twenty-five horses, but only twenty-two men rode, with lances in their hands and bows slung from their saddles. The three other saddles, in the midst of the column, had limp shapes lashed across them, under red-stained sacking. At sight of the banner, a trumpet sounded from the castle walls. They were expected. The riders reined in at the bridgehead, while their leader pulled down the scarf over his nose and mouth to call across the water. 'From my Lord Kermorvan! Prisoners and escort, for the Lord Warden!'

At the answering hail the bridge began slowly

swinging out towards them. They waited in patience as sentries ran down to make it fast, and saluted the little riding as it clumped on to the walkway. 'Escort, eh?' grinned one, wrinkling his nose at the smell from under the blankets. 'Faugh! Good an' ripe! Had your work cut out looking after them lively lads, eh?'

'That's right!' growled the captain, glaring from under his bushy brows. 'Seems they're just what's wanted for sentry-go round here!'

'Don't bloody joke about it!' groaned the soldier. 'Or they will recruit 'em. We're all on double-stag as it is!'

'That's soldierin' for you, my lad!' said the captain, not unsympathetically, and passed on, resting his lance in its saddle socket like the rest. At the castle gate the stocky figure of Captain Erlan was waiting, and they exchanged salutes, fist to heart, then outthrust. 'Welcome back, Ferlias! Come on in!' He sniffed and recoiled as the horses bearing the bodies came past into the tunnel. 'Stars above, you must've had a merry ride!'

'Sorry we couldn't deliver 'em alive and kicking!' grunted Ferlias.

Merthian's captain shrugged. ''Tween you and me, all for the best! The Marchwarden wouldn't be saying this right out, mind, but he was well pleased with old Kermorvan's message!' He led them out into the courtyard, almost empty at this hour save for some grooms and a few mailed figures lounging on the walls, eyeing the newcomers. 'So now you can leave your stiffs and your mounts to the lads, and come wash the stench out! My Lord Warden orders you're to enjoy our hospitality ere you bear the old bugger back his thanks and compliments!'

'Not necessary!' said a deep voice from the end of the column. A bulky figure removed his helm and scarf to let white hair straggle down. 'The old bugger has come in person to receive them – and to have a few words with my daughter and her betrothed! So, captain, if you'd do Lord Ieran Kermorvan the honour of calling them down?'

The effect on Merthian's captain was immediate and

obvious. Like most sothrans, Erlan's upbringing had dictated obedience to the great lords of the realm; and the name of Kermorvan still retained its power. He stood open-mouthed, and looked wildly about. 'My lord . . . He's not here, he's . . . And she—'

Kermorvan booted his horse forward, and Erlan quailed at the look on his face. It was not lost on one or two of the loungers, men with a touch of Northern copper skin. They sprang up and began shouting.

'*Shut the gate! Pull back the bridge! The bastards're on to us!*'

'Some tender consciences here!' grated Kermorvan, and bellowed, '*Stand back from that gate! I'll skewer the man who disobeys!*'

With not the slightest surprise or hesitation his riders snatched up their bows, and drew. At the same moment, so suddenly the horses plunged and whinnied, the three inert bodies kicked free of their looped ropes and slid out from beneath the blood-stinking sacking, plucking out swords as they landed. Kermorvan snatched up a great horn and blew a blast which echoed across the lake. '*Alert, Morvannen! Morvan morlanhal!*' The loungers cowered from the arrows that threatened them and yelled frantically to the captain.

He, however, was grey-faced with panic. 'Treachery!' he shouted, ducking behind a pillar. 'Guard! Back that bloody bridge! Cut them down!'

That was easier said than done. There were barely ten men down in the courtyard, and they were on foot and unarmed; the rest were on the walls, and few had bows to hand. The riders wheeled, sending the captain scurrying, and the guards on the wall ducked or ran as arrows whistled up at them. Kunrad and the prentices, keeping low, made for the bridge mechanism just as the two nervous loungers came clattering down off the wall to reach it, swords in hand. Kunrad cut down the first one as he spun the windlass wheel, while Olvar, parrying the first blow aimed at him, smashed his opponent on the nose with a huge mailed fist, picked him up as he staggered and threw him at the wall. Gille snatched up their fallen swords and passed them to Kunrad, who studied the mechanism a moment, confirming his memory, then thrust a sword in with such force that it stuck deep in the wooden frame, and beside it another. There was a fearful rumble from the bridge outside. A cog crunched down on the blades, seized and jammed. Olvar was already pounding ponderously up the stairs to the wall.

Other guards were crawling along the battlement on their bellies to the drawbridge winches, when Olvar arrived. Lying flat put them at a terrible disadvantage, and by the time Gille and Kunrad caught up, Olvar was already winding the drawbridge down again. The rumble grew to a reverberating thunder as the rest of Kermorvan's housetroop galloped across it into the tunnel and came flooding out into the courtyard.

Kunrad and the prentices gathered up the writhing guards' swords and helms to jam the mechanism, then ran back out on to the wall, expecting a flood of guards from the towers or the heart of the castle. Instead they saw only a few, appearing in small groups or even ones and twos. The firstcomers on the wall showed some fight, but Kunrad's sword toppled one over into the lake with a scream, another down into the courtyard among the milling hooves, and sent the rest scattering. Others stood gaping wildly, unable to sort out who was fighting who, or why, in the noise and confusion, since all the liveries were the same. Men milled around the trees, screaming out questions while they dodged the horsemen, or tried to escape back into the castle interior.

From the wall Kunrad could see one or two of the guards who had fled him, hard-faced bullies who looked more like corsairs than soldiers, sneaking along the courtyard towards the gate, not to close it but to escape. One had already made it through, and was bolting back across the bridge. That did not concern him. Even as he watched, the man spun around and fell backward on the walkway, with one arm dangling towards the water and a crossbow bolt in his chest. Kermorvan's troops were already dismounting and leading charges up on to the walls and along, chasing little knots of disunited guards.

'Know something?' breathed Olvar. 'I think we're bloody winning!'

'Already!' said Gille disbelievingly. 'Where are they all? And where's Merthian?'

'Bugger that!' said Kunrad without warning, and ran to a stair. The prentices kept up, but before he reached the foot, the mastersmith literally threw himself off, on to the back of a figure who was trying to slip by underneath. A moment later Kermorvan's huge warhorse breasted the mêlée, stamping furiously with its great fringed hooves, and Captain Erlan found himself flat on the cobbles with Kunrad's sword and Kermorvan's lance at his throat. Around them they were vaguely aware of other men dropping their swords and holding up their hands, and a movement that spread across the courtyard like a great ripple. Voices protested, women screamed, but the sound of combat was gone almost in a moment, replaced by silence and heavy breathing.

'Well, captain?' demanded Lord Kermorvan. 'How about some of that hospitality we were promised? And to start with, where in Hella's name's my daughter?'

The captain glared and twisted about, and said nothing. Kermorvan growled. 'Think a moment, soldier! Here's your impregnable castle taken in ten minutes flat! Maybe a whole heap of other things you're relying on ain't so secure, either!' He jabbed the spear-point into the man's neck, hard enough to make Kunrad wince.

'And consider!' added the Mastersmith mildly. 'Even assuming Merthian could get you out, somehow, what's he going to do to you after this? What reward for your loyalty then? Maybe you should be thinking of clearing the slate with us, eh, Erlan?'

'She's alive!' gurgled the captain, holding up his hands. 'She's all right, she's well, not a scratch! Nobody would – My Lord Warden gave orders – uk!'

'And where's he?' demanded Kunrad.

'Left – days 'go, after Kerm – your lordship's word reached him! Took two third parts of the garrison with him. left the lady locked up safe—'

'Well then,' said Kunrad. 'You can take us to her, can't you? And quick!'

The captain scrambled up, clutching at his throat, and nodded awkwardly. Kermorvan detailed a couple of men, and, leaving Ferlias in command, they followed him, not towards the tower Kunrad had scaled, but the next along, squatter and stubbier but still dauntingly high and featureless, its windows much smaller and set high beneath the frowning eaves. The door at its base stood unlocked, and Kermorvan thrust it booming back. Almost at once, as they set their feet on the winding stair, there was a shriek from above, an echo of tearing fear.

The captain looked as startled as they. '*What? There's nobody up there with them – my lady! My lady!*' He went bounding up the worn steps, so fast Kunrad had no need to drive him, and Kermorvan was left puffing and panting behind, with his men bearing him up. Erlan was fumbling at his belt for keys as he went, half weeping. They reached the top, breathless.

'My lady! If anything's happened to her my lord will slay me like a dog!'

'No he won't!' snarled Kunrad. 'Because I'll do it first! That the door? *Get it open, man!*'

The captain twisted the key, but it stuck in the lock, and he let it go with a yelp, shaking his fingers. '*Break it down!*' snarled Kunrad, and kicked at the lock with such force that the whole door shook, and the latch bent inward. The captain threw himself against it; it shot back and he went staggering in, off balance on the worn carpet.

The room was a bedroom, darker and less richly furnished than Alais's own room, but comfortable enough. Only the air was strangely, shockingly cold, so cold their breath smoked suddenly. And there was Alais, whole and alive in her lace-trimmed nightgown, but shrunk back behind the bed with her face tear-streaked and crumpled up with terror, holding a great cushion before her as if to shield against some fearsome blow. But the person who was striding towards her with every aspect of intent menace, hand raised as if to strike her down, was no more than Mistress Nolys, the delicate old Nanny herself.

Her look, as she glanced back at them, was a glare of haughty disgust and high-minded annoyance, eyebrows raised as if they were dirty little children who had come bursting in on a private matter. But there was something so awful in it, the sheer force of revulsion and hatred etched in the folds of the withered old face, that it stopped both men in their tracks.

The captain gaped, half laughing, and scuttled in front of her, stretching out a hand to stop her, babbling incoherently. 'My lady – please, whatever, don't be angry – Nanny, please stop and listen – there's been trouble, we must—' He caught her by the shoulders to pull her back.

The old woman's purple lips hissed like a snake, and she lashed out and slapped his face.

The captain stiffened, arms outflung, almost on tiptoe, and let out a shriek that rattled the yellowed glass in the high window. And then stopped, instantly. The heavy man crashed backward to the carpet in a cloud of dust, limbs quivering in sudden rictus, mouth gaping but utterly breathless. Kermorvan and his men, at the door, stood in blank horror. So also Kunrad; but from a deeper cause, from the memory of such a scream sharply cut off. And from seeing once again the glassy print upon a dead man's face, the milky, opaque eyes, the rime that whitened the red-grey bristles and aged him even in death.

Kunrad looked up and into the old woman's dim green eyes. He sprang back barely in time as she bore down upon him. Behind her Alais threw the cushion; it hit the floor by her feet, and shattered like glass. Kunrad slashed wildly with his sword, only to twist it violently around as she tried to snatch hold of it. But Kermorvan had his sword out, too, and it was her turn to writhe away from his stroke. 'Go ahead!' panted Kunrad, slashing the air before her. 'Just you try and strike one of us down! Go on! Even if you succeed, the others will have you! Whatever you wanted to do, you can't do it now! Not now!'

'Nanny!' croaked Kermorvan, circling with her. His face was ghastly, but his voice was firm. 'What's got into you, old woman? I don't want to hurt you, but I will if I have to—' He staggered back as she gave a wild whinnying laugh and grabbed at his sword. Beside him his men were green with fright, but they were fumbling anxiously with their crossbows, and got them levelled.

'Shoot her!' shouted Kunrad.

'No!' roared Kermorvan.

'*Yes!*' screamed Alais, in such a voice that they all turned to her. Then, barely in time, Kunrad threw himself back as the nurse's crooked fingers slashed the air an inch in front of his nose. He slipped on the carpet, fell heavily, flung up his sword to ward himself, and she caught it. He let go barely in time. The hilt froze in his fingers and took some skin with it. The blade dulled to a dead white, shattered in the air and fell in a ringing shower, like glass. The crossbows snapped, one, two, and both bolts thumped home with a force that should have bowled the fragile body over and over. She only staggered, bent, then straightened and continued to straighten; for she was growing taller even as they watched.

The long features lengthened, the high cheekbones spread and became angular and sharp. The lips empurpled, then paled to a livid tinge, thinning as they changed, until they were no more than a snarling line around long narrow teeth. The stooped shoulders swelled and grew bony, distorted; the slender arms crooked, and muscles stood out on them like twisted cord. The skin coarsened, yellowed, sprouted thin wiry hairs like a beast-fell. The elaborately raised hair wound and uncoiled with a serpentine slither and became a sleekly pulsing mass, framing the still lengthening face. The eyes . . .

It was impossible to look at them. They were three

times their normal size now and still swelling, milky and opaque as the dead man's, yet they moved and saw clearly, a greenish glitter within darting from one assailant to another with gloating menace, echoed by the writhing mouth. She spat suddenly at one of the bowmen, and he screamed and dodged as a stream of mist whitened the side of his mail. He fell down, beating at it and writhing. The other, who had managed to reload in the confusion, loosed again, and caught the apparition of the woman in the side of her face. She reared up with a howl, and her tangled head crashed against the plastered ceiling and brought down showers of it. She shrieked, and raised up hands that had become massive, elongated, the shape of the mark on Haldin's face. Kunrad rolled out of the way barely in time as a great clawed foot, no longer human at all, kicked out at him. The pale claws ripped up the carpet and left furrows in the wood beneath; and those furrows filled with solid ice.

The nurse's body, still thin and withered-looking, twisted and thrashed in pain, as she struggled to pull out the barbed bolts. Kermorvan, throwing off his shocked paralysis, struck out at her. His sword jarred as it touched her side, as if there was scale-mail beneath the shredding cloth, and he jumped back, tossing his whitened sword frantically from hand to hand. There were shouts from below; more of his troops, drawn by the commotion, were forcing their way up. The other crossbowman, greatly emboldened, darted across the room to the shelter of a heavy chair, and drawing his bow again, rested it on the chairback to aim. She saw him even as she plucked out his last shot, and breathed harder at him, just as he loosed yet again. He ducked down; the chair blossomed white in an instant, glazed with bitter rime. The arrow blanched in the air as it flew, becoming an arrow of ice in itself, and this time, by luck or judgement, struck the creature in one great opalescent eye.

The shriek crazed the window-glass and stabbed their eardrums like sleeting icicles. The creature reared up, whipping back and forth, and smashed and thrashed against the wall, bringing down the columns of the bed in splintered ruin. Alais leapt for safety, diving out past the thrashing creature. Kunrad caught her up as she came past, and, snatching the fallen bowman's sword, he backed off with her, towards Kermorvan. With a single whipping motion the creature dragged the dart from her face and flung it, smoking with blood, to the floor. It stuck there as if bowshot, and she rose like a snake, fixing her good eye on the little group that huddled towards the door.

The pale lips writhed, and the air smoked around her, awesome, towering. She wore the bitter haze like a falling robe, swelling still in size, even as dark blood trickled from the torn eyesocket. 'Flock, sheep!' crackled a voice as inhuman as a winter gust. 'Huddle, vermin! Share your warmth and your stink! Chatter your little defiance, while events unfold that were planned and determined ages before you were whelped, from filth into filth! Determined in minds as ancient as the world you infest, the selfsame minds that first shaped and steered the stone beneath your feet, and are its rightful masters still. The first breath you drew was already too late to stop us! Man will wrestle man for scraps of gold amid the trodden dung, and both will go down into emptiness. So it is foreseen, so it is decreed, by your own vile nature as much as any act of ours! With the poison of your own blood you shall sting yourselves, and like the worm in agony you shall devour your own tails, and wipe your own wasting imperfection from the tormented earth!'

Shaking violently, the young crossbowman nonetheless managed to draw and load, whole others milled in the door. Kermorvan and Kunrad, picking up small tables as improvised shields, were inching forward. The creature hissed mist about them, and laughed, with an eerie ripple like chiming icicles. 'Spit your sharp sticks, scratch with your steel claws! Can they so much as scratch the Ice itself? The Walls of Winter will crush you, and the shroud of the eternal Ice will still even the corruption eating at your forgotten bones, and you can no more alter this than turn back the flow of your own rotten mortality. *It is foredoomed!*'

The last words blew across them all like a winter gale. Kunrad threw himself to the floor, over Alais, dragging Kermorvan down with him. Some of the men were fast enough also, but others reeled, screaming, clawing at their ice-bitten faces and hands, croaking out of frozen throats and beating at frozen eyelids. The sound grew till it was no longer a voice or even a windrush, but a mighty screaming blast that blew the window out of the wall and sent the cold column of mist boiling up and outward behind it. Kunrad and the others saw the shadow within it swell, blur and disperse into the rushing mist, an insubstantial torrent like a mirrored waterfall, pouring its last wisp out of the chamber and into the air. Men cried out and pointed then, as it went spurting across the lake in the tower's shadow, keeping out of the morning sun. Over the forest they saw it pass, and the trees in its path shivered into momentary whiteness; then, as they thawed again, their drooping, blackened leaves sank slowly into death.

Kunrad clutched Alais in his arms as she shook and sobbed, trying to comfort her. He could say little more than that it was all right now, that the creature had gone, that she was safe now and he was here; but he said it over and over. It was nothing more than has been said in so many terrible times and places since the shaping of the world; but it was something Kunrad had never said to a woman, nor Alais heard from any man. It seemed strange and new-minted to them both, and very precious. For in truth she was giving trust and comfort as much as she took, whatever the outward appearance; and perhaps that also was as old as the world. They clung, and felt one another breathe, and their bodies blend into one expanding warmth that held back the room's awful chill, and it seemed entirely natural. It was a long, long moment before Kermorvan's explosive cough called them back to themselves, and their situation, and the awful look on his empurpled face.

A Lord and a Lady

Alais tore loose from Kunrad, and flung herself upon her father with tactful enthusiasm. 'Father, dearest! I knew you'd come for me!'

In the room it felt as if a cloud had lifted, and the lake air that streamed in though the shattered window tasted sweet. Kunrad levered himself upright, finding to his surprise that he was trembling. Around him those who had escaped the last bitter blast were helping their less lucky fellows, whose skin was seared red as if by flame; and there were two who lay as still as the captain. The crossbowman was emerging nervously on all fours from behind his chair, as if astonished to find himself still alive.

'You there!' rumbled Kermorvan over his daughter's back, which he was absent-mindedly patting. 'Well done, that man! Go find Ferlias, have him scare up a healer for these lads – oh, and tell him you're a troop-leader as of now! Well, stand up, man, or somebody'll slap a saddle on you!'

As the soldiers staggered out, he turned to Kunrad. 'So, sirrah, good of you to unhand my daughter! Eventually!'

Kunrad drew a deep breath. 'Yes, my lord. We were both a bit . . .'

'I know, I know! Just not in front of the troops, that's all. At least not so enthusiastically. Felt like hugging myself to see nothing'd dropped off.'

'You were safe enough!' said Kunrad, light-headedly. 'Wine's slower to freeze.'

'*What?* Why you impertinent young dog's arse!' He considered a moment, then gave an explosive chuckle. 'Slower, eh? Well, you Northerners'd know about that. Go round all winter with icicles in your pants, I suppose! Still,' he admitted, rubbing Alais's back again, 'sooner have you jawin' me outright than that little sniveller Merthian being so terribly bloody correct, and sniffin' behind his hand all the while! Sooner have you all over Alais than him. Not a license, mind!'

She looked up from Kermorvan's shoulder suddenly, and fixed them both with wild eyes. 'Daddy – Kunrad –

what was she? She—' She pushed them away, clearly struggling to get a grip on herself.

'Nolys – Nanny – she . . .' She swallowed and looked at Kunrad, almost defiantly. 'I was right! They wouldn't hurt me. I held them off, I felled at least four of them before somebody hit me in the stomach with a spear-butt – I've got a huge bruise, right here, see? Oh, sorry, Father. Well, they didn't do anything at all even when I bit them all, and I was a bit sorry. They just put me on a horse and brought me to Merthian, and he was all mud and leaves after combing the forest, and he flew into a sort of cold rage. It was funny, really, except it wasn't. He's the only man I've ever seen who could have a screaming fit without even raising his voice, or speaking less clearly. And he said, well, all sorts of things about me helping enemies of the South and being a whore and well, warped and all that, but he never even stopped knitting his fingers. Then he seemed to go all cool again and said he'd forgive me, but he couldn't trust me, and we'd have to be wedded at once to stop scandal, and he'd drag me off and lock me up where nobody could get at me. Then he seemed to think better of that, and said he'd have to slap me up here with Nanny to look after me. And she, she was sort of kind at first, and trying to win me back over for him, that was obvious; and I didn't mind that so much . . . But then she brought me word that . . . that you'd been killed, Kunrad! And the whole place seemed to empty! And she turned very strange and grim, but still I c-couldn't . . .'

'You'd better sit down,' said Kunrad. 'If the chair's thawed. If there's any wine here . . . oh you've found it, my lord.'

Alais took a gulp her father could not have bettered, coughed violently and went red in the face. 'Then there was all that noise that woke me up – and she was at the door, listening. And then she turned really strange, and said I shouldn't hope to be rescued, whatever Merthian might want. And then when the noise died down she

A Lord and a Lady

rounded on me suddenly, tried to slap my face and the air turned so cold . . . I put a cushion up and she hit that, and I felt it go all solid . . . What happened to her, Father?'

'Powers alone know, sweetheart,' rumbled Kermorvan. 'Something from the Ice, that's for sure. I've heard of Ice-hags, Ice-witches, in fairytales. Maybe you'd know more of these things up north, youngster!'

'Not much, mercifully. They do say the Powers that rule the Ice can walk in man's shape, or woman's for that matter, at times. And we've heard of the hags and the witches, too; there's all sorts of silly tales about them. They're usually, well, made out to be seductresses, though. It's said you can see their inner selves in mirrors at sunset and sunrise, that kind of thing, but no two tales agree. I wouldn't have credited it, either – until what happened to Olvar back in Saldenborg. You remember I told you, Alais?'

She shuddered. 'Yes, but . . . this, here, this wasn't really Nanny, was it? Just something horrible in her shape – wasn't it?'

' 'Course, 'course!' rumbled Kermorvan soothingly, patting her hand. But Kunrad shook his head.

'My lady, your father's kind, but I think you'd see through any lie we told you. I think it always was her. She . . .'

'What?' rumbled Kermorvan irritably.

'She brought Merthian up, didn't she?'

'She did,' agreed Kermorvan. 'From when he was a child. Knew his parents; decent old family, nice couple. Died young, from some sickness – very suddenly,' he added, in a strange tone. 'Like my poor wife, a few years after. So?'

'I was just thinking that there might be more than one kind of seduction. All in the upbringing, my lord, as you said yourself.'

Kermorvan glared at him. 'Doesn't mean a thing—'

Alais cut in. 'Yes – but, she brought me up as well! Don't you remember? For years on end! You're saying poor

Merthian was just a creature of the Ice, aren't you? Trained up from birth to become ... what he is? Well, what am I, then? I don't know it – but then does he?' Her voice was faltering again, breathless and shaky. 'Don't you see it? I'm part of the pattern too. I must be! I was marked from birth to be the ideal wife, the one who could legitimise his claim. And to give them another hold over him. She must have been preparing me too! Oh Powers—' She clutched her father by the arms. 'Maybe they started early! Maybe Mother's death – and you losing your estates—'

'What was left of them!' said Kermorvan sternly. 'Your foolish old father just rounded off what his grandsires began, that was all! So you can put all that out of your—'

'No!' she said stridently. 'You never could lie to me! You believe it, don't you? We were ruined, and my mother died, and I was broken to bridle like a colt without knowing it! Kunrad, you know it's true, don't you? The way I brought you to Merthian, that was my idea, she planted it in my mind! Whatever I say or do, I'm just a puppet, just another tool of the Ice!'

Her hand clutched Kunrad's wrist strongly enough to cut off the blood; but it was her pain that made him wince. He clasped the cold fingers in his, and stared into her wild eyes. 'Really, truly, my princess, I do not believe that's true at all. You are nothing of theirs – or why would the nurse have felt the need to harm you?' Beside him he was acutely aware of a slight sigh, no more; but knew it was Kermorvan relaxing, lowering the barriers against his own dark suspicions. 'No! Whatever they did to Merthian, you're free of it, that I know. And even he's not completely in their power, I'll wager. It's just that they know how to feed his worst instincts and make use of his higher ones.' He laughed a little, although he had seldom felt less like it. 'A good man going wrong would always suit them better than an outright villain. For one thing, he's harder to unmask!'

The vice about his wrist relaxed, slowly, and Alais sank back in the chair, and put her hands up to her face.

Then she looked up, quite suddenly. 'You said – what happened in *Saldenborg*? Was *that* where what you told me about – Olvar nearly getting frozen?'

'After we were set on by a band of cutthroats, yes!' said Kunrad, puzzled. 'They had somebody or something with them—'

Alais flushed excitedly. 'Saldenborg! That was where Merthian took ship back from the North – he told me! And Nanny was there with him!'

'In Saldenborg?'

'All the time he was in the North!'

Kunrad sat down hard on the bed. 'I assumed he'd gone by land. Took ship? It makes sense. With the corsairs, I'll be bound! Powers, what sense! They must have informers there, spying out which ships are departing, sending word to their raiders. Poor Ceinor! He never had a chance! And they must have spotted us, through him, maybe; and Merthian sent them to attack the ship and waylay us ... or she did. She came to watch. Powers, she could have killed us all ...'

'Didn't want to give herself away,' shrugged Kermorvan. 'With so many folk about.'

Kunrad shook his head. 'Maybe she wasn't worried about giving herself away to men. Maybe it was somebody else – somebody who came looking. And found us ...' He shook his head. 'She was with Merthian all the time? Not at the Athalby fair. But maybe where he headed afterwards, where we chased him, Haldin and I ... Sense, indeed. All too much sense, now.'

Kermorvan was still flushed with anger. 'No doubt you'll explain eventually. But speakin' of which, where is the little bastard? He hopped off, they said – where to?'

Kunrad looked at him, surprised. 'No mystery about that. To the corsairs, of course! He hadn't any choice, had he? The moment he was sure I'd escaped, his plan was in terrible danger. As long as there was even a chance I'd got word out, there'd be only one way for him to save it – advance it! Hearing we'd been killed might have eased his mind a little, but he still couldn't be sure we hadn't already blown the gaff. He's got to bring the corsairs out now, ready or not, and march south to stake his claim – or risk meeting an army coming the other way! That's why he took so many men. He'll need all the trained soldiers he can muster to keep that pack of cutthroats under his thumb!'

'Yes!' said Alais, surfacing. 'Yes, you're right! That's why he didn't want to take me! He thought of it, then realised he didn't dare!'

'Or the nurse told him,' Kunrad said. 'Pointed out you're far too precious. I can just imagine that jewel-encrusted chieftain of theirs slavering to get his paws on you. He'd have a deadly hold over Merthian then!'

'He might want hold of a few other things, as well!' said Alais, with a wan smile. 'At the least I might cause quarrels. And you know, Merthian still has hopes of me! He was going on about it when he left – how he'd show me he was right. He must be desperate now. Maybe he's already on the march!'

'No!' said Kermorvan grimly. 'He's got to do one more thing first.' He twitched his moustache impatiently as they looked at him. 'Come on, infants, let's get out of this garret. I need some air. That's the trouble with this thick-walled place, no decent draughts! Not healthy, not having a few good whistlin' draughts. Air gets stagnant. Sling some clothes on, girl, and come down!'

The old man lumbered cheerfully down the stairwell, his sheathed sword clanking on every step as his short legs rolled him from side to side. He threw open doors as he went, exposing what seemed to be mostly storerooms full of sacks, and muttered to himself. 'That's it, that's it. Makes sense, the little prick!'

At last he came to one which opened out on to the wall, and trundled out into the open with a roaring sigh of relief. After that dingy chamber and its horrors, the light seemed very clear and the air fresh and clean. It was still early morning, and a track of unexpected gold glittered across the deep blue waters. The forest beyond gleamed with dew against the tumbled clouds. A heron flashed brilliantly in the air, catching the sun on its white underwings as it came in to land. The unceasing wind ruffled Kunrad's hair, and it seemed to him again that this place was some enamelled jewel, impossibly bright and perfect; only now he was a part of it.

He felt very strange, giddy almost; and why not? He had lived hard now and on short commons for longer than he cared to think. But it was more than that. Something had changed, something within him. That he knew; but he was not willing to seek it out. He was almost afraid of it. It was not the armour. That nagged at him more than ever now, if anything, because it was part of the greater problem. It was not his worries about his future, or the prentices; he had others more immediate. Yet now something made them both more urgent and less important. Something, somewhere, had sapped some of the grim determination that had driven him so far, and put in its place a painful gift. Its name was hope.

On the bridge, the troopers Kermorvan had left on shore were dragging off the bodies they had shot down. The old man gave them a merry wave. One of them waggled a corpse's arm back at him, and he bellowed at the joke.

'See here?' he said, turning to Kunrad and Alais as she caught them up. 'Magnificent view, ain't it? Mountains back there, hills there, woodland through to the margins of the Marshlands.'

'Wonderful,' said Kunrad, 'I love it – but you were saying—'

'I still am! Knew what he was about, old Badgerbeard, when he built this place. Not much leeway for good roads, is there? Nothing a full-scale army can get along, for sure, 'cept through this lake country. Now d'you see it? Eh?'

Kermorvan laughed at their blank looks, and waved a hand southward. 'You're thinking of him seizing the southern half of Bryhaine – but what good'll that do him unless the north is firm at his back? That's his biggest threat against the south. And where's the heart of it all?' His fat finger stabbed downwards. 'Here! The Castle of the Winds! Right here!'

The old man thumped the massive stonework. 'All the armies of the South could batter themselves senseless against this fortress, if a good garrison holds it! That's well known, and that's the foundation of his power. This castle commands the land ways south. It's the only safe place for his food stores, if they try the scorched-earth retreat against him. All his supply lines, his tactical retreats – all his careful strategies will rest on having this castle at his back. As much or more as having that precious armour of yours upon it! The principle's the same. It makes him untouchable, not worth the resisting!'

The old lord grinned evilly. 'And equally, if the little bugger doesn't have it – or worse, if it's held by his enemies – then, by the Raven banner, he's dipped deep in the dungheap!' He slapped his fat palms joyously. 'Classic problem in the art, see? Horns of the Ram, they called it when I was a squire studyin' at my father's stirrup. Even a small garrison here could harry his advance. And if even a small force was on its way northward, he'd be caught between them. And then? Then he's just another rootless brigand with no fortifications, no supplies, nothing at his back but the Marshes!'

He leaned on the crenellations, and stared out at the bright sky. 'No, this – this here beneath your feet! – is the heart of his whole device! He's always assumed it's impregnable. Don't I know that, listening to him! He could never have dreamed he might lose it so easily – with his own co-operation, as you might say! So before he can make a move south, he's going to have to come back here to the Castle of the Winds – and get it back again!'

Alais and Kunrad were struck silent; but Kermorvan, full of his own idea, was strutting up and down the parapet, chuckling to himself. It was Kunrad who spoke,

A Lord and a Lady

finally. 'You're very sure of this, aren't you, my lord? You've thought it through long since.'

Kermorvan stopped suddenly and wheeled about. 'Oh! So, clever bugger, eh?' He laughed. 'You're right, by Saithana's round pink – well, you're right, anyway. All those long wasted years, first here as castellan, then out there in the hills, trailing back here to bend the knee and take my orders from goody-goody little Master Merthian – yes, and see my little princess!' His face softened a moment, and he put a hand on Alais's shoulder. 'Oh yes, Northerner, I've thought of it all right. How it might be managed. If I only had this place, the revenues, the men – but I'd never have stooped to using outlaws! Let alone encouraging them, raising them a fortress – ach! It doesn't bear thinking of, the little—' He suddenly gave a great whoop of laughter.

Alais took him by the arm. 'Be serious, Father!'

'It's just the thought of his face when he hears! Ah, here's these boys of yours, smith!' Kermorvan waved them over. 'Handsomely done, my lads! Any time you get weary of bashing metal, you come to me and I'll learn you the fine art of headbeating. Though you've a decent start – What's this, a little looting?' He prodded the bundle under Olvar's arm. 'You're learning fast, all right!'

'Not exactly, sir!' said Gille cheerfully. 'We got a touch weary of Galdred's cheap-jack mailshirts, and found some of our captives wore good Northern work – some of it very familiar!'

Kunrad smiled. 'Ours, you mean?'

'Seems to be. Officer's choice, we are. So we helped ourselves to a couple, and brought one more for you. And that put us in mind of another thing or two, and we managed to persuade one helpful fellow to remember where your gear had gone. Your tools were in the farriery, and Erlan had your sword; but he wasn't prone to argue. Which we present to you now, in token of all else.'

'Along with some news,' said Olvar, holding out the weapon Kunrad had made among the corsairs. 'Armouries here are damn near stripped. Apparently Merthian hauled all his thousands of hauberks off with him.'

'Doesn't surprise me,' said Kunrad, taking the sword gratefully, and told them what had happened, and what had been learned. They grew graver as they listened, and all Kunrad's new-found joy could not suppress a rising sense of panic.

Alais took her father's arm again. 'We're going to have to think of something, Father. If you're right, and Merthian's going to be bringing his whole army back here . . .'

'Yes!' said Gille shakily. 'Hammer of Ilmarinen, how soon could he manage it? How soon?'

'Weeks?' suggested the old man, his ebullience fading. 'Days? Your guess or mine, boy! However long he needs to hear the castle's been taken, whip up his pack of strays and bring them howling down on us – that's how soon! And they won't have the time or patience for a long siege. They'll be out to roll over us, fast, whatever the cost in men. Time's more costly to them!'

'We've got to go, then!' said Alais. 'Get out of here before the corsairs come, get away southward! Or take refuge somewhere else—'

Kermorvan shook his head. 'There's no refuge safer than this within reach. And if we hand Merthian his castle back, we're handing him the trump. He could cover up his plans then, or fight off any force from Ker Bryhaine till it grows weary and compounds with him. Joins him, even. It's happened before.' He straightened up again. 'And besides, I for one ain't willing to hop away south'ard like a hunted coney. That little prick wants his grubby paws on what's mine, if it's anybody's. Dammit, I want to fight him! It's a matter of honour! At least until Ker Bryhaine can get the lead out of its rear end and deal with him!'

Kunrad glared at him. 'Will honour ward off arrows? Or the touch of the Ice? That sounds pretty stupid to me!'

'Oh yes?' demanded Alais. 'And what about the matter of a certain armour?'

Kunrad glared out across the lake. 'That's different! I mean, yes; but . . . well, there are more important things!'

'More important than your heap of clever tinkering?' she inquired sweetly. 'Do my girlish ears deceive me?'

'People's lives!' roared the mastersmith. 'Your life, damnation! We've got to get you away, at least!'

'My life?' she said, and her manner was no longer mocking. 'Does that mean something to you, Mastersmith? Then understand that yours might also mean something to me. And consider that my honour is also at issue here, more than anyone's. I am stricken deeper even than you with your armour, perhaps. The taint of the Ice is upon me, and I shall see it washed away, or never feel clean again. I too must fight!'

Kermorvan had been hissing and bubbling like a kettle-lid, eager to protest; but he said nothing, when he had the chance. Instead the strength seemed to sap out of him. 'Words,' he said, as he had before. 'If we could man our walls with words, we might stand a chance.'

Alais bridled. 'But, Father, if this place is so strong—'

'With a proper garrison, blast and blind it! Even if I rope in Merthian's own men and these cutgullet wretches he's been trying to train, I couldn't muster a full siege garrison! Not nearly! There's not enough men to be had this far north!'

'Maybe you're not looking far enough north,' suggested Kunrad. 'Dunmarhas, the last great city before the Marshes – send word to them, for their guard! They love the corsairs as little as you. They may not strip their own defences, but they'll send some aid, at least!'

Kermorvan was making little bubbling noises. '*What?* An army of bloody Nordeney sheepshaggers? On Suderney ground? In our damned castle?'

'Your precious forebears wouldn't have said that!' Kunrad pointed out acidly. 'We were their subjects, too! Until Syndics drove us out, and stripped the throne from under you. They did that, not we!'

'Besides,' put in Olvar practically, 'Dunmarhas is full of sothran blood, being so close.'

'They're right, Father!' said Alais forcefully. 'And remember, if it wasn't for some of those sheepshaggers being so brave, Merthian would still be about his business, and me ready to hop into his bed with a crown on! And while we're about that, why not remind a few other people we once wore one? It was always our right to raise levies of the people. Why shouldn't you do so now?'

'*Eh?* Call up the peasants? Powers above us, first the sheepshaggers, now the sheep!'

'They may have more spirit than you give them credit for!' suggested Kunrad, remembering the hound and the dung-fork.

Kermorvan's face twisted into a horrible scowl. 'That so? Ever tried running an impressment on 'em? All the young'uns take to the hills, and anyone with a wrinkle is suddenly over sixty and has Grandpa's papers to prove it!'

'Well,' demanded Kunrad, 'wouldn't you say that was showing some spirit? Come to the North, old man! There are divisions everywhere, I suppose; but there high's not so far from low. All folk there will unite to defend their own, if they're given enough of a stake in it!'

'Way they did with you and your thrice-damned armour?'

'That wasn't everyone's problem, not directly. I shouldn't have expected it to be. You give the peasants a chance at the corsairs, and you'll see.'

'That's right!' chipped in Gille. 'After all, it's not the lords behind their castle walls who're suffering worst, is it? Not yet! It's the farmers and the village folk, isn't it?'

Kermorvan's face creased up horribly. 'That's so. Never dispute it. That's why they need lords to protect 'em, train soldiers to fight for 'em.'

'Well,' said Olvar, 'Gille's lot, for all their fat rent-rolls, still spend half their lives up to their arses in dung; as do mine in fishguts! Yet, lord, you say we fight well enough!'

'That's so, truly!' said Kermorvan heartily. 'And, Old Raven himself knows, we've little enough to lose! But suppose we can make the shitkickers fight – what *with*?

Maybe in your land a peasant can afford a sword, but not here. Metal goes where it's needed. They've got – what? Scythes, billhooks, maybe weaving-swords and suchlike, and a few hunting-bows, but no real manslayers.'

Kunrad grinned at him. 'They must have smiths, then – of a sort!'

'Of course! What d'you think we are? No big towns round here, of course, and the Castle man's gone; but all the bigger villages'd have at least one. Plenty more lads who can turn a hand to it along with all the other farm tasks. Have to, among the outlivers. But they're hardly weaponsmiths!'

'I'm sure!' said Kunrad. 'But we'll see how they work under my instruction. And under Olvar and Gille here!'

'But what'll they work *on*?' demanded Alais. 'This isn't like Ker Bryhaine or one of our other cities, Kunrad. There's no markets to bring metal in, no great mines. I don't suppose there's any metal to be mined in these parts—'

Kunrad laughed aloud. It was a touch grim, perhaps, as suited his mood; but there was that in his voice which startled the prentices. 'No metal? And you said you knew the hills, princess! Your guidance led us well, but had you only seen them with my eyes . . . My lady, all along your favourite woodland ways the very pebbles speak of iron, the earth is red with the rust and dust of it! Not more than two days' ride among those foothills, and I'll find you iron as rich as currants in a marriage-cake! If you can find me men to mine it, beasts to bear it, you shall have it flow in rivers before you!' He laughed again. 'I laboured years to shape one suit of armour, and was damned for it! Well, now I'll make a thousand blades to lift against it!'

'If you have the time!' said Kermorvan, whose mood had sunk even as the mastersmith's arose. 'And if you don't?'

Alais looked from one to another, and seemed startled by what she saw, there in the growing brightness. 'Why then,' said Kunrad, more softly, 'then what we have must serve. I came here dead, and awoke to new life; and I'll not let go of it so easily, ever again!'

CHAPTER NINE
The Voice of the Winds

FOR ALL LORD KERMORVAN'S pessimism, he could bestir himself. Before noon of that day scouts were sent out towards the Marches and the Great River, and a trusted messenger was being despatched northward to Dunmarhas, picking up a guard at Kermorvan's tower on the way. This far inland, and in the advancing summer, he could skirt the top of the Marshes with little enough peril, and come to Dunmarhas from the east. With him he carried letters, and which would bear more weight was hard to say. One was from Kermorvan to the Guildmaster and notables, but another from Kunrad to the head of the Smiths' Guild in that city. He had signed and sealed it with his name and character, Kunrad, Mastersmith of Athalby; yet as he looked at that once-familiar title he felt a deep inner stirring. Was he in truth that man, any longer? Was he, who had travelled the length of the Northlands, across the great Marshes and the paths of the Southlands, truly of Athalby any more?

He sat back, and sighed. He could hardly see the place, in his mind's eye. The land around it, yes. Scenes from his childhood, his lost home, the long years of peace, those he could see; even some familiar faces. But the town itself he saw only distant, shrunken, grey and small. Something was not in it, not any more. It was his heart. He had torn it up by the roots, to follow a mad quest, not realising that to have any chance of winning, one must also, always, lose. He had become Kunrad of the Armour for a while. He still was; but he was Kunrad of some other thing now, something that he could never quite grasp.

He listened to the music of the waters below the window of the tower room. These had been Merthian's chambers. He had them now, not least because Kermorvan refused to climb all those stairs. He had Merthian's chair, Merthian's bed, even with Merthian's chamberpot underneath – a childish thing in bright yellow glaze he had put back hastily, and would never use. He had something else, though; and what that was, also, he could not think.

A hand touched his shoulder, and the very lightness of it made him jump. 'It's not an Ice-witch!' smiled Alais. 'Father says the messenger's ready!'

Together they watched him go, the young crossbowman who had kept his nerve in the tower. 'I hope his way north is less perilous!' said Alais. 'And now we had better lay plans for our own journey.'

Kunrad blinked '*Our*...'

'Of course. For iron, you great windbag! Father doesn't know the hills half as well as I do! If you're going to go blundering around them, you'll need a good guide!'

Lord Kermorvan did not absorb the idea at first. He was already busy sending as many men as he could spare out among the peasantry, with trumpets and declarations that Alais had helped him draft. He treated the problem like a scouting expedition in wartime, covering the most ground with the least men, and spent the rest of the day with Merthian's great maps of the region spread out on tables all around him. Occasionally he would lose his temper and throw everything in the air, but the effort appeared to agree with him; and, rather to Kunrad's surprise, he seemed to be making sense of the business. It was only at the hastily prepared dinner they shared with Alais, Ferlias and the prentices, that he caught the drift of what was planned; and for a moment they thought he was going to throw the table in the air.

'You're schemin' to take my daughter off on this bloody mining trip? With Powers know what roamin' those hills, and a full-scale war brewin'? Northerner, if I wasn't that grateful to you I'd call you out and chop your head off, first strike! Or your—'

'Father, he isn't scheming anything,' said Alais patiently. 'I am!'

'*You?*' exploded the old man. 'Never schemed anything in your life, you! Wish you did, more – no, not that! Just wish you thought a mite about things! Just rushed at 'em, head down, all you've ever done! Same as your poor dear mother, 'n' look what happened to her!'

'Yes, Father dear,' she answered sweetly. 'She ran off with you.'

Kermorvan's purple deepened to bursting point, then faded just as swiftly. 'So she did. Silly little biddy! Fine prospect I was. Just like her, you. Same's when you took a header into the lake to see if you would swim, 'n' you couldn't. Or took that hedge high at the jump and damn near left your brains on that branch . . . Ah well. I can't talk, you'll be sayin'! Almost let you marry Merthian 'cause I thought that was what you wanted. Just tryin' to stop you makin' another mistake, that's all! But then, well, maybe it isn't a mistake at that . . . Eh?'

Kunrad had tried in vain to stem the flow. 'What isn't a mistake?'

'Oh . . .' Kermorvan looked shifty. 'Swimmin', minin' trips, that sort of thing. But this ain't any pleasure jaunt, see? We go out, we get what we can and back here quick, and no hanky-panky or you'll have a damn great pain in the panky! The pair of you!'

And Kermorvan turned back to his joking with the prentices, with whom he was already a great favourite. He left Kunrad feeling battered and confused, unable to understand half of what the old man was prattling about. He gulped at one of Merthian's choice vintages and longed for Northern beer. He and the old man had become allies, but it was with the young men that Kermorvan was making friends. Alais echoed his thoughts. 'Look at Father! That was why my brothers were such a disappointment to him. They're so staid and careful, and he's still half a boy himself – but then I suppose most men are, really.' She hesitated, and looked at him sidelong. 'Except you, perhaps, Kunrad. And I almost wish you were, so I could understand you better. I thought this obsession with the armour was childish, but now ... I don't know. There's something worse about it, something dark. You grew up so near the Ice, didn't you? I could almost imagine you could have been shaped, as Merthian and I were. Shaped to make that awful thing, shaped to make things for war, things that kill ...'

Kunrad was becoming reconciled to the wine, beginning to notice how the flavour changed as it grew warmer in his mouth. It no longer tasted like ink. Subtle fragrances swirled across his palate and seemed to dissolve directly into his blood. Alais's comment brought him back to earth with a bump, a little hurt. 'You know I'm no bloodthirsty manslayer, lady. And as for that accursed armour, I heartily wish I'd never laid maul to metal. Now, if you'll excuse me, I'm going to bed. I'd suggest you do the same. We've an early start in the morning.'

He stalked off, winecup in hand, giving her no chance to reply. She looked after him for a long moment, only to become aware that all conversation had stopped, and that everyone else was looking at her.

She was there on the steps at dawn, though, in her riding clothes, now somewhat stained and rumpled, glaring defiantly at her father. He sighed and waved her to her horse, then looked to Ferlias. 'Look, cap'n, I don't like bein' away, but you should be all right. Chances are his Wardenship hasn't even reached the corsairs yet.'

'It'll be well enough, my lord,' said Ferlias patiently. They had thrashed all this out the night before, but Kermorvan was clearly worried. 'I'll keep myself busy with the peasants, as they come in.'

'If any do!' rumbled Kermorvan.

The captain allowed himself a brief smile. 'I'd say you need have no concern about that, my lord. The first are already waiting at the lakeside there, come in with the wagon levy. The recruiters tell me there'll be many more. Seems our Marchwarden's not as universally beloved as everyone seemed to think. A good many guessed at some dirty doings with the corsairs, what with midnight comings and goings!'

Kermorvan's bleary eyes widened. 'Eh? And never thought of reporting it?'

Ferlias shrugged. 'Never. Dead afraid of them as they are, too! There's peasants for you!'

'Be reasonable, Ferlias!' protested Alais. 'Who could they report to? Who would ever have listened to the country folk?'

'I would!' snapped Kermorvan.

'Well, sir, you weren't too hasty with us, sir!' Gille reminded him. 'And that although we had her ladyship's word, too!'

Kermorvan shook his head. 'Mmph! Still listened, didn't I? This, this is the turn things have taken in this bright new commonwealth of ours! All that tattle about abolishing the distinction 'twixt man and master, yet the gulf grows ever wider! And me too sunk in my own miseries to see it!' He blew a great shuddering breath. 'Well, we'll improve things a mickle around here, right now! Bridge out, captain!'

Ferlias's men bent to the wheels, now freed, and the drawbridge swung out across the deep blue water. The lead rider raised his banner, and Kermorvan led the little cavalcade out of the gate. There on the shore awaiting them were all the wagons that could be raised in the area – Merthian had taken many already – and around them some hundred men and women, dressed as roughly as the farmers the smiths had seen. 'Hope our friend with the dung-fork's not in that lot!' hissed Olvar.

'You've got mail on now!' grinned Gille. 'Should keep your saddle-polisher intact, more or less!'

When the watchers saw Kermorvan's black banner they cheered and capered, and some rushed on to the bridge to meet him. 'Get your ratty arses off, you silly buggers!' was his greeting. 'You'll have us all in the water!'

They laughed, and drew back. The old man reined in by the wagons, and glared around from beneath his bristling brows. 'Thanks for your aid!' he growled. 'If we get all this done aright, you'll have your carts back in time to load your harvest in – and with no sweat keepin' it from thievin' corsairs, neither! But look'ee here, you—' He fixed one inoffensive man with a terrible glare and jabbed a knob-knuckled finger. 'None o' this skulkin' and mutterin' from now on, see? I'll not have it! Anything smells, no matter who's got his boot in it, it's my business to know, see? And yours to come runnin', rumour or no! That's called duty, that is, and don't you dare forget it! That's what lords are for!' His scowl turned to a horrible grin, evidently meant to be reassuring. 'I won't bite your heads off. Not that you'd miss 'em! My gate's open to any man, be it Lord Muck or the muck-shoveller. That's how my folk ordered it in the East, that's how it'll be now I'm here – or I'll know why!' He treated them to another glare. 'Right then! Piss off inside with you and report to the captain!'

No gem of oratory, but it roused a healthy cheer – far more, Kunrad realised, than Merthian's polished politeness would have done. Kermorvan's bluntness spoke more directly, and with more authority. But as his men rode by, he muttered, 'Let's hope we're still behind the bloody gate!'

'You will be,' said Kunrad encouragingly. 'We'll see to that! That gulf you spoke of – it's the same between North and South, isn't it?'

'First things first!' said Kermorvan. 'Let's find this ore of yours and put an edge on it first. There's a mort of cutting comes before the mending!'

The riders moved on past the slower wagons with their tall ox-teams, man-high at the shoulder, which were to meet them at a camping place just below the mouth of the main pass into the mountains. 'I'll need somewhere where the earth is cut into, and the layers of rock beneath laid bare,' Kunrad explained to Alais. 'Then I can look for the types of stone best suited to bearing metal, and find the seam the pebbles come from!'

'Long as it's not all been worn to pebbles long since,' said Kermorvan. He had turned gloomy again, and all Alais's prodding and persuasion couldn't cheer him up. The few folk who lived out in these parts, most of them hunters and outlivers, looked with little favour on their search. They were afraid of the high passes, not so much for the mountains themselves as the mountain spirits who dwelt there, whom they feared might well be angered by any such intrusion. But as they reached the camping-ground Alais had picked out and halted to make fire and feed, Kunrad surveyed the mighty walls of stone before him with deep satisfaction, and the valley mouths that opened within them.

'Up there!' said Alais. 'The tallest. I think that's a place after your mind. When I was a girl the rock layers always looked to me like birthday cake.'

Kunrad nodded. 'Like enough. We could take a ride up there, look around and be back before dark! Come, lads!'

The prentices surveyed the high cliff walls, and the greying cloud that swirled above their summits and streamed like winter's banner from the peaks. 'Looks like a perfect place for your mountain spirits, doesn't it?' groaned Olvar. 'Lots of nice pointy rocks to drop on us, clouds to lose us in, cliffs to lead us over!'

'That's so!' admitted Gille. 'But you're forgetting one thing. If there are any mountain spirits up there, they're between the Mastersmith and something he wants!'

Olvar though for a moment. 'Feel a touch sorry for 'em, now you mention it.'

'Me too,' said Gille.

'You think he's like that?' inquired Alais, a little wanly. 'When he really, truly wants something?'

The prentices greeted her warmly. 'My lady,' said Gille after a moment. 'He's like an awful lot of men, really. He has to know he wants it, first.'

The light was greying as they rode up the steep paths, but it still shone bright on the upper slopes, and would hold until long into the summer evening. It was a beautiful ride, though rather a steep one; but Kunrad had eyes for neither heights nor depths – only the path around him, and the scattered falls of rock from the mountain wall. Every so often he would leap down, ignoring the drop to his right, and exclaim with satisfaction over some rock or other.

'There's a whole fall of them here!' he exclaimed, as they emerged into a wide gorge at the foot of two real peaks, in the centre of which a mountain stream had worn a shallow tarn before escaping to the vales below. He pointed to a brownish slash among the white rubble of the hillside. 'See, scattered like that, right out across the slope there. Strange, that . . . Such a lot of it, and so regular. Almost as if . . .'

'As if someone's been mining it already?' demanded Gille, rubbing his neck as the hairs prickled. The wind was whistling through the gorge now, and but for the stream's dull splashing, it was the only voice they heard. Yet each and every one of them felt as if they had overheard the echo of a whisper, a departing footfall, glimpsed a flicker of movement. It was as if the gorge had just that moment fallen empty, and its watchers remained alert and expectant around them.

It was an eerie moment; but the next sound they heard carried a more definite fear. Every man's back twitched at the faint clickings that carried down the wind, as if stiffening his shoulders might somehow stop the crossbow bolts aimed between them. Kermorvan swung around with a stifled oath, caught Kunrad's arm and pointed. A single pebble was tumbling down from the high outcrops along the right-hand wall, impossibly high for a man to climb, down in great bouncing leaps across the barren stoneface, until it rebounded off a shelf some thirty feet above their heads and down through the rubble of the fall, to roll across the path immediately before their horses' hooves. A trickle of disturbed pebbles pattered down behind it. In the silence it left there was a new sound, a kind of faint insistent sizzle, and the wind carried a sudden acrid whiff of burning.

'Who d'you think this is?' whispered Kermorvan.

'Not spirits, anyhow,' said Kunrad. 'Too material. A penny piece to a pint mug it's . . .'

Kermorvan gestured, as if he did not want the name spoken. He rose in his stirrups to shout out, but his throat was evidently ash-dry. He swallowed as best he could, and called out between his cupped hands. 'We mean no harm! We come in peace! Metal is all we seek!'

He had not bargained for the effect of the echoes. The sounds they had magnified must have been very faint, for they made his loud words boom alarmingly off the walls and into the wind. **SEEK... HARM... METAL ...** from every direction around them, like titanic mockery. The effect was not exactly reassuring.

'Let me!' said Kunrad swiftly. 'If they turn us away now, we're done. But if *not* ... Will you go along with whatever I say?'

'Well ... it depends ...'

'*Will you?* Nothing dishonourable, that I promise – but there's no time to explain!'

Kermorvan groaned. 'More hot water for you to tip me into ... But I've trusted you this far, boy. Say on – but have a care!'

Kunrad raised his hands and took a deep breath. '*Hear me!* I am no enemy to the duergar race, whom I guess you to be! I have spoken with your kind before!' He pitched his voice higher than Kermorvan's boom, and it carried more clearly through the echoes. 'I am the mastersmith out of Nordeney who helped two of your kind escape the corsairs' fortress! And though I claim no special credit, let it stand that it was me and mine who threw down the gibbets at a certain crossways!'

He sagged down, listening to the silence. 'Nothing's happening!'

'That can be a lot better than something, believe me!' rumbled Kermorvan softly. 'Try again!'

'We face the corsairs now!' he called again. 'Your foe and ours! We need metal for sword and spear-point! If you will not aid us, at least do not hinder us!'

There was only silence.

'The corsairs!' he shouted again. 'And behind them,

the Ice whose instruments they are! Would you have the high vales and foothills under their cruel hand? This man at my side is a great lord of the Southlands, of their line of kings. If you help us, actively help us, he'll give you his word to forbid the killing of your kind like vermin. The killing and the gibbeting – forbid it, by law. Will the corsairs ever do that?'

'*What?*' rumbled Kermorvan.

'*Do it!*' snapped Alais. 'Do it, Father. We've no choice now.'

Kermorvan's cheeks flared for a moment, then he subsided. 'Well, well. Never did like that, I'll allow. One o' those beastly sheepshagger customs.' The old man raised his hand in solemn assent.

'You've done something!' said Alais shakily, almost at once.

After a moment longer Gille nodded. 'Something's changed!'

It was strange how the quality of silence could alter. It had not lost its menace, but it seemed less immediate now, more expectant.

'Thank you!' shouted Kunrad, and added under his breath, 'Now for the push!'

He cupped his hands again. 'You! You could find the iron for us, far faster than we could!' He drew breath. That was what had changed! The vicious hiss had stilled. 'If we return here, say tomorrow at noon, with our men and beasts, will you guide us to what we need?'

Silence; and now it was hard to read. But then suddenly, from high on the left-hand walls of the gorge, another and smaller pebble came falling, freely now, arcing high out into space to strike nothing until it exploded before their feet. Their horses shied; and as they struggled to soothe them, they saw, impossibly high above, gleams of metal. All along the precipitous slopes they stood out in the low long sunbeams, and lower, from minor rock and hidden crevice, until the gorge winked and sparkled like a mine of jewels. They were squat, burly figures all clad in shining armour, and Kunrad's mouth watered as he longed to get at it and winkle out its secrets and shapings. He peered and squinted, missing completely what everyone else saw at once.

'There's bloody hundreds of 'em!' wheezed Kermorvan shakily. 'And what's that bugger up i' the top doing?'

Kunrad strained his eyes as the bright shape raised a hand, palm outward. He could almost make out the articulation. It was a segmented scale construction, sprung on sliding rivets probably, like his! It was only then he recognised the gesture. It looked like an echo of Kermorvan's. Then the armour flashed again, and there was no mistaking that calm downward wave. They were being told to go. Again the open palm; again the wave. Then the figure turned away, and almost as one the gleams along the gorge winked out. It was as if the hillside had swallowed them.

Kermorvan wheeled his horse, and chivvied the others. Alais and Olvar pulled Kunrad along, because he kept turning to look back up the gorge into the deepening shadows. Kermorvan rode his horse close, demanding under his breath, 'Did the little bugger really accept?'

'I don't know!' admitted Kunrad. 'I hope so. It looked like it. If the duergar can keep so close a watch and summon such a force, there'll be nowhere else we can go, not in the time. And you saw them! That armour is superb . . . Kermorvan, these aren't wild men!'

'They ain't exactly chambermaids, boy!' rumbled the older man.

'I mean they've arts and crafts of civilisation. And numbers. They can keep us out of the mountains if they want. Kermorvan, you'd be well advised to stop this killing anyway, whether they help or not.'

'Mmmh. You mean to go back?'

'Yes! What else can I do? That gesture . . . And that armour! It could hold the answer . . . We'll have to see, won't we?'

Kunrad hardly heard the call to supper that evening.

Alais went in search of him with a steaming bowl, and found him sitting under a tree some way off, the smith's book on his knee, scratching figures in the earth with a stick. 'One minute more and you can wear this as a helmet!' she warned him. 'About fit for keeping those addled brains of yours in! Is it that accursed armour again?'

Kunrad's stick slashed away what he had been drawing, and he sprang to his feet. 'Why not?' he demanded savagely. 'I was shaped to make it, wasn't I?'

'I'm sorry!' she said, backing off. 'I should never have said anything so stupid! There's more to you than that, more that – that I admire. You're strong and valiant, yet you're not cruel and you're not a bloody-minded soldier. You're a craftsman, and yet you're a scholar and more of a nobleman than many who bear the name. You have eyes, and you see – sometimes. It's just that it upsets me so, to find, at the heart of all that, nothing but this evil bloody *armour!*'

The twilight shadowed her face, but he could see the change in her whole stance, and the way the bowl shook. 'I'm sorry. It was not the armour I was drawing but something else, an idea I had from that old book, and the notes of the duergar . . . Lady, this hold the armour has on me, it pains me also. Worse, because it so distresses you. I would never have that.' He put out his hands to steady the bowl, and they met hers around it. She almost jerked them away, then realised that would spill the soup and held them there, stiff and tense.

'What would you have, then?' she demanded.

He gave a laugh that was almost a scoff, bitter and uneasy. 'Oh, Powers! Many things! Peace of mind. Freedom. A new life! My old one's eaten up like a fire that runs behind me. I am left only today, and what is to come. I could wish so many things – if only I felt I should!'

Her voice was unusually low and serious. 'Maybe you should worry less about could and should. The future is hardly certain for any of us, is it? Perhaps the things you could wish are the making of it. If only you have the vision to reach out and take them.'

The bowl struck the ground with a soft thud, spilling its contents unheeded. His grip on her was almost violent, his hands twisting in her hair, forcing her head back as his encircling arms crushed her against him. Her hands were flat against his shoulders, her long fingers splayed and taut, yet she was not pushing him away so much as trying to hold off the same fierce movement in herself. His lips came down on hers and hesitated, for hers were drawn back in a fierce fixed grin, and he met only her sharp teeth. But at the first hint of withdrawal, her mouth clamped against his, wide open so that her tongue reached out and lapped against his lips. She drew him in as if he was the very air of life itself, and her startled shivers were as much at herself and the surging force within her. Her fingers clutched and clenched, then grabbed at his own trailing hair around the back of his neck. His grip relaxed an instant, and he felt her arms fly up, free, and lock around his neck as she ground her breasts against him, and then her thighs, almost shocking him with the animality of it, and the heat it aroused in answer.

Shadow claimed the world, but the blackness that took him was deeper. He saw and felt nothing save the pattern of her body as it moved against his own, almost as clearly as if they were naked. That thought set the darkness roaring, and tightened his temples. He was drowning in her; he had no breath but hers. He clutched at her, and they swayed, crumpling one another's clothes in great handfuls, pulling the flesh bare. His hands slid over her, clothed, and she caught her breath at the intimacy of it; but when his hands returned there was no longer any barrier. Their mouths tore apart then, because they had to breathe; and they clung, dizzy, head to shoulder, his legs braced apart to bring them one against another. Instinct busied her hands as her head spun, and it was only gradually she felt him hesitate, and still his own questing fingers. She threw her head back, looking a wild question into his face. His eyes avoided hers; he jerked his head in the direction of the firelight, startlingly near.

'We'll go farther away, then . . .' she said, and tugged at his hand. He shook his head. 'What is it, then?' she hissed, still trying to draw him on. 'What's the matter with you? I . . . You know, plague you! You love me, too!'

'This isn't right,' Kunrad said slowly. 'Yes, of course I . . . but this is ridiculous! You, me – you being what you are! Your father . . . I'm a foreigner, princess. An enemy, practically. Not even rich or important. I've made enough problems for other people already.' He ran down, uneasily aware she was not saying anything. He had been ready for fury, a slap even. That would have made it easier. He was dreading a sob. Silence left him helpless.

'And you're not making them for me?' she whispered suddenly and savagely. 'Look at me! Look!' It was a rhetorical question, in the darkness, but he could see the odd flash of flesh and white linen as she strove to tuck her disordered clothes back together. Her voice was gravelly with controlled misery. 'I've never let any man do that, not even the least any girl might! You think I don't know who I am? You think I'm not reminded of that every time I see some snotty serving-girl enjoy a little slap and tickle with the first lad who ventures? You think I didn't know whose hands those were, or what I was doing myself? Any man! Ever! And *you* have the raw cheek to turn all principled upon *me*? You . . . *Northerner!* Nothing but salt cod in your belly and the Ice in your veins! I should have known I was wasting my time!'

'Not that!' His hands gripped her shoulders. 'There've been other women, but what I felt about you . . . what I feel . . . never anything like that. I never knew I could. That was why. I'm not going to drag you down, too.'

'I'm too important, that's it, is it?' She cursed under her breath, standing awkwardly among the low undergrowth, struggling to straighten her breeches. 'Well, I suppose I should feel honoured. At least you wouldn't hang back from the armour . . . Blast this hook!'

'Here,' he said. 'Let me.'

The touch of the back of his fingers against the

warmth of her belly was enough. Neither was the least in thrall now, and yet there was no space to argue. 'Oh damn it!' she hissed, and slammed him against her as she might a door.

They walked back to the camp in sullen silence. 'I feel humiliated,' was all she said.

'That it was your turn to hesitate?' he said. 'After so many plaints?'

'I only baulked at a leap,' she said. 'As a spirited horse might. You could have ... gone on.'

'You don't know much about the game, do you?'

'Game,' she muttered. 'Very well! I hope you still enjoyed your play.'

'Of course,' he said.

'Fine! So now you know what a princess feels like. Tell your friends!'

He took hold of her and swung her to face him. 'My instinct was right,' he said softly. 'This was neither the place nor the time. Later ... we'll see. A princess ... well, I know now that she feels like everything I have ever wished.'

'Except one thing,' she said acidly.

'No. That's no matter of wanting. That's something I have to have. That armour is my knowledge. That armour is my achievement. Without it I have neither. What I *want* is you. But ...'

She began to cry a little. 'Kunrad, things are bound to happen before we come through this. Aren't they? Horrible things.'

He put his arm around her shoulders. They felt stiff and unyielding. 'Yes, princess. Yes.'

They rode apart as the morning sun climbed the sky, until the narrowing path forced them together. Kermorvan squinted at them from under yellowed eyelids, and grumbled to himself, or turned to bellow at the trail of workers with the carts and teams. Kunrad was none too happy with them himself. They looked willing, these sothran peasants, but they were not overly well fed, and they mostly bore farm shovels and mattocks, poor stuff for mining.

Again the gorge opened before them, and in this early light it was a sun-struck channel glowing in the grey rock, as if the bare layers of brown and yellow and purple-red were those mysterious minerals said in smithlore to lock in the secrets of the sun. It was a splendid sight, but it swiftly soured upon him as their horses crested the path, and he saw the length of it. It was empty. The gorge held nothing but that light, and the warm wind sighing against the wall.

Kermorvan dangled a sun-bracelet and snorted. 'Knew you couldn't trust the little . . .'

Kunrad leaned closer, peering at the curious workmanship of the bracelet, and the sharp-edged shadow the perforations cast across it. 'This is a fine antique piece of work. Very precise. We're a few minutes short of the hour.'

'If you say so. Can't see it that close – *what's that?*'

Kunrad was already looking around, and Alais. The sense of sudden watchfulness was back. Something had triggered it. Something was stirring the hairs on his neck. Something in the wind . . .

Kunrad rose in his saddle, and shouted. 'What's this? Did you never mean to help us?'

Silence. Then he heard it clearly; that faint sizzle once again, louder now and easier to locate, spitting and fizzing from high above to their right.

There was no more warning than that. The noise was a thunderclap, and in the narrow gorge it was redoubled, not echoing but shivering the cliffs like a vast stone gong. The horses shied, and kicked, the peasants dropped their tools and fled screaming down the path. Red flame and grey smoke spurted out of the cliff, and for a moment Kunrad half expected to see a dragon burst out on gigantic batwings. Instead he flinched as he saw a long streak of the hillside shiver and slip downwards. He yelled to Alais, tried to get control of his horse and for his pains was sent flying from the saddle to land painfully upon the path. Alais turned to him, but Kermorvan thrust her back and sprang from his saddle with a thump. His huge hands clamped on Kunrad's arm with bruising force and, as the others scattered, the old man more or less hurled the smith back down the path, then threw himself flat by his side. Some ways beyond their feet the slip of brownish rock went rolling and rumbling and crashing across in a tongue of dust and rubble, and smashed like a wave against the further side. Lesser rocks came bounding down in its wake, and the men yelped and covered their heads, and took the bruises, hoping that nothing bigger was following.

The silence that fell was of a different kind again, the shocked and empty echo of riven air. It was broken by a harsh cawing sound, a deep-throated crow-laugh that had too much resonance for the voice of a bird. It might have been the mountain itself mocking the plundering pretensions of mere men. Cautiously the two of them heaved themselves up from a tide of gravel, coughing and choking at the dust. 'Bastards!' groaned Kermorvan, trying to shake his fist skyward, and falling over.

Alais came running up to them, 'Daddy! K— Are you all right?'

'Just mocking us, the louseridden little rockfuckers—' Kermorvan's voice streamed away into some remarkable cursing and coughing. Kunrad caught his arm and shook his head. He too was coughing, but he was laughing.

'Bastards!' spat Gille, as he and Olvar stumbled through the stones to help. 'Ambushing us like that!'

'No!' Kunrad hacked. 'Wrong, wrong – all wrong – couldn't be more wrong—' He clutched at the rocks and roared, a little hysterically. 'Not ambushing!' He brandished a stone. 'Whassat look like?'

'My umbels!' groaned Kermorvan. 'Damn near strewed 'em across the hillside, too!'

'Yes!' panted Kunrad. 'Kidneys!' He hurled the stone at Gille, who fielded it neatly, and stared. 'What they call kidney stone, boys – remember?'

The Voice of the Winds

'Powers above!' said Olvar, peering over Gille's shoulder.

Kunrad suppressed his coughing a little. 'What you did—' he said to Kermorvan, clapping the old man's shoulder. 'Never forget! But that was a controlled slide. They set those fires of theirs in the mountainside like that, very careful – see? It'd never have hit us. And these rocks—' He shook his head. 'That up there, it must be a huge seam. They've been working it a long time, maybe, very carefully. That's why I only found a few fragments. But I never dared hope – Kidney stone!'

'One of the purest iron ores there is!' grinned Gille. 'And in nice convenient pieces! We've no more than to shovel it up, and be on our way!'

Olvar was peering into the margins of the fall. 'There's something else—' He plunged forward, and took up what looked like a heavy sack. 'Two or three of these!' He delved, swore, and held up a bleeding finger. 'Spearheads! Fine ones, if my hide's any test.'

Kunrad nodded, dislodging a great avalanche of dust from his hair. He stood up, painfully, and waved his arms. 'Wish they'd show themselves! If I could only get a closer look at that arm articulation – *Thank you! Thank you very much!*'

It was a listening silence, for a second; and then, just as certainly, it was no longer. 'Well,' humphed Kermorvan, dusting off his paunch. 'A help and a warning both, if I'm not mistaken! Now we round up those yellow-livered dungdancers and set 'em shovelling. And best you don't shout at those friends of yours any more, my lad. Or they might get generous!'

It was long hours into the night before the train of weary peasants left, their carts groaning under the load, as also the huge oxen that drew them away. Of the duergar they saw and heard no more; save, as they quitted the gap for the last time, the sound of many deep voices echoing away among the peaks, deeper than human tones and in a close harmony that throbbed through the darkness.

'Might be a marching song,' said Kermorvan. 'It has that beat. It comes to me that I'll be keeping my word indeed, if we come through this, lest one night I hear it marching to my door.'

'I think you are wise, my Lord Kermorvan,' said Kunrad.

The older man brushed some more dust out of his moustache, and looked along the line of carts. 'Well, at any rate you have your metal now.'

'Not quite,' said Alais acidly. She was still not speaking to Kunrad. 'Our gallant smiths still have to render it down, don't they? Smelting, is that the word? I wonder how they plan to manage that, in time. Gille? Olvar?'

'Well,' said Gille uneasily. 'It does take time, it could be difficult – but I'm sure the Mastersmith has something clever in mind . . .'

'I'm sure he has, too,' she said. 'The Mastersmith's mind is deep enough to hold many strange things, and dark enough, alas, so mere mortals trip over them. I'm sure he'll be only too ready to enlighten us, when he manages to remember we exist!'

Kermorvan stared at her as she turned her horse to the far side of the wagons. 'Beak of the Raven!' he rumbled to the prentices. 'Now what's this all about? There I was frettin' about . . . Ah, never mind! Never mind! Soon enough when we're back at the castle. Probably all asleep in their nice warm beds, rot 'em! Like any man of sense.'

When they came to the hilltops above the lake, though, it was clear that nobody had been idle. 'The walls are manned!' exclaimed Kermorvan; and as they looked down to the bristling hedge of spears about the ramparts they shared an instant of common dread, that the Marchwarden might have returned and retaken it in their absence.

Olvar broke it with a chuckle. 'Don't think one in ten of those pigstickers has got a head on it. Not much use 'gainst corsair tinplate. Well, we can fit them out a bit fancier now!'

Nonetheless they all watched warily as the bridge was run out. All save Kunrad, who was gazing absently around the lakeshore, contemplating the trees, plucking leaves from bushes and watching how they fell.

'What're you up to now?' boomed Kermorvan.

'There's a prevailing wind in these parts, isn't there?'

Kermorvan stared. ''Course, yes. What the lake's named for, and the castle. Whistles off the sea, straight across the Marches, bounces back off the mountains and forms a sort of eddy around the lake, see? Strongest up on the ridges there. Worse in winter. Get a sea-gale'll freeze your—'

'Yes, I thought so. It's very like the land where I used to live, rolling country with a mountain background. And I remember the Marsh winds ... My lord, I don't think we need to take the carts into the castle.'

'What? Well, where then?'

Kunrad pointed. 'Down around the shoreline there and up to the hilltop beyond.'

'Overlooking the castle? That's the ridge I meant. Yn Aruel – Hill o' the Winds. What in Raven's name d'you want the ore up there for?'

'An idea. Something that came through a note in that smith's book, and a coughing corsair ... Gille, Olvar, you go with them! My lord, I'll need the working party still, and another for tree felling. Another over to where they cut peat. And are there clay beds in the area?'

Kermorvan roared. 'Why, man, how would I know? What's pottery to me? The farmland south o' the lake's heavy river clay. I know that; murder to plough! But—'

'There's clay along the south shore,' put in Alais stiffly, looking at nobody in particular. 'Fine clay. I used to play with it. One of the peasants could show you.'

Kunrad looked at her. 'Won't you?'

She glared at him. 'A shame. I'm otherwise engaged. I'll await you at the castle, Father!'

She turned her horse and went cantering away down the shore while Kermorvan was still spluttering. 'Now what's got into her? Ah well, no arguin' with her in this mood. Just like her mother!' He leaned over to the prentices and gave a conspiratorial whisper. 'Take my advice, lads. Never have a daughter!'

Olvar's stolid features cracked in a brief flash of teeth. 'No need to tell Gille, my lord. He just has other people's.'

Kermorvan gave a great snort, stifled it and took on a look of moustache-bristling disapproval. 'Well, better watch himself in the Southlands here. No laughing matter. Cut a man's – cut him off in his prime, some fathers will!' He rounded on the peasants. 'All right, you heard the Mastersmith, take your wagons along to that hilltop there with these lads! Come on, look lively, it's barely a step further, it won't kill you!'

'Why there?' Olvar wondered aloud over the groaning chorale of wagons, oxen and wagoneers. 'Why that hill in particular? And all that about the wind? Maybe he'll try laying a furnace chimney up the hillside to strengthen the draught. I've heard something of that. What d'you think, Gille? Gille?'

For once Gille was the silent and morose one. 'You shouldn't have joked like that! I was wondering . . . what if I *do* have a daughter one day? I mean, what's it going to be like?'

Olvar, unusually, threw back his head and roared with laughter. 'The searing justice of the Powers, is what! A poacher turned gamekeeper! You'll lock the poor lass up in an iron cage!'

'Better than a gilded one,' said Gille seriously. 'Think that's what's bothering the Mastersmith? About the princess?'

Olvar looked askance at him. 'Maybe. Ask him, and beware of your ears. He's a lot else to bother him right now.'

Gille brushed him off. 'Not him, you oaf! Her! You wait!'

When the carts toiled up to the hilltop, an hour or so later, Gille found it already a mass of activity. The few bent trees on its upper slope were fallen or being felled, and a trench was being cut along past their roots, right across the lakeward slope. Kunrad, standing on a great displaced bole, caught sight of him and waved. 'Just the men! Olvar, I need the ore dumped on the hilltop above, but so none of it rolls down – not yet! And Gille, will you take my compliments to Lord Kermorvan and say I need some lengths of that earthen piping they use for drains? About ten good armspans will do! That's it, lads! Hurry along! A few more days' grace and we'll set a ring of steel about the castle!'

It was three hours more before Gille returned, and when he did the hilltop was already changed still further. The trench now ran in a great halfmoon around the summit, easily two hundred paces long, and was still being widened. The sun was high, and even in the strong lake breeze men were sweating and flagging; but Kunrad drove them like sheep.

'We tore up the drains themselves, Mastersmith!' called Gille. 'That was all they had!'

'No matter,' Kunrad shouted back. 'If we can't make this work they'll have worse worries! Now—' He stopped dead. There, leading the packhorse that carried the malodorous earthenware pipe, was Alais. He sprang down and came running.

'My lady, I—' He stopped in confusion. 'What I want is this, Gille! Get Olvar and his lads. See those slots? There's loads of clay coming up from the lakeside. What we're going to do is line those slots with stones, separated so there's a thin course between them, and then a thick layer of clay with stones in it, about kneehigh. Through that, as we lay it, a length of pipe to make a hole, right through to the trench, but we shape a wide mouth in the clay at the front, like a trumpet. Got it? Then we'll get brushwood and fire each, lightly, so that it's solid, like making a clay mould – right?'

Gille looked around wildly. 'Mastersmith, I think I begin to understand. But nobody's ever made such a thing! Would not a tall flue—'

'Not in a hundred ways!' snapped Kunrad, eyes gleaming. 'Go to it, lad! Go! Run! And you, my lady—'

'Yes, Mastersmith? Where would you have me?'

'Safe within walls, far from strife, like anything a man holds dear. But failing that, anywhere you wish, my lady. Command me as you like.'

She gave a wry smile. 'I meant to say as much to you. Your prentice all but haled me out by the hair. He said you needed me.'

'I never told him to do that!' blurted Kunrad, deeply shocked. 'I'll have his hide!' And then, subsiding, 'But he was right, the little sod.'

'I didn't quite believe him. But, yes, he was right. He said something about having a daughter himself.'

'That's a new one. But then this danger sets us all to thinking, doesn't it? It's no time for love, not if you're practical. I tried to be practical; it's all I know. I was wrong.'

'No more than I was.' She seized his hands. 'Kunrad, I promise you this – I will be jealous of that armour no longer. Not enough to stand in your way, anyhow. What now? Time is riding hard at our back. We may have wasted what little we had. Is there anything left for us, amid all this?'

The first load of clay arrived, in panniers across the shoulders of more packhorses. From up the hill came the sound of Gille and Olvar swearing at one another, and the clatter of shovels.

Kunrad managed a smile. 'Maybe not. But if we gain through to the other side, maybe. And my lady . . .' He squeezed her hands, gently, and felt the wiry strength of her own grip. 'This I promise you. I will not abandon my quest; but if ever it comes to a choice between that armour and you – then my choice is already made. Let it rot and rust before you come to harm!'

She stared. 'But . . . even if you know no peace again, as you foretold?'

He shrugged. 'I would know as little, or less. I have grown, my lady, and it is your doing.'

She pulled him to her then, and they kissed there on the hilltop amid the noise and confusion of the building, and it fell away around them and faded from their minds. Only when their embrace ended did they realise it had stilled in truth, and saw every eye in the site turned upon them, men standing statue-like with earth still upon their spades.

They looked at one another in horror. 'There's only one thing we can do!' panted Kunrad.

'Yes. Kiss me again.'

Manhandling a lady of quality – probably something a man would get flayed or impaled for in this stiffnecked Southland, thought Kunrad cheerfully. Well, let them stare. There was something to be said for more immediate worries.

'What're you gawping at?' he snarled at his audience, when he came up for air again. 'Idling till the corsairs come for you? Work! Work till you drop! Get those slots cut as we marked them out! And stack up that wood there – d'you want it rolling down the hill? Get those timbers to length, and stripped!' He turned back to Alais. 'And best I follow my own orders,' he added ruefully.

'I also,' she said cheerfully. 'Answering to Father's. But with a better heart. And when we come through it all . . .'

'Then we may truly set the woods afire!' he grinned. 'Let it startle whom it may!'

When Kermorvan came bustling up the hill at nightfall, sat high on his huge warhorse with its feathered legs, he stopped dead in astonishment at what confronted him. The trench now stood at some two hundred paces long, and three wide, and deeper than the height of a man. The back wall was being built up with drystones, by peasants skilled in the work. The fore wall was lower, a bank in the earth, and men were driving narrow slots through it at regular intervals, while others carried up stones from the lakeside, some of them wide flat slabs from the outcrops.

'Missing your drainpipes?' laughed Kunrad, though his dry voice cracked a little.

'Bugger the pipes! What in Hella's name's all this?' demanded the old man, heaving a leg laboriously over the saddle. 'More fortifications?'

'Not exactly,' grinned Kunrad, helping him down with encaked hands.

Kermorvan fastidiously brushed off the lumps of mud. 'Could be some kind of earthfort, such as our forefathers built when they first came to this land. You still see remains of them, here and there, on hilltops just like this. Burned out, mostly, so hot the stones themselves have fused like glass!'

Kunrad paused. 'Burned out? Well, well. Then they may not have been forts!' He looked along the trench. 'This too is an ancient thing, such as Northern smiths no longer use. My prentices have never heard of it, and I only from an old book, and some older wisdom! But it should serve us here, thanks to the strong arms of your folk. The last loads of clay and fuel come tonight, and it should be in use within a day.' He licked a finger, and help it up. 'If the Powers are on our side, and the wind holds. And the corsairs keep away!'

'The wind'll hold, at this season,' said Kermorvan. He said nothing of the corsairs. 'Gets stronger toward midnight, in the spring and summer. Comes singing round the old towers and moaning in the wells. It'll be there, all right. But will you? A long ride and no sleep last night, long day's labour and no more tonight – Alais is worried about you, you know!'

'I'll be all right,' said Kunrad wearily. 'Where is she, anyhow?'

Kermorvan winked. 'The kitchens! 'Bout time she was put to some proper woman's work!'

Kunrad looked askance. Kermorvan had some very sothran attitudes. 'And she stood for that?'

Kermorvan shrugged. 'Never a cheep! Bossing around a whole bevvy of clucking peasant women. They'll be sending up some grub soon, and you look as if you could use some. And speaking of Alais, my lad—'

Kunrad lunged past him suddenly, his voice edged with strain. '*Easy with that stone, there!* You'll cave in the bloody channels!'

'Never mind!' muttered Kermorvan gruffly. 'It'll keep!'

Yet it, whatever it might be, churned over and over in Kunrad's mind as they laboured on into the dark. Torches were lit, and by their light men hauled up great bundles of dry firewood from the castle, and the still larger bales of brush and branch and peat. Some were stacked, but after a time more went into the trench, till the weary labourers fell down among them and were almost buried. Their fellows had to probe with sticks to make sure none were left. Even the hardened peasants were beginning to collapse now, sprawling insensible to the curses and kicks of their overseers, and Kunrad felt shame at using them as roughly as their masters did. He knew he could not have stood such treatment, for all the toughening the long journey had given him, and the old strength he had regained. Yet he dared spare none of them, any more than himself. When their labours were done, his would only be beginning.

And now there was Alais – sothran lady, princess of the old royal line, fair, brave and powerful, whom he had come so near losing, and might still. What was it Kermorvan meant to say? The obvious, probably. That Kunrad was a foreigner, a commoner, poor. That however much he liked and respected him . . .

'*Olvar!* Get that bank shored up before it falls on someone!'

The obvious. Hands off Alais. And what would Alais say? She might be willing to run away with him, back to the North.

'Overseers! Bring up those end timbers now. 'Ware, and don't catch the lip of the trench!'

Back to the North. And *that* might be all the pretext some sothran lords would need. Wars had started over less.

Over and over as the figures came and went across

the torchlit hilltop, bringing supporting timbers for the wall and the brushwood for the firing of the clay, he seemed to see her face. Over and over in the darkness, until suddenly it was no longer fleeting and flickering but there, steady against the dark, staring at what had sprung into being so swiftly. Her red hair whipped like the torch-flames.

He sprang down and ran to meet her, seeing suddenly that her slender shape was outlined in glinting mail, with a bow at her back. Her eyes were grim. 'The scouts we sent out,' she said. 'The first word came back not long since. There's activity deep within the Marches – ships mustering on the river, many of them. That was all they could make out at the distance, but it's enough!'

Kunrad drew breath, striving to clear his mind and marry time and distance. The scouts had been sent out . . . 'Four days since?' His back grew chill as he caught her meaning. 'And the word returned in—'

'Less than a day. Relayed by flag and sun-glass. They dared not use smoke.'

He drew breath. 'That's something. But they could still be on us in a matter of days, with scant warning! Seems Merthian has blood in his eye, all right!'

'He may have more yet. Father has placed the land on a war footing. He's preparing an advance guard in case they come too swiftly, to stave them off for as long as he can; though he said that was a counsel of desperation. All men save those labouring must carry their arms at all times and wear armour, if they have it. I've brought yours, and the boys'.' She pointed to a cart behind her. 'With shirts and breeches, so we may wash the stinkards you stand in! And food for your men. They look as if they need it.'

He nodded. 'Gille! Olvar! Have the overseers stand down their men! An hour to eat and rest. But only half of each team at a time! We've got to get that earth tamped back, at once! You've no notion what that wall will have to withstand!'

'They need more than that!' protested Gille, shocked. 'You'll kill somebody soon!'

'The corsairs will do it better!' snapped Kunrad, then shook his head. 'Yes! Yes, of course, I'm sorry. Two hours now, then three later. A little more for those who must wait. And my lady, if you would send down to the castle for fresh men. Half as many, if Ferlias can get no more. But we must not stop! We dare not!'

It was near dawn before the last heap of earth was packed and tamped down around the foot of the great arced wall, leaving proud the upper rim and the row of strange slots along its face, each with its vent and channel. Kunrad inspected every inch, kicking, prodding, never leaving any small crack or slide in doubt. Then he took one of the unlit torches, and went by himself to a campfire. Those near by thought he was warming himself, until they heard him singing and saw the torch burst suddenly into flame. As soon as he was sure of it, Kunrad clambered on to one of the rough tree trunks set astride the great trench. He held the flame high, watching it gutter and flicker in the warm lake wind, and he sang words that none save Gille and Olvar understood, in the Northern tongue.

> *Spirit of light in the brightness feasting!*
> *Friend of the smith at his hearthside feeding,*
> *Come to the feast that I spread before you!*
> *Kindle the hearts of the sturdy ash-logs,*
> *All the long years of their captured sunlight!*
> *Crack the bark*
> *And curl the needle*
> *Glut yourselves on*
> *Saps of springs past!*
> *Gleaned glow of a hundred summers!*
> *Cleanse it, that it shine eternal,*
> *Undying, in the heart of metal!*

Yet as he sang them, over and over, the labourers

trembled, such was the command they heard even in his voice, that fatigue made harsh. When he began to shift his feet in time, and slap and stamp on the top of the walls, the sothrans crouched wearily and whispered among themselves, old tales their overlords had long forgotten, of the wonderworking smiths of the Northern folk. They watched, wide-eyed, as Kunrad, almost dancing with the intensity of his words, swept the torch about his head in a great corona of flame.

All at once it flared higher and faster than it should. With a cracked shout he plunged the torch down between his feet, into the top layer of brush. The fire seemed to leap to the wood almost before the torch even touched it. Kunrad tottered an instant astride the fire, off-balance, unable to jump either way. Then a gust blew, awakening a breath almost of eerie music along the line of pipes. Along the trench, before and behind, rushed great hissing plumes of flame, and the mastersmith was engulfed in an uprush of fire. The watchers sprang up with horrified cries, but Gille and Olvar were already running up around the end of the trench. The flame danced, guttered and parted, and they saw Kunrad stretched out against the last of the slope, beneath the high mounds of ore. The prentices half carried him down to a water-butt, and splashed his scarlet cheeks. His eyes flashed suddenly open, and the labourers drew back as if from the presence of some inhuman spirit.

He laughed a little before it became a cough. '*Friend of the smith at his hearthside feeding!*' he choked. 'Damn near bit the hand there, eh?'

'You almost overdid it,' said Gille reproachfully. The pipes sighed again, the flame flared and soughed, and it seemed as if the whole hillside breathed like a great beast. Smoke billowed skyward, and the sweet smell of burning wood. The front wall popped and cracked, but it held firm.

'Almost!' Kunrad exulted. 'But it works, lads! It works! Now we'll smother the vents – it's charcoal we want, not ashes! And—'

'And it's a smith we want, not an invalid!' said Gille severely. 'When that's done, you rest!'

With the dawn new lines of men came toiling up the hill, stopping in shock as they saw the stumbling scarecrows, mud-caked and mindless, who shambled down past them. Kunrad himself looked little better, freshly clad but still haggard and weary, with his face all smoke-blackened once again. He had grudgingly stretched out for a brief nap, but he was already on his feet again, peering down into the smoky pit, poking around with a pole, ordering this or that vent opened or stopped. 'Charring bravely!' he said, smacking the cinders from his arms. 'It'd take days of slow burning, normally, but we can't spare that now – what's this, Olvar, fresh hands?'

'Yes. But scarce half the number, as you feared. Some too old or too young.'

'No matter! They'll serve!' He waved to the new arrivals as they squatted down, whispering among themselves, and shouted. 'Welcome! We need you!' He rubbed an arm over his face. 'Is it my smoky eyes, or are there some more—'

'Yes. The overseers stayed, and some of the others said they'd be back after a dip down below. Tough buggers, these whiteskin boys.'

'Let's hope we can make their sweat worthwhile!' said Kunrad feelingly, and waved the peasants to their feet. 'Half the teams to the fuel stacks there, the others to the ore mounds! We're going to heave 'em in layer upon layer – so we keep in the juices! We've built the hearth – now we'll bake the pies! Just like your mamma's best!'

There was some laughter at that, but not much. The labourers were too much in awe of this tall Northerner who dared to kiss their princess in public, as the whisper ran, and kindled fire with song, as in a folktale. They ran to work at his word, averting their eyes, and shovelled with desperate force, as if a Power bade them.

As the fire was stifled Olvar and some of the strongest men sprang down into the trench to level off the layers as they came down, at constant risk of being overwhelmed by the great cascades of purple stone. The wood beneath, still charring, was forced lower and lower, compressed more tightly till the song of the wind in the vents rose to a high seething whistle. The heat in the trench grew more intense, and some of the fuel layers caught as they were laid, flaring briefly until more shining ore came crashing down to stifle them. All this while Kunrad was running back and forth along the front wall, lost in clouds of dust and smoke, leaping in and out of the trench with manic energy to direct the laying of the layers.

Slowly, as the day wore away to the afternoon, the trench filled almost to the brim, and the labour grew slower with the terrible need for care. Delays grew while a collapse was filled, or an overlarge boulder was hammered into pieces, let it cause a blockage. Over one such Kunrad stood, directing the hammers and wedges, a wild, smoke-blackened figure with a colourful rag tied round his head where cascading ore had cut it. In the low golden light of early evening his spidery shadow waved and gestured across the whole hillside. Gille and Olvar, snatching a hard-earned rest, watched him in mild amazement.

'Say now, brother prentice,' enquired Olvar. 'D'you remember a time when he was just a nice amiable workaday weaponsmith? Instead of a mighty warrior, wonderworker, groper of princesses in the public gaze? Don't seem possible, do it?'

Gille shrugged. 'Remember when we were two innocent lads who knew nothing of the world, but all about sleeping under the same roof two nights running?'

'*Same* roof be damned!' groaned Olvar. '*Roof*, short and simple. Bed, for that matter; or hayloft in your case. I envy these folk! Never mind the hue of the skin, they're just like mine. Hey there, lad!' he called to a nearby worker, a shock-haired young farmhand hardly smaller than himself.

'Yer will, me lord?'

'Don't call me that!' snapped Olvar. 'I was born in a two-room fisherman's shack, with three brothers. Expected

I'd die there, if I 'scaped drowning! Guess you feel the same about your homestead?'

' 'Ud do, zur. If they bastard corsairs hain't burned 'en down. Out 'o the night, never a word. Killed my mam, stole old cow.'

'Sorry I am,' said Olvar, in a memory of his own dialect. 'Flayed they'll be for it, with your good help!'

The young man knuckled his forelock, making Olvar bridle, and stooped to his shovel. 'And there's our answer, I suppose,' sighed Gille. 'If we'd sat still and done nothing, you in your cottage, me in our manor, all this'd have come down about our heads soon enough. And we worse prepared for it. At least this way we'll strike a harder blow!'

'And take one!' said Olvar gloomily, as Kunrad hailed them back. 'Coming, Master! We must be near done, surely?'

They were. The ore piles had shrunk to mere gleanings, and the last scraps of fuel and kindling were being laid carefully across the top. Kunrad seemed calm now, save for the heaving of his chest and the gleam in his eyes. 'See, boys! See? It's holding! The first firing settled the clay! The wall's so firm it'd stand without the earth! It's time to fire her properly!'

'That'll take a while, won't it, master? To light a mass like this, evenly?'

'No. Not with your help and craft.' He looked at his labourers, sprawling exhausted over the matted and trampled grass. 'They think we can conjure fire. Would that we could! But what we sing into the flame, the steel will remember.'

When the labourers saw the torches lit again, they clustered close to sit and watch, half fascinated, half fearful. Gille and Olvar were pouring water over themselves at a waterbutt, and over Kunrad without waiting to be asked. The watchers drew breath, half expecting him to steam, as if he were himself a sizzling glede. Instead the water washed the soot from his countenance, and showed it fired by exhaustion into a pale hard mask of effort. He turned his reddened eyes on the crouching labourers. 'On your feet, lads!' he shouted. 'The last long stretch, and then we're home!'

The labourers heaved themselves up from the matted grass, with little of the customary groaning and grunting and complaining. They parted before him silently as he picked out the overseers and stationed them, each with a few of the steadier men, at the mouths of the vents. 'On my word!' he was repeating, over and over. 'Not before! Not after! Just then! And when you're done, fall back, to the side, away! Anywhere but before the wall, or I'll not be answerable!'

'But, lord, what'll yer word be?' asked one of them awkwardly.

Kunrad's mouth twisted in a smile. The man shrank back. 'Believe me,' Kunrad said, 'you'll know.'

Gille and Olvar were lighting torches, as he had bade them. They offered him one, but he shook his head wearily. 'The first fire is the master's, remember? Always, even when so many hands are in the work. The burden of it remains his.' He turned the torch in his fingers, almost numbly, ignoring the sparks that struck him, singing to himself as before.

> *Light of the past returning!*
> *Sun of the forest set free!*
> *Heat of a newer burning –*
> *Heed and hearken to me!*
> *Kindle my thought in the flame of thy breathing,*
> *Carry my words to the heart of the fire,*
> *Command all the elements mingled and seething,*
> *Coupling deep in the furnace desire.*
> *By the smith's will let them conceive a child there,*
> *Blood of the stone and black bone of the tree,*
> *Like and unlike in thy heat reconciled there,*
> *Bursting forth fiercer and brighter than thee.*
> *Light of the past returning!*
> *Sun of the forest made free!*
> *Setting the cold stone burning,*
> *Bow down and obey me!*

* * *

He rose up, twirling the pitch-coated wood, looking to the prentices. Without a word they scurried to either end of the wall, standing on the hillside and the tall endstones thrusting spear-smooth from the soil. Weariness bowed their shoulders, but all the watchers could see it dragging Kunrad's feet like invisible fetters as he trudged down the slope and stepped out on to the rear wall. The later afternoon wind whistled about him, whipping his dark hair in the same way as the pale flames of the torches. Still he sang, never relenting, and the words became clear to those who knew the Nordeney tongue. They heard, and whispered them to their neighbours, so that it became an echo, out of step as echoes always are, running rustling around the scarred hillcrest like the airs it spoke of. Gille and Olvar took up the chant, and they tapped their feet and patted their lips and wove the tune together in the manner of Northern mouth-music, while in the middle of the trench Kunrad hovered with his flaming branch.

> *Drink!*
> *Drink in the flame as you drank up sunlight!*
> *Blossom and leaf in the furnace springtide!*
> *Dance with stone in drunken frenzy!*
> *Crack its bones in hot embracing!*
> *Crush the veins and spill the heartsblood!*
> *Drink! Burn and be born together!*
> *Flow!*
> *Free as you flowed in the world's bright*
>   *birthpangs!*
> *Run as you ran before earth's blood*
>   *hardened!*
> *Shining river, winter's ending!*
> *Ice is melting, banks are bursting!*
> *Feed the trees in brilliant blossom!*
> *Flow! Burn and be born together!*

Share the same ordeal,
Shatter in the fire!
Shriven and cleansed in the furnace—
Be reborn as Steel!

All of a sudden he stopped, gestured sharply. Gille and Olvar downed their torches into the extreme ends of the trench. Small flames caught in the kindling, crackled and grew a little, sending up thin threads of steamy smoke. The fuel was too damp, too fresh; it would take time to catch. A little sigh of sympathetic disappointment went up from the watchers. But Kunrad stood, back bent and blade-tense, listening and looking out across the lake. The trees on the slope opposite bowed their heads as if they heard him, and across the wide waters lines of grey ripples arose and grew long, like the wake of a ship invisible. The first fingers of the gust riffled his hair, and with a shout to the men below he sprang down, straight on to the top of that mass of caged fire, and plunged down the torch like a spear into the back of some great beast.

At his shout the team crouching below hurled themselves into the channel and with frenzied speed tore away the stones and wadding they had so carefully set there. Then they sprang back as another voice spoke, loud and urgent. The rising lake wind rushed among the watchers and broke like a wave against the wall.

Into the centre slot it blew deep, and sang a whining, wheezing song in the vent; over the wall it flowed, and drew the air along, up and through from the vent below. Where Kunrad's torch broke the layer, flame fountained manhigh, with an eerie howl, as if to devour the summoner. But Kunrad was already away, stabbing down with the torch, springing aside from the spray of smoky flame that spewed up as he shouted for the next channel to be opened. The wind plucked at the flames, and flattened them; but as it roared through the channels beneath, the newly opened vents, they straightened and spread, and others rose to join them like a field of deadly flowers, fiercer and faster than the torches could ever have lit. Many, perhaps, of the onlookers understood that this was the first fire, left smouldering among the charcoal far below until fed anew by the channeled force of the wind. Yet still it seemed like magic, and so it was told in their tales a thousand years on.

Another note, a deeper one, sang in the wall; another joined its voice in eerie thrumming harmony with the first, and another, as Kunrad opened the breath of fire all along the trench, still chanting, skipping and stamping between the flames as a child might among rain-puddles. His soaking clothes were steaming now, and the sweat on his cheeks glittered in the malign glare of the fire-spouts. His voice joined in the weird harmonies of the rising wind as it both sang in the vents and skipped and dipped over the rim. The angle of its coming he had had no time to observe and calculate properly, but the eerie music that shivered through the trench told him how well he had guessed. A trail of fire whined at his heels, but he was almost at the end now. Olvar followed his master along the rear wall; at no small risk to himself, for this was the lee edge, and the flames roared over his head. A wet rag shielded his streaming copper cheeks, an arm his eyes from the blazing air and stinging sparks. Beyond the blaze Gille watched them both, tense and scared, ready to spring but never moving. The whole huge trench hummed and roared with the dual breath of the wind and Kunrad was above the last wide vent, truly dancing to the whistling song now, whirling and yelling like a man possessed. Suddenly the onlookers screamed in horror. The men below, poised on the edge of panic, moved one whit too fast and tore the channel clear. Even as his torch touched it the red worm's tongue darted out and licked across his sleeve, as if to drag him down. His shirt blazed. With main strength he tore it bodily off his back. It fluttered away in the updraught like some agonised bat and crackled to flying ash in an instant.

The furnace sang a deep dragon chorus. The hillside shuddered to the music. Kunrad hurled himself onward, but the surface gave beneath him at the edge. He landed, swaying, as the flame boiled up. Gille sprang, right across the flame-breath at the angle of the trench; Olvar reached out. His shirt smoked; Gille yelled as a spark caught his face. But their hands closed on Kunrad's, and together they fell forward off the wall's end and on to the muddied slope below. Men emptied the water-butts bodily over them as they rolled, and their clothes spat steam. There was a unison sigh from the watchers.

After a moment Kunrad sat up, sought to speak and fell coughing. They gave him water, and he sighed harshly. Gille, dabbing his cheek, gave him a lopsided grin. 'What's so funny?' growled Kunrad. 'Have I no eyebrows left?'

'They're untouched, Mastersmith. But you stood in sore need of a shave before. Not now!'

Kunrad slumped forward. 'I could not believe the fire could grow so swiftly as the old accounts suggested. I should have paid better heed. I might never have shaved again.'

'Hear it!' croaked Olvar, exulting. 'The furnace-song!'

Kunrad rose to his feet in the twilight, his clothes half flayed from him, his skin glistening with the water; and some of the watchers gave a great wail. Many fled, careering down the paths to the castle; and even the overseers gave back in great shock. At his back the trench that was now a raging furnace roared in animal contempt at their terror, and darted insolent claws at the man who had dared to summon up its power. Smoke billowed up from the hilltop, so high that the newly fallen sun shone on it like a scarlet banner.

Under the fire-music Kunrad heard the crackle and spit of the ore. He knelt down as near the furnace as he dared to go, feeling as much as hearing the heat and thunder in the earth.

'Enjoy your rage!' he whispered. 'Spill me my earth's blood, press me out the wine of smiths! I have fed you almost to the limits of my own life. Now you must pour me out life in return!'

CHAPTER TEN
Ice and Steel

A HAND TOUCHED HIS shoulder, startlingly cool, and recoiled with a gasp at the raw patches of skin.

'Are you all right?' Alais breathed. 'You're all burned . . . Will it work as you wish?'

'I'm well enough,' said Kunrad, almost dreamily. 'And I've done all I can, for now.' She helped him to his feet, and he winced at her touch. 'They're not real burns, the most of them. They do smart, though. I could go down to the lake.'

'Fine idea. I brought some salves and bandages. And your clothes. Lean on me.'

'I'm sorry I weigh so heavy on you,' he said, as they made their slow way downwards.

'You do not. Not really, for such a great lump! As if you've been burning yourself up.'

'Maybe I have. I feel as if I could just cast myself on the lake and drift away.'

When they came to the shore he clambered slowly down to an overhanging rock and dabbled his scorched feet awhile before lowering himself painfully in, gasping at the shock of the cool water. After a little while he rolled over on his back in the shallows, floating gently, and was startled to see how beautiful his handiwork looked, and how eerie. About the hilltop lay a high crown of blazing gold, and above it a veil of shimmering air in which the very stars seemed to dance. The strange tuned roar thundered like a great organ across the night. It was an awesome sight, one it seemed impossible he could have created.

'All I sought was to build the best furnace I could

with what was at hand,' he mused, as he sat on the rock, letting the cool night wind dry him.

'You did that, and more,' said Alais. He felt her long clever fingers slide the salve across his burned arm, and sighed as the stinging lessened. 'You've made an emblem of power.'

'I didn't make it. Your people's backs and limbs, they did the making.'

'But your mind shaped it, your will drove them. You have wrought an amazing thing, Kunrad. You are an amazing man.'

He looked away, across the waters to where the castle brooded, with the hill-fire dancing along its white walls. 'Am I, princess? I don't feel it. Strange to see those towers, and think that only a few weeks past I lay a fettered prisoner beneath, with none but my poor lads to think of me.'

'Not so!' she said softly, and then, teasingly, 'Merthian was, you may be sure! And the corsairs!'

'I meant, with concern,' he chuckled. 'Nobody else at all?'

She tossed her hair back, and flicked a spot of salve on to his nose. 'Not I! For there I was, thinking you'd settled your bill with my dear betrothed and gone jogging away happily back to your Northlands! And what did I care? I had my world secure about me. That's what I kept telling myself. If I thought of you, I grew annoyed.'

'And then I came dripping in your window and turned it all upside down!' he chuckled.

'Yes. You stand in my debt. With a stiff rate of use!'

He winced as she wound the bandage round his shoulder and bound it tight. 'There! At least your mail shouldn't chafe. You'd better get dressed swiftly, so you don't get a chill.' But her fingers lingered on his bare skin. He reached an arm around to draw her in, but let it fall.

'Princess, princess. I must go back to the furnace. It needs watching, and careful feeding. There is a substance in the charring of wood that stiffens iron into steel.

It makes the metal more springy and better able to hold an edge, but if there is too much it turns brittle. In this fashion of furnace it forms in odd ways. I must go test the balance, add some other metals – and soon there will be slag to run off, waste and debris.'

'So difficult,' she sighed, drawing the arm back about her waist. 'I hoped you could simply rest and let it burn.'

'No, princess. And after that, of course, comes casting, shaping, forging – though there your local smiths can lend a hand. Till then, the steel cannot serve us. A week, at the least. Two—' He laughed. They both knew how likely that was. 'Ah, then we might achieve some real miracles for men to sing of. This above is only a beginning.'

'But a bright one.'

Later, when they had eaten and rested, they sent the prentices for a swim, and sat themselves down to watch the flames. The greedy song of the vents had sunk to a low roaring hum, changing pitch only as the wind veered or flawed a little. Kunrad found it strangely soothing, and let his mind ease in its courses. The first indications were good. The flames were a fine colour, the coals burned steady, more fuel had been heaped in and the first tricklings of slag were being leached out along the channels below the vents.

'Past midnight now. Not long till dawn,' remarked Alais sleepily, leaning on his shoulder, where he had folded his cloak to prevent the mailrings digging into her face.

'No. And we should have our first spillings of metal soon. And then . . . just give me that week . . .'

They nodded together, half into sleep, as the stars rolled across the sky above, and the River sank slowly from its height towards the horizon. It had fallen only a little way, though, when the new sound jolted them awake and to their feet, jarred and frightened; and Kunrad knew his wish was not to be.

It was the voice of trumpets, sounding from the hills about the lake. Shrill and swift, across the dark waters they rang, from the watchers set there; and they were echoed and answered in the towers.

'The alarum!' Alais spoke almost in a whisper. Instinctively they were clutching hands, like children before some mystery or danger. 'But the scouts . . .'

Red beacon-flames kindled, and mirrors flashed with their greedy light, spelling messages the watchers could not read.

'Overrun, maybe. Or simply overtaken. It could happen, in that awful country!' Kunrad cursed. 'Or they may only have fallen back to the watchposts. That would give us a little longer!' He cast an anguished glance back at the furnace. 'But how long?'

The girl pointed, wordlessly. Lights were awakening in the castle, and against the black waters of the lake the bridge was beginning to swing outward. Already there seemed to be movement in the gate. More trumpets sounded, and the shadowy cluster of men came pouring out across the bridge.

'What's happening?' demanded Gille, running up to their side. Olvar followed, cursing as his ill-adjusted mailshirt pinched him. Every man on the hill was awake, and fearful voices surrounded them. 'They're not running away?'

'No,' said Alais, her voice shaking. 'They're marching in order. That's the advance guard.'

They looked at one another. A counsel of desperation, Kermorvan had called it.

'Must be damn close!' whispered Olvar. 'What do we do?'

'Wait!' said Kunrad. 'Until we know!'

Before long they heard hooves on the hill, and saw the shadows of riders toiling up the long path; almost every horseman they had, it appeared. As their leader crested the hill's brow his silhouette against the greyly gleaming water was unmistakable.

'Well, the dung's flying good and proper!' was Lord Kermorvan's wheezy greeting, as he swung from his saddle. 'And your home-made firemountain here? Any yield?'

'All we would have needed!' said Kunrad bitterly. 'But not soon enough!'

'Ah well. Always in the fall of the dice, eh? You did your level best. Now we'll have to do as much. That's why I'm up here!'

'How long have we got?' demanded Alais.

Kermorvan tugged at his moustaches. 'There's the sticking point. Scouts, such of 'em as got away, say there's a big force coming upriver, as you'd expect. Could be landing in a day or two. But there's something else, a vanguard maybe that was landed early and's been moving overland from the south, fast. That's what got the scouts, them that didn't run fast enough. But how large, how swift, that's hard to say. We just know they're coming hard. Could be the whole force, even, and the river just a feint.'

'But why?'

'Surprise, most likely. Save a long siege; they must know that's dangerous for them. But it could be a worse purpose. The scouts – well, the messages are garbled, but they say there's men and something more than men. Something fell, they say, something cold.'

Kunrad and Alais exchanged glances. 'Her! The Ice-witch!' exclaimed Alais. 'It has to be!'

Kermorvan nodded, watching his foot soldiers march out along the shore below. 'That's what I thought, too. Dunno what the bitch expects she'll do to a castle, though!'

'Her arts are Winter's,' said Kunrad, 'if the legends are true. Winter freezes water and cracks stone. One such as her might; they say some are more powerful than others. But Winter also chills men's hearts.' He shivered suddenly in his mail, and remembered the careful padding and venting he had designed to keep his own armour at a stable warmth. He cast a quick look at the furnace in which he had sunk his hopes. 'The River roll them off to Hella! Do we have a few hours more, at least? We could bleed off what metal there is, and work it in the castle!'

'Can't promise you a thing, lad! The scouts that got away were the ones that didn't linger around to count.'

'Then we'll try it! Better that than see it all to waste! *Hoi, Gille, Olvar! All you men!*' His voice echoed across the hill. 'Every man jack who's still up here! Up to the wall and the vents! We'll tap her as she stands!'

Men ran this way and that in shouting confusion, jostling among the legs of the horsemen as they sought to watch the approaches. 'Quiet!' bellowed Kermorvan. '*Quiet!* Or I'll have your heads! Silently, sod you, how'd you expect us to keep watch?'

Everyone froze momentarily at his furious voice; and in the unnatural moment of silence that followed the night seemed to pulse and throb like a driven heart. Then Kunrad realised it was more than the blood in his own ears. There really was a sound, soft, thudding, unrelenting. Riding the wind, it echoed off the hills; it pulsed across the lake. The night was alive with drums.

'Well,' said Kermorvan quietly. 'That's it. They're here. Ferlias! From the south, there, if I mistake not?'

'Cut around and come up between the hills,' said Ferlias grimly. 'And that'd make it the main force, most likely, and the ships a feint. As we suspected.'

'So be it! Fat's in the flame. Order the guard deployed around the base of the hill here, and along the shore. Stall the outlaw swine as far from the castle as we can! Now, let me see – archers. Send me up every one you can spare from the battlements, every second man, say? And then get you within and captain the castle against our retreat, understood?' He turned to his daughter and Kunrad. 'And best you go with him!'

Alais glared at him in the furnace light. 'Why should I, and not you? Do you tell me there's no hope in what you're planning?'

'I' the long view, damned little,' admitted the old man quietly. He rubbed her shoulders awkwardly. 'Castle's our best hope, but only if we can stop them sweeping over it. It's worth the try. My lads down there, they may be more than half of 'em peasants, but they're game! And the corsairs may be better armed, but they'll not have the discipline; it's not in their nature. If they're coming by straitened paths and along the shore, they'll be strung out and straggling a long way back. I can hold the lads together long enough to break the first assault, I'm sure. That may count for much, if it stops 'em dead.' He raked down his hair, as the chill wind whipped at it. 'And at worst we'll leave such scars upon 'em as will give the Southlands a better chance when the time comes! But there's little more you can do, my lass, you or the Mastersmith. And if I should happen not to return, well, Ferlias may need some leadership there within.'

She caught her breath, but Kunrad grew grim. 'Well, there's one thing! I'll not leave them our hard-won steel!' he growled. 'Not till I must!' He ran to the wall, where the men were huddled, casting fearful glances into the night. Some were already slipping away down the hill.

'A blessing to be single-minded!' said Kermorvan sourly. 'What about you lads?'

Anguish stood on Gille's face, but he shrugged helplessly. 'We're with him!' he said, and the prentices turned sheepishly to follow their master.

Alais pulled free of her father, and unslung her bow. 'I'll keep an eye on him, Father. Raven bring the sun for you!'

Kermorvan grunted. 'I fear we're due for something else first! See down there?'

It seemed shockingly close, less than a thousand paces down the shore. Lights were breaking out, as if lanterns cunningly shielded were being suddenly unveiled, and torches kindled. From a narrow gap the lights spread backwards like a train of fire, right back into the shapeless shadows. The night sparkled with sudden dazzling glints of burnished metal.

'The whole force, for sure!' whispered Alais.

'Aye, but stretched out at length, the fools!' rumbled Kermorvan. 'Just as I'd guessed! So they must come at us in small files, with the rest pressing at their backs. That'll cost 'em dear!'

'Unless they can break us on that first push. And if our fears are true . . .'

Kermorvan snorted. 'We'll find out soon enough – What in Hella's name?'

Light flared, voices gabbled, men scattered. 'It's nothing!' came Kunrad's voice. 'The grass is heat-dried, the slag-tap set it afire!'

There came a sudden blast of icy wind, so chill it made even Kunrad catch his breath. The sothrans had never felt anything like that fire in their lungs; they coughed and yelled. The grass blazed and blew out, the furnace drank it in and blazed high, flooding the hill with light.

'A fine target that'll make us!' roared Kermorvan. 'Put it out!'

Again the gust, colder this time, stinging men's faces and sucking the moisture from their eyes; and again. Olvar swore, and pointed. Down along the shore, not five hundred paces distant, the trees had turned a silent, shimmering white beneath the moon.

Against the wind that bowed their fellows they stood stiff and still, as if they were made of glass. A faint icy music shivered from their leafy crowns. The grassy shoreline shimmered. The low lake swell froze even as it climbed the narrow beaches, and did not fall back.

And suddenly, as if the sky mirrored the earth, pale light awoke there also, and men howled with fear and hid their eyes. Rippling curtains of light were drawn across the stars, shivering sheets of transparent radiance, one moment in faint cool rainbow hues, the next in dazzling white edged with green or blue. To impossible heights they flew and shook, the banners of cold, dwarfing the distant mountains with ethereal, potent majesty.

In the lake they danced, as if pointing a way or outlining a path, so that the castle no longer seemed a separate solid thing, but a tiny speck at the centre of a vast enweaving web.

'They're nothing!' roared Kunrad. 'Only North-Lights! We see them all the time! Stand and don't fear them!'

'You hear?' bellowed Kermorvan to his forces below. 'Stand, my brave lads! Nothing to fear! Just a mountebank trick, see? Stand, you sons of bitches! See me pissing my britches? Stand as I do, and keep ranks. *Morvan morlanhal!*'

Had he been down among them, he might have had some effect. The archers on the hill held firm, by the old man's iron will and the aura of his name; but the men below heard him only from afar, and they faltered. As well they might; for they saw, now, what was coming upon them, racing with that tide of terrible frost.

All along the shore a mile or more streamed the corsair host, men of fell and terrible name, and for the most part in war-gear as hardy as any in the lands. Swords of Nordeney many bore, and Northern armour upon many backs, and the fell wind whitened the steel with a faint rime, so that they shone ghostly in the auroral glare.

They were running, in time to that drumbeat, heavily but steadily. The narrow strip of open shore forced them to come in narrow files, as Kermorvan had predicted; but those files seemed endless, for what came on was a force of above three thousand men, with only a few left behind to hold their ships. Against the full strength Ker Bryhaine the City might have mustered, it was small; but Ker Bryhaine lay far to the south, and this was the greatest force then in those lands. And out before the corsair files, like a spearhead, ran what was worth many a thousand more; and it was named terror.

Among their vanguard there was only one horseman, riding at their head; and in the auroral light he shone above their shouldered spear-points like a god of war. From head to toe bright steel ensheathed him, yet he rode with fluent ease, as if it weighed no more than silk. His high-crowned helm hid his face with a mask of such calm, commanding aspect that few men could have endured the contrast with their own; yet so poised was he that it seemed wholly natural and right. Up to a rise above the shore he rode, where he could be seen, and there rose in his stirrups and brandished his long lance with pennons flying at its tip, shouting a command to his men like the personification of righteous wrath. The men of the castle-lands who stood against him felt their hearts falter. Doubt gripped even those who had so long suspected him. They had raised their hands against their lord, which had long been made the basest of crimes in sothran lore. What now advanced against them looked like the retribution their hearts had been taught to fear. Mouths dried, throats choked up, and they shrank back in dumb dismay.

From the hillside broke a great cry in answer, but in one voice alone. Kunrad stood there, shaking in his rough mail, panting with open mouth. Alais seized his arm. 'Is that it? That which you made? That draws you on?'

Unable to speak, he nodded, breast heaving. She held to him fast, but could not tear her eyes from the shore. 'I begin to understand, at last,' she said, and her voice also shook. 'And not you alone. Poor Merthian, to see such a thing presented to him, and as soon snatched away! He believes he is strong, you know. But no man is stronger than his dream. Now he has clad himself in it.'

Kunrad's voice, when it came, was bleaker than the winds. 'And not poor Kunrad, to have shaped such a dream, and had it torn from him?'

'No,' she said. 'Not wholly. For Merthian only has what he could take. He wears it, but he has not become it. You made that awful, awesome thing, and yet you have it still. You poured yourself into it, body and spirit, that I see. But what I see there he could not steal, for I see it here also, in that mighty flame – and in its creator.' She laughed. 'I am given better sight than Olvar's. Kunrad, you said once it bore no man's face, that armour. Did you not recognise your own?'

He stood in blank astonishment, until a sudden outcry from below turned every head. For the figure of the Marchwarden was only a harbinger of fear; and his command had been a summons, to the still greater terrors at his hand. They came now; and the ranks fell wide apart to let them pass.

There were two great beasts there, that loped along on heavy legs, so fast the teams of men who clutched their trace-chains could scarce restrain them. Like outriders they ran out before the column, scaly beasts, long of body, wide of jaw, like dragons bound to the earth. But for all that, they moved as beings of hotter blood, high on their legs; and among their snout-scales, over their wide-spaced dagger teeth, long bristles stood stiff. Bright red were their eyes, bright as lacquer, rolling and flashing as the creatures snarled their goaded fury. Spawn of the elder ages they were, from one of those ancient eras when the Powers of Ice, it was said, had in their extremity called down the Celestial ice, causing the heavens themselves to fall, and for a brief while thrown back the Eternal Winter about the world. Such terrible times bred strong and savage creatures, and the worst of them the Ice would sometimes preserve and nurture, in wastelands such as the Marshes, that they might be hurled against its foes, striking at the Life it hated with the raw stuff of life itself. About their scale-lined legs steel claws were bound, across their bony brows and on their thrashing tails steel spikes were set; but it was those steaming, snarling jaws that awoke the primal fears of men as brand or blade could never do.

Yet overtaking them, so that they bayed and bucked, and Merthian's great horse reared under him and screamed, there came a vision that struck deeper still, deepest of all into the hearts of those who had heard rumour, or remembered. A vision; for even the chain-beasts were natural things of flesh and blood; but this had the semblance and movement of a nightmare. Stark, scrawny, twice the height of mortal men, though it leaped and danced and capered like a demonic ape, it was a woman still. Its likeness seemed a deliberate distortion, its very derangement shaping an image of insane fear.

Wild hair streamed grey as glaciers, bejewelled with rime and alight with green sky-fires. In the taut dark skin, seamed with strange traceries like an arcane script, the eyes blazed the green of lucent ice-caves, lustrous as corrupted pearl. Thin black lips yelled and gibbered words in breath that rolled like heavy steam, colder far than the air, and boiled around her curses. Great spidery hands clawed and clutched their black narrow nails at the air as if to tear the last warmth out of it. It was at her passing that the forest stiffened and shone white; and beneath her very feet the ground cracked and shattered like ground glass. Any leaf or twig that brushed her sagged, blackened and shrivelled even as the rime enveloped it. Even the running beasts cringed low as she passed; and the men fell back, and raised their shields to hide their averted eyes.

Save one; for, mastering his frightened mount, Merthian rode down proudly at her back, between the beasts, as if it were the natural place for such a lord among men.

It seemed for a moment as if Kunrad the Mastersmith would hurl himself down from the height into their path. Instead, pulling free from Alais, he turned, he ran, across the scarred brow of the hill to the front of the fiery coronet he had set there. He seized one of the labourers' great mattocks, and threw himself upon the tall stone that crowned its central vent. '*Stop the channels!*' he yelled to his men, and even as the prentices leaped to obey, he swung the mattock like the hammer of Ilmarinen.

One blow, and the stone cracked and sagged; but the pick flew asunder, and men ducked the fragments of the blade. Then Kunrad, armoured as he was, sprang from the ground and threw his main weight upon the stone, and with his great strength pulled it backwards over and on to himself.

A woman shrieked aloud. Tearing through the earth, driven by the pressure behind, the stone slab sagged outward and crashed to the ground, and with it opened a narrow gap to the heart of the furnace. Even the freezing wind that blasted through it had only served to revive and freshen the fires that seethed within, and the gap was like an artery opened in the living earth. The release was sudden and violent, far greater than the gradual tapping it was made for. A sear-white stream bubbled, boiled and fountained outwards in exultant freedom, overleaping the stone that blocked the channels dug deep to contain it. The spout of white-hot steel spewed defiantly into the freezing air, and, like the avalanche that gave it birth, went racing down the slope in a torrential waterfall of pure fire.

No cold could have withstood it. The very winds had fed it, and the heart of trees, and the will of a master-smith. And that will, perhaps, held it to its path, and the trees that were dead and whitening sprang up before it in a sudden blossoming of fire. Beneath an arch of flame the stream raced onward, struck the low rise where Merthian had stood, and leapt again with the force of the fall behind it, into a spattering, searing rain.

So swiftly it came that none was ready, least of all the leaders. The great beasts, touched by its first fine spatter, screamed and plunged, and beyond all restraint swept among their handlers, even as they too were borne down by the fiery rain. They stumbled screaming and beating at themselves, and were rent and crushed by the claws of their fell charges. One, snapping furiously at the burning spots, plunged into the lake and sank, towing its last handlers, tangled in the traces. The other reared up, flailing at the air, and charged straight at Merthian. His horse rose and kicked, and that alone saved him, for the beast ran by beneath and so, oblivious to the bite of spear and blade, into the horrified men behind. The horse bolted for the lake.

Not so the creature of Ice before him. Like some thrawn beast it also sprang high in the air to avoid that glaring rain, higher than a man could leap; and came close to missing all but the lightest touch. Yet a single such agony would shrivel any mortal flesh; and to the strange body that a spirit of the endless chill had shaped around itself, its kiss could have been far more devastating. However that may be, the leap was broken. The tree above spurted fire, and the grey shape convulsed and fell, even as the main stream of steel welled down in one wash of scarifying light across the narrow shore before it.

The creature's feet landed square in the spreading stream.

The scream that went up drowned the howlings of the beasts, drowned the very roaring of the fire, split the very air around men's ears. The exhausted howl of the furnace vents, like some creature bleeding to death, was lost in it. It shook the air as a thunderclap might; and the eerie glows above were blasted out like a guttering candle. The grey shape staggered and capered like an unstrung puppet. Still the metal poured, lower now yet still white at its heart, spilling swiftly down a conduit formed of its own cooler self, spreading in fiery pools across the path.

Around it even the damp soil sprang into flame, as if it were peat. From tree to tree the fire leaped, like lightning through the clouds, and the white stain that had blighted the forest's crown flared swiftly to leaves of licking orange, more fair, more alive, more perilous. Branches already dead where they hung burst asunder in the sudden change and crashed flaming among the heads of the outlaws. A wall of fire sprang up around the pooling metal; and at its heart the ice-witch swelled, blackened and sank down. The mouth gaped wide, and spewed a shrieking jet of steam skyward to the hidden stars.

The white column blasted upward. The shape was momentarily borne up within it, stiffened like a bow drawn taut. The sound shrank to an ear-piercing whine. The column shot skyward, free of the flames, while on the path beneath something that no longer had a shape folded, shrivelled and fell in a swift spurt of fire. Yet the column did not disperse, but lifted, sourceless but clinging, neither widening nor dispersing, till it caught the moonlight high above the lake. Then a warm gust off the mountains took it, toyed with it like a stray leaf and sent it tumbling off outwards, towards the Marshes and the endless sea beyond. No trail of ice followed it, no blast of frozen air; and no one marked its passing.

On the hill, all eyes were upon that awful stream, and upon the stone that had unleashed it. Even as the first outpouring slackened, Alais and the prentices were leading a chain of men with water-butts. Yet as they reached it the stone lifted, and again she screamed; for it seemed as if the armoured figure climbed from the heart of the flame. 'The channel!' she screamed, as if it was an accusation. 'You dove into the channel!' And she threw the water she carried anyway, for sheer joy, and rushed into his arms.

'Of course!' said Kunrad, a little surprised, shaking his dripping head. 'What'd you expect? I'm a Northerner, I'm not that daft!'

She let him go at once. 'Be thankful I don't bloody well push you in!' she yelled, and then grabbed him and hugged him again. Together they stared down at the havoc on the path below.

'Waste of good metal!' grunted the mastersmith. Then she heard the blare of trumpets, and felt him grow tense in her arms. She had no need to ask; that was a warning from the castle, and their peril was all too clear.

Their own ranks, unprepared for the fire, were as scared and scattered as the foe's, and beginning to break for the castle. Among the corsairs, no more than thirty paces off, there was terrible disorder, yet not one man fled; they could not. So long was their column that the rear ranks, far back around the curve of the shore, had seen little of the terror of the iron-fall, or the eventual bloody slaying of the war-beasts. They held, blocking their fellows' flight, and even pressed on, edging them closer to the fire. Panic was spreading, nonetheless; those in the vanguard were threatening those who pressed them, some even turning their weapons on their fellows. Others were running down into the lake, throwing off their arms to swim. But at the trumpets they halted, and turned to point down the shore.

Riding in a wash through the shallows came a little knot of horsemen, led by the shining rider, his armour still gleaming bright in the starlight. He had no trumpeters, and they could hear him shouting to crack his voice; but men saw him in that glittering array, an image of command and strength, and in their blindness they heeded him. He and his captains reined in around the disordered vanguard, railing them, berating them, crowding them back in line with their horses. He bade them stand fast, form up and follow to a swift victory; and clearly they heard. Even those already fleeing faltered and looked back.

Kunrad's heart grew cold within him. Order forgotten, discipline gone, banners fallen, courage broken; yet there was that armour, and even that band of cutthroats would follow it still. Bile rose in his throat. Where was Kermorvan? Now was the time to strike. He could see it, just as he could see when it was right to pour metal or lay down the first decisive hammer-stroke, that would make a piece or mar it. He forgot all else around.

'*Archers!*' he screamed suddenly. '*To me!*'

And such was the power of the sight they had seen on that hilltop, and the voice they had heard, that the ranks of Kermorvan's archers came surging forward to the breast of the slope, drawing as they came.

'*Bring down those horsemen!*'

As one, with a hiss of silken menace, the longbows swung up, and Kunrad felt the mighty tension in his own arms. Only about two hundred archers, but they were soldiers and hunters, men whose lives depended on the strength of their bows; they pulled the weight of a fair-sized man, and their eyes and hands were steady. Kunrad realised suddenly he had no idea of the sothran commands, but he could not wait to ask; he shouted *'Loose!'* in the Northern fashion, and they obeyed.

The night sang around his head, a great wing thrashed the air, a pale cloud glittered above the fire, and fell. The horsemen, looking up, saw what was descending, and their cries and exhortations broke off in yelling panic. Those who had shields swung them over their heads and spurred back; one or two fell or sprang headlong from their saddles into the lake. The ranks on the path mirrored the change. Men dived heedlessly for cover in either direction, or simply cowered down where they were. The arrows plunged among them in shining, rattling rain. They plucked captains from their saddles, or toppled the poor beasts themselves kicking into the darkening water. Men on the path jerked where they lay and went limp, or ran clawing frantically at the shafts that transfixed them. But the bright figure neither fled nor fell, but raised his shield high against the fall, and bent over his charger's armoured head to ward it. Kunrad clearly saw at least two shafts shatter against the backplates he had case-hardened with such care, and go bouncing away. Then Merthian was upright again, and leading his surviving captains out of shot. Only one did not follow, a tall figure with a fantastically ornamented helm; he shook his fist at them, shouted as if he had lost patience, and turned his horse to the shore.

'Follow me!' yelled Kunrad, clapping on his helm, and went leaping and slipping away down the slope. The men of the castle's advance guard heard him also, and stopped in their milling half-retreat; hands pointed to the hill, and the archers coming down surefooted behind him. But from his vantage he could see the corsairs also steadying and regrouping around the tall horseman as he rode up and down, heading off deserters and quelling disorders.

'Halt!' shouted Kunrad to the archers. *'Draw! Into the vanguard this time! Into their faces! Loose!'*

This time the trajectory was lower, the sound harsher, a spitting, sawing breath of death that made Kunrad duck involuntarily as it rushed past him. Corsairs at the fore screamed, turned and were struck down in the same moment. But fewer fell at the volley, and behind the fire a sound was swelling, a savage chant of acclaim. Above the flame he saw the rider with the gaudy helm come driving forward, with a tight knot of men behind him; and despite the arrows the corsairs followed. More and more of them, not in orderly ranks but in a tight-knit spearhead that looked almost as dangerous. The decorations on the tall man's helm were the great spreading wings of a seabird, beating as he rode; and they sparkled weirdly in the night. He swept up an arm, pointing at the hill, and Kunrad caught his breath as he saw the flash and glitter of jewels at wrist and neck, and across the armoured chest.

'*That one!*' shouted Kunrad. '*Mark him!*' Then he flinched, as something sang past his face. The nearest archer coughed and fell writhing, clutching at the stiff fletches of a crossbow bolt thrusting out through his red beard. Another plucked at Kunrad's breech-leg, and the archers scattered as more thudded into the dark hillside around them. He ducked and ran to one side, waving the archers to do likewise, and an instant later the night sang again; they were being pinned down, unable to aim. The corsair chieftain swept out his sword and waved again, forward now towards the fire. Kunrad saw the crossbowmen bunch together behind him with the rest, shielding their faces against the heat of the flame. Once past they would have a clear shot at the hill.

'*Archers!*' he yelled again, but knew there was no time for another volley. '*Their chieftain! Fire at will!*' The chieftain was already at the dwindling metal-flow, pulling back on his reins for the jump across the pools of fire. His horse lifted him high against the lurid smoke, a huge menacing shadow, his sword upraised as if to strike the flames asunder. The jewels on mail and scabbard glistened blood-bright in the glare.

Beside Kunrad's ear a single bowstring snapped the air. So strong was the firelight he clearly saw the arrow in its flight, whipping its tail like a fish. Beneath the blazing foliage its arc took it, and its resined fletches flashed into flame, yet straight it flew to meet the crest of another leap. Straight under that upraised arm it struck, and no jewel or mailring turned it. The fire flashed and vanished, the sword flew up, wheeling against the light, and the reins snaked free as the impact shot the corsair chieftain from his stirrups and down into the roaring pools beneath. An uprush of blazing debris, like a fount of firegems, marked his fall. The horse bolted, mad with fright, and men shrank back at the terrible sight.

'Well shot, that man!' gasped Kunrad. Across his mind, for an instant, came those bloody moments in the ship. 'See, that's held them! Well shot, man, well shot!'

'And it's kind of you to say so!' said Alais calmly from his side, choosing another shaft from her belt.

'*You?*'

'The others were running all over the place. And I'd promised to keep an eye on you. Somebody has to!'

'But you can't – I won't—' Kunrad's tongue seemed to stick in his mouth. He looked from her to the shore, and back again, unable to form his words for excitement. The front ranks faltering, the rear in disorder, Merthian nowhere to be seen – surely now, if ever, the iron was spitting hot.

That thought freed his voice.

'*You below!*' he screamed. '*Up and into them! Attack, damn you, attack!*'

The men on the shore looked up doubtfully, and for an awful moment he thought they would not obey this Northern voice with the strange commands. He could see it in their very stance, tense as runners, unsure they had heard the start. He hauled out his own sword, brandished it above his head and went running down the slope, still shouting, dancing almost as he had at the furnace, to summon up the fire. '*On! Now!*'

The archers were running with him, shooting as they went; and seeing that, the front ranks stepped hesitantly forward, one pace, two, like pawns on a game-board. The next rank followed – and then, all at once, high on the hill the trumpets sounded. The great war-horns from the castle echoed them across the water and off the distant mountains, to wake the duergar in their beds of stone.

With a bloodcurling howl the whole mass of men began to pour forward. At most in that vanguard there was half the corsair strength; but on their chosen stretch of lakeshore they had formed wider ranks that made them appear more numerous. And while many behind still had only wooden spears, a fearsome wall of pikes and bills glittered before the front ranks, and among them many of the long spearheads of the duergar.

'*So!*' yelled Kunrad, leaping in the air. '*Archers, forward! Give them cover!*'

He could order volleys no longer; but this close, and in the firelight, the hunters could move and skirmish, and pick their targets. Arrows whined overhead as he went bounding down the lower slope, still brandishing his sword. He promptly caught his foot in a tussock and fell headlong, sending his helm flying.

Winded, he fought to struggle up. The ground drummed under him, and he found himself surrounded by the legs of horses shifting excitedly. A hand caught him by the hair, and he looked up into Kermorvan's baleful glare, pop-eyed with fury.

'Since when were you made commander here, my lad? You'll need a horse for that game!' He more or less threw Kunrad against the horse behind him, whose saddle was empty. Kunrad struggled up into the stirrups, his boot slipped and he sprawled double over the saddle, to harsh laughter from around him.

'*Sit up!*' growled Kermorvan, in a furious whisper. 'Straighten your back, stop coughing! *Look* like a bloody commander!' Then he added, as he hauled Kunrad up by the scruff of the neck, 'Not that you're not playing it well! Or else I wouldn't have given you the trumpets. You saw the moment to strike, every time. I – well, I'm getting old.

You've the command now, lad. You'll do.'

Alais rode up beside them, winding her wild hair down beneath her helm. Somebody handed Kunrad his. He looked around, still gasping for breath. The lines on the shore were well ahead now.

'Well then! My lord . . . Very well. Archers – you stay above the fight as long as you've arrows, then close with your blades! The rest of us' – he copied the corsair leader's sweeping wave – '*Forward!*'

He dug in his heels, and the horse went bounding easily down the slope. The soldiers saw him and Kermorvan at his side, and the black banner rising among the horsemen thundering behind, and raised a great cheer. But even as they parted to let him through, so another great shout arose from their foes. Through the barrier of fire another rider sprang, and through the mirroring metal he wore, the flames seemed to flow and kindle anew.

Not till then, perhaps, did Kunrad wholly understand what he had shaped, or perceive what had so immediately dazzled Merthian's sight and scruple. Now, himself a leader, he faced a steely, impenetrable image of victory, a vision for foe to quail at, for friend to follow, even over such a barrier as he himself had created. Into the fight he had poured raw steel; but now it was hurled back at him, forged hard and bright about his foe.

And after Merthian the corsairs came streaming, crossing the fires at last. The flames were dying now, and they sprang through, or ducked and weaved between the pools of metal that still glowed and shimmered in the red air. Some trod on smaller fragments, screamed and fell, but with that bright vision to follow their fellows sprang across them as they writhed, and ran on. On came Merthian still, his few remaining horsemen gathering at his back, and the defenders' spear-fence swept up to meet him. The first he met and dashed aside with his shield, slashed out with his lance and felled its wielder and the man beside him. The corsairs poured past his horse to engage the line, while pikes and spears clanged helplessly off his shoulders. Then, pulling his horse around, he picked out the captain of the line and rode at him. Again he batted aside the pikes to left and right, and as the captain thrust at him Merthian's lance took him in the breastplate and transfixed the man, black pennons and all, and stuck in the ground behind. Out came his sword and slashed down the pikeshafts, and the corsairs pressed forward under the shadow of his shield.

'Gathered them from the rear again!' growled Kermorvan. 'Where we couldn't see him!'

'He'll break our line!' said Kunrad. 'We'll have to try and hold him! *Horsemen, forward!*'

He had learned the principles of war for his weaponry; he had led one charge in a mock battle, one small group of town guardsmen against another, in bright day and unencumbered ground. Here in the firelight, with men striking and dying in the lakeshore mud under the very hooves of his horse, it was a confused, demonic vision in which that radiant armour was the only spot of clarity. The charge stalled in a milling tangle of foot-soldiers, a rough line that swayed this way and that like waving wheat. A mounted corsair plunged by him, driven by the press of men. They cut at one another, missed, and were driven apart in the mêlée. The sky was shedding its blackness, but in the firelight it was still hard to tell friend from foe.

Merthian, ranging up and down the line, suddenly waved to his horsemen, set the long shield before him and charged straight at the centre. There were fewer pikes now, and his sword scythed them away like very wheatstalks. His tall warhorse breasted the crush with its steel gorget, and bore down all in its way, while he hewed at the heads to either flank. The corsairs roared and drove in behind him, horse and footmen together, in the swift fast fighting they understood.

'They'll be through any moment!' coughed Kunrad. 'Kermorvan! Fall our men back, back towards the bridge! Hold the front lines as a rearguard! We've done what we could. I'm going to try and deal with *him*!'

The horns sounded, and the defenders checked and gave back, slowly, in good order as Kunrad forced his horse through. '*Merthian!*' he roared. '*Merthian! Marchwarden, master of naught! Thief and traitor! Ice-puppet!*' One or two crossbow bolts whirred past him, but he was too angry to notice, hot in pursuit of that shining vision that plagued his dreams and poisoned his life. '*Merthian, you thieving get of a bitch! Give me back my armour!*'

The high helm turned, its plumes bobbing, and seemed to hesitate. Then it reined in, keeping well back, and shouted to the footmen around, waving them furiously forward. Ignoring their retreating enemies, they swarmed towards Kunrad's horse. Over his head a glimmer passed, and down into that living mirror. It struck the shield, but this was no arrow; its weight turned the shield sharply and clanged hard against the helm, rocking its wearer in his saddle. Shield and sword dropped from his hand, but the javelin simply glanced off that frozen light and fell with them. Merthian swayed drunkenly where he sat.

Beside Kunrad Alais yelled in thwarted fury, and snatched another javelin from her saddle. 'Lock me up with your tame Ice-bitch, will you? Come, my darling bridegroom, come and be kissed!'

The advance halted. The corsairs looked around anxiously, expecting some new assault from the side, and the last of the castle rearguard took the opportunity to disengage and fall hastily back. But the corsair horsemen swiftly gathered in a knot around Merthian, shielding and supporting him, and the footmen came streaming towards Kunrad and Alais. More crossbow bolts sang around them.

'Time to get back, my lad!' snapped Kermorvan, waving the rest of his horsemen away. 'But daughter, that was warmly kissed!'

Together they wheeled and spurred back, with screams of violent derision behind them. But the distraction and delay had gained the defenders the moment they needed. Most of them were already within the castle gate, and in the greying dimness he could see the rearguard streaming on to the bridge now, under the eye of the few archers to whom any arrows yet remained. Even as Kunrad glanced back over his shoulder, though, he saw the protective knot part and Merthian come charging forward, arms in hand once more, no sign of blood or marring about him. Kunrad had made his armour all too well. After him galloped the corsair horsemen, with footmen clinging to their stirrup-leathers, and Kunrad realised they could be overtaken in minutes.

Arrows sailed over their heads as Kermorvan's archers shot their last, but though another rider fell it did not break the pursuit.

'We can't let them reach the bridge!' gasped Kunrad.

'So!' wheezed the old man, and waved wildly. '*Pull back the bridge! We'll swim for it!*'

'Speak for yourself!' groaned Kunrad, but he knew the old man was right. So did Ferlias in the castle, evidently; the bridge was already hauling away from the shore. Even as it did so, two men sprang back off it, and ran to meet them. More bolts sang by, a horse screamed and the others baulked and collided in confusion. Alais slid from her saddle, Kunrad half fell from his, and they landed among the others, already tearing off their mail-shirts and springing into the water.

'Mastersmith!' shouted Gille, as he and Olvar came puffing up. 'Come on! We'll help you!'

'I can manage!' he growled, as he hauled Alais's mail over her head, and disproved it instantly by struggling with his own. The prentices yanked it off him, and as his ears came clear he heard the approaching hoofbeats. Without an instant's delay he scooped up Alais in her shirt and britches, and jumped.

The lake was an icy slap, a flooding, bewildering fog about the eyes, a panicky straining for breath. Alais was no longer in his arms, and he could not even tell which way was up. He kicked out, and burst up coughing and sneezing among a mass of other streaming heads. Through bubbling ears he heard Alais, next to him, calling out, 'Father? *Father?*' He tried to speak, sank again and was scooped up by Olvar's huge paw on his arm.

'Don't fight it, boss! I'll tow you!'

'Kermorvan?' spluttered Kunrad, and then, as he swung about to face the shore, he saw the old man stagger to his feet on the bank, from beside the tangled bodies of two horses.

'*Father!*' shouted Alais, but Kermorvan only waved irritably. Shaking his head as if to clear some noise in his ear, he tugged at his sword, freed it. Then with the limping walk of a man grown too old, too fat to run any more, he stepped out into the path of the onrushing corsairs, and his former lord.

It was at Merthian that he struck, and his slashing blow drove past the shield and rocked the Marchwarden in his saddle. But the blade skipped free, and Merthian's shield spun the old man around in the narrow way. Another horse struck him, and he was ridden down, tumbled over and flung aside in a flurry of cloak. Alais shrieked, but the corsairs pouring past hid him from sight. They reached the bridgehead and swirled out along the shore in complete disorder, every man jostling to the fore. Merthian reined up at the water's edge, pointing furiously to the swimmers, the first of whom had already reached the bridge.

'*Sink me those swine!*' they heard him scream. It was nothing like his normal voice. '*Every last one!*'

Already crossbows were being drawn, and bolts were hissing into the water among them. A swimmer clambering aboard the bridge shook and went down with an agonised gasp. Other bolts struck the water at a low angle, and went skipping off across it as boys skim stones. Another found a mark in a swimmer's shoulder. Kunrad snatched at Alais, Gille came to their side, and they struck out clumsily for the bridge. They were behind the others, for Kunrad had no buoyancy of his own, and Alais was dead weight at first. But as the bolts struck closer she began to swim for herself, a fierce stroke, breathing in great rasping gasps. If there had been more crossbowmen, or better light, they would have been dead at once, but they flailed on, while the men on the bridge shouted and cheered, and shook their fists at the shore. Some of the castle's bowmen were running down to lend cover, but such was the crush on the bridge that they could not get near enough.

Olvar, gasping, was flagging, and the bolts were coming closer; and Kunrad's anger and shame grew. Suddenly he broke the big prentice's grip on his arm, and kicked free. In that moment he had little hope, and cursed himself yet again for having brought all this upon those who had trusted him. The first faint gleam of light shone between the deep mountain notches, and touched the armour Merthian bore with brilliant, triumphant gold. Kunrad, barely keeping above water, could not forbear to shake his fist and shout some fool's defiance, but his folly was made clear to him at once. Merthian saw him, heard him, and gesticulated frantically to the crossbowmen. Suddenly the bolts were raining down around him alone, and it would be only a matter of time. But no less suddenly they were flying wide again, and faltering.

A rumour came from the shore, and from the bridge still more excited shouts. Kunrad saw heads turn among the jostling corsairs. Olvar, rested, reached out and pulled him irresistibly the few remaining strokes to the bridge, but Kunrad shook him off and clambered around to its shoreward side, dipping now as men rushed to the rail. Somewhere up the shore there was noise and movement, and there was no mistaking the tone of dismay in the corsairs' shouts. The grey light was growing by the second, and suddenly it was clear – a line of horsemen coming down out of the hills to the north, whence Kunrad had fled. A double line, he realised, or treble, moving at a swift trot; and he saw banners, and the cold glint of lanceheads. Three hundred at the very most; but that was ten times the corsair horse he could see, and nearing fast.

Kunrad caught hold of the rail, and with an arm-tearing effort he hauled himself from the water. Hands reached out to him, but he hung there, staring. Alais fought her way through with Gille, who cried out and pointed to the bank. The corsairs, their attention held by the bridge that moment too long, were in milling disorder. Merthian's mount plunged this way and that as he fought to chivvy them back into line, but they flowed around him like oil. His shouting carried across the water, but not his words; maybe there were none. He was too far back, and too late. As the newcomers came out on to the wider shore war-horns brayed, harsh and cold, and they opened out into mailed ranks of six, and then of twelve, sweeping the shore from wood to water. Another blast, and the lances dipped in a single rippling wave, the trot became a swift canter, the canter, with almost eerie ease, a gallop. The dull tremor of hooves reached the men on the bridge.

'That's order!' sobbed Alais, drumming her fists on the rail. 'That's true cavalry!'

The first rank crashed into the corsairs.

On the bridge they leaped and capered and shouted, until the timbers creaked and cracked, and Kunrad was almost tipped off. The corsair ranks flew apart like a rotten fruit. The first corsairs went down before they could level pike or sword; the ones behind did not try, but sprang wildly for the steep hillside, or spilled into the lake. The water there was deep, and they had no time to remove their mail.

The bridge shook to the shouting, but Olvar's voice rose above it. 'Look at them! Look! Fur cloaks over their mail, and a few honest brownskins among them! They're Northerners, Gille!'

'Dunmarhas!' sighed Gille, half laughing his relief. 'The Dunmarhas City Guard! Your message got through, Kunrad!'

'Northerners!' ran the ripple of voices through the crowd. 'Nordeney horse-soldiers! On our side!'

Men pounded Kunrad's back as he struggled over the rail, and the prentices as they helped him, and cheered the Lady Alais whom, they said, had brought the wild men of the North to their aid.

'*Wild men!*' sniffed Gille.

Up to the bridgehead the horsemen drove, as a chisel bites a trough through soft-grained wood. There, though, they ran into Merthian, and the men he had been able to gather about him – his own guard, probably, barring the path in a close double shield-wall. Their onrush stalled, and the corsairs, as quick to turn one way as another, swirled in around them. Merthian waved up the tail of the column.

'They're in toils!' hissed Olvar.

Kunrad scrambled clumsily up on to the rail. 'Hey, you sothran lads! Are you going to let the Dunmarhas men have all the fun?'

'No!' roared another.

'Let us back ashore!'

Kunrad waved to the castle. 'Gate, there! In the name of the Lord Kermorvan – *Swing back the bridge!*'

The bridge had already stopped, as even the winch-crews ran to see the providential new arrivals. Now, suddenly, it juddered into reverse, and the massive chains and cables roared in torment as the overladen mass was sent sweeping in towards shore again. The undue weight grounded it with a jar some ten feet short of the landing stage, almost throwing Kunrad off again. It was Alais, leaping up and down in her sodden shirt until she all but danced, who waved her people on, screaming out, '*Butcher the bastards! For the Lord Kermorvan!*'

And then, almost cracking her throat, '*Morvan morlanhal!*'

There, in that tormented voice, the ancient battle cry brought chills even to Northern spines. On the sothrans it stung like a goad, and in a single crash of sound they echoed it off the mountains.

'*Morvan morlanhal! Morvan shall arise!*'

And even as they shouted, brandishing their weapons, the first of them streamed back off the bridge. Across the gap they sprang, or straight down into the breast-high water; it made little difference. The obstacles seemed not to be there. As they poured off the end, the bridge lifted again, swung swiftly and crashed into place. Kunrad and the others, precariously placed, fell in a heap. The defenders needed no leader now, and their blood was up. In one great flow, like a dam unleashed, they went roaring out past the exhausted swimmers and, mad for revenge, hurled themselves into the confusion on the shore. Down from the castle gate, against all orders, came half the garrison after them, roaring and bellowing past.

Into the midst of the corsairs they drove, and suddenly it was the outlaws of the Marshes who were caught. Merthian's immediate line held, but the looser ranks of the rest were driven in by sheer press of men, and staggered back, crushed too closely to offer fight. The defenders, driven on by the same, rammed through them, right across the shore to where the Dunmarhas horses were being encircled. Right to the woods they came, and the hillside; and the corsair force, though greater in numbers still, was sliced in two like a serpent.

To Kunrad's eyes, as he looked exhausted from the bridge, it writhed thus. The upper half gave back from the Dunmarhas men in alarm. Merthian pulled back his precious lines to let more of the rear column through. But they had heard the shift from triumph to panic, seen the charge from the bridge, and few were so eager to follow now; while some already engaged seized the moment to break and slip to the rear, spreading the panic further. Robbed of their own chieftain, baulked of the swift and overwhelming slaughter they did best, the corsair force milled and boiled in confusion. But so might the defenders, in the developing skirmish; and then the corsair numbers, with Merthian to rally them, would surely tell. Again it seemed to Kunrad that he saw molten metal quiver and boil on the edge of the mould.

He had no trumpeters, and needed none. Exhaustion fled; he swung himself to his feet, balanced on the rail, and shouted his commands with all the force of his forge-bellow lungs. *'Kermorvannians! Shields, men with shields! Form a shield-wall! Around the horsemen! A shield-wall, quick!'*

Without thinking he had translated a Northern word. A happy accident, if accident it was; for the image struck deep and immediate into the minds of untrained men to whom martial terms meant little, and showed them at once what they must do. Enough men obeyed for the few trained soldiers to rally the rest. The shapeless arrow of men hesitated, seemed to shiver an instant and then flowed right through the disordered corsairs to form a hardening ring of steel about the beleaguered horsemen. To the front crouched men who had shields, or had snatched them from corsair dead; and behind, close enough to strike over them, clustered the rest, so that each shield sheltered many bodies. The struggling outlaws suddenly found themselves facing a ragged but deadly hedge. Kunrad swayed on the rail. There would be no mistaking these commands, anyhow.

'*Riders! Prepare to advance! Shield-wall – forward!*'

For a moment he feared they would ignore his directing arm, and rush out in all directions. But the riders shouted, the lances dipped, and the whole shield-wall around them, still holding, surged slowly forward like some sluggish armoured beast. The corsairs in its path tried to strike at it, but were caught by the lances that stabbed out across the shields, or, trying to avoid them, fell to the blades that licked out between them. Over them the wall passed, bristling like a porcupine. Fewer dared to challenge it, and let themselves be swirled away in disorder along its flanks.

'*Now!*' shouted Kunrad. '*Shield-wall – ready! Horsemen, ready! Then open and let them through!*'

An instant's confusion, and he held his breath. Then the Northern war-horns blared again, the defenders peeled back, and out of their midst the lances poured forward, lunging down at the already hard-pressed corsair line with the height and weight of horse. Merthian was lifting his visor-mask to scream orders, the line swayed an instant – then broke. The lances stabbed, the bright blades rose and fell like threshing flails, and suddenly the corsairs were turning their backs, spilling to left and right, uphill, along the shore, even into the lake again. '*That's it!*' roared Kunrad, waving so hard he almost overbalanced. A single crossbow bolt sang past his leg and stuck quivering in the rail, but he ignored it. '*Shield-wall! Close!*'

The wall was ragged now, for many men were streaming after the horsemen, striking their advantage home; but with a great clatter of shields it happened. '*Good! Good! That's it, that's the way! Now – turn to the north!*'

Northward the great beast turned, bristling and unstoppable; and now the defenders hammered hilt and haft on their shields in a deadly thudding rhythm, and to that they advanced. The corsairs there, who had taken the brunt of the horsemen's first charge, saw what bore down upon them. Before them were the hills, and beyond them to the east, the river and the ships that were a feint, and bore their supplies; for they had carried as little as possible, to let them march far and fast. That way was safety, whatever else befell; and in the swarming chaos of a shattered hive, they turned and fled.

The shield-wall might have broken then, and pursued them; but Kunrad was watching. '*No! Let them go! Shield-wall – southward! And harry all before you!*'

So great was the roar that went up that his words might have been drowned; but his gesture could not be mistaken. It was the last he gave in that fight; and it was decisive. He had split the corsairs, rescued the hard-pressed horses and brought them forward to break Merthian's guard, the last core of order among the invaders. Now he would shatter them entirely. Southward the shield-wall turned, and the corsairs, already struggling to keep clear of the horsemen, faced that sweeping line of metal as it bore down on them, heard that dull relentless pounding, and gave back, swiftly.

Olvar gave a great shout, and pointed. Merthian, by the sheer power of his will and word, still held fast a square of footmen together around his remaining horse, no more than twenty or so. But the sheer press was pushing them back from the bridgehead, back along the shoreline, almost to where the flames still smouldered. Here he sought to hold his men, screaming at them to but stand in this narrow way, and the day would still be theirs. Now, though, the rest of his force flowed around him like loose sand in the tide, and shook their fists at him as they did so, and brandished weapons, so that his defences were as much against his own as his enemies. Riches and conquest he had promised them, and now they were failing to regain what they had thought their own.

Back into the fire the ragged square was pushed; and though most of the metal was dull now, it still held a fearsome heat. The rear of Merthian's square disintegrated suddenly as men backed on to it unwarily, and screamed as their boots caught fire, and jumped for the lake, or fell and were further burned; till even the faintest touch of heat made men leap and run. The last semblance of order broke, and to the south, too, the corsairs turned tail and bolted. But in their traces, with baying horns and savage cries, ran the cavalry, and at their backs the shield-wall broke ranks and charged. Few could escape in time, not with Merthian's remnant still blocking the path. The struggle dwindled from a battle to a hunt and a slaughter; and that too was by in a moment, leaving only a strew of bodies, as chaff on a threshing floor.

Kunrad jerked his head wearily. 'We'd better get ashore too. Find some weapons, and our armour, maybe, before somebody takes a shot at us!'

With an arm around Olvar's shoulder and another round Alais, he limped off the bridge and up the trodden way, sticky with bloodsoaked mud. He was glad now he had had no time to shed his boots, though they squelched uncomfortably. Gille stopped dead so suddenly they all barged into him. Kunrad, seeing the cause, tried to hold Alais back.

She shook off his arm and ran to the hunched heap by the pathside, one leg impossibly twisted beneath the trampled black cloak. The bulky body had slumped into shapelessness, and the white hairs that escaped from beneath the shattered helm were sticky with blood, though the puddle beneath seemed absurdly small. Alais fell on him, sobbing wildly, while Kunrad and the others stood awkwardly by.

At the sudden ripple of hooves, though, she sprang up. The others caught up swords and spears from the dead hands around them. But the horse that came trotting back around the corner of the shore was of a dark, shaggy heavy-shouldered breed, with no armour on it but a breastplate and headpiece. Its rider's skin matched the bronzed gleam of his mail. He was a lean-faced man with a broad brow and dark straggling hair and beard that almost concealed the gold collar about his neck; a gold-hilted sword hung sheathed at his saddle-bow. Other horsemen followed him, keeping a watchful eye around. He rode up to the party and saluted them, in strongly accented sothran speech.

'I'm told it'd be some among you folk that's in charge here? Aye, Mastersmith Kunrad, it would be. And the Lord Kermorvan?'

'This is Lady Alais Kermorvan,' said Kunrad. 'The Lord Ieran, we fear . . .'

'I see. My sympathies, my lady. I'm Arin Hergesson, captain of the Dunmarhas Guard, with two hundred horse and eighty to your aid. I'm sorry we could come no sooner. We rode as fast as we dared when we saw your great beacon.'

Kunrad felt as if his grin would crack his exhausted cheeks. 'It wasn't a beacon, exactly. But it served us better than I dared hope. Thank you, captain. You broke them.'

'Aye, that's true enough, but yon gaberlunzies might not have stayed broken. Now it's chiefly a matter of subduing the raggletag. These sothrans lads laid into them with a will, I'll say.'

Alais's voice was bleak. 'They had mortal wrongs to avenge, captain Arin. As have I. I am deeply grateful for your help, but I ask one thing more. I want . . .' she swallowed. 'I want the Marchwarden Merthian taken, on the counts of treason and murder. I set a price upon his head—'

Olvar caught her arm and pointed. Far down the shore, beyond the farthest reach of the straggling battle, a small group of horsemen was speeding away down the shore. Into the first long rays of dawn they rode, and a blinding spot of fire flashed among them.

'The armour!' snapped Kunrad. 'That marks him!'

Arin shouted to his sergeant, and the man spurred away. 'We'll set men on his heels, lady! But he has a fine start on him,' Arin added, 'and we dare not hunt him far into the Southlands, for reasons you'll understand, I think.' He looked about him keenly. 'As it is, we must look to our safety. With your leave, I think I had best be about securing the castle—'

'*Never!*'

The voice made Kunrad's skin crawl. He knew whose it was; but it was horribly changed. Alais choked and half screamed.

'Never!' it rasped, as they turned to see the ruin of Lord Ieran Kermorvan, helm falling from a bleeding scalp, half raise himself in the dust, blood trickling from his broken mouth, and fall back with a groan. 'Never! Northmen holding Ker an Aruel – never, never! Blank treason . . . heads roll . . .'

Alais, cheeks bloodless, caught his head as he collapsed into the dust once again. She looked up. 'Olvar, Gille, get men from the castle, and something to carry my father in. And find a healer!'

'We have two with us,' said Arin, 'if they're not away getting their fool throats cut. Go, Hodir, bring 'em back! As to the castle, surely it's best that it's we who take command, with a strong force of—'

She lowered her father's head gently on to his pillowed cloak, and stood up. She was half dressed in a blood-smudged undershirt, her red hair was plastered about her like damp weed, her face was streaked with dust and tears and smears of blood, but she stood erect and unshakeable. 'No, Captain Arin! My father is right. Could you allow a sothran force to hold your chiefest castle? You could not. No more can we, and however great our gratitude we would fight to prevent it, as we have fought here. We would far rather not, and welcome you as you deserve.'

'She's right, Arin,' said Kunrad, and stepped to her side. 'We've built a bridge here, of sorts. No point in breaking it down, all for one piece of brazen cheek! If anything can fire up the war again, that will; and Dunmarhas will be the first to suffer! And how long could you reasonably hold the place?'

Arin swung his horse impatiently, while eagerness and greed flickered across his features. 'Aye, well,' he said at last. 'It'd be a main fine place to be lord of, even for a little while. Still, you've the right of it, Mastersmith. We'll not be the ones to start the stramash, not just yet. But what then? Are we to camp out yet another night on the damp sod?'

'By no means!' said Alais. 'I will tell captain Ferlias to find quarters in the castle for you and your men. As, let it be said, our honoured guests.'

'And in that,' said Gille wryly, as he slumped down wearily at the waterside, 'lies all the difference in the world.' He stared down the lakeshore, where the screaming and shouting was swiftly dying down. 'Well, Master, we seem to have won. But it's not how I imagined victory, exactly.'

'No,' Kunrad agreed. 'Nor I. It's not how they sing about it, that's for sure.' There was a nasty snapping sound, and a groan, and he glanced over to where the healers and Alais were busying themselves over old Kermorvan. 'It seems a sad and sorry thing. But of course I myself have not won. Not yet.'

'You've done more than anyone else, boss!' said Olvar, surprised. 'And you've paid Merthian back the bloody nose he gave you, and more besides. Now you've thrown him out of his home, you've ruined the stratagems he'd staked his whole life and fortune upon, and left him a fugitive in his land, far worse than ever you were.'

'And you think that gives me any satisfaction? Look at the cost! And I still don't have the armour.' He signalled to one of the healers, as Kermorvan was lifted up and borne away towards the bridge. 'How does his lordship fare?'

'Ill, I fear, Mastersmith. He was more flung aside than trampled, and his helm shielded his head. His hip was thrown from its joint, that we have set aright. But he has also many broken ribs, and blows to the face and body, losing some teeth and a fair measure of blood. It may be inner cords have also parted. Naught to kill you or I outright, I guess; but he is an old man and infirm. We'll do what we may.'

Kunrad nodded, and fell in beside Alais. 'You are castellaine here now, my lady.'

She smiled wearily. 'But you command, Mastersmith.'

'I command what? That?' He jerked his thumb at the skirmishing down the shore. 'That needs no commander. That's as simple as sweeping the ways clear of filth. It all happened without me.'

'But it must have an end, and what then? Someone must give commands for what happens next, and I trust your vision as much as my own.'

'Even with the armour?'

She turned to face him, and took his hands. 'Kunrad, I had not seen it when I spoke so harshly. Now ... really, truly I understand. Your inner flame shines out of it, and all that makes you the wonder-worker you are.'

He laughed, though his throat was painfully dry. 'Lady, I am all but burned out, and little remains save the char. Yet you revive me. If in all the wide world only you understand me, then that is more than enough!'

He put an arm around her shoulders, and they followed Kermorvan's bed in its slow progress across the bridge. When they came to the gate Ferlias awaited, who by virtue of his trust had not been able to leave the castle, with the small reserve of his garrison he had been able to keep. He bowed his head to Kermorvan, who saw him not; but to Alais he offered his keys, and she refused them. 'By order of my father, the Mastersmith Kunrad commands here now! Obey him in all, as you would my father or myself!'

Ferlias blinked in surprise, but made no hesitation, and bowed deeply. 'What then is your command, my lord?'

'I'm no lord, Ferlias. If you need any title, master is enough. And my command is that you take your men out and set some order in that bloody butcher's yard out there. The Dunmarhas fellow, Arin, has his horsemen in check; we should look to ours. Such of the outlaws as are left, you may offer their lives. Let them earn their pardon, we'll have need of labour. When you're done, return with Arin. There's counsels to be taken.'

Ferlias saluted smartly. 'At your command – Master!' His stern face twitched in what might have been a smile; then, casting a glance after Kermorvan, he ordered his men out.

'You said "we" and "ours",' remarked Alais, as they passed within. 'Yet Arin and his men are your countrymen, are they not?'

'Dunmarhas is about as far from my home as you can get, and still be in the North. I've never been there. And while I command here, these are my people. And while I love you.'

She rested her head on his shoulder as they came out into the courtyard. It looked bright and welcoming in the morning sun, with the lake wind stirring the trees, almost like a peaceful village square in its own right. 'I always wanted this place to be my home. It feels like it now. It is yours, Kunrad, and all within it. So am I.'

'Mine for a little while, maybe. But I cannot see myself being allowed to keep it, for the very good reasons you gave. My kingdom might soon be a smoky Northern smithy once again. And you—'

'I will be at home there too. Provided you let the smoke out, now and again.'

They kept watch all that morning, while the healers cared for Lord Kermorvan. The castle's own healer seemed more than anxious to please now that his lord had fled. They found no worse wounding; the old man's head was whole, his jaw fast save where the teeth had been lost, and it was clear the ribs had not pierced his lungs. His side and head were bound up, his leg was splinted and compressed, and his lesser wounds bandaged, till he looked like a great swaddled baby. Around this time he began to awaken, and put the point more forcibly; but the healers' infusions of herbs and bark seemed to relieve him greatly. By the afternoon, when Ferlias and Arin returned, he was propped up on a huge oaken settle under the afternoon sun, drifting in and out of a fitful sleep. But though Ferlias knelt to him, much moved, it was Kunrad they saluted, and Alais, and to them they delivered their report.

It was short in the telling; how they had some two hundred outlaws under guard, mostly wounded, and another thousand, maybe, fled, wounded and disarmed and in total disarray. Some sought the ships on the river, but most the margins of the Marshes; and when Ferlias guessed that not one in five would survive the week, Kunrad shuddered his agreement. For the rest, some thousand and more lay dead along the lakestrand, and all their leaders save Merthian among them. The defenders had more than three hundred of their own to bury, nearly another hundred gravely wounded; but Arin's men, though eight horses had fallen, had no man dead and few in any danger.

'And that's better than we dared hope!' said Kunrad decisively. 'The men must eat, from the drawn stores, and then take the corsair dead to the hilltop, where the furnace should still serve. Their comrades can be made to help.'

'Being done, Mastersmith,' said Arin. 'They're portioning out the food now.'

'Then we can eat, also, and talk. Find ways we can relieve the families of the slain, from Merthian's coffers, or by forgoing rent, some such thing. Alais, you understand how these things are managed here. First, though, we must consider Merthian.'

'He is not taken,' said Alais coldly, 'or you would have told me.'

Arin shrugged. 'My men came within sight of him. He has maybe fifteen riders with him, no more, and he rides like one possessed, along these wide dusty roads of yours. Southward, as far as they could tell. They must needs turn back when they came to a town. I am sorry, lady, but they could do no more. Why not let him go, for now? A fugitive can do little harm.'

'But will he stay a fugitive?' They turned in surprise, for the voice, faint and rasping, was Kermorvan's. 'Think, man!' he urged, with a shred of his former vigour, and tried to thump the flat arm of the settle. 'Why does he ride south so fast? He has a purpose. He goes somewhere. Where, but to Ker Bryhaine itself?'

'Father, calm yourself!' urged Alais. 'Why there, of all places? When they hear what he's done, they'll hang him from the walls . . . Oh.'

Kunrad nodded grimly. 'You lend words to my fears, my lord. They'll hear from him first. And who knows what tale he'll tell?'

'Driven from his castle by corsairs and Northerners, no doubt!' Kermorvan half laughed, coughed suddenly and clutched his side, his face glistening with sudden sweat. He lay back in his chair. 'In alliance with his rascally old castellan, who has royal ambitions!'

'But the warnings you sent!' protested Ferlias.

'Part of the scheme, he'll say!' croaked Kermorvan. 'Aye, he'll be there, all his old plausible self, with Bryheren, who loves him and is ever swift to believe the worst of me!'

'We have to go after him,' said Kunrad. 'And soon. He has the start of us, that cannot be helped. We should be able to lessen it. We will have fresh horses and better supply, though I don't doubt a great lord can find all he needs along the way. I will go. I must, for he still has the armour. Olvar and Gille will no doubt wish to come with me. But your sothran lords will surely be slow to take any Northerner's word over his. We will need some voice that carries weight, one of their own; and Alais, I think—'

'They'll have one!' wheezed Kermorvan. 'Mine! Order up my horses and my housetroops! Somebody help me out of this mantrap of a settle!'

Alais ran to do the opposite. 'Father, don't be ridiculous! There is no way you could ride, and if you did, it's three weeks' journey at the least! It would kill you!'

He glared at her. 'What if it does? My duty, ain't it, as much as getting stiffened in battle? There's hundreds of my lads lying out there in worse fettle than I am. What'll folk say of them an' what they died for, if Merthian gets his lies in first? And what'll he do to the living who know the truth?'

'He wouldn't surely!' she protested. 'Even he—'

'Think not? A year or two back I'd never have thought he'd flee and leave his men! Why'd he do it now? Had to! What else might he do – 'cause he has to?' Kermorvan scowled. 'He's on the slippery slope down, and slidin' too fast to stop. At best he'll needs cow and muzzle the folk here. Even then – well, he can't afford to have naysayers hangin' around, can he? Doesn't leave me much choice. Die in harness, or helpless in a chair. And seein' that little prick with ears sendin' you and all else I care for skimmin' down the River? No, daughter. The Kermorvannen will face their foes once again, as they're supposed to. Master Kunrad, I await your marchin' orders.'

Kunrad stood up. He wore his smith's garb once again, and the battered sheepskin jacket as before, but his face was weary and stern. 'Ferlias, you command the Castle of the Winds, while we are gone. Take every measure to preserve the truth of what happened here, the more so if we do not return. Captain Arin, I'd be

Ice and Steel

grateful if you would remain to help him – as our guest. And see that Nordeney, at least, is left in no doubt of the truth. Have horses made ready, then, and the best horse-litter that can be contrived, and a healer to accompany it. An escort of Lord Kermorvan's housetroops, as many as you can spare, with full arms, supplies and all else for a long journey. We leave this night!'

CHAPTER ELEVEN
Armour of Proof

KUNRAD REINED IN HIS HORSE atop the ridge, and waited as the dawn light grew. So it had been, all the way southward. Kermorvan, slung in his litter between two horses, was forever chafing at their slowness, always urging them to a trot, a gallop even. Then the effort would leave him so drained that they would have to ride slow again, often losing all the advantage. Kermorvan would recover in some degree, and demand with lurid oaths that he be put into a saddle like a man; but this the Dunmarhas healer who rode with them sternly forbade. 'If you ride, you will fall, old man,' he said, nodding his bald head with grim satisfaction, 'and if you fall you will surely die, and your cause be lost. And that's all there is to be said about it, so you may spare your insults. Aye, *imphm!*'

Kermorvan would subside, muttering about Nordeney vultures. Then an hour later he would be roaring himself red-faced for more speed, and the arguments would begin all over again. 'Am I red in the face?' demanded Alais after such a shouting contest.

'No,' said Kunrad mildly. 'Purple, as befits a princess. You never look like him normally, but . . .'

'Be serious, Kunrad! He'll kill himself. Can't we leave him somewhere, a day or two at least, to follow when . . .'

Kunrad put an arm around her shoulders. 'He would work himself into such a fury he'd undo any good rest could do him. Or come after us on horseback. At least here we can keep him under our eye.'

So it was that Kunrad waited, watching the road ahead become a faint pale line as the sky lightened. Somewhere on the slope below, untouched by the light, Kermorvan was growling, 'Take your hands off me, girl! I want to sit up! I want to see!'

'See what, my lord?' asked Gille.

'Hah! You wait, my lad! Just from the crest here – if we're ever allowed to get up it! The bastard Marchwarden's probably a week ahead of us by now!'

They knew, though, that that was unlikely. Merthian's horses had already been weary before the battle, tired by the long trek overland, his ill-judged cast of the dice. It had been some five days, they found out, before he could get any fresh ones, and by then the beasts had been barely able to walk. Kunrad's party, on much fresher mounts, found they were less than a day behind. And while Merthian's name and office could commandeer fresh mounts at any castle or garrison along the road, it could not for his corsair officers, some of whom were all too obviously outlaws. His name had shielded them, but suspicions were aroused, and when Kunrad arrived with Kermorvan they grew stronger. The pursuers were given every help, and sometimes guides and escorts to speed them over shorter ways. Merthian, held to high roads and the pace of his lamest horse, might have made up another day's lead, but little more.

How much damage he could do in two days remained to be seen.

Kermorvan arrived just as the first faint sun-gleam stained the clouds beyond the mountains. Kunrad shifted uneasily in his mail, feeling the sweat stirring already. He had not thought the Southlands could get any hotter, but they had. Even his cherished jacket had been relegated to his saddle-roll. 'What is it you want to see, my lord?' he asked. 'You must be able to see some ten leagues or more from this height.'

'More, if I remember aright!' rumbled Kermorvan painfully. 'It was always here I used to stand. You wait. You'll see.'

Kunrad had seen a great deal of the Southlands already; and, like Northerners before and after, he had been impressed against his will. He had thought Nordeney a fair and fruitful place; and so it was, where generations of men had laboured, and ground their bones against the land till at last they were laid in it. Elsewhere, though, it seemed harsh and stony and unyielding, compared to this rich and generous country. All the way southward the mountains loomed purple at his left hand, a high fountain from which a thousand rivers and myriad smaller streams ran down rich burdens of soil into sheltered vale and spreading plain below. On the valley flanks grew vines and orchards, and sheep were pastured. Over the plains spread great fields of corn and other crops. Castles on eminence and outcrop loomed with sunlit majesty over village and cornfield, visions of authority and order, established and unchanging. To the Northern eye they looked oppressive, but the peasants who served them welcomed the strength and security the towers represented, and the binding core of custom and law.

Even Kunrad had to admit that the lesser nobles who dwelt there were no great oppressors. They lived at hardly any remove from their folk, and shared their country language, livelihoods and concerns as a farmer might with his labourers, keeping only a rustic kind of state that was small burden to support. Together lord and man watched the seasons turn, and asked little more from them than that their flocks should increase and granaries swell, and that a man should live as his fathers had. That in part was the doing of the Syndicacy, and their restraining hand. If a lord should exceed his rights, or neglect his folk, or turn unduly cruel, his produce failed, taxes were not paid, and complaints would flow to their high courts in the city of Ker Bryhaine. Then inquisition would be done, as it had been by the kings of old, and in extreme case the land and title given to another lord. That the peace should be kept, the taxes flow and each man know his place was the ideal of the Syndicacy, as if the Powers, whom they often invoked, had commanded it. And that was natural; for the place of the Syndics, the great lords and wealthiest men of Ker Bryhaine, was at the summit.

So the peasants toiled in their little patchwork fields, and gave day-labour in their lords' wide lands, and grudged it only a little and for the sake of grumbling. They grew ample food and a rough sufficiency of comforts, but it left them little leisure to grow in themselves. That was for the lords; a breadth of crafts and arts flourished in their castles that the North could rarely afford to maintain. If a peasant showed some unusual talent, he might well find a patron to pay his way to freedom, whereas a Northerner, as Kunrad was only too aware, must fend for himself. 'If I can no longer help you,' he told Olvar and Gille, 'you must stay, and live well here at some lord's expense. Sooner that, than waste your talents sweeping your father's stables or gutting your brothers' catches.'

'Maybe, Mastersmith,' Gille had said. 'And yourself?'

Kunrad stared into the distance. 'I am a leaf in the wind, blown towards I know not what.' He would say no more.

Now he strained his eyes, watching for what Kermorvan wished to see. Fingers of light reached between the peaks in brief sharp contrast with the blackness of the land they shadowed. The long beams showed him why this height was so important; it was the last of the tall ridges, the roots of the mountains thrust out across the land. From here on they grew lower and wider, becoming lines of rolling hills that sank at last to wide plains, stretching out in blue haze to the distant sea coasts. As dawn brought colour back to the world, he saw that their slopes were clear, for the most part, save where a dull shadow spread outward from the mountains along a deep vale.

'Aithennec!' said Kermorvan grimly. 'The last arm of the Great Forest beyond the mountains, that once covered all these hills in the days before the coming of men. Our ancestors had had enough of the Forest and its perils. They cleared it all, save that one deep glen, and that is kept well clear of the roads. But if war and division return, I doubt not Tapiau's gloomy hand will stretch forth again.'

Kunrad nodded, fascinated. 'Worth seeing, indeed. I've heard so many tales about that place.'

'Most of them short of the reality,' wheezed the old man. 'But it was not that I sought to show you, lads. Look now south and west, where the land lies like a cloak! Look, and feast your eyes!'

The land to the southwest lay like a cloak indeed, a garment flung down careless and wrinkled, and left bleaching in the sun, so that spring greenery mingled in a strange patchwork with dry yellows. Kunrad guessed the summer would bake it yellower, killing the grass and ripening what must be fields. But as he looked more keenly he saw a faint gleam, as though some brooch or fastening had been left in the cloak's wide shoulder – ivory, perhaps, with a grey-green tinge, and flecks of bronze and gold that flashed suddenly in the first long sunbeams.

Kunrad smiled at the sight. It seemed tiny and distant, another piece of jeweller's work; then his smile faded as he realised how wide that cloak truly was, and what size that brooch must be.

Kermorvan nodded. 'They say Morvan was greater, and Kerys the Lost beyond the seas, where my forefathers were kings. That may be; but this is Ker Bryhaine, the Stronghold of the Land of Freedom as they call it, the greatest city of all this realm of men. My home.'

Alais brought her horse up to Kunrad's side. 'And mine, I suppose; though I scarcely remember it. I was – what? – seven when I was brought back here, briefly; and I hated every moment of it. Except our ancient house, perhaps, with its lemon tree in the court. But Father and my brothers were quarrelling . . .'

Kermorvan did not seem to hear; but he levered himself as upright as he could in the sling, and sighed. 'Aye, my home. Some ten years since I have seen it, and I feared I might never do so again; for I would not return in shame and defeat.'

Alais stroked his matted hair. 'None can say so now.'

Kermorvan snorted. 'One can. One little bastard, in fact, is probably busy saying just that at this very moment! I've looked enough. Why do we hang about here? Ride!'

'We've ridden half the night to get you here at dawn!' said Alais severely. 'You need to rest!'

Kermorvan grumped and grumbled. 'Later! Nearer noon, if you must, to let these Northerners find some shade. Under the Forest's edge, maybe! Surely we could reach that in a few hours?'

Alais threw her hands in the air. Gille swallowed. 'The Forest? Is that safe, so close?'

Kermorvan chuckled, though it seemed to pain him. 'Oh aye! The High Road passes by it, there's no way quicker. At noon, anyhow. By night, or in winter, I confess I'd as soon not cross that way myself, but some do; the coast road's poorer, and it adds three or four days to the journey, at least.'

'So be it,' Kunrad nodded. 'We'll breakfast at the bottom of the hill, and go on then till we near the Forest. Forward!'

He was more willing to take risks with Kermorvan now. The old man was weakening, visibly. His wounds kept opening, and shedding more blood; and fevers shook him, for all the healer could do. In the North such a journey would have killed him for sure; but here the climes were milder and the going easier upon the great high roads of the Southlands. If they were to get him anywhere it should be soon.

The road down the hill was the best they had found so far, its surface of packed yellow clay already growing warm in the sun. 'How do you make your roads like this?' Kunrad marvelled. 'We've no such skill in the North. Shaped to the hill, so we always ride level and clear of trips and tangles! Even,' he coughed, 'if it is a bit dusty!'

'Our artificers brought the skill from Kerys, they say,' Alais told him. 'Something to do with laying a bed of many layers, and drainage. And great labour; the lords must send peasants out during the growing season, when the women can tend the fields.'

Olvar's impassive face twitched. 'We couldn't do that in the North. The first work they'd do is bury the man who suggested it!'

Gille, riding behind the leaders, coughed violently. 'At least our clime keeps the dust down. Look out there! In this heat you can see people using the roads, just by the little clouds they kick up!'

Olvar nodded. 'I wonder if Merthian's one of them? It's too far for me to make out, now. But I'll be watching for a flash from the master's armour!'

'He's gone, I'll be bound!' groaned Kermorvan. 'Flicking his forked tongue around the city, no doubt! But we'll stuff it back down his throat yet!'

Alais, Kunrad noticed, said nothing. But even in the warm radiance of sunrise she seemed pale.

None of them grew any happier as they neared the Forest. For much of the way it was hidden from them by the rolling hills, save for a few straggling trees at the vale's end; but it grew in their minds. To the Northerners the Forest was a name of fear and horror greater than the Ice. Few had much reason to seek the glaciers; but the fishing and trapping by the banks of the Westflood and the Forest margins were rich, and every year hardy souls would cross the Meneth Scahas and camp along the Forest edge. Some returned with rich loads of furs, scoffing at the terrible tales; but others returned not at all, or broken by fear and hardship. To approach even its outmost arm so lightly was disturbing, although the road was wide and well established, and the prospect of shade welcome; the high sun smote their necks. They looked warily about, loosening swords in scabbards, before they at length chose a place they might dismount.

And that was as well. They crossed now between the two walls of the glen, and the Forest filled it from edge to edge like a dark wall. Near the foremost edge many stumps showed where vast and ancient trees had been felled, fir and pine and massive redwoods, some as wide as a small house. Lesser trees and bushes were scattered like shrunken remnants about those vast ruins; but in the glen's mouth the great trees still towered, and beneath them heavy bushes of thorn and briar, and dank tangles of fern and bracken. Even the wind and the sunlight seemed to glance off their brooding gloom, leaving the stillness beneath untouched. Only the outermost trees glowed with a faint green corona, and the waving lines of alder and hazel that overhung a small shallow river flowing out of the wood. On a green sward by a sunlit pool, affording clear views in all directions, they dismounted with groans of relief. It had been a long ride, and many men went off among the trees, Alais in another direction, while the healer tended Kermorvan and clicked his tongue in disapproval of the old man's oaths. Kunrad sprawled face-down by the river and splashed water over his head, though he had more sense than to drink anything from this eerie place unboiled. The coolness cleared his mind, and when he heard the first distant crashing he sprang up at once, and shouted.

That saved them, and their care in resting well away from the trees. If the horsemen who came charging from the shade had had bows, it might have gone otherwise; but they had to break cover too soon. Even the men among the trees had enough warning, and in the minute it took the attackers to reach the Forest margin, Kunrad's men ran to their horses. One, spurring ahead of the rest, made straight for him as he remounted, stabbing at him with a long spear. Kunrad, sword in hand but one foot in the stirrup, ducked down behind his saddle and slashed out at the spear, smashing it. The rider reined in hard, but Kunrad hauled himself up and with little hesitation hewed him from the saddle. Mail rings flew, and the man fell dead to the ground. Swallowing hard, Kunrad stared at the dead face. Small wonder the man had singled him out; it was the scarfaced corsair who had first captured him.

The little river-mead was a mêlée, the corsair horsemen slashing this way and that, careless even of their own, but they were already outnumbered and encircled by Kunrad's men, holding back and stabbing at every opening with their heavy lances. The men caught in the trees came rushing back now, not bothering with their horses, but hurling stones and hauling unwary assailants bodily from the saddle to fall on them, daggers flashing. Kunrad heard Alais scream his name, and saw two attackers riding around the main fight, towards Kermorvan's litter; and one of them, even in the shadows, glittered like a statue of living steel.

With a wild shout Kunrad spurred forward, into their path. The shining man pointed, and more or less pushed the other towards him, while he rode on. Kunrad shouted again, and it came out as a slavering wolf-howl. The corsair took one look at what was coming at him, and hauled his horse's head around, goading the staggering animal back towards the trees. Kunrad passed without a glance, charging after Merthian, still yelling like a man possessed; and so in a sense he was. Merthian saw him and spurred on, faster and faster. He gave one wild slash at the litter as he passed, sending the healer diving for cover, but he did not stop. Off towards the high road he galloped, and away in a cloud of shining yellow dust, while behind him his corsairs were beaten from their horses, or lifted kicking on the ends of spears.

Three or four, seeing this sight, broke away, but they did not follow. To the trees they fled, belabouring their horses with the flat of their swords, or to the northern edge of the vale, and the hills beyond.

'And a warm welcome they'll get, either way!' said Kunrad grimly. He stared after the dust cloud, and decided he was not a good enough horseman to catch it up. 'Let them go!'

'Eleven dead!' said Olvar, rubbing his knuckles in grim satisfaction. 'Must be every man jack he had with him, counting the tail-turners, and not one of us more than scratched. Silly bugger, to throw his men away on a worthless ambush!'

'Did he?' Kermorvan sat up, in high good humour after his entertainment, as he put it; but his pale eyes were very cold. 'I wonder. He's off to tell his tale in Bryhaine – which he couldn't very well do with a tail of known outlaws, could he now?'

Alais looked sick. 'You don't mean—'

'Couldn't just ditch them, could he? They'd have killed him, then; or denounced him! They must have been relying on him to buy them pardon. Whereas goading them into a convenient ambush – if it worked, so much the better; if it didn't . . . Well, either way he's rid of a nuisance, ain't he?'

Olvar grimaced. 'Makes perfect sense – if you're Merthian.'

'It does now,' said Alais bitterly. 'He wouldn't always have acted so basely.'

Kunrad was still contemplating the dust. 'Perhaps not, princess. And yet he was just as base in his plundering, wasn't he? It was there always. Now he will be less able to deceive himself about his reasons. And so, hopefully, others.'

Alais considered. 'Well, we'll soon know, won't we? It's cost him most of his lead. If he ever had it. Look at these poor horses, at death's door, most of them! Take off their tackle and let them, at least, run free!'

The land grew ever lower from there on, but still a rolling mass of valleys and rises, the wrinkles in the cloak. They came among villages once again, and tall houses set among their own lands, more splendid and less heavily fortified than those further north. Here and there, though, loomed massive, ancient-looking fortresses, though none as huge and solid as the Castle of the Winds. Their sentries kept a careful watch on the road, challenging this armed band as to its business – giving Merthian, as Gille pointed out, even more reason to be rid of his late friends. Of towns, as in all their way south, they saw nothing at all, to the Northerners' surprise.

Alais was amused. 'We have only a few – chiefly ports, like Bryhannec to the south, near Merthian's lordship of Anlaithann. Larger than any Northern town I've heard of, mind you, save Dunmarhas and perhaps Saldenborg – if that's how you pronounce it! And some of the villages on the great estates are quite towns in their own right.'

Kermorvan was struggling to sit up again. 'That's right! We had one once, in my great-grandpa's day. We let the peasants run it on their own. Nice place, all little wooden cottages, carved and painted—' He sagged back on to his pillow with a deep sigh. His fat had dwindled, and the skin around his jowls hung loose and bloodless. 'All gone before my time, of course. All gone.'

Alais leaned over and stroked the grey hair tenderly, avoiding the bloodstained bandages. 'Does it seem so strange to you, Kunrad? But who would need more, when we have Ker Bryhaine the city? Even I who have hardly set foot there count myself its daughter. For better, for worse, it is the heart of all that happens in this land, the focus of government, trade, wealth, of learning and amusement also. It stands for us; it *is* us!'

Kunrad nodded. 'And that is why you must have a Marchwarden in the north, eh? Too far away to be governed directly; but another great city would become a rival, and a focus for rivalry. Better to vest the power in one lord, one your Syndics can place or remove at will. No doubt the powers of the Ice saw that long ago, in searching out your weaknesses, and moulded an ideal man for the post, as I would beat out a blade on my anvil.'

'And made me a part of it!' Alais writhed. Kunrad took her hand in silence, and she looked at him, hard. 'Kunrad, how shall we ever make them believe us?'

'They will, in time, when they look into the matter. Making sure they take that time may be the best we can do. How long do we have, now?'

'Two days, no more. Merthian will be there soon.' She cast an anxious glance at the grey-faced figure in the litter. One of his cuts was leaking a thin red trickle down his temple. 'But that is not the least of my fears.'

The days that followed did not see them stilled. At every rise they crossed the wind now brought them the cool savour of the sea, and only Olvar thought it any different from the North. And as they turned their faces to it, drying their sweat under its salty caress, it showed them a gleam of light, a shining pinnacle that lifted like a lone mountain out of the low lying lands about. Always it was that trace nearer, that trace brighter, shining in many colours according to the time of day – in the morning an ivory glow, under the noon sun a hot ruddy gleam with a dazzling heart, and at evening ivory once again, shot with the pallid grey-green. At last, on the second morning after the ambush, as they came over the last long wrinkle in the land, the Northerners saw why.

They stood now within less than a league of the outer walls. And if these were not yet so wide as they would be, still they covered a vast span, spreading outward like ripples of stone from the low rocky outcrop on which the citadel was built. This outcrop, sloping gently up from the landward side, fell sheer away into the deep blue of the harbour beyond. Beneath the landward side the rooftops clustered in great swathes, just as to seaward gathered the tall masts of many ships. Those rooftops of slate and glazed tile, grey-green, blue and white, formed the setting of the brooch they had seen from so far; but the gem itself stood high and airy atop the outcrop, so graceful in form that its strength was not at once apparent.

This was the Citadel of Ker Bryhaine, crown of the city, heart of the land, sentinel of the sea beyond. Above the smooth grey stone of the outcrop there arose seven towers of increasing height, with walls and rooftops to link them, like a coronet encircling the frowning brow of the cliffs. And those towers were of pale stone brought from afar at great cost and effort, and shaped so seamlessly that, less than two centuries since it was raised, it might have been carven from one monstrous block of ivory. A thousand years hence the greatest armies were to break against that crowned stone still; and only when the Ice was at last thrown back, and all the lands were changed, were those walls at last overwhelmed by nature and by time, and by no human hand.

This Kunrad could never have known; but he might well have expected it, standing and shading his eyes. In part this was against the glare of the sun; for it leaped and danced about those tall pinnacles, sheathed in ruddy bronze and crowned, beneath the banners that curled and snapped from tall white staves, in circlets of blazing gold. But he shaded them also against a power and a majesty he had never seen the like of, save in Ker an Aruel itself. Here, though, it encompassed a city that could have swallowed all the cities of the North and still outnumbered them; that was stone where they were wood, and graven deep and majestic along its walls, where they were painted bright.

This was the city he had seen on Merthian's gold coin, in another life, and thought impossibly great. He felt as wild and coarse as any of the gulls that wheeled and yelled in the blue above, or the great ravens that beat and croaked above the hill they stood on. But the feeling passed, or rather grew to a greater wonder; for these people, with all their strength, had come closer to being conquered than his own, and from within.

'They need us,' he muttered to Gille and Olvar, who stood no less dazzled and gaping at his side.

'I hardly see how,' whispered Gille, 'though I'd die before I admitted it! What are we to *that?*'

'Free?' suggested Olvar; but he too looked deeply daunted.

'That's part of it!' said Kunrad. 'But not what would please the Syndics, I think. We'll have to show them something else.'

He turned to Kermorvan, expecting him to be glorying in the view. But the old man lay sprawled in the litter, his face grey beneath its bruises, his wrinkled eyelids fluttering. Saliva trickled from one side of his fluttering lips, thinly laced with red; blood had blossomed through the bandage around his ribs. Alais, bathing his brow with water, looked up anxiously. 'He can't go on!'

'He must!' said Kunrad harshly. 'What can we do for him here? Within those walls at least he may find better care, even if he cannot speak for us he—'

'*Speak!*' whispered Kermorvan's voice, thin and dry as old parchment. 'Why are we halted, so close? Go on! Go on, damn you!'

'Father? You—'

'*Go on!*'

Kunrad looked to the healer. The bald man shrugged. 'Well,' said Kunrad. 'As his lordship commands, Alais. Mount up, all! And keep your weapons to hand! We may find Merthian's lies stand sentinel at the gate!'

Sentinels there were, in great numbers, outside the massive double valves that stood on their tall pivots of blackened steel, on the crenellations above, and on the tall wooden gallery capping that ivorine wall. Kunrad thought there must be some alarum, but Alais told him there were always as many, at every gate. More than anything else, that brought home to him the sheer scale of life within these vast walls, beyond which buildings were already beginning to spread. The next generation would be adding another circle of walls, no doubt. So much casual strength seemed reflected in the manner of the watchers, relaxed and unsuspicious before open gates. But when they caught sight of the little band, the change was instantly visible. The loungers snapped to alertness, weapons flew to hands, and there was a growing turmoil of voices which the officer who appeared did his best to ignore. He stepped out before a low barrier and held up his hand.

'Halt there! Your name and your business!'

Alais rode forward, as they had agreed. 'The Lady Alais Kermorvan of Morvan,' she said coolly. 'And this is the Mastersmith Kunrad of Nordeney, our guest and friend.'

There was an even greater stir among the sentries, and the captain's brow darkened. 'Kunrad, you say? I've heard that name lately! By the Wing of the Raven, Northerner, you've a damned cool nerve riding straight up to our gate—'

Kunrad kept his calm. 'I do so at the behest of the Lady Alais,' he said stiffly. 'And the Prince Kermorvan her father, whom we bear in the litter there—'

'The Prince – Watch 'em, lads!' The captain stamped forward, peered into the litter. 'That's the pri— the lord himself!' He smote his brow angrily. 'What in Hella's name's in train here? Here's a day since we had his lordship the Marchwarden come tearing through, howling for the Syndics and saying some Nordeney corsair of your name had attacked the Castle of the Winds, and Lord Kermorvan was slain, and his daughter carried off! And now you bring them here to us, alive!'

'Barely!' said Alais with a glassy command that shone though her travel-stained appearance. 'And if he should die because we're kept waiting at the gate, who will be the one to pay, captain?'

The captain's face twitched. 'Lady, believe me – but it seems there's more to be said!'

'Indeed there is,' replied Alais calmly, looking down her nose. 'And we have come to say it to the Syndics, as soon as we may. Why exclude us, save to shut out the sound of many voices where only one is now heard?'

'Maybe, my lady, maybe! But the Marchwarden ordered that we arrest—'

'*Arrest?*' Alais's face remained cold as marble. 'I see. And what authority did he give? He has none within the City, for many good reasons. Have the Syndics confirmed those orders?'

'Well, no, my lady. They couldn't. Not enough of 'em in the City these hot days, y'see. Off on their estates. So it took a day to convene the Syndicacy, and it's only just in session about now—'

Kunrad slapped hand to palm. The captain jumped,

and Kunrad was suddenly conscious that a hundred sharp points were aimed at him. 'My pardon, captain! But that being so, why should you have to decide anything your good self? Surely there could be no objection to giving us an escort direct to the Syndicacy? Let them pronounce upon us!'

The captain squinted at him, then nodded jerkily. 'That I may do, nor – er, Mastersmith. No tricks, mind!'

Alais flayed him with her eyes. 'You will note that these are not outlaws at our back, but my father's men, some from the City here. Our Northern friends I vouch for, and you will use them with proper respect. Neatly done!' she added in an undertone, as the captain scurried off to summon his men. 'Lords and prisoners are both escorted, so he need not decide which we are.'

'I had only to trail a way of avoiding the responsibility before him, and he snapped at the lure. I guessed even soldiers would be less self-reliant in such a place as this.'

'Shrewd thinking,' she said, looking at him askance. 'Would a young Mastersmith of Athalby have seen so keenly, I wonder?'

Within minutes armed men were forming a double file on either side, and the barriers were swung back. The soldier in charge gave the order to march, and Alais did not gainsay him. But as they entered the wide street beyond the gate, and could no longer be forced back, she gave a sharp order of her own, and the man behind her unfurled the black Kermorvan pennant from his lance, with its design of Raven stealing the Sun for mankind. Clearly they were not prisoners; and as people in the street saw it, they came pressing forward excitedly between the tall stone buildings, or hanging out of the high windows and iron-rallied balconies. There were even some cheers. The soldiers winced nervously, for the Syndics hated the old royal emblems, but they did not dare try to pull it down – the more so as the cheers were growing for the Raven pennant, and sympathetic muttering as they saw Kermorvan lolling in his sling. Their escort led them around the corner of the spacious Seaking's Square, circling a fountain wrought of writhing naked forms, and were entering the steep Ravensgate leading up to the Citadel, when a tall man at the rear of the crowd, white-bearded and stooped with age, struck staff to ground and called out in a great voice that belied his years, 'Ravens, awake! *Morvan morlanhal!*'

The crowd roared out the ancient battle cry, and Kermorvan seemed to hear. His eyes fluttered open a moment, and widened as he realised where he was. Kunrad thought he saw the old man try to raise a hand, and let it fall. He seemed to be breathing deeply; and Kunrad feared it might be the gasps of a fading life.

The Syndicacy at the time met in the Great Hall of the Citadel, ranged between the two tallest towers, which was only later made into a special chamber. At that time its exterior was a single flat wall, without the layered colonnades and painted portico and later symbols of self-importance the Syndics assumed. But across the full height of that wall was ranged a great carving in relief that depicted a city with another citadel at its heart; a city, if Kunrad read the image aright, far greater even than this one. Behind its tallest tower the sun blazed long rays, as if it was a mere banner flying.

He nudged Gille. 'Know what that is?' he said quietly. 'That's the city of Morvan, Morvan the Lost from which our ancestors all fled. We built that, both our peoples together; and nothing less than the full force of the Ice could destroy it.'

'There's long been talk of removing that image,' said Alais sourly. 'Or covering it over, on the grounds that it encourages folk to yearn for a vanished past, and not face up to the demands of the present.'

'I'm not surprised,' grunted Kunrad. 'The rag-seller would rather you forgot the feel of silk.'

'We have that proverb too,' said Alais. 'A sign in itself, no doubt . . .' She stopped. 'What's this around the door? *Escort, halt!*'

They had been about to do so, anyway; and before her crisp command the soldiers could hardly help themselves. The double file stamped to a halt upon the cobbles, and Alais and the others immediately rode out from between them to confront the ring of sentries stationed about the door.

'What's this?' she demanded of their commander.

'Your pardon, lady!' he said politely but firmly. 'By order of the Syndics, they sit in closed session, and none may enter! Any who attempt it I must arrest!'

'Be damned to that!' said Alais, sounding remarkably like her father. 'Can you not see the banner? Are you so ignorant that the name Kermorvan means nothing to you? My father is a Syndic, and I head his retinue. He has the right to enter any session, and I to bring him therein!'

Kunrad, Olvar and Gille rode up beside her. The sentry commander stared past her at the bloodstained figure in the litter, and at the impressive ranks of soldiery, not realising they were as nonplussed as he was. 'I – I don't know! No, you must wait here until the lords—'

'Enough of this insolence!' she snapped, and urged her horse forward, pushing him out of the way. He opened his mouth to shout; but Olvar stooped from the saddle and swung a fist. His mailed glove caught the commander in the face, lifted him off the ground and sent him skimming along the cobbles on his back, unconscious. One of his sentries stepped hastily aside to let him pass. None of the others moved. Alais rode through the gap and dismounted. 'See to our horses!' she said loftily. 'We go to announce his lordship's arrival!' She snapped her fingers to the others, and they fell in behind her, cloaks flying, as she strode up the steps and into the wide-arched doorway.

Kunrad was about to congratulate her on the arrogance of her bluff, when she turned a flushed face to him and snapped, 'Keeping a Kermorvan out of their damned council! The idea!'

Hastily he changed his mind. 'It's not done, then?'

'It's an outrage! Against the ancient laws! Against all custom, unless matters have sunk further than I thought possible! I'll wager half the Syndics don't know about it, too. Some underhanded little scheme hatched by Merthian's friends!'

They were in a high-ceilinged antechamber here, gloomily lit by wide windows above the stairs that went off to either side, above a shadowy arch. Sentries standing in the gloom snapped to the alert as Alais stamped forward, then froze as they saw the armed men behind her. 'In the name of the Lord Kermorvan!' she hissed. They made the best of the situation by presenting arms.

Beyond the heavy wooden doors ahead they could hear voices, one louder than the rest. She seized the iron-ringed latch, and seemed about to thrust the doors apart, when Kunrad's hand prevented her. 'Olvar, Gille!' he said softly. 'Watch the way here!' He lifted the latch, careful to make no sound, then opened the door the merest crack. A dazzling flash of light met his eyes.

From high windows the rays of the afternoon sun fell slanted across the cool shadowy dimness of the chamber beyond, creating a blazon of harsh contrasts, hard light and deep dark. Between them, striding back and forth, Merthian passed, as he harangued the dark silhouttes seated in tiered rows beyond him. He was bareheaded, but wore the armour, as Kunrad had guessed he might; and as he passed in and out of the sun, raging in his newly strident voice, a mighty flash punctuated his emphatic gestures, like an embodiment of pure and righteous wrath. The dust motes in the sunbeams swirled this way and that before his arm.

But before Kunrad could catch what he was saying, he paused for breath, and another figure rose among the benches, with long grey locks and a voice grave and cool.

'My Lord Bryheren, may I address the Marchwarden? I thank you. Sir, this is a grievous tale indeed, and clearly must be looked into. But know you, it now appears that we had some earnest of troubles not eight days since, when messages reached us from the north.'

'My Lord Carthen, I have heard this also!' snapped a more belligerent voice, as a small grey-bearded man sprang to his feet across the chamber. 'Only these despatches came not from your Lordship the Marchwarden, but under the seal of the Lord Ieran Kermorvan, your castellan whom you accuse. And they told just such a tale of treason and outlawry brewing, but placed the blame for it upon yourself! How may you account for those?'

Merthian tossed his head, and gave a quick dry chuckle. 'All too easily, my Lord Ternyan. Lies and falsehoods, sent to confuse the issue in the event of the failure these traitors feared. As it seems they have done! Was no action taken?'

There was an excited rumble of discussion. Another figure leaned forward from the high dais at the centre, into the clear light. The rumblings ceased. A lean face, of early middle age, no more, but deeply lined, with a ring of short-cut grey-black hair around a high bald crown. Narrow green eyes regarded Merthian evenly.

'Such is the regard you are held in by many in this chamber, my lord, that we could not credit them, and suspected some drunken tomfoolery, or motives more sinister.'

There was a stir beside him, and Alais caught her breath. Kermorvan saw why; for among the men seated behind the Chief Syndic, two were leaning over to whisper to one another. And though one was young and short, the other tall, with his dark-red hair receding, and both were plump and soft of outline, it was not hard to see the likeness between them, and to Alais. They turned uncertainly to their master, who did not appear to heed them, looking gravely down at the chamber over steepled fingers. 'This being the summer recess, it did not then seem necessary to bring these messages to the attention of this chamber until they had been investigated. A small force is even now being prepared.'

Merthian blazed. 'I thank you for that regard, my Lord Bryheren! You know now it was greater treachery than you could imagine! I dare ask only one thing more of you, that I take command of that force as is my right of office, that I may wipe away this slur upon my honour, and free the Castle of the Winds from the barbarian hordes that infest it. My late castellan Kermorvan has already paid the price of his treachery, as I told you, but there remains his daughter with whom he sought to ensnare me, and this Nordeney adventurer who calls himself a smith—'

'And from whom you stole the very armour you wear!' said Kunrad, just loudly enough to be heard, as he pushed the door quietly open, and stepped into the chamber. At the edge of the tiers of seated figures he paused, contemplating the staring Merthian, and bowed low to the Lord Bryheren. 'My Lord Chief Syndic, I am the Northerner Kunrad, Mastersmith of Athalby, the man he names, and was never anything more until he came to my small smithy to steal and burn. What I have become, his treachery has made me, and I am come to throw it in his face!'

'And I am Alais Kermorvan, Lady of Morvan!' Behind Bryheren the two men sprang to their feet, but did nothing more. She did not stop as Kunrad had, but went stalking down the shallow stairs to the floor. Kunrad caught her by the arm, and she stopped, face scarlet and breast heaving under her mail. 'I am she, my Lord Bryheren, whom this creature all but seduced to his ways, whom he misused, imprisoned and sought to destroy. I loved him once, and grieve for him still; for I know the root of his corruption, which touched me also. Yet I hear him here pile evil of his own upon that evil beginning, traducing the name of the lord my father, when I watched this traitor and his corsair henchmen ride him down like any dog! And I know that he must be judged as what he is. I ask that you hear me as you have heard him.'

Merthian, mouth working, stumbled forward, and raised one shining arm to strike; but he let it fall, and snorted with contempt. 'You backstabbing little jade! You corsair's trull, you whore of a Nordeney ditch! You've no right of audience here! I cannot in honour prove your lies upon you, I leave that to the chamber, and the headsman! But as well your father died when he did—'

'*Or what would you say to him then?*'

Merthian sagged, and his already pale cheeks turned ashen. Alais made a small ridiculous sound and spun around, biting at the back of her hand. Behind Kunrad the whole chamber rose to its feet in one rush as, supported unevenly by Gille and Olvar, the bloodstained figure of Kermorvan limped to the head of the stairs. He had pulled some of the bandages from his face, and the blood was trickling down from a dozen places; the bruise on his cheek stood out livid with the half-imprint of a horseshoe. His skin was grey, his lip curled swollen around a wide gap in his discoloured teeth; he winced every time he put any weight on his injured hip. But his eyes, no longer yellow, shone in that ruined countenance like a young man's, fiery and alert; and they were fixed upon Merthian. His voice grated, he spluttered his words, but they rang clear in the silent chamber for all to hear.

'You said you saw me die, you get of a gutter bitch! But you didn't hang around to make sure, did you? No, you were too busy running to save your miserable skin, and get your word in first!' A chattering hubbub raced through the tiers of richly dressed men, and he found voice to rise above it. 'Doesn't square with what he told you, does it? I guessed not. Wouldn't put himself in that light, not when he was lying anyhow!'

There were protesting shouts from the far side of the hall, but Kermorvan simply waved impatiently. 'Merthian Anlaithann, for no lord or warden I'll call you any longer, I denounce you to this chamber and to your miserable face as oathbreaker, outlaw and traitor!'

Merthian rounded on the Chief Syndic. 'Are you going to permit this? Am I expected to stand still and hear this slur upon my honour? Out and to jail with him, or I'll needs take my own measures!'

'You will do nothing at all to bring disgrace upon this chamber and your office!' said Bryheren quietly, over sounds of sympathetic outrage. 'My Lord Kermorvan, you are not a familiar sight in this chamber, but you have right of audience here, in due form – but neither your daughter nor these' – he waved his hand vaguely at Kunrad – '*they* do not.'

'They are my witnesses and my supports, my Lord Bryheren.'

'Then we shall examine them in due course and proper form. Would you not be better to rest now, until you are recovered?'

'My lord, I have not let myself be dragged all these long leagues southward for my recovery! I came to see justice done, and to reassure you—'

'To reassure them?' screamed Merthian. 'When my fair castle is left in the hands of Northern bandits?'

'*Your* castle?' sneered Alais.

The Chief Syndic flashed her a black look, but nodded. 'Your pride is pardonable, my lord, but remember that it is *our* castle, given into your charge. My Lord Kermorvan, is it indeed in Northern hands?'

Kermorvan gave a gap-toothed leer. 'It's in the hands of my old captain of horse Ferlias, whom many of you will remember. Think you could get *him* to endorse any treasonous shenanigans? The Northerners there are barely three hundred horse who came to help us kick master Merthian's little arse out from under him. They're our guests, they're under Ferlias's command, and if they ever think any different they're outnumbered thrice over. The only other Northerners are here by me, and welcome. Anyhow, most of Merthian's chums were our own home-grown breed of sewer falcon!'

The roar of protest was louder, but again Kermorvan

carried over it, snorting and growling like an angry bull. 'Send north! Send to know what manner of outlaw scum he draggled south with him, then abandoned to die! Send to ask Ferlias how the Castle stands! Send to ask the peasantry what their beloved master's been up to all these years—'

Merthian swung a fist. Alais stepped in his way and struck him once, across the mouth, with the force that flung her javelin. It sent him staggering, with split lip.

'*Enough!*' spat the Chief Syndic, springing up and gesturing to an official, who rapped a great pikestaff on the boards. 'The next to break order I'll have flogged, whatever their other guilt or innocence!'

'My lord!' howled Merthian, thrusting Alais back. 'I demand in the name of my office that you put an end to these irregular accusations at once! They seek only to delay the inevitable!' The number of shouts in his support was disturbing.

'What have we to gain by that, Master Thief?' growled Kunrad, half drawing his sword. 'Leave off fighting with women, and answer! I'll abide the truth when it comes. Dare you do the same?'

'I dare!' shouted Merthian above the uproar. 'But that does not mean I have to bow the neck and be traduced! My lord – in the name of this chamber, which as you hear is behind me, I demand that you silence these intruders, and stop that traitor's mouth until his trial! And that I be sent at once to save what I can from the wreck he has brought about!'

'To bury the evidence, you mean!' spat Gille.

'Kermorvan, silence your servants or I'll hear you no longer!' shouted Bryheren.

Alais pushed past Merthian, and called up to the dais. 'Arenyn! Kerynan! Will you stand to hear your father and your sister dragged down in such a fashion? And your family name trodden down in a mire of lies?'

The younger brother looked uncertainly at the Chief Syndic, and suddenly he pattered down to the floor. His sword looked largely ornamental, part of the livery he wore, but he set hand to hilt readily enough. 'I will not, sister!' he barked, in a younger version of Kermorvan's voice. 'My Lord Bryheren, your pardon; but I'd stand for my father's good faith if the heavens fell! Brother Kerynan, what say you?'

The taller man swallowed nervously. 'My lord, any man may be mistaken in anything, I allow – but though my father may be many things, and we in little accord, yet I know he is not traitor and betrayer! And my sister is an honest woman!' Having taken the plunge seemed to give him courage; he also stepped down to the floor, tugging at a sword stuck in its scabbard. 'And . . . and also those witnesses they vouch for, Northerners or whatever they may be! Let them have their hearing, my lord!'

Alais ran to embrace her brothers, leaping up and down and weeping aloud. They gathered around Kermorvan; and taking him from the prentices, they helped the old man to a particular seat in the tiers immediately to the right of Bryheren. Kermorvan's face was limp and sweat-streaked as they settled him down, and he gripped the wooden barrier before him with whitened knuckles; but then he settled back and breathed deeply, like a man content, with his children around him.

Bryheren's narrowed eyes grew wide with surprise; and Kunrad saw with a sudden thrill that the reaction of his aides had impressed him more deeply than anything else. He sat back in his great chair with a loud sigh; and that quelled the uproar in the chamber as surely as his bailiff's rapping staff. He drummed his fingers on the chair arm.

'If we hear lies, it is no disgrace to us, but only to the forsworn. My Lord Merthian, we shall hear you to your satisfaction.' There was an approving growl in the hall, but by no means a majority; and as he went on, it died. 'And then we shall hear the Lord Kermorvan, and his witnesses. I find that there is a case to answer on both sides. And we shall reserve judgement and all else until the truth is made clear.'

Merthian choked with anger; but Bryheren leaned forward, and the expression in those eyes was hard. 'And before you start, my Lord Marchwarden, there can no longer be any question of your commanding the relief. It is no reflection upon yourself, but a simple demand of justice. You must – how did the Northerner put it – abide the truth.'

The shouts of protest from Merthian's supporters seemed to die stillborn, such was the change in Merthian's countenance; and not of colour alone. One look after another flickered across it with the transience of flame, too fast to be given a name – horror was there, and burning shame, and sudden, revealing fear, and desperation that blossomed rapidly into fury. He knew what must happen now; and Kunrad believed he saw murder come into that look, at the Chief Syndic first of all. Then a great calm seemed to descend, like a shutter closing. Merthian spread his arms in a gesture of reason and resignation, and turned to address the Syndicacy, unaware of what he had so nakedly revealed.

'As you will, my lord. I shall be happy to accompany the force as its guide—'

Bryheren's face was impassive, his voice pedantically precise. 'By no means would we so inconvenience you, my Lord Merthian. Many lords know the region well enough, Lord Ternyan for one. I should prefer you to remain here and at my behest until this matter is resolved. Lodgings will be found for you within the Citadel. My Lord Kermorvan will also wish to remain, but as he is clearly suffering he may reside at his home, if he wishes.'

Merthian seemed to be struggling violently to swallow something. 'You – you'd imprison me? And not him? Whose side do you take, Bryheren?'

'I seek only to act for the best interests of Bryhaine.'

Merthian made a desperate gesture. 'When I was appointed – you promised me – anything I may have done was with your approval, in spirit—'

Bryheren did not raise his voice, but his tone was inexorable. 'Then you must have nothing to fear, my lord, must you?'

Merthian was standing half stooped, chest hollow, panting with baffled rage. 'All right! So that's the way of it! I am betrayed to my enemies and yours! But I have been insulted, my honour traduced, and I may still claim my right of retribution!'

'Not against my father!' protested Kerynan Kermorvan angrily. 'He is old and wounded! And besides, you cannot challenge your accuser in a case!'

'Certainly!' said Bryheren, in his dry, even manner. 'That would in effect be trial by combat, and that, of course, was abolished even in ancient Kerys. The precedents are clear.'

Merthian stood straighter now, and his eyes glittered. 'Him? I'll leave him to his wounds, and the poisons he's filled himself with! No, I threaten no kin or decent countryman, my Lord Bryheren. But that Nordeney bandit there put the name of thief upon me, and I will have his head for it — here and now!'

Bryheren frowned. 'The challenge is allowable, and a time and place may be fixed for its answer. Yet it is customary to allow time for thought and redress, and an opportunity for mediators to settle the quarrel by other means, or to agree rules and limits for the fight — to first blood alone, for example—'

'That's for men of breeding,' said Merthian stiffly. 'This is ridding our clean air of a scabby Northern cur!'

'He's gone stark mad!' said Olvar incredulously. 'What'll he gain that's worth the risk?'

'No, not mad!' said Alais, leaping down the steps to clutch Kunrad by the arm. 'Can't you see? He thinks — if my father—'

'Yes,' said Kunrad. 'I was thinking much the same.' Merthian might be desperate, but his mind was still working away, coldly balancing probabilities. If old Kermorvan died — and it was a miracle he still lived — and he could silence Kunrad . . .

'Then there's only my word against him,' said Alais, 'until the investigation is complete. And as a witness only, since I'm a woman. He thinks that would let his supporters turn the tide.'

'He may not have so many now,' said Gille. 'Look at their faces.'

'But he doesn't seem to see that!' shivered Alais. 'He still means to try. You've got to keep out of this, Kunrad! You can refuse, you don't live by our laws—'

'He doesn't think it's a risk!' said Kunrad slowly. 'And if I back down, I may be within your law, but my guess is it would make me a less credible witness. Wouldn't it, princess?'

'Yes,' she whispered.

Kunrad nodded. 'Well then.'

'But you will still be there to speak! You are a brave fighter, but you were not raised as one, as he was! You're more than his match as a leader, you've proven that – but hand-to-hand, and armed as he is? He'll kill you! And what then? What of us all?'

'What must be,' said Kunrad, still slowly. 'More than one can calculate, princess. Remember that!'

Bryheren was on his feet, and beckoning to Kunrad. 'Well, Master . . . ah, Mastersmith Kunrad? What say you to this challenge? And to its immediate settlement? I advise you against it, the more so as you are a material witness and an outlander; and not, I guess, a warrior of an order such as ours. You may refuse without stain upon your honour.'

Kunrad bowed. 'My Lord Bryheren, I do not feel that is so. I had a home once, and a name for my craft, gold enough for my needs, and a place of honour in my own land. And I made that armour, the dearest of my craft that I would never sell! This man stole all these things from me, and when I pursued him, a close friend was slain by his allies – of the Ice.'

Bryheren rounded sharply on Merthian. 'What's this? The *Ice*?'

'More lies,' said Merthian dully. He had lost interest in argument, Kunrad saw. His hope now was in killing.

'Best you hear that from my Lady Alais, my lord,' said Kunrad. 'She has the most to say on the point. But I made that armour on that man's back, and he dishonours it. Let him say how else he came by it, or fight me as he threatens!'

Merthian shrugged. Bryheren shook his head. 'I am half minded to have you answer these charges before me, Merthian, this instant! But the challenge is issued and accepted. Where will you fight?'

Kunrad was about to open his mouth, when Merthian snapped, 'Here. Now. Before the Syndicacy, armed as we are.'

'Outside in the square, then,' began Bryheren. 'And you must wear the same w—'

Merthian shook his head, and suddenly drew his sword, tossing aside the scabbard. Kunrad stepped hastily back and drew his. Merthian tugged up the mailhood from around his neck, and snatched up his helm. It fitted him only too well.

'This cannot be allowed!' snapped Bryheren, and then dodged back as Merthian came on guard. The onlookers scattered, Olvar pulling Alais back.

'There is precedent,' Merthian said flatly. 'Lords have fought and killed here. Did not Vayde the Necromancer slay three upon these same boards, to the great shame of all Suderney? I will wash them clean with the blood of this his lying disciple!'

Kunrad, backing away, realised Merthian was again being cleverer than he had guessed. He sought not only the Northerner's death for a grudge, but a symbolic, patriotic gesture that would swing his following behind him once again; and it might very well work. Merthian slashed at him suddenly, a superbly controlled stroke; he countered it, but the tip rang across his mailshirt, and somewhere he heard a link give. 'My Lord Bryheren!' he called. 'This isn't a fair fight! He has my armour, while mine is ordinary mail—'

'What's the matter, Mastersmith?' Merthian jeered. 'Couldn't make yourself another set?'

That raised more than one laugh from around the chamber, and Kunrad knew any further appeal would come to little. Anger drove his hand, and he struck out and under Merthian's guard, aiming for the mailed joints at his elbow. His sword skipped helplessly along the overlapping plates, and he barely managed to slip aside as Merthian lunged in answer. He saw Gille and Olvar alongside Alais on the steps, faces grimacing, intent. She was bunching her fists and hammering the air in front of her, while they swung empty punches. He laughed a little, to reassure them; but also giving voice to a sudden strange elation. 'Remember how we worried over those plates, lads? Look at the flexion in 'em!'

Merthian hewed at him again, a great overhand swipe; Kunrad threw up his sword two-handed to counter it, but the stroke hissed down to his hilt with jarring effect. He fell back against the low wall encircling the first tier, braced himself and used his great strength to heave Merthian's sword back at him. Merthian staggered, Kunrad swung at his hip and caught him with a jangling crash. But again the mirrored metal sent the sword skipping away, down over the studs that anchored the plate to the mail and heading for the floorboards. 'See how important it was to shape those studs?' Kunrad demanded. 'So the sword doesn't snag and spend its force, but is directed harmlessly away—'

Merthian's sword hammered his down into the wood, biting deep, then swung up at Kunrad's unprotected neck. But that had been obvious, and instead of pulling up Kunrad plunged forward, under the stroke, levering his own blade free and bringing it up, as he whirled around, to strike Merthian's from the rear, speeding it on its way. Merthian was half spun around by the sheer force, managed to catch himself, only to find Kunrad's sword already sweeping towards his breast. The breastplate did not ring, but thudded and rose slightly under the impact, catching Merthian a smart blow under the chin.

'See that?' said Kunrad keenly. 'That's why it's got to fit perfectly. He must be wearing more padding under there—'

A stroke raked at his shoulder. It was slow by Merthian's standards, but Kunrad's counter was too late, and he was thrown backward on to the dais stairs, fighting to keep his balance again. Merthian thrust like a striking snake. Kunrad's parry deflected it only a little, and the sword smashed the panelling at his flank. He rolled aside, feeling fiery heat at his shoulder from the first blow, where the mailrings had been driven through the padding. Merthian freed his sword, but Kunrad had just time enough to hack at his neck. It was a hefty blow, near his hardest; but the strange-shaped shoulderplates caught it and sent the blade flying up in the air, while Merthian himself was no more shaken. 'See that? See that?' crowed Kunrad, obviously rejoicing in the perfection he had created. 'Just the way we planned it after that first one cracked!'

Merthian swung at him furiously, but with less skill than he might, somehow, and Kunrad parried it. For a moment they closed; then it was pointwork, fast stabs and short spitting slashes with the first few inches of the blades. Kunrad was getting the worst of it, stinging beneath his mail with the repeated impacts. A trickle of blood was running down from his injured shoulder, and it ached with every impact. Any minute one might get through. Then, by chance, he managed to bar a thrust, bound Merthian's sword and heaved hard. His huge strength bore Merthian's blade back, to bring his own point below the breastplate's lower edge. It lodged in the mail beneath a moment, Merthian was flung back; but then the point was skittering away to the side, and Kunrad staggering past.

'The mail held!' he called to the prentices. 'See? Never rely on the plate entirely, even when—'

'*My lord!*' panted Merthian. 'Make him stop! He's taunting me!'

'I know of nothing in code or custom against such exchanges,' said Bryheren calmly. 'Proceed!'

They faced one another, legs apart, swords levelled, grinning mirthlessly with the violent need to breathe. Merthian was having the best of it so far, and not solely due to the armour, either; only Kunrad's greater strength had saved his life against the other man's coldly fluent skill. That strength had carried him thus far; but he had come straight from the high roads, without rest or food for hours since. And something more than mere exhaustion was plucking at the edges of his mind.

Kunrad found himself being pulled this way and that by his feelings. He never wished to kill anyone; and yet for a hundred reasons over and above his own safety, he desperately needed to bring Merthian down. And all the while he was striking at his own greatest achievement, the thing that had torn his life apart and led him this terrifying dance; striking, frustrated by its strength and craft and glorying in it, all at once, striving to expose the weakness he suspected, and proud when he failed to find it. The tensions and the effort, and the cold fire in his shoulder, were making his head roar like the wind furnace. He strained to think of some craft of his own he could bring to bear, some of the things he had learned for the shaping of swords. What had old Kennas taught him – of the edge and the point that must be able to act as one . . .

With all the lightness he could, he leaped forward, body in line with his sword, thrusting hard at Merthian's unprotected face. Merthian sprang aside and launched a parry in the same catlike movement – but Kunrad's wrist flicked, and the lunge became a backhanded slash. The parry went by beneath, and all Merthian could do was fling up his arm. The blow landed on it with a jarring crash, echoed almost instantly as the point struck square upon his shoulderplate. Instantly Kunrad heaved back the blade in a slash that should have carried across Merthian's throat or face; but the Marchwarden had had time to learn the ways of the armour, and ducked his head in the manner Kunrad had planned. Helm and collar met and joined as one to form a smooth surface that would turn the impact; the visor came down with a clang, and the sword was sent skidding away. Merthian, recovering fast, swung up his sword in a wide over-the-shoulder wheel that sent Kunrad leaping back. It crashed into the heavy panelling where he had been, and clove it to the floor in a shower of splinters.

'You saw that, Gille?' Kunrad shouted, almost laughing with delight. 'How the gorget locked under the blow?'

'Every piece as you designed it, Mastersmith!' called Gille. 'The buffered hinge, and the virtue of integrity!'

Merthian slammed up the visor once again, and screamed so loudly Kunrad could hardly make out the words in it. *'He's driving me out of my wits! For the love of all the Powers, make him stop!'*

'For all I know, it is legal to chant a hymn of praise in such proceedings,' said Bryheren coolly.

'Or a bawdy song!' suggested Kermorvan unexpectedly, at his side. The old man was slumped back in his seat, but his eyes flicked keenly between the combatants.

Bryheren cast him a disapproving glance. 'Be that as it may, Lord Merthian, you have chosen your ground, and a contest without mitigation or prior rules. Now you must abide by it. Proceed, or confess yourself defeated and forsworn!'

The lack of sympathy in his voice was startling, and Kunrad understood suddenly that his enthusiasm had been doing Merthian more harm than merely infuriating him. All unwittingly, the mastersmith had been demonstrating beyond all doubt who was the true maker of that armour. And, through that, all else, as well.

Merthian's cheeks looked sunken, his eyes wild. He knew. He cast Bryheren one hate-filled glance, and then slid down the stern mask-visor and hefted his sword, blade up, with an air of finality. Kunrad waited for him to to strike, but the lean Marchwarden made no such move, only paced sideways easily, circling him like a great hunting cat.

Kunrad, in his dizziness, found himself thinking the thoughts behind that mask. Truth mattered less to Merthian than carrying his supporters. With the Syndicacy behind him, even the failed bid for a kingdom might be washed over as a necessary act of patriotism, in the face of greater treasons. Truth would follow where he led. Kunrad was the first barrier he had to break. He circled, waited, watched.

Kunrad held his sword out in both hands, watching Merthian's eyes beneath the mask; but that constant predatory circling was making his head and stomach swim worse than ever. He could feel tremors building in his sword-arm. Merthian's sword darted out suddenly, and he swung to meet it. It was a feint, and he almost overbalanced. Again, and he twisted to meet it, and again it was a feint. Again they circled, again Merthian stabbed out at him, withdrew as a feint – then suddenly, as Kunrad's defensive cut swept by, he slid and twisted, supple as a serpent, past his blade, and in.

It was a move of consummate skill; and though Kunrad tried to twist away in his turn, he had neither the build nor the finesse born of long training and skilled instruction. A terrible cut came at him, he parried, it became another and another, a fearful chopping rain of broadside blows that came now high, now low, now from this side or that with a speed he could not possibly match, and sent him staggering backwards across the boards. He could not parry them completely. Now an edge struck him here, now a point there, bruising and stinging and destroying his control. The voices around him were a continuous roar, and somewhere among them a tearing scream. A ringing slash smashed across his chest, sending mailrings flying up into his face, and it was the end. He spun around, able to resist no longer, and fell heavily on his back, arms outflung. His unprotected head hit the floor a stunning bang.

Above him Merthian loomed, and the air seemed full of fog, somehow; or was it the smoke of a forge? Another scream, and the young lord swung the bright sword high in the air, back across his shoulder, twisting back. The sword hovered at the crest of what must surely be a single devastating blow, a harbinger of night. But the blade did not fall.

There was a single strangled cry from within the scowling mask, and the eyes showed wide and white. There was a faint squeal and clank of stressed metal, and a brief painful grunt of effort.

In that instant Kunrad should have struck. He did not.

His sword wavered in his hand, and the look of frozen horror on his face could have mirrored the one beneath the mask.

The onlookers were struck silent, in the knowledge that something strange and terrible beyond their comprehension was taking place. Then abruptly, with a yell of frustrated anguish and a peculiar grating squeal of metal, Merthian twisted free, and his blow fell.

Kunrad's had less far to travel.

It was not a slash or a cut, but a thrust as with a spear, straight up into Merthian's side, as the blow he aimed exposed it. With the two men's strength united it rammed home, just where the flat of Olvar's blade had struck, in another land long ago. But this was no slash with a blunted trial weapon. This was the deadly point forged upon the corsair anvil so long since; and though there was no special spell within it, there was the strength of Kunrad's will, and the longing to be free, and the deadly bond of love and hate that drew him ever after the shining thing he had created.

This he had made the core and focus of his life, and it had pulled him along roads he never wished to take, and made him other then he had been. He had come to hate it even as he longed for it, almost more than the man who had riven it from him. And now he struck at it, straight up against those loricated sideplates; and where one, now, was the slightest fraction raised, the point went home.

The mail beneath it, stretched to bursting point, tore like ripped cotton. The plates exploded outwards, peeling away before the widening body of the blade. Straight through the leather base it sliced, through padding and silken shirt and without distinction into the skin beneath. Between the ribs the edges passed, peeling them apart like the armour plates that had protected them. The sheer impaling force of that blow lifted Merthian bodily from the ground.

His own last stroke fell wide. The sword he had bought that day long since flew by its maker, smashed down and stuck among the floorboards, half its length deep. And the onlookers, even Kunrad's partisans, could not suppress a gasp of horror as the Mastersmith's blade burst out in a spray of blood beneath the lower edge of the visor. The stern features flew back to reveal Merthian's own, convulsed in silent agony as, impaled from rib to jaw, he slid down on to the crosspiece of Kunrad's sword and sagged there, supported only by Kunrad's upraised arm.

Kunrad, aghast, flung the bloodied grip from his hand and rolled aside. With the ghost of a gurgling cry the Marchwarden toppled on to his face, and a strangely dull clatter of metal, as if the bright thing that had brought him to his end also lost its life. He lay kicking in his agony before the dais, while his blood welled out in a slow pool across the boards.

Alais came flying down into the makeshift arena. Gille and Olvar capered wildly on the steps behind her. Kunrad himself rose on his hands and remained there, fell and cold, the blood fallen from his face and his eyes wide and stark as he contemplated the ruin he had wrought, like a man who beholds a demon in the seat of reason.

Alais stood over them, but it was to the Marchwarden she stooped, and spoke in a low voice. 'For those you slew and might have slain. For all the wrong you persuaded yourself to do, in the name of right. This had to be. Sleep now, and forget your pain.' She rose then, with a face of set steel, and took Kunrad by the arm and drew him to his feet.

He took one ragged, bewildered breath, and then his eyes seemed to fix on her, as a lost man's upon a single light. And he flung his arms around her and kissed her there before the lords of her land, and she laughed and wept even as she embraced him in her turn, hungrily. Gille and Olvar danced around them, slapping them on the back, half weeping themselves. When Kunrad raised his head once more, his look was so strange that they faltered.

'Boss, you did it!' said Olvar urgently, as if to reassure him. 'You triumphed!'

'Though for a moment I feared you wouldn't!' added Gille. 'Master, what happened? Why were you so slow to strike?'

'Because it seemed as if I was fighting myself,' said Kunrad. 'And I saw why. I have not triumphed.'

'But you have your armour now!' protested Alais. 'Justice, revenge – though I know you wanted that least of all. Your gold and the rest you can claim from Merthian's estate, and the Syndics will reward you still more richly, I'm sure. And if you want more, Kunrad,' she added, a little tremulously, 'there is more. If you want it. So, Kunrad, what greater triumph will you seek now? What did you ever mean to?'

He could not meet her gaze, and stood silent awhile, oblivious to the furore in the chamber. 'What I thought . . . once . . . I thought I would go home, put a new roof on my forge, make new forms and swages and tools, and set to work again. Just as before, on the same quest. To find the last little flaw, to eliminate it entirely, to make – oh, not a perfect armour, of course. Perfection is lifeless. But one that fulfilled the power within me, that perfected me as a mastersmith. To make something that would live in legend, and be a standard and a challenge to those who came after me.'

'And that was the reason you have done all this, Northman?' Alais stepped back. Lord Bryheren stood before them, his narrow countenance expressionless. 'Let me see, have I understood this aright, from his lordship's somewhat excited account? Chased Merthian the length of your land, got yourself into the corsairs' hands and out again, into Merthian's hands and out again, alerted Lord Kermorvan, helped him seize the Castle of the Winds, and led his forces to rout the corsairs with some magical river of metal I scarcely comprehend? And finally, of course . . .' He gestured.

The body before the dais lay very still now, and the dust settled slowly on the brilliant metal, and dulled the shining surface of the blood-pool. One of the officials was lowering a cloak over the face. Kunrad would not look. Bryheren turned to the Kermorvannen. 'Chief Secretary Kerynan! Would you please have *that* removed. And cleaned up. All that, sir, simply to return to the labours of a craftsman?'

'Well,' said Kunrad, slightly surprised. 'Naturally. In all my worst moments I dreamed of it, believe me! I had other reasons, of course. To help my lads there – and later, well, my Lady Alais, who befriended me. And her father . . .' He seemed to search back into a distance, and then raised his head suddenly to look the Chief Syndic in the eye. 'And other dreams. To avoid one more damnfool drop of bad blood between North and South. War! Everyone talking of it, nobody wanting it, nobody willing to stop it. How could that ever be right? There can't be – mustn't be – war between us. That carving of yours, out there – Morvan! We were the same people when we built that! Two metals mingled in a hard alloy! We let the Ice tear it apart, and we've been weaker ever since!'

'Maybe,' said Bryheren cautiously. 'You are not the first to believe so. But too many errors have been made, on both sides perhaps. Such a division cannot be – what is the term – soldered together so easily, in one generation, or ten perhaps.'

'But must it be torn wider? We were brothers! We could be again!'

There was an uneasy stir around him, and Kunrad became aware he had the attention of the whole chamber. Even the officials tending to the corpse looked up.

'Simple words,' said Bryheren, not unkindly. 'Bold ideas, flowing from the heart, not the head. You are more than a mere craftsman, clearly; but you cannot hammer the hearts of men true upon your anvil, however worthy your intention. Simple ideas, believe me, have cost more lives and more prosperity than deeper insights, careful and considered.'

'You mean, like your bloody Warden's, here?' The gruff voice made them turn. Kermorvan, to Kunrad's astonishment, was standing up, and very slowly, very painfully, making his way out of his seat.

'You should be in bed!' cried Alais, 'And being tended!'

The old man's eyes glittered, and his moustache bristled. 'Not after such a tonic as this day. You've eased a greater pain than any wound, my lad!' His sons were at his side again, helping him slowly down the stairs. 'He's right, Bryheren. War was part of Merthian's plan, wasn't it? The plan of the Ice, that means. Well? Why should you want to do the Ice's dirty work for it? The North helped us. The bloody duergar helped us, even. Are we going to show nothing in return but ingratitude and suspicion? Listen for the glaciers laughing, then, as they lie over Morvan! Or can we not at least try to be friends?'

Bryheren's face did not change, but the voices around him were less certain now, less harsh. 'We must debate this at leisure, my Lord Kermorvan. But your contribution will be . . . valued. For now we will make no hasty moves, one way or the other.'

'That's enough,' said Kermorvan curtly. 'For now.'

He sagged suddenly, but less drastically than before. Arenyn eased him back to the nearest bench, and he subsided on to the cushions with a great sigh of relief, and an agonised wince. He shot out a ham hand and closed it about Kunrad's arm. 'But his lordship's question was fair, my lad! I've a mind to ask you your intentions, myself. D'you mean to drag my daughter all the way back to that little smokehole of yours on the edges of the Ice?'

'Anywhere he wishes!' said Alais contentedly, seizing Kunrad's other arm. 'If it gave birth to him, it must be a wonderful place.'

'It is, in many ways,' said Kunrad sadly. 'But I see now how small it is, and how confining. I have looked on a wider world, and gained a wider understanding; but the price was high. I can never be content there again. Neither in the place, nor in myself as I was. I have found my armour. But I have also found the flaw.'

'Well then!' said Gille brightly. 'You can make it anew, master. Olvar'll be only too happy to test it again, won't you, Olvar?'

'You don't understand!' said Kunrad with a bleak insistence. 'I told you, I felt, suddenly, there at that last moment, that I was fighting myself. I was. I found the flaw in that armour, all right. I suspected I would, calculated I might use it, even, never dreaming . . . I know now why it haunted me. Why I felt I needed to find it so badly.'

'Mastersmith, how *can* we understand?' protested Olvar. 'What is this flaw? How'd you come to see it?'

Kunrad laughed, but there was little warmth in it. 'Oh, that was easy. I hesitated. I designed that armour around myself; and I hesitated. It seems I always do. Oh, I have slain when I must, but never gladly, never without that first instant of hesitation; even deep down in my mind, I guess, beneath the surface of my thoughts. But when I pretended to strike a killing blow at you, Olvar, I did not hesitate; for at any level of thought I would never truly wish to harm you. And what happened then?'

'Powers defend us.' said Gille shakily. 'Master, it can't be that!'

'It can, and it is. In every slightest facet of the shape, and in every virtue. It must run all through the structure of that armour, like a warning graven deep in the metal. Small wonder I could not find it! If I hammered it out in one place, it would only show up again in another!'

'What are you *talking* about?' demanded Alais.

Kunrad shook his head, as if trying to loose a clinging thought. 'I will try to explain it. There is – an assumption, say, that I have, without intending it, embodied in the shaping of that armour, at every stage from the first vague image in my mind to the last, minutest refinement. An assumption that, before an extreme blow that takes the armour to the limits of its flexibility, a blow that must inevitably kill, the one who wears the armour will make one slight – instinctive – hesitation.'

Bryheren stared. 'Can such an idea live in a mere thing of metal?'

'Doubly so. In the deep refinement of the shape, and in the virtues I have poured into it, out of my deepest self, my inborn craft.'

'There's something to it, Bryheren,' rumbled Kermorvan. 'Believe me!'

Alais looked wide-eyed at Kunrad. 'And if whoever it is *doesn't* hesitate?'

'Then the flow of the whole armour is destroyed! Every joint, every sliding plate, every ring perhaps, is suddenly set in an adverse position, abutting, clashing, jamming, locking, one against the other. I made that suit a living, flowing thing, and sought to test such possible adversities out of it. But there was one I never could; one, or a hundred, who knows? Merthian did little real fighting in that armour, and mostly from horseback in a mêlée, where it was not tested to extremes; or he would have discovered it sooner. But you saw it come to pass!'

'It looked as if he froze to stone,' said Bryheren wonderingly.

'And then struggled against it,' breathed Alais. 'Struggled fearfully . . .'

'Can you wonder?' shivered Gille. 'What that moment must have been like to him, struck suddenly rigid, expecting death at any instant?'

'The loose fit may have worsened the condition,' said Kunrad grimly. 'All he needed to do, though, was relax. But he could not, not then! He fought free, as I tried to, and at the cost of bending those sideplates a little, again as I must have done. I saw, and I understood; and though the seeing of it felt like death to my own heart, I struck.'

'But you hesitated first,' said Alais. 'We all saw that. Almost too long.'

Kunrad nodded. 'Yes. And that was all the confirmation I needed. I did not make the perfect armour, that I guessed. I know now I never could have, and now—' he swallowed violently. 'Now, I never will. You had clear sight, Alais, when you saw my face in that mask. The flaw is not in the metal. It lies deeper. It lies in me.'

Kerynan Kermorvan contemplated him gravely. 'Sir, many would not call that a flaw at all.'

'No, brother!' laughed Alais, in sudden joy. 'Not I, for one! I love you ten times the more for it, my lord of men!'

'Then it's worth it,' said Kunrad, 'whatever the cost!' And again he embraced her. But she saw clearly the bleakness that still lay in his eyes.

'Not wholly a flaw,' he said, his voice choked. 'Not as such. I would far sooner be as I am, than a slayer without conscience, or a self-deceiver. But in the life I chose, and the craft I loved, I stand condemned.' He stroked Alais's hair, but his voice did not change. 'A voice spoke to me, an age ago as it seems, naming a price, a price I might have to pay, worth more than the matter I sought to win. A life I must lose; or a way of life. I did not understand him then; now I do, and my note is called in. I cannot ever be the greatest of weaponsmiths in my day, a name to last the centuries among armourers. And if I cannot, then where is the fuel that must feed my furnaces? I abandon my craft, and all the vain ambition that made me live. I cannot be a man of peace, and live to make the weapons of war.'

He raised his eyes to Bryheren. 'My lord, will you see to it that Merthian is entombed in the armour he wears? For I give it him now, and wish to see it no more. I will strive at smithcraft no longer.'

Gille and Olvar stood open-mouthed with shock. Alais gaped, unable to speak. Even Kermorvan goggled. Only Bryheren, who understood him the least, spoke.

'For such a man as you, Northerner, there will always be valuable work to be done. In my service, for example. A man who knows the ways of Nordeney — No? Well, perhaps you are right. I have nothing against trustworthiness, in its proper place. But in the service of the new Marchwarden, then. For one must be appointed without delay, to heal the damage that has been done, to root out these corsairs and, yes, to mend our fences with the North. If we are not to have immediate war, we must have peace no less swiftly. Come, we must talk.'

Without waiting for an answer, he turned to the benches where Kermorvan sat. 'My lord, the last holder of the Marchwarden's office died in disgrace, and without nominating any successor. In a time of danger such as this we need not delay. I appoint you to the office.'

Alais gave a little gasp of delight. Kermorvan's roar turned into a cough, and he hugged his side and rocked an instant before he answered '*Me?* My lord, you hate me about as much as I loathe you. And if I were any nearer dead you could save time and bury me! If it hadn't been for that loudmouthed beggar and his battle cry I might have slipped into my last sleep ere now.'

'You seem stronger by the minute,' observed Bryheren. 'I am sure you will recover. And as to matters of feeling, Merthian . . . A proper man, I thought, an upright young man, as so few are. One I could risk, there being no other safe contenders. Well, I am proven wrong. A man without faction, a man who can be trusted — these are what the office demands. You have proven yourself, and earned a great reward. Perhaps, since I cannot trust my favour, I must rely on my dislike.' There was a trace of a wintry smile, but the tone beneath was bitter.

Kermorvan said nothing for a moment; and then he sighed wearily. 'I might accept, my lord. Provided that I may resign when I wish, upon the grounds of my health; and that I enjoy immediately all the privileges of my office, the castle, the estates, the nomination of my deputy, my successor and so on.'

'That is only reasonable,' said Bryheren, with an air of some relief. He stalked back up to his chair, skirting the wide patch where the blood had been swabbed up, and turned to the Syndics around the chamber. 'My lords, you have heard. In such a time as this I urge you not to debate. I do not doubt my own judgement, and I know of none of you who would not arouse too much rancour to fill the place safely. This is a Kermorvan, you may say; but he has one invaluable recommendation. By his actions in exposing a conspiracy he could very well have joined to his advantage, he has proven that he has no interest in establishing any kingship. Are you therefore content that my Lord Kermorvan of Morvan should this day enter into the place of Lord Warden of the Northern Marches, and all the titles and estates thereunto appertaining?'

The chamber fell silent. The lord called Carthen looked momentarily very black, but silenced his followers with a shake of those long locks, like a dog's ears. Only the old lord Ternyan appeared disposed to argue, whispering urgently among those around him, as if seeking support. He found little, it seemed, and sat back angrily.

'Not one contrary voice, my lords?' said Bryheren evenly. 'Then let the question be passed as answered. My Lord Kermorvan, you may take the oath seated, in consideration of your wounds . . .'

Repeating the oath seemed to go on for a very long time, but Kermorvan's voice, if anything, grew stronger.

Alais looked on with shining eyes, and hugged Kunrad's arm. He forgot his own troubles in his gladness for his friends; and watched in astonishment as, when the oath ended, and Kermorvan was confirmed in his office, the old man levered himself to his feet, and treated the assembled Syndics to his most unpleasant glare.

'My lords! I thank you for your confidence. It makes a change, believe me! You need have no fear, it shall not be abused. I shall take better care of your northern lands than you have done, perhaps. For there is no better way I can do so than by appointing my deputy at once, and my successor; and I name Kunrad of Athalby, Master-smith of the North, and our proven friend.'

Bryheren jerked to his feet like a string-pulled puppet. Kunrad sat down hard on the end of a bench, as if his strings had been cut.

'You cannot!' snapped the Chief Syndic. 'He is a foreigner, neither lord nor citizen!'

'Not so, my lord. For before you and all these noble witnesses – and who could be more fitting? – I give him my only daughter in marriage. And so adopt him into our clan and blood, as a lord of the line of Morvan. And may he bring it increase!'

Uproar rolled over them, but Kunrad hardly heeded it. A voice rang in his ears, but he fought it down. 'Has anybody bothered to ask me about this? Or Alais? Alais, do you want this?' he demanded. She struggled to say something, and then kicked him on the shin, hard.

'Well, that's all right, then,' remarked Gille.

Alais embraced Kunrad tearfully, while Bryheren rested his head in his hands. '*If we gainsay this*,' he said, in carefully modulated tones that cut through every shouting voice in the chamber, and left a jarring silence. 'If we gainsay this, then my Lord Kermorvan will only resign, and we will be left without a trustworthy hand in the north. And no, my Lord Ternyan, neither your friends nor your foes will tolerate you in the place, any more than you them. Can you advance a candidate of proven worth or trust, Lord Carthen? I thought not.'

'If we must have a Kermorvan,' suggested Carthen smoothly, 'might not his sons—'

The brothers looked startled, and then alarmed. Bryheren smiled. 'I could not manage without my First Secretary and Lord Treasurer, my lord; although I am sure you would be eager to nominate replacements. Besides, the rigours of such a remote life might not suit them.'

Alais stifled a giggle.

'Moreover,' added Bryheren, 'we need a man capable of war, yet not dominated by it. No, we could debate a month, and end with drawn swords, and still be no nearer a trustworthy candidate. Speaking for myself, I would prefer the Northerner. A new landholder is needed for the estates of Anlaithann, and they will supply enough to maintain him without further drain upon the common purse. But one thing concerns me. My Lord Kermorvan, if we honour this, will you not resign the next moment, and leave us to install your successor?'

Kermorvan, settling painfully back in his seat, savoured his moment. 'Yes, my Lord Bryheren. I will.'

Kunrad felt as if the bench slid out from beneath him, into a bottomless pit that opened up. The chamber was shocked into silence.

Bryheren heaved a deep sigh. 'Then in the name of all the Powers about us, let us save time and trouble!'

Carthen was on his feet, tugging at his long grey curls, almost stammering in outrage. 'One of our highest offices? Passed to an – an—'

'—*outsider?*' sputtered Ternyan.

'Precisely,' said Byheren, without expression; and it dawned on Kunrad that he too was savouring the moment. 'Because, in large part due to yourselves and your perpetual factions, my lords, there is no insider we dare trust. Destiny has plucked this man from obscurity and tossed him into our laps; and I am not such a fool as to waste him. After all, he has already achieved something unheard-of in this chamber; and that is to make you two noble gentlemen agree. My Lord Kunrad, will you rise? And repeat after me—'

Giddily, wondering if he could command the rolling phrases of the sothran tongue, Kunrad rose. He tried to hold on to the panelled railing before him, but Merthian's blow had smashed it, and it wobbled. But the ancient words he heard were closer to the book-language he had learned than the spoken tongue of the day, and the lords around him whispered in surprise as he spoke.

He found himself swearing loyalty to the land of Bryhaine; and as he thought of the mountains and the forests, and all the wide lands he had trod in his long quest, and most of all the Lake of the Winds, it no longer seemed as strange to him as it might have. Athalby, its lands and folk lay far behind him. They had rejected him, and he had outgrown them as the child outgrows the womb, or the bird the shell. He had passed through the horror of the Marshlands into a new life, and these lands had shaped him anew. And, more than anything else, they had given him their own, Alais. He looked upon her, shaking with delight and wonder, and knew no regret at all.

Kermorvan was nodding proudly to himself. The two brothers contemplated Kunrad with mingled amusement and suspicion, but no more than a sister's suitor might expect. That would be the least of his problems.

'—and thus, into thy hands it is given, by the Syndicacy and State of this Land of Freedom, to fortify, hold and defend in all honour, with all its subject lands, estates and strongholds, the Castle of the Northern Marches, called the Castle of the Winds, to be thine own while life and office last. Kunrad of Athalby, now Kunrad, Lord Kermorvan of the line of Morvan – it is fulfilled!'

Bryheren's voice turned to a dry croak under the strain, and sweat spangled his bald head. The chamber was silent, and deathly tense. Lord Ternyan rose suddenly, and stalked out of his seat. Kunrad was uneasily reminded that his sword had gone with Merthian. The white-haired little man looked him up and down, and snorted. 'Forty years! And cheated by a . . . a *savage*!'

He hawked and spat at Kunrad's boots; but he missed. He turned on his heel and stamped out, with an imperious wave; but only two lords made as if to follow him. Carthen half rose, appeared to see something, and sat down. He was looking at the splintered floorboards.

Relief, tangible as a breeze, lightened the dusty air. No other lord moved, or spoke. Kunrad caught Kermorvan's eye, and realised with horror that he was expected to make some address in answer. His mouth opened, and almost without thinking, he spoke.

'My lords! I thank you, the more so as you do not know me, yet, or what to expect from me. You think I may favour my own land, or the line which has made me one of you. My lords, I will not, save as it is for the benefit of all. That must be so, because I need some such aim to pursue. I had a great talent once, that I let rule my life to the exclusion of all else. I studied metal, and scarcely knew men – still less women. I shaped the means to kill, and never truly understood what must lie behind them. I found, today, that that talent was ruled by a need still greater – a need to reflect before I act, to be sure of that action, to hesitate. I will hew and shape metal no longer. I will put it behind me, as a childhood thing; and strive with sterner stuff. My Lord Bryheren said to me, I could not hammer out the hearts and minds of men upon my anvil. *But I will!*'

The words seemed to flow from within him, from the same fount and source as the words he sang over metal; but now they came more freely than ever before. The hammer was no longer in his hand; but it rang true in his voice.

'What is dull and cold now, I will heat, and purify of dross, and shape as truly and justly as I am able. I will make men sweat in my fires, and hammer them into correction, if I must; but I will never use such blows for their own sake, or let them warp or weaken my purpose.

That, I will follow with as much care as I lavished upon that armour, and as much determination as when I pursued it. I will shape the steel you entrust to me, not this way or that, by fashion or favour, but to make the best of it that can be made, most useful – and most fair. I could no more betray that purpose than I could make a mean and unsound work. Judge me by my actions, my lords.'

A sudden quiet settled upon the hall. Then the dust motes swirled as the Syndics rose, one after another. Kunrad caught his breath. But one after another, they bowed to him. Some bowed deeply, with hand to heart, some stiffly, some with the merest inclination of the head, barely willing; but they bowed nonetheless. Kermorvan's pale eyes glittered, and he hauled himself to his feet, and bowed also. Last of all rose Bryheren, and they bowed to him; and began to file out, quietly, avoiding the stain where the blood had been washed off the boards.

Kunrad bowed his head; but it was only partly in answer to the accolade. A truth had been brought home to him. He held the Marchwarden's castle now, his lands and goods. Merthian had paid him his asking price for the armour, after all.

The Chief Syndic paused in front of Kermorvan, expressionless, but it was to Kunrad he spoke. 'You and the Lady Alais shall dine with me this evening. No banquet; there are concerns we must discuss. There is much you will need to learn, and urgently.'

'Alais will be my teacher,' said Kunrad happily.

'I do not doubt it!' said Bryheren dryly. 'She is a Kermorvan, with all that that implies. But perhaps she brings us a greater gift than we know. Until this even, then.'

He bowed again, and strode on his way. The younger lords Kermorvan, with apologetic nods, busied themselves with clerks and papers of record. Their father grinned at them tolerantly, raked his matted hair, sighed luxuriantly, and hauled his stiff leg up on the vacant bench.

'And you, my lord?' asked Kunrad.

'I? Still feeling every last hoofprint! Pain, weakness, ill knit at every seam. But not a trace of fever, after my sleep. That beggar, wakening me with that deafening war-cry! I began to feel hungry. So it seems I may linger a few days longer – few enough if you throttle me that hard, girl!'

'Years and years and years!' Alais carolled, spreading her arms as it to embrace the world. 'The beggar, you said ? He worked a miracle, waking you! Kerynan, send out after him, we must reward him!'

Kunrad shook his head. 'I do not think you will find him. Any more than we could, that night in Saldenborg. I should have known him as we passed, if I had not been so worried. The stance was the same, and the voice. *You may lose even if you succeed – and gain even if you fail . . .* If you wish to thank him – well, you might feed the ravens that wheel about your towers.'

The touch of the unknown, cool but thrilling, laid silence about them once again. Alais frowned. 'They say the Powers rarely intervene to help mankind without some counterbalance, some service or debt in return; for they wish us to learn reliance on ourselves. What will he ask of us?'

'What we have given already, perhaps,' said Kunrad. 'The Ice frustrated, the realms of men made more secure. My old life lost, my new life found. So he set the price; and it was high enough, by Raven's name! But there is more to be done yet. More than our lives will hold, maybe. We must set out for the north again soon.'

Kermorvan chuckled. 'You may. I'll see it no more. My bones are too old and broken to stir any further. My sons and I are agreed. I'll come back here, to my old house with its lemon tree, and live out my days, whatever's left of them. The north and the castle, I leave it to you. May you dwell there in good fortune!'

And it was as if that wish brought it all home to Kunrad. Land, mountains, forest, lake, the white walls and towers below which he had languished in deepest despair, and on which he had felt the fresh touch of light and freedom – all, now, were his own, in boundless lordship, ultimate mastery. And at their head, all of them together and more, the girl with the dark red hair and bright eyes, whom he had first set sight on out of night and horror, the princess who had stood against his pursuers, and delivered him out of darkness and despair to win a new hope and a new destiny. It was more than his heart could contain.

He took her hands, carefully. 'You always wished Ker an Aruel could be your home, princess, didn't you? It is, now; and your children's. Our children's.'

They trembled. 'You don't . . . regret it? All you are giving up?'

He laughed, aloud, and it echoed beneath the high roof of the empty hall, loud and free. 'Gille and Olvar will fill my place! For, given their toils in the forges, and on the great furnace, I can now name them journeymen!'

'A mighty long journey we had to earn it!' said Gille, and they bowed. 'But we thank you – my Lord Marchwarden!'

They draped his old jacket around his shoulders with all the pomp of a ceremonial robe. He hardly noticed, unable to take his eyes from Alais. 'For me, I'll seek out gentler things. A weaponsmith's house is not one to raise children in. Too many sharp edges!'

'You'll have enough of those yet!' said Kermorvan dryly. 'The Castle of the Winds is no lordly bed of ease! But with the pair of you to look after it, it may hold. It may hold!'

And so it came to pass. Of Kunrad's reign as Warden, the Chronicles record much; for he lived long, and through their many children he and his lady became renewers of the royal line. It is said to be through him that that ancient house of Morvan acquired a glimmer of the true smithcraft in the blood. He governed well, striving always to lessen the gulf between lord and man, and deal justly with both; and under his wise guidance the two lands gradually lost much of their distrust, and lived in harmony, at worst, for hundreds of years. He was the first of many to become citizens of both Nordeney and the Southlands, and owe allegiance to both. His name soon became honoured in the Northlands also, even as far as Athalby, which derived great lustre from it – though he never did find the time to go back. Gille and Olvar did; but all their lives they passed between North and South as the bravest and most determined of merchant smiths, and at last the richest. This also, as they acknowledged, they owed to their old master.

The Marshlands he scoured of the remaining corsairs, and threw down their citadel; and though the inhuman terrors of that realm were never overcome, it became far safer for trade to pass, both by land and sea. In Kunrad's lifetime, as he foretold, he saw the Great Causeway across the Marshlands begun, with its inns and hostels made safe for travellers by the powers of the Northern smiths, and the strong arms of sothran warriors. The Ice remained as it had been, a threat behind the mountains; and it was slow thereafter to meddle so directly in the affairs of men. These were no small achievements, and Kunrad lived content to the end of his days.

Most of the time. For in moments of anger or frustration, even into his old age, he would don an ancient and barbarous coat of fleece, and retreat to his most secret chambers, in the castle's highest tower. And the commoners in the estates around, it is said, would tremble at the lights that came therefrom, and the screech and clangour of tormented metal that drifted across the lake, and the strange and terrible oaths. But the wise ones remembered how he had once conjured a river of fire from the very hillside to shrivel up their foes, in the place that could still be seen today. And they were sure that their strange lord was once more making his Northern magic for their prosperity and protection, and the growing of the crops and swelling of the herds; and they too were content.

Only the smiths of the North, then and in later years, were left to grieve over what might have been, and the wonders Kunrad might have achieved, if he had only taken heart and let all lesser concerns fall by the wayside, as a true smith should. They wagged their beards sadly over their winecups, debating the flaw that was in him. They never ceased to bewail the lures of women, and power, and suchlike worldly trifles that can so seduce a man from his true path, and make him betray his inborn art.

For any man, they said, might become a hero, a lord of men and shaper of destinies, if the chances were but tossed in his way. But once only in a generation, if then, is born a man who really knows how to shape a mailring.

Appendix

Of the land of Brasayhal at the time these events took place, its nature and climate, and the then state of its several peoples, such as are set forth in the volumes of the Winter Chronicles called the Book of Settlement, and the Book of Sundering.

The tales of Kunrad, and of his apprentices, appear in the Chronicles mostly as anecdotes and sidelights to the events of the time. It has been necessary to piece them together across two volumes, adding much that later readers would not know, and leaving out what now needs no explanation. This anecdotal origin, though, made the narration more colloquial and less formal than the body of the Chronicles, preserving character and speech in the manner of the time. Voices can be heard, and faces glimpsed, across the gulf, and the winds of Ker an Aruel blow between the pages still. They show us the same land in which Elof was to awaken, and which is described in the Books of Sword and Helm and Armring that tell his story; and yet younger, and less troubled.

Many aspects of that land, its history and peoples are beyond the compass of these stories, and so to those books some further accounts are attached. Much may be found there that concerns this also; of the origins of the Long Winter, and the nature of smithcraft, the languages of North and South, and the Guilds in both lands. Here, though, new things demand new explanations, or in deeper detail; for this tale and this world are seen though very different eyes. And however much may be told, or guessed, still more must remain a mystery.

THE LAND

Kunrad and his fellows lived and died some thousand years before the coming of Elof, but to the land, as to the Long Winter, a mere millennium meant little. The narrow western seaboards of Brasayhal were much the same in their fabric and outline. Some seven hundred leagues they stretched from the chill North to the Southern deserts, blasted and impenetrable barrier to any lands beneath the world's curve; yet at their widest they spanned no more than one hundred and thirty leagues between the summits of the Meneth Scahas, rendered Shield-Range, and the Sea which had uncovered them as the Ice consumed it. They were the thin edge of the blade upon which the Kingdoms of Men in that quarter of the world now balanced; and, for all those men knew, they were alone.

The Long Winter

To the North and South the glaciers had closed in, many millennia since, cold fingers of squeezing fists. This was an Ice Age, though which one the Chronicles treat of remains uncertain. That at least one such earlier age had occurred, in which the fathers of the duergar fled first to the hollow hills opened for them by Ilmarinen, is well established in the Chronicles. There are hints, though, of an earlier still, and other realms whose fragmentary relics could still be found in remote corners of the lands; and the tales of the duergar agree.

It is the image of such ages that the whole world was caught beneath an eternity of cold, an unchanging winter landscape; but this was not so, not even on the strips of half-frozen country that marked the margins of the Ice, that would now be called tundra. The glaciers that clamped tight about the world from either pole had long since halted, seldom further south than the 45th parallel, and until Elof's day it seemed they would come no further. A great band of land and sea still lay open and free; but within that band their weight had compressed the very weather, so that the climes were crushed closer together, and ran to extremes, with less graduation between them. So the equatorial regions, for all that the icecap lay twice as close, became far hotter, a belt of burning desert. Yet these realms of Ice and fire were the more sharply boundaried, and between them there lay still a temperate zone where life endured, and in which men, and many other creatures, strove to survive.

The Lands of Men

The heart of the continent, where the realm of Morvan had been carved out, lay once again crushed beneath the Ice and shrouded by the vast forests of Tapiau, and the Eastern seaboard was cut off and forgotten. Only the West, shielded by the high peaks of the Meneth Scahas, young, raw and jagged, still offered lands clear for men.

It was the deserts that marked the southernmost boundary of Ker Bryhaine, mirrored at sea by an area of fierce tempest and baking, terrible calms; both, it was said, under the rule of great and secretive Powers. Whether by sea or land, men who strayed into this realm seldom returned. Yet along the desert's rim broad rivers flowed, making the land more fertile for all its heat, and with careful cultivation great fields and orchards throve. North of this region the climes grew swiftly more temperate, until they achieved the balmy warmth in which the great city of Ker Bryhaine was founded and flourished. No snow ever fell there, and winter was mild and wet; summer was long and easy, and the Ice seemed like a distant dream. Beyond the city the land grew slowly cooler, yet remained warm and fruitful to the northernmost boundaries, the Marchwarden's realm. Beyond this lay only the barren Debatable Lands, encompassing the Great Marshes; and to the early settlers of the South, themselves of warm-country stock, it seemed that the lands beyond could hardly be worth exploring. Yet it proved otherwise.

The Northlands, for the most part, were only slightly colder than the South, and though the land was more rugged and the soil less rich, in their southern regions life flourished as freely. But once again the compression of climes was very sudden, and towards the north they grew swiftly colder. Like today's Northlands they suffered bitter winters and fierce summers; yet because they lay along more southerly latitudes, the balance was different. Winters were shorter and less destructive, summers longer, and they were divided by true autumns and springs. The best of Northern climes lay along the coasts, warmed perhaps by ocean currents; yet some of those washed the feet of the sea-glaciers, and bore south the fearsome ice-islands that were their heralds. The coastlands, too, lay further from the winds that blew off the great Ice, and the water that flowed from it. The far North inland, Kunrad's country, was proverbially chill; wind and water rarely felt warm, even under a high summer sun. North of that, at the mountains' feet, the land became tundra, beneath whose shallow soil ice lay and never wholly thawed. In places, as at the pass Kunrad came to, this was hardly noticeable; but as the Meneth Scahas spread out into the wider, northward-reaching Nordenbergen, so at their feet it spread out across the high rolling moors of the Starkenfells, unforgiving country where only wild and hardy men dared dwell.

Kunrad's homeland was healthy enough for the young; but in a long-lived era few achieved any great span. The old marked out their lives by winters.

The Ice

For most men at this time the Ice was barely a presence. Even to Kunrad's folk, who dwelt some six or seven leagues from its mountain frontiers, it was no more than a rumour, a chill taint on the wind and a cold light below the horizon on winter nights. They knew enough to fear it, and not even their boldest huntsmen or ore-hungry smiths went near it. The courage of those who stayed with Kunrad is all the more remarkable.

That it made an impression is evident from the unusually detailed description of the terrain at the glacier's foot. It corresponds to many that can still be seen, not least in its abrupt and startling barrenness and sterility. Haldin's description of how the characteristic rockfield was formed shows that much had been learned in the bleak years around Morvan. The tearing power of a glacier upon solid rock is terrible to contemplate, and its effect upon the landscape, the hollowed-out mountainsides and sccoped-out vales, the scarred rocks and scattered debris from vast distances, is awesome to behold even after the passage of many millennia.

Only the colour of the outflow pools is at all unusual. The greenish tinge may possibly result from some mineral such as olivine dolerite, not uncommon in raw granites. It could also derive from some heavy concentration of metallic ore, such as copper, ground out by the glacier's passage; that would certainly create the unpleasant taste noted, and in sufficient concentration would be poisonous. However, both of these might tend to settle in particles, rather than create a uniform hue. It is possible, therefore, that the green was some strain of algae or other microscopic life, sufficiently small to be ignored by the Ice, or poisonous enough to be of service to it in clearing away all higher forms.

Appendix

Flora and Fauna

Living things were also much as Elof knew them; but Kunrad's viewpoint was more limited. His travels, wide as they were, took him mostly through land inhabited, or at least explored, by men, and, save in the Marshes, he encountered less of the era's more remarkable animal life. Having spent most of his life in a harsh, narrow land, however, he seems to have been deeply impressed by the abundance of nature further south, and not least by the trees. He loved them, and one of his first acts was to replant Yn Aruel where the furnace had burned. The Marshes made an impression of a different kind.

Trees

In Kunrad's country trees were sparse, with none of the wide evergreen woodlands found nearer the coast. Pines seem to have been dominant, mostly tougher and more thrawn varieties like the whitebark, and even the gnarled bristlecone pine, much commoner then than today. Only in the more sheltered valleys was there some mixed woodland, chiefly aspens, birches, and elms, and a few tall red cedars and other junipers. The sugar maple, or a sweet-sapped relative, also grew there, although none are found so far west today, and also the deciduous redwood *Metasequoia glyptostroboides*, now gone from the land altogether. There may have been a few evergreen redwoods (probably the coast species, *Sequoia sempervirens*, since most others had already been wiped out by the Ice), but at nothing like their full growth.

Little wonder, therefore, that he was so struck by the redwood forests of southern Nordeney. The original descriptions are detailed enough to name these as probably the giant redwood, *Sequoiadendron giganteum*, but even larger than present specimens. The ring phenomenon he saw, in which redwood saplings grow up round the stump of their fallen ancestor, is still visible in surviving forests, and in the fossil record. Such ghostly presences testify to trees some ten to thirty per cent broader, if not taller, than the present record. In Kunrad's day they still dominated the landscape; his impression was that men dwelt among them, rather than the reverse. By Elof's time, however, the growing population had drastically shifted the balance to farmland, and the woods, though still extensive, existed almost on sufferance. After the fall of the Western Realms and the return of the Sea, they revived somewhat; but never again achieved their primal grandeur.

Coastal redwoods were also common in the north of Bryhaine, the Marchwarden's dominions. In the low lying terrain around the Marshlands oaks grew thickly, along with hickory, hazel, sycamore and riverine species such as alders, but as the land climbed towards the mountains the redwoods and other evergreens returned. The lake of Ker an Aruel was quite high-lying, among the mountain's roots, and surrounded by mixed forests which must have seemed like richer versions of those Kunrad was used to, the white and green and yellow of birches against the darker walls of evergreens; the colours of the castle and the Wardenship were green and gold. It may be one reason he felt so much at home there.

The redwoods extended some way south, but Ker Bryhaine's main woodlands were almost entirely deciduous, with a wealth of species, save for the swampy delta lands along the southern coast, where exotic varieties flourished such as magnolia, gums, cypress, fiddlewood and even mangroves. Many trees were cultivated, often on huge plantations, including species of nuts, and some kinds of citrus (called lemons and oranges in the text), possibly introduced from further south, as were tomatoes, or from Kerys.

Only in one small area did the giant redwoods linger. This was Aithennec, the Great Forest's lesser arm, which extended through the lower passes of the Meneth Scahas and out along a deep river vale like shadowy fingers into the coastlands. At its margins and along its streams lower riverine species flourished; but behind them the various northerly species which dominated the heart of the continent reigned supreme, barring the southern sun with their own cool shadows. At this time Aithennec's extent was least and its power weakest; for Ker Bryhaine in its youth felt confident enough to challenge the Forest Lord. Every few years a force of brave men went out to cut back the lesser trees around the river, and even fell the tall evergreens beyond. They had to work swiftly, and always in groups, for those who strayed might easily vanish.

Sometimes their corpses would be found among the branches of a fallen giant; or worse, they would reappear days later, witless and hunted. Despite this, the Forest was gradually beaten back into the vale, making passage possible by the inland road; and by day, as long as the trees were not disturbed, a bold man might venture beneath them. Nonetheless, to risk lying in wait there, Merthian's men must have been desperate indeed.

In later years the watch waned, and the Forest slowly returned, with the fear of Tapiau. The inland road fell from use and was overwhelmed, by Elof's day forgotten. It may be the clime also favoured Aithennec's trees; for the magnolias and mangroves had greatly dwindled, and the citruses were much rarer, suggesting a land growing steadily but consistently colder. Even so far from its bounds, the inexorable breath of the Ice was being felt.

The Saltmarshes

Like most people, the smiths seem to have drawn little distinction between the kinds of plant that carpeted this bleak, depressing and perilous region, calling them reed and rush interchangeably. Towards the seaward side these would mostly have been grasses, probably of the *Puccinellia* and *Spartina* species, and the vicious black rushes (*Juncus gerardii* and *roemerianus*), that still torment walkers in such habitats today. Only occasional clumps of plants such as sea lavender and sea pinks on firmer ground would have broken the monotony. Further inland, however, where the channels were less tidal and the flow fresh, true reeds, *Phragmites australis*, took over, with transitionals such as marsh elder and *Salicornia* species on drier ground. The fallen tree trunks that scattered the inland regions may well have been large cedars.

The animal life of the Marshlands, under the malign influences that reigned there, was deeply distorted. Only smaller wetland species such as fish and amphibians remained unaffected. Birds, free to fly in and out, were also safe; but it is noticeable that they flocked only in the upper reaches. The main Marshes were dominated by less normal forms.

The glimpse of the dragon corresponds closely to those of Elof's day, unnatural creatures which could hardly be called animals at all, so evident and malign was their intelligence. The reaction of the corsairs suggests that this one, though, had established predictable hunting patterns and times. Experience of drastic genetic modifications suggests that they tend to revert to their natural forms, and perhaps this was happening here. Other forms encountered, such as the monster with its 'family', suggest some terrible human origin, beside which the giant snake seems almost natural by comparison. The shed skin leaves little doubt that it was a snake, and not some other serpentine form, such as a 'legless lizard' or eel (which can wriggle easily enough across damp land). It may not have been as big as the trackway suggests, broadened possibly by the body flattening under its own weight. Anaconda-like species approaching this size have been reported from South America, but never conclusively; the best documented, filmed from a helicopter, appears to rise and snap in much the manner described.

OF THE BEGINNINGS OF BOTH LANDS, THEIR SETTLEMENT & GROWTH

While the lands themselves were much as Elof knew them, their populations were often very different; towns waxed that would later fade and dwindle while others were barely founded, country was cleared that would later return to the Wild, forests grew where fields would come, and the High Roads and Causeway were not yet built. The lands were yet young, and with the growing pains of youth.

Ker Bryhaine

The first founders of the Southlands drew boundaries to encompass all the land they thought fit for themselves and their descendants: for they meant to found a mighty realm to equal Morvan, whence they had fled, or even Kerys, lost beyond the eastern Seas.

For the most part these first-comers were men of the race stemming from southern Kerys, the Penruthya. They dwelt in Morvan's warm southern provinces, last to suffer as the Ice laid seige to it, yet first to drift away. Passing through the perils of the Forest Realms in ever increasing numbers, and at last in one mass flight, they found a land far more like that of their forefathers, and better suited to their traditional farming of fruits and roots and vines, corn and fattened beasts. There they built their greatest cities and their widest estates, of which Anlaithann was once one, though like many it dwindled through family division and the slow encroachment of the burning Wastes.

So, by the time the latecomers from Morvan reached the coast, those who endured until its fall was certain, or even until its last terrible hours, they found the land of Ker Bryhaine well established, ruled by a new order, and scarcely welcoming. These latecomers were mainly of the north Kerys stock, the Svarhath, which had helped them endure the chilling of Morvan for longer. Some with sothran blood and kin were accepted by the Penruthya, among them the surviving children of the royal line. These were allotted lands and fair treatment, but denied their kingship; for the kings, who insisted on defending Morvan, had fallen from favour, and power on the coasts had been vested in a self-appointed syndicacy of lords and leading citizens.

Most of the latecomers, though, were treated like beggars, sheltered and fed, but grudgingly. And they were forbidden to settle land of their own – not only in the well-settled south, but even the still empty regions south of the Debatable Lands, around Ker an Aruel. These the sothran lords claimed for their children to come; but shame, as well as selfishness, lay behind their treatment of the latecomers, more steadfast than they and a living reproach.

This could not be borne. Men began to fight and die; but throughout the better part of an ordinary lifetime the leader of the latecomers, Lord Vayde the Great, already old, threw his terrible energies into finding his people a home. Forcing a shaky truce on the sothrans, he launched ambitious projects to explore the little-known areas beyond the Marshes, which the sothrans scorned. He built or began a great chain of castles and waypoints, picking out paths through the Marshes and clearing great tracts of marginal woodland and scrub. He found the North a land nowhere near as desolate as the sothrans had assumed – its clime well suited, in fact, for the newcomers. He was too late to prevent the outbreak of civil war, and in it he perished at the last; but in aiding his people's great exodus northward.

So the two lands were born, in strife and hatred; and in their way they both prospered. The sothrans grew rich, or rather their lords did; and their power increased, until they held the hand of life and death above a population poor and ignorant, in thrall to the land and their masters, save in the cities where the merchant and craftsmen classes flourished. The lords were not evil, or especially oppressive; but the natural run of such a society, without the restraining influence of the kings, was towards vassalage and serfdom. By Kunrad's time the process was well advanced.

Nordeney

This the Northerners had seen, and hated. They might have accepted a monarchy; but most of the Kermorvannen chose their surer life in the South to an uncertain future in the North, and those who did not, felt unfit to take the sceptre. So the Northerners, without Vayde to unite them, formed independent settlements. One or two cities arose around Vayde's castles, but more towns were founded by a few familes at most, a good distance from neighbours and sternly independent of them. They also prospered and grew, but never wholly as Vayde had intended. The land in itself was poorer, but they used it well, and more systematically than in the South, in chains of family farms rather than great estates. The men who worked it always had some stake in it, labouring for their gain and their families, and not a remote lord. Arts of cool-weather farming, brought from Kerys and developed in the decline of Morvan, brought them richer harvests, though with harder labour. Trade and craft, a lesser occupation in the South, came to dominate the North, through the mechanism of the Guilds. And, to ease the lives of all, there were the incomparable benefits of smithcraft. That strange art had grown up in Kerys and Morvan, among the Svarhath most of all. In Nordeney, though, it attained its peak of achievement, and what had been a select and secretive study became of benefit to all.

Thus the Northlands grew; and soon its population was swelled by the arrival from over sea of another folk, also fleeing the Ice and their persecuting kin. Some of these had been in the land when Vayde arrived, fishermen and sealers merely beaching for the season in what they thought of as perilous wasteland. When, however, they saw what wonders he and those who came after him worked, and how the land was changing, they brought word to their families across the ocean, and many returned with them to stay. They were a plainer folk, still living as tribe and clan, with less craft and skill, and only the simplest farming; but they were hardy and strong, good seamen and woodsmen and tireless labourers. To the pale-skinned kind of Kerys they looked somewhat strange, having skin the hue of fired copper and eyes curiously lidded, heavy of body and face; but mindful of their own late troubles, the Northerners gave them unstinting welcome, and at times helped them rout the cruel kin who harried them, the tribes later to be known as the Akia'wahsa, or Ekwesh. Their first great coming was in the time of Kunrad's grandfather, and by his day the races were already mingling; until in Elof's time a pale face was rare in the north. The sothrans made that one more ground for derision.

It was almost inevitable that the two lands should come into conflict; and less than twenty years after the exodus, it began. Most sothrans were content to be rid of their inconvenient kin, even a little ashamed. There were lords who had suffered in the strife, however, or feared the growth of a rival state, or were simply consumed by hatred. They were hard to restrain, for even the poorest lords maintained a personal guard, and one of only middling fortune could command some two to three hundred troops. These determined lords pieced together an expeditionary force, and sent it under noble commanders northward by sea. This force made the mistake of attacking Vayde's fortress of Tensborg. The resulting battle left the North in possesion of such ships as they could salvage, and the commanders, dearly ransomed to their friends. Too dearly, for the humiliation roused the South, and a legitimate force was sent, this time by land, around the end of the Marshes. This allowed the North ample warning, and they were met, not with pitched battle, but with skirmishes, harrying, lightning assaults by night; and, most lethally, a combination of scorched-earth tactics and the cutting of their supply lines. Plagued by disease from the Marshes and famine from the North, wandering aimlessly in unfamiliar country, the army mutinied and retreated in disorder before it had reached the first Northern towns. The next year a larger force beat back similar tactics to reach and burn Dunmarhas; but a confederacy of the Northern towns descended on them as they triumphed, and drove their rearguard back into the Marshes, where it was decimated. Similar incursions over the next thirty years met with more success, often beating back Northern armies and burning a few small towns, but never achieving anything significant; and this story became the story of conflict between the two lands. Numerically the Syndicacy's forces could have crushed the North, but the cost would have been too great. The North was not strong enough to touch the South, except with swift freebooting raids by land or sea. These were returned, and became common enough to sustain bodies of corsairs who claimed a nominal allegiance, or none at all. Gradually conflict subsided; but bitter memories lingered on both sides of the Marshes.

Nonetheless, after a century of squabbling and brief inconclusive flares of war, the lands drew nearer a mutual tolerance; but still not to Vayde's plan. Much he had hoped for was neglected. His chain of defences was never completed, and most fortresses never built. Thus it was at Asenby, where the King's sister Ase the Deep-Minded settled with the remnant of her household, and where Elof was one day to awaken. After her death it dwindled to a parochial townlet behind a wooden palisade. Had it indeed become the stronghold Vayde planned, its subsequent history, and that of the whole Long Winter, might have been very different. In beginning the Great Causeway, however, Kunrad was destined to fulfil a crucial part of Vayde's strategy; but in drawing the two lands closer he achieved still more.

Kunrad's Rule

Most important of all, perhaps, was his effect on sothran society; for in his wide domains, both by intent and by his own Northern attitudes, he sharply reversed the trend towards serfdom. Often he did this by harking back to ancient laws and customs which had never been repealed. The rights of the peasants had been increasingly eroded; so he encouraged his people to form communities (such as Alais describes) which could still be granted charters of right. Peasants had become increasingly bound to the land, so they were often sold with it, like chattels; some even sought this, because it meant they could not be expelled from the land, either. He contrived to loosen those bonds, and those that held a man to the occupation of his fathers, so that men of ability could seek their own livelihoods in skills and crafts and trades, which he encouraged. Those who wished to remain with the land he gave rights in it, and the incentive to work for themselves.

Such practices Kunrad wisely confined to his own domains, never offending his fellow lords by seeking to spread them, openly at least. Yet spread they did; for the whole land came to hear of them, and many of the wiser lords noted that by some mysterious alchemy the Marchwarden's revenues were swelling, not shrinking, and he was growing unexpectedly richer. They too began to perceive that taxing a free man is kinder than stripping a slave, and incidentally more profitable; and when their own peasants began to murmur about such matters, they found their demands greeted with gracious acquiescence, often before they were actually made.

The gulf between lord and man remained wide. Kunrad was not so foolish as to think it could ever be otherwise; but his good sense turned a tide, and left a stronger, more united land that endured until Elof's day and after, and the end of both realms.

THE DUERGAR

Of these uncanny folk and their history more is said elsewhere in the Chronicles. The glimpses of them here reflect how they were perceived and treated even in Elof's day, as near animals. Duergar were in fact human enough to breed with men, though neither folk looked kindly upon the idea. The sinister aspect, barely capable of speech, they cultivated for their own protection, and so that knowledge should not be forced from them. For all their power and wisdom they feared men, for their sheer numbers and their rapacity. Kunrad had neither the chance nor the genius to draw as close to them as did Elof; but humanity and kindness alone led him to look beyond the mask, and he was rewarded for it. When he came into his Lord Wardenship, he sternly enforced Kermorvan's promise, and persecution was stamped out for many years thereafter. Yet in all his years dwelling at Ker an Aruel, in the shadow of the mountains, he never again saw the Folk of the Hollow Hills; or at least, there is no account of it. But he did wander freely in the high passes, to the marvel of many; and whether he could have done so, without at least the goodwill of their guardians, is to be doubted.

OF ARTS AND WISDOM IN THE NORTH

Smithcraft

To other accounts of this singular art Kunrad's tale adds some informative sidelights. Next to legendary masters such as Elof

Valantor, greatest master of all mastersmiths, and his strange precursor Lord Vayde, his achievements were modest; yet few if any ordinary masters could have achieved what he did in the dungeon, for example, with such scanty resources. In a sense they were incidental; it was the power inborn in him, and the singular concentration with which he was able to direct it. Yet without the shreds of material and the craftwork to focus this power it would have been useless; he could have stared at the bars till he perished, without effect. Such was smithcraft, a power that manifested itself solely through the mind of the talented smith and the metals and forces he worked.

As Kunrad claimed, that power could appear in either sex; but equally, as Alais divined, it was considered man's work. Women smiths were uncommon but, in fairness to the Guilds, they were generally accepted, especially if they favoured finer work such as jewellery. Usually their worst problem was finding a master to let them serve their apprenticeship.

In the majority of smiths the craft flowed modestly. To most it gave only an ability to influence simple artefacts, enhancing their normal function – a deeper-striking hoe, a ploughshare which did not shatter in stony Northland soils. The charm against rust Kunrad used was only slightly more sophisticated. The text here is a highly simplified rendering of one quoted elsewhere in the Chronicles, as is the account of its action, couched in the terminology and philosophy of the craft. To later eyes this is about as intelligible as a discussion of electron shells might have been to mastersmiths; although there is evidence to suggest they might surprise us there also. It is certainly clear that such simple charms depended as much on physical and chemical action – and knowledge – as on more arcane craft. Some mildly and specifically corrosive substance was employed to bond with the iron's oxidisation layer. That this might be an acid of phosphorus is a guess, but an informed one, for such acids are commonly used in ablative rust treatment. Such virtues as the smith added would only intensify its action – or, in Kunrad's case, its absence.

Most masters, and the better journeymen, could create more remarkable works, as for example vessels, lined hogsheads even, which could keep their contents cool or hot, or preserve them for long periods; cunning hinges and locks; harness to control difficult horses and oxen; small works such as jewels to enhance the wearer, or the remarkable musical instruments Gille is said to have made; and large ones such as fastenings to secure house walls against damp, roof staves to ward off thunderbolts, stoves that would channel heat where needed and be safe to touch. They also made filters to freshen water, on many different patterns and principles. Kunrad's, it seems, was unusually good. He appears to have known of the properties of activated charcoal, but also its limitations, preferring silver. This is often a constituent of water filters, but he must have had some way to enhance its properties. It may not have been very efficacious on a microbial level, but served against parasitic infections such as *Giardia*, possibly what afflicted Olvar after his ducking. Folk of that time, accustomed to less thoroughly treated water, would probably have had more resistance to infections, so the filter might well have been enough to tip the scales of survival in the smiths' favour.

Beyond such everyday smithcraft came less conventional creations such as sobriety goblets, love brooches, bracelets and other tokens, fertility girdles, and curiously shaped amulets whose virtues, if that is the word, were intended to have the opposite effect. Serious mastersmiths often looked askance at these, unless they were in need of money, in which case they traditionally had their journeymen make them as test pieces. There was no doubt that such things worked; but even apart from the ethical aspects, the question, as at least one incident in Gille's career was to show, was how well – and for how long.

More reputable and more striking, though, were the so-called direction bracelets. Sothrans tended or pretended to confuse these with ordinary magnetic-needle compasses, and the uncannily precise astrolabe-like navigational instruments fashioned by a few specialist smiths. A direction bracelet, though, was deeply imbued with subtler virtues, depending on its maker's skill. The simplest would swing for a long period in any set direction, for example to mark a path in the dark, or note the sun's direction behind cloud; but more advanced ones would indicate the direction of a place the user held in his mind. The most powerful models, made, with some difficulty, by practised masters like Kunrad, could often follow a person or a thing, if only the holder set it fixedly enough in their mind, and most surely if the mind was their maker's. In later years, as the High Roads were extended, and cheaper magnetic compasses became more sophisticated, the sheer expense and effort of making direction bracelets led them to fall from use, until the art was all but forgotten.

The greatest masters of all, however, those most revered by their fellows, sought to develop one special skill, often to new limits. Sometimes they achieved great leaps forward, discoveries without precedent. Often this was innate genius, but equally often the evidence suggests they were inspired, if nothing more, by contact with the ancient knowledge of the duergar. In this context the smith's book that Kunrad found, full of marginal hints and scribbles, is especially interesting; the casual references here make little of what it was to become.

No record of its maker's name has been preserved. It seems he was a young man, probably a journeyman of scholarly mind well on the road to mastership when he was taken captive. Gille always believed it was the duergar woman who disclosed so much knowledge to him, out of pity for his distress; it is no bad guess. He felt also that it was the very possession of that knowledge that went to the man's head, and led him to betray the duergar, and also, perhaps, terror at discovering how far superior they were to men. That too is not unlikely.

Kunrad, when he forswore his craft, seems to have given the book to his prentices, and with them it returned to the North. Its fate is uncertain, unless there is a clue in a text called the *Skolnhere-Book*. This was a recondite work by a mastersmith of Morvan's eastern highlands; but it was revised, some seventy years after these events, by another mastersmith of ability called Skolne, who extended and amplified it with strange and highly original observations, theories and experiments. Some were half-intelligible puzzles, only gradually solved, if ever, hundreds of years later. This book renewed the scholarship of smithlore, and was consulted and pondered by the great mastersmiths down to Elof's day and after. And Skolne, it seems, was one of Gille's many grandsons.

Gille himself became better known as a trader and a flamboyant musician and singer of rare skill, and save for his instruments he made only one contribution to the scholarship of smithcraft. That was to commission and take part in an attempt to duplicate the duergar's strange contracting wire, no doubt for its commercial potential. Apparently the basis was one or more dramatically expansive alloys, woven as wires of varying gauge into loose, subtle webs, which were held between interwoven sheaths – a structure not unlike living muscle. Even with what Kunrad could remember, though, Gille created only feeble structures, apparently little better than modern 'muscle wire' alloys.

Iron and Steel

What Kunrad, significantly, came to consider his truest achievement was not the armour, or any actual metalwork, but smithcraft in the wider sense – the great furnace. It was all the more remarkable, certainly, because accounts suggest that smelting and steelworking were nowhere near as advanced as in Elof's time. In both North and South each smith or group of smiths would make what they needed for themselves, often by the co-fusion process, melting cast iron with 'seeds' of wrought iron. This could be done in a crucible at the forge hearth, allowing the smith to control the crucial carbon content and any other alloying with great precision. The cast iron itself was smelted on a largely local scale, in small so-called natural-draught furnaces which used low temperatures and relied for their draught on gas buoyancy in a long chimney flue, usually too long to be self-supporting and so built as a shaft of stone or brick running up the side of a hill. More advanced models used various bellows mechanisms to increase the pressure; the largest of these were water-driven, like mills, and could, at their best, produce high-carbon steels of modern quality. It was this kind which the prentices may have expected Kunrad to build. He, however, had been inspired by the smith's book, perhaps some elementary reference or some duergar comment, and saw how, with the constant lake winds to help, an older and simpler method could be vastly expanded for both smelting and steel-making of unusual quantity and speed.

This was the 'frontal' wind-draught principle. Northerners in particular used this during the first settlements, but later it fell from use. Rather than forced in a chimney, the wind was captured and directed through a series of cells, technically called tuyaus, spread over a wide front along a relatively shallow furnace, essentially a walled open trench. Modern authorities have assumed that such a design could not produce sufficient temperatures for anything more than charcoal-burning. Supposedly wind and pressure fluctuations would disrupt the furnace action and 'freeze' the interior, and the open top would let too much heat escape. In fact the open top is part of the operation, the flow both drawing air through the tuyaus and creating a recirculating eddy between the walls which rolls the hot air more evenly through the furnace. The result, by a process still not wholly understood, is a 'bloom' of lower-carbon steel in the middle of the furnace, with a layer of high-carbon steel at the bottom, in quantities as great or greater than other designs. Wind-furnace operation turns out to be highly efficient, and probably the only reason it fell from use was that natural-draught furnaces could be built on lower ground, the base rather than the summit of a hill. It is not unlikely that the duergar, favouring the windy mountain heights, would have developed the design further.

Moreover, increasing the scale of the furnace, as Kunrad did, has a marked effect on its operation. As the area of the frontal wall increases, so does the wind pressure along it, and the speed of the flow over the top, increasing the already fierce pressure gradient which draws air through the tuyaus. One can easily imagine this producing the weird organ effect the Chronicles mention. The furnace's hot core area becomes larger and therefore more self-sustaining, easily maintaining temperatures of 1,500°C and higher (the melting point of steel) over a long period. While much depends on factors such as the ratio of ore to fuel and the size of the ore fragments, there is little doubt that this design could far outclass anything else of the time. With the subtle enhancements of smithcraft, it might well match (though with less mechanical control and convenience) early designs of the modern blast furnace, and with many times the capacity. The wash of metal it could unleash, therefore, needs little confirmation.

The ore Kunrad was so alarmingly given seems, from the description, to have been some form of haematite, a ferric oxide mineral, often occurring very pure and easy to smelt, and a favourite industrial-era source. While it was well chosen by the duergar, it also says something for Kunrad's own knowledge that he selected such a likely area to search.

Armour

While the armour of the time is well documented, relatively little is known of the techniques which produced it. Most of the great weaponsmiths were men of Kunrad's stamp, single-minded to the point of monomania and often intensely secretive, inclined to pass on their craft, if at all, by whispers. *The Daybook of Ambrys*, which Elof made use of more than once, was one of the few texts of any depth, and chiefly a collection of useful material from ancient sources otherwise lost, with minutely detailed illustrations and patterns. Designs and fashions changed, but one fact is immediately apparent; that although this was an old and sophisticated culture, plate armour never ousted mail, as it did elsewhere. Ringmail remained the basis throughout North and South, as it had in Morvan of old, and even in Kerys. Plate was added to it as a reinforcement, and only on more expensive suits. Now and again a master armourer such as Kunrad, or Elof in his captivity, would actually incorporate plate and mail into a single unit, using the mail as an underlay for joints and other flexible areas; but this was held to be most difficult, in which none but a master could be trusted.

It is hard to be sure why this was; not lack of ability, certainly. Many descriptions suggest a skill at shaping subtle joints and mechanisms far in advance of later cultures. One possibility is the fighting style that was passed down through the centuries by the aristocratic warrior orders of Morvan and Ker Bryhaine, brought thence from Kerys itself. There are innumerable accounts of the startling speed and fluency of the fighting skills they drilled into their elite warriors, with a deadly dancer's grace which plate suits might have hampered. The same preference is found, surprisingly, in astronauts, who consistently prefer more cumbersome flexible suits to solid armour, even though this is demonstrably lighter and less restrictive. It may simply be that mail developed to such a pitch that plate's lightness and strength were never commanding advantages. Even if their mail was heavier, which is doubtful, it allowed the body to bend and stretch and flex its limbs with a life that plate could not match. Also, it allowed a greater flow of air, especially important in hot climates such as Ker Bryhaine's. It is known that medieval knights armed *cap-à-pie* in plate would sometimes suffocate or die of heatstroke in the crush of battle.

In the North the demand for plate armour would anyway have been limited. Nordeney town guards, usually more of an armed watch than an army, tended to reserve even their mail for parades or battle array, and preferred it as light as possible.

Otherwise they wore jerkins of leather, stiffened or studded with riveted metal, of which surplates were also made. Armour such as Kunrad made was mostly worn by the important – and wealthy – citizens and professional captains who commanded such forces.

Throughout the tale the terminology of armour has been rendered in terms of the medieval European equivalents – vambrace, gardbrace, greave and so on. However, the actual pieces would not always have looked the same. The calf protection corresponding to a greave, for example, was almost always jointed or otherwise flexible, conforming more closely to the flexion of the muscle without yielding to blade or blow, and probably transferring much of the force of such a blow to the shinguard. The better mastersmiths evidently understood such mechanical principles, and the lesser ones imitated them. In general, armour seems to have been made more living and expressive than the kinds we are accustomed to, more like an enhancement of the body within; and in that, as in all else, Kunrad's creation excelled.

Smithcraft and Trade

Smiths, like most craftsmen, generally settled in a particular town or district, but many travelled, some or all of the time. As journeymen they would often spend time with different masters to broaden their skills, or seek somewhere their special abilities were in demand. Others travelled to sell their wares, many into the Southlands; there Northland gold and worked metal fetched high prices, however little men professed to believe in its power. The majority of smiths, less adventurous like Kunrad, simply sold their wares to ordinary traders, often on commission, to be sold on in the Southlands alongside Nordeney's rich furs and skins, wool, wood and paper, waterproof ropes of seabeast hide, spices, whalebone and oil, dried fish and distilled drink. Sothran merchants, also the great travellers of their land, would come north bearing the trappings of a richer, more leisured country – cheap grain, fine leather, sophisticated furnishings and fabrics, tapestry hanging for draughty walls, carven wood, books (some of them printed), glass, sugar, wine, preserves and other sweetmeats. Yet all of these treasures could not outprice the works of Northern smithcraft.

Healers

In both Nordeney and Ker Bryhaine healing was a specialised skill, but the healers did not correspond exactly to doctors and surgeons of later days. Many folk professed wisdom in the care of sickness and wounds; but above and beyond them there were a few who possessed an innate talent or power for such things, very like smithcraft, but rarer. Whether any such link existed cannot now be said, but it was thought of in much the same way, as an innate ability bequeathed by the Powers to man and passed down along particular bloodlines. Like smithcraft, it could be heightened by study and labour, and often lay latent without them; and it could appear in either sex. Culturally, however, just as smithcraft was largely reserved to men, so healing was thought of as women's work. Very occasionally a smith would also display powers of healing, and would make extraordinary surgical instruments or other devices that only he could use to their full.

Metrye was a well-known character of the Northlands who features in other tales of the time, both as healer and seeress, a sour and ambiguous, but basically benign creature. She may simply have been incorporated in Kunrad's story by the usual process of heroic accretion; but it is by no means impossible that she knew him.

OF BELIEF AND WORSHIP IN THE TWO LANDS

There are only casual references in Kunrad's tale to the beliefs of the time, because these seem to have been largely taken for granted, and not dominated society as they did, for example, in medieval Europe. Paradoxically this may have been easier in a world where supernatural potencies were an accepted and everyday fact, but appeared very rarely to ordinary men. Belief centred on two main areas – the governance of the world, and the destiny of mankind.

The latter was thought to have been given into the hands of a wide range of intelligent forces considered benevolent, hostile or simply indifferent. These, usually called Powers, were thought of as animistic but anthropomorphic beings of many kinds, greater or lesser, who dwelt in nature but sometimes walked among men. At times they would manipulate men's destinies, for better or for worse, in pursuit of higher causes and according to laws largely hidden.

The Powers of the Ice were considered to be older, steerers of the world in its lifeless youth and hating the life that had come to defile it, most of all the creature called man. Another, less ancient group espoused life but displayed little special sympathy for man, and in some instances even outright hostility, especially as his realms encroached upon theirs. Only a select few of the greatest seemed to care for man at all, among them Ilmarinen, giver of smithcraft, and Raven, a wandering spirit of strange mien and stranger disposition. It was rarely safe to call upon him, unless it were to repay some obligation, for his aid could be almost worse than the original predicament. Others could be kinder, but usually only in individual, exceptional ways – those who most often took human shape, and with it, perhaps, some human empathy.

Often these were the lesser Powers, vassals, servants or soldiers of their higher brethren, for to them a bodily form, human or otherwise, was comfortable enough. Many enjoyed the appetites and sensations that came with it. The Ice Powers affected to despise these, and be disgusted by flesh; yet they all too often fell victim to it. Their greater fellows, of hostile or friendly persuasion, rarely assumed human form. It seems to have been as uncomfortable for them as being crushed into a small container would be for a human, and as limiting; for it distanced much of their perceptions and powers, their memories even. This, and their unfamiliarity with form and sensation, may account for the peculiar quirks and characteristics many of them, such as Raven, displayed.

Far more often they would inhabit their chosen medium, as Niarad the great oceans, or Tapiau the forests. By his own account Tapiau was present in every tree, and every growing thing that made up the forest life-cycle, but only in fairly large concentrations, their root systems interwoven like nerve ganglia, did he have enough presence to be fully aware.

The other fundamental aspect of belief was more personal, and taken more seriously. This was a concept of life after death, and perhaps also before birth, most often referred to as the River. At its simplest this was an image of the passage to the afterlife, which the common folk of both lands often identified with the Milky Way. More sophisticated thinkers took darker, more abstract metaphysical views, in which the River seems to have been an image of Time, often incorporating concepts of reincarnation. Yet for them, too, the astral image was never wholly abandoned. It may have had its roots in a tradition that their ancestors had stemmed from the stars, and tales of a celestial army that had once descended to earth to help their estranged kin. A similar story linked to the Milky Way, of two halves of a sundered people led by brother princes, is found among the mythologies of the Magyar peoples, and curiously enough also among the Finno-Baltic peoples who were indeed estranged from them, some eighteen hundred years earlier.

These beliefs were fundamentally common to both the Svarhath and Penruthya, and pervaded all their cultures. In Kerys they had been observed as a religion in the fullest sense, held personally but also identified with the state, having temples, worship and formal beliefs and schools of doctrine. In Morvan the state aspect had grown, and in Ker Bryhaine it became the chief element, with little left to personal belief. In Nordeney, by contrast, worship became more relaxed, often to the point of superstition, and often ignored or derided as myth. Often cults were related to trades, sailors praying for safe voyages and farmers offering for a good harvest. Seasonal festivals, such as Athalby's Spring Fair, originally celebrated the Powers, but were now chiefly occasions for meeting, marketing and merry-making. Neither state ever had a formal priesthood; lords, guildmasters and other leading citizens officiated at major rites, but ordinary folk worshipped for themselves.

The existence is also established, almost exclusively in the South, of an ancient, small and necessarily secretive cult of the Ice. This was a direct worship which practised rites and rituals possibly derived from certain cult practices of the Ekwesh, or sharing their roots. Its philosophy and purpose was a hatred of mankind based on quasi-aesthetic disgust, and a worship of pure sterile mind, as represented by the Ice powers. Its rites, though profoundly solemn, appear to have demanded mortification of the flesh in ordeals imposed to harden bodies and stiffen wills – and, no doubt, like so many medieval practices, for sado-masochistic gratification. They also included isolating cruelty, acts so unpleasant they set their celebrants apart from humanity, in a brotherhood of atrocity. The rites of terrorist groups such as certain Serbian secret societies and the Mau-Mau often display the same characteristics.

Like many smiths, Kunrad was not especially religious, perhaps because their educated skills diminished their acceptance of superstition. As far as can be told he swore by the Powers occasionally, drank deep at Guild feasts to celebrate the great patron of smiths Ilmarinen, and otherwise thought little about them – at least in his early life. Others displayed even less respect, as witness Gille's irreverent little song. It was probably original, extempore even; but may have followed a familiar model. There is some evidence, in the North especially, of riotous misrule festivals, like the Roman Saturnalia or its medieval descendants, at which satirical songs were sung about the Powers. This, though, seems to have been basically affectionate. Nobody wrote rude songs, or any other kind, about the Ice.

These festivals the South considered very barbaric. They tended to honour the Powers with great solemnity and pomp in ceremonies descended from the rites of Kerys, but more in celebration of their own self-importance than the Powers concerned. These were considered chiefly aristocratic rituals, linked with their warrior-cult and their belief in their own manifest destiny. Only at regular festivals or times of national joy or disaster did the common folk share in them.

Which view, if any, the Powers themselves preferred is not recorded.